Deep Obsession

Deep Obsession

Mike L. Van Natter

Library of Congress Control Number:		2014904687
ISBN:	Hardcover	978-1-4931-8389-0
	Softcover	978-1-4931-8390-6
	eBook	978-1-4931-8388-3

This is a work of fiction. Names, characters, places and incidents either are the product of the author's imagination or are used fictitiously, and any resemblance to any actual persons, living or dead, events, or locales is entirely coincidental.

This book was printed in the United States of America.

Rev. date: 04/16/2014

To order additional copies of this book, contact:
Xlibris LLC
1-888-795-4274
www.Xlibris.com
Orders@Xlibris.com
543976

Contents

"Forgive your enemies,
but never forget their names . . ."

–President John F. Kennedy, 1962

Dedication

I always enjoy reading the dedication page of a book. It's great to see the encouragement and support given an author by family members, friends, and professionals in their respective fields.

This book is no different. I wish to dedicate this work to my wife *Gloria*, who has been a good and faithful companion and dive buddy for over twelve years. Our innumerable wreck diving exploits under the waters of the Great Lakes, the Caribbean Sea, and the Atlantic Ocean have been a major source of inspiration for the underwater adventures in this novel. I love you dearly, Little Glo.

The interest and encouragement of our children; *Mindie*, *Nathan*, and *Maegan* have been my inspiration through many months of research, drafting, proof editing, and revision so vital to the successful completion of the finished work you now hold in your hand. I love you guys and I'm so very proud of each one of you.

To granddaughters *Charity* and *Jade*, and my inexhaustible grandson, *Aiden*: I hope this book will make you proud of a grandpa who has never wanted to grow up. Thanks for keeping me young at heart. You are all so precious to me.

To *you*, the reader. It's gratifying to know that even in the 21st Century, and despite all the technological gizmos sucking up the precious moments of our lives, there are still folks out there who enjoy the tactile feel, smell, and adventure of a good old fashioned book.

Finally, the author wishes to thank the *North American Bureau of Security* without whose assistance this book would not have been possible.

Author's Note

Deep Obsession is a work of fiction. The events described herein are imaginary and have not (as yet) taken place. The characters, except for the Castro brothers, are fictitious and not intended to represent any persons, living or dead. In addition, much of the technology contained within these pages is excitingly real but not common public knowledge.

Due to the nature of the book's plot, several international government organizations have been mentioned. The author in no way wishes to portray any of them in a bad light.

The reality is that each of the organizations mentioned in the novel is highly efficient and commands the respect of those they serve and protect. The functions they perform within our society are what make ours the great democracy that it is.

My humble gratitude and thanks goes out to these fine dedicated men and women who do their utmost to ensure that crises such as the one contained within these pages have no chance to succeed.

CASE # 143854

PROJECT VECTOR

1

The Pursuit

In the late 1930s, Winston Churchill described the parkway on the Canadian side of the Niagara River as "the prettiest Sunday afternoon drive in the world." Under normal conditions, Sir Winston would be right.

The shimmering water of the mighty river *is* a breathtaking sight even on a normal moonlit eve. But there was nothing normal about this eve. For tonight Lee Hartley was both chased and shot at, neither being conducive to sightseeing. For reasons unknown, someone wanted to take his breath away—permanently.

It was a hot Friday night in August, and the twenty-mile Ontario riverside road linking Fort Erie in the south with Niagara Falls to the north was Lee's only avenue of survival. The two-lane parkway runs parallel to the river that rushes north on its ravenous path over the world-famous Horseshoe Falls.

Lee knew that the winding Niagara Parkway never took kindly to vehicles traveling at high rates of speed. The default penalty for rejecting prudence along this winding road was a choice of two fates. The first was to crash horrifically into a tree. The second was to careen off the road and drop twenty feet below into the swift-moving, swirling waters. Either option more often than not ended in fatality. Lee was interested in neither.

Gravel exploded in protest from beneath the rubber paws of Hartley's navy blue 1987 Cadillac Sedan de Ville, as he narrowly negotiated another abrupt bend in the road at breakneck speed. He glanced into the rearview mirror. Another flash, then another thud as bullet penetrated metal; this time the lid of his trunk.

The Caddy's ancient engine growled in protest as he downshifted to negotiate another curve at high speed. He nearly missed flying over an embankment, tires screeching their reluctance at just the right moment. One thought burned in his mind as he fought to keep the lumbering leviathan on the road: *who had pissed in this guy's sandbox, and why was he taking it out on me?*

The road was dark but as they sped past a streetlight, Lee noticed that his pursuer piloted a dark sports car of some sort. He instinctively ducked when he heard another shot, answered this time by the disintegration of the Caddy's rear-deck window. He was still alive and driving, so where the bullet ended up was of little concern.

Fortunately, every time the driver made an attempt to pull out for a clear shot, another curve came up and foiled the attempt. Lee chided himself for neglecting to bring his .40 caliber Beretta Centurion on the trip. But hindsight was twenty/twenty and so was the pursuing driver's vision.

As Lee rounded a tight curve, he had to slow down. Lee cursed as the Caddy's driver side mirror was atomized by another round. *Too close for comfort!* Hartley cursed under his breath that he had neglected to charge his cell phone earlier in the day.

Another yank of the wheel, another downshift, and the venerable old Cadillac was reluctantly coaxed around a serpentine bend before soaring over a small bridge immediately thereafter. Sparks flew as the Cadillac experienced quick coitus with the road when its undercarriage returned to ground. Blinding lights reflected off Lee's rearview mirror. The pursuing driver was good Lee reflected, much to his dismay.

Other cars had begun to fill the two-lane parkway as both vehicles neared the little village of Chippewa, James Cameron's hometown. Lee embraced his steering wheel in the classic white-knuckled death grip. In warning, he laid on the horn with an elbow, swerved around a delivery truck, and nearly clipped an oncoming pickup in the process.

Looking again into the rearview, Lee rejoiced when the sports car nearly spun out of control in an attempt to avoid a head-on with the same pickup. The truck was forced off the parkway and around a small grove of trees before jumping the ditch and reclaiming the road. From his rearview mirror Lee saw smoke, dust, and dirt that billowed up from the incident. The once glistening streetlights clouded into obscurity.

Lee spotted a fork in the road ahead. In blind desperation, he drew a chance card and swerved a tight left down the wrong lane of a one-way street. He careened to a halt up a lengthy driveway framed by high, well-manicured bushes. Lee quickly powered down the Caddy and switched off its lights. The sports car roared through the right side of the fork, its driver oblivious to the Caddy's abrupt and desperate evasive action.

For the first time Lee Hartley sensed the perspiration, cold and wet, drizzling down from the locks of his long dark hair, stinging his eyes. He folded his arms around the top of the steering wheel and dropped his head heavily upon them, more from exhaustion than the need to mop his leaking brow.

He then reached over and pulled out a little silver flask from the glove compartment. He opened it and took a deep swig before tossing it, empty, to the passenger floor.

Lee sat there for several minutes. His mind scanned the activities of the past few days in a vain effort to make sense of the night's bizarre ordeal. Drawing a blank, Lee fired the Caddy up, backed out of the driveway, switched on his headlights, and then laid in a course for the return trip to Fort Erie and home.

It was nearly ten o'clock the next morning when the handsome, sturdy, six-foot-tall Lee Hartley awoke from a fitful sleep to a dazzlingly beautiful sunny day.

The forty-something commercial diver rose from his bed, and wearing only short navy microfiber boxers, smoothed back his dark, long, black hair, and took in the morning's cloudless deep blue sky. It held the promise of a fresh new day. The leaves on the mature red maple trees that framed his bedroom window purred silkily as a gentle westerly wind caressed them into ecstasy.

Waiving his usual early-morning workout, the powerfully built freelance diver made a change to his usual itinerary.

Today, a call to Alan Exner at NABS headquarters would be his first order of business.

2

NABS

Following the terrorist attacks in New York on September 11, 2001, little was done to fortify security at Canada's border crossings in response. With the Niagara River a natural international boundary between Canada and the United States, the Peace Bridge was built to connect the city of Fort Erie, Ontario to its American counterpart, Buffalo, New York.

Canadian border crossings were deemed a security concern by the United States in the days and weeks following the attack. While the U.S. vastly improved security protocol at their end, Canada did little to fortify her side.

The Peace Bridge, built in 1927, had soon become one of the busiest crossing points between the U.S. and Canada. It was some eighty years later that much political wheel spinning and international haggling led to heated debates concerning the need for an additional route as vehicles often backed up for miles on the Queen Elizabeth Way on the Canadian side, as they waited to clear U.S. Customs.

The current single-bridge traffic restrictions resulted in several fatal accidents. When U.S. Customs would have an inspection blitz, it was not uncommon for America-bound vehicles to careen into traffic stopped on the far side of a blind hill near the border on the Canadian side.

A second span would double the requirements for border protection at this port, which from an American perspective, meant that the Canada Customs and Revenue Agency would be double the security risk. The project unsurprisingly never came to fruition.

Even Canadian residents believed that their revenue agency's true *raison d'être* was not one of security, but of nickel-and-diming them upon reentry into their country by imposing heavy duties on items purchased at greatly reduced costs from the United States.

This bad rap was to change when Canada Customs morphed into the Canada Border Services Agency. Severe pressure had been applied by the U.S. government to ensure that restructuring was put in place to shore up lax Canadian border security. However, in true Canadian fashion, little else changed save the flashes on border guard uniforms.

Adding insult to injury, U.S. Customs officials were literally up in arms when they discovered their unarmed Canadian counterparts would sometimes walk off the job when alerted to dangerous fugitives coming their way.

It took a simple, direct, albeit heated memo from the office of the president of the United States to the Canadian prime minister in Ottawa for Canadian bureaucrats to see the light. The curt memo simply stated that if Canada couldn't get her act together on border security, the Americans would do it for them.

The Canadian government finally relented. Soon after, CBSA initiated firearms training, which provided their personnel with the confidence needed to effectively do their jobs. A much needed start, but it seemed to end there.

This eventually led to the formation of the North American Bureau of Security. A joint endeavor between the two countries, NABS was officially developed to enhance and coordinate all border operations between the two countries, and provided invaluable assistance to both existing Canadian and U.S. border services.

The *reality* was that this newly formed international agency's prime directive was terrorist intelligence. However, its duties were soon expanded to include the monitoring and acting upon other illicit operations as well. On the Southern Ontario side of the border, Intel was funneled to the Niagara-On-The-Lake section station of NABS.

Once suspect groups or individuals were identified as potential threats to North American security, information on their activities was then disseminated to the big four agencies, notably the CIA and the Department of Homeland Security (DHS) in the United States, CSIS and the Communications Security Establishment Canada (CSEC) in Canada.

Several months back while conducting a routine bridge abutment stability study of the pilings under the Peace Bridge, a team of underwater experts from the Niagara Underwater Recovery Unit organized and led by Lee Hartley came upon a semtex-based explosive planted at the base of the bridge's central pier.

His experience as a commercial diver came in most handy that day. In spite of a seven-knot current attempting to dismember him, Lee had managed to disarm and remove the professionally designed and shaped military-type charge within ten hours of its intended detonation.

This led to an international investigation, which recommended that NURU be commissioned into active full-time duty as a sub agency of NABS to assist in ensuring waterway security for the whole of the Niagara River. Maintaining diligent surveillance both above and below the surface from the Peace Bridge in the south to the brink of Niagara Falls some twenty miles to the north was a daunting task. However, the unit quickly adapted and became extremely useful in providing invaluable assistance and intelligence to NABS.

For Hartley's quick and efficient actions that day, he was put on a sizeable retainer with NABS as their foremost underwater consultant.

NURU's previous mandate of seeking and reclaiming local drowning victims and property lost to the river was downloaded to the local volunteer fire department and police marine unit, leaving it to focus directly on matters of international marine security.

There was a definite need for increased border security along the shores of the Niagara River, and thanks to NABS, jurisdictional squabbles between the two countries' various law enforcement agencies was eliminated.

Although the acronym for the bureau was the cause for much guffaw when first announced, the agency proved worthy of the moniker, *NABS*. Smugglers of both illicit goods and illegal immigrants attempting to cross the border were 'nabbed' with increasing frequency and dealt with both swiftly and severely.

Drug cartels, counterfeiters, gun runners, human slave traffickers, and the like were forced to find other means of cross-border logistics. Seizures ran into the millions of dollars during the first year of the bureau's inception alone, not to mention the incarceration of key members of several nefarious operations.

The Neighbors to the North had finally made good on their pledge to contribute greatly to international security along their undefended border with the United States.

3

Background Checks

Alan Exner was control for the Niagara Station of NABS, situated on the sixth floor of an office complex overlooking Lake Ontario at Niagara-On-The-Lake. On such a clear day, he looked out over the lake and viewed the Toronto skyline. It shimmered in greedy corporate splendor as the sun's rays reflected off the myriad windows of the city's innumerable office buildings.

Exner was a former officer in the highly secretive Communications Security Establishment Canada (CSEC). He was awarded NABS' top position due to his diligence and tenacity in the line of duty, as well as his past ability at successfully coordinating activities of other field agents while under conditions of extreme duress.

CSEC's intelligence is routinely shared with Britain's GCHQ, Australia's DSD, New Zealand's GCSB, and America's NSA. Together, these agencies and their shared intelligence form the basis of the ECHELON system. ECHELON's responsibilities include monitoring an enormous proportion of all the world's transmitted data, cell, and fax traffic. The intercepted data, or *dictionaries*, are then linked and disseminated through a massive array of computers known as *Sequoia.*

Exner's hair was on the longish side and grayed at the temples, which gave him an air of mature sophistication. He was tough and efficient, and possessed both a razor sharp intellect and dry sense of humor. He had zero tolerance in dealing with those who profited from the misery of others. His piercing steel gray eyes and deep bass voice underscored this fact, and combined with his no-nonsense attitude, he had the innate ability to break the toughest of them.

A product of the early 1960s, Alan Exner cast an imposing figure. His tall, strong frame belied muscles of steel and an attitude to match. He was a rare breed of man who meant what he said and said what he meant. This garnered much respect from his peers, although no one ever took his good nature for granted. Alan Exner was not one to tolerate either fools or the insincere.

While firm with his operatives, Exner was nonetheless a fair man who loved his job, valued his friends, and treasured the memory of his deceased wife Marlissa. In a botched home invasion a few years back, his wife had been murdered. No one had yet been brought to justice for the crime.

It was midevening several years earlier, and Exner was in the upstairs shower at the time, music blaring, when Marlissa answered the doorbell. From the evidence obtained, CSEC forensics believed that the door had been violently kicked in just as she began to open it. She was thrown backward and apparently struck her head on the marble of the bottom step of their spiral staircase.

Marlissa should have died from the severe skull fracture suffered when she fell, but may have attempted to yell a warning to her husband. This may have been the reason the interlopers slit her throat from ear to ear. If that wasn't enough, she'd apparently been yanked to her feet by her long blonde hair. Investigators found a sizable clump mired in a bloodied boot print just past the stairway Exner was to later descend.

The murderers had ransacked Exner's downstairs office, apparently leaving with nothing save a complete and utter mess. It was obvious they had been looking for something specific, as nothing valuable was taken other than his wife's life. No fingerprints had been found at the scene.

When he finally came downstairs, Exner was totally unprepared for the horrific scene that awaited him below. Investigators found no leads, no witnesses, and no closure for Exner. The break-in was brazen, professional, and untraceable. An unsolved case, it had all the earmarks of the perfect crime.

Although Exner's job had earned him many enemies over the years, he couldn't come up with the name of anyone desperate enough to violate his home and murder his wife in cold blood, let alone what they could possibly have been looking for.

Alan Exner had never allowed himself the pleasure of another woman since. The deep-seated, traumatically imbedded sense of loss and sorrow in the belief that he felt directly responsible for her death (after all, *he was right there),* was to become a self-imposed curse he felt compelled to endure for the rest of his life.

Marlissa was still and forever the love of Alan's life, as evidenced by the myriad photos of them still prominent around both home and office. It was also evidenced by the fact that he still wore the wedding ring she had placed on his finger so many years before.

A beautiful person both inside and out, ever sensitive and protective of their marriage, Marlissa was the quintessential woman. She was vivacious, successful, intelligent, competent, and athletic. She was a very giving individual and totally uninhibited in meeting his needs; truly one of a kind.

No; her memory would never fade, never die. Neither would his quest to bring her murderers to justice at worst, to a violent death at best. It was only a matter of time.

Exner was surveying the beauty of Lake Ontario from his office window, nursing a steaming hot cup of café mocha, when his desk phone flashed to announce an incoming call from a secure line.

Carefully placing the hot cup of liquid down beside an "eyes only" file folder on his dark mahogany desk, Exner hit the speakerphone button. He then plopped his derriere down onto the corner nearest the folder, knocking the cup over in his haste.

"Ex . . . Ex, you there?"

Jumping up with blinding speed, Exner grabbed the important folder and tossed it onto the far end of the desk before he let out a huge sigh of relief.

"Yes. Oh hi, Lee, I—"

"I can call back if you're busy, Ex. You're . . . ah, you're not, you know, with your secretary or anything like that, are you, buddy?" Lee kidded.

"No. *NO*, I am not, thank you very much. I almost . . . never mind. What's on yours?"

"I need a favor, man. Some crazy just about ran me off the Parkway heading into the Falls last night."

"And this is different than any other night of yours, because . . . ?"

"Alan, I'm serious. The guy was a pro. He tried ramming me into the drink. When that didn't work, he started shooting."

The silence was almost deafening, and Exner knew Hartley was serious the moment Lee called him by his first name.

"You okay, Lee?"

"You mean other than having the Caddy strafed with bullets?"

"Lee, the thing's a relic anyway. Now this may come as a shock to you, but it doesn't owe you a thing!"

"What d'ya mean? It's only a few decades old, and just broke in nice. Hey, you're missing the point here. The guy was *shooting* at me, Ex. I'm *not* a happy camper, and last night's experience was the direct antithesis of fun . . ."

The control of NABS Niagara came back around to sit behind the large desk, a look of concern sweeping his visage. Exner listened quietly as his old chum detailed the recent events.

"Okay, okay. Got a description of the vehicle? Tag number? What about the driver? Listen . . . can you get down to headquarters as soon as possible? We need to talk, and not over the phone."

"Right, then . . . be there in an hour. You *were,* you know, with your secretary, weren't you?"

"One hour, Hartley."

Tossing the portable phone onto the top of his living room coffee table stacked with dive magazines, Lee grabbed his wallet and keys before going out the front door. Locking up, he made his way to the driveway. Conducting a slow circle check of the Cadillac, Lee suddenly felt sick to his stomach.

The venerable old vehicle had several hefty dings in its heavy chrome rear bumper. Paint had given way in places to bare metal where several deep scrapes were incurred along the passenger side. Lee had side-swiped several trees during last night's escape from impending death. Those at the rear of the car occurred when his pursuer had rammed him on several occasions.

"*Unbelievable*!"

Lee stared at the remnants of the driver's side mirror, a bullet hole in its supporting mount. He kicked the left front tire out of anger and disgust. Immediately, he began hopping around, cradling his now damaged foot.

Climbing into the voluminous cockpit, he brought the leviathan to life, uttering words that would make a sailor blush.

A pair of indelibly inscribed black tire marks on the pavement behind bore mute testimony to Lee's displeasure as he matted the accelerator upon clearing his driveway. Someone was going to pay. Someone was going to pay *big-time.*

Lee felt like he was more in a library than the office of NABS control. There were several bookcases stocked with publications and periodicals, file folders of various colors and thicknesses on a stand by the doorway, and a multi-slotted in/out rack mounted by the entrance door that was full to overflowing. Lee noticed that the "in" rack was currently empty.

Flanking the large triple-paned bulletproof glass window that overlooked the lake were two large live palm trees. Several paintings hung on the walls, primarily rustic beach scenes and rugged seascapes.

The most striking of all, however, was a large breathtaking painting of Marlissa above and behind his desk. She appeared well tanned, and wore a red rose above her right temple. Her hair flowed down and into her deep cleavage. Marlissa was adorned as a Spanish *señorita* in a deliciously short ruffled dress.

But it was her sensuous warm smile and hungry eyes that drew you into the painting. Surreal to the casual observer, but as Lee knew firsthand, genuine. The artist had almost supernaturally captured both Marlissa's spirit and her unearthly beauty.

It all added up to the office of a man who had "arrived." But of the depth of Exner's grief knew no man, not even his closest friend, Lee Hartley.

Early in their high school years, both developed an affinity for the more intense individual sports offered: karate, boxing, and gymnastics, through which they became fast friends. Each tried to better the other in everything he did. But Alan could never breach Lee's indomitable *kamikaze* spirit and obsession to dominate.

It was the strict discipline and technique of the old venerable Japanese martial art of karate that Lee enjoyed most, however. He had eagerly embraced the "way of the empty hand," along with its exotic philosophy. The *kata* (set patterns of various one-man routines that had to be perfected before graduating to the next belt level), were a challenge Lee enjoyed. *They were* perceived as "an outward expression of the inner peace within," a portal through which the practitioner could develop the ability to know himself.

Lee's hungry passion for karate led to the promotion of black belt one year earlier than his contemporaries. Karate became for Lee the prime philosophy of life that enabled him to be at peace with himself throughout the succeeding years.

Following high school, the two parted company when Exner left for university to study political science. Lee attended a community college north of Toronto to pursue a career in commercial diving.

Their times together became fewer and farther in between. Alan hit the books in earnest; Lee was away for weeks at a time apprenticing in the underwater skills trade.

Following graduation, Lee travelled the world and quickly developed bonds with locals of various ports, who invariably referred him to underwater contractors that needed a good diver for a "tough job." Such networking built up a profitable business for Lee that garnered him much success in his chosen field of employment.

Lee continued to perform kata as often as possible, even when on assignments to remote locations. Their assiduous practice afforded not only cardio fitness, but also fluency in fighting technique as well.

But it was Alan who seemed to come out on top both scholastically and vocationally. He landed a job with CSEC even before he completed his thesis. Unbeknown to Exner at the time, the ultra-secretive Canadian agency regularly canvassed the university for its best and brightest.

They recruited young men and women who not only displayed keen interest in both domestic and foreign affairs, but more importantly, were found to be intellectual loners. Such individuals they deemed ideal for the rigors of intelligence gathering both at home and abroad.

Initially, Exner didn't quite grasp the overall ramifications of aligning himself with CSEC. He met Marlissa indirectly while working a case, and then fell deeply in love with her. Following a whirlwind courtship, Marlissa and Alan got married in a private ceremony in Niagara Falls, dubbed "the Honeymoon Capital of the World."

Exner soon realized he couldn't share his work at the end of the day with Marlissa, and that bothered him greatly. He had to develop the fine art of lying to account for unexplained absences and dangers while working on cases of a sensitive nature.

Alan resented having to do this to the love of his life. But he was under almost constant surveillance, if not from his own organization, from others, both hostile and friendly. As a result, he and Marlissa had no close lasting ties to anyone outside of immediate family.

By necessity, Exner's life was his work. But following the successful completion of his more lengthy assignments, he couldn't wait to come home to Marlissa.

Now he returned home nightly to her memory. How he would have done things differently had he the chance! But life is cruel; indeed, second chances are but evaporating mists of hope to those who have lost that which can never be regained.

Seated in a plush leather chair within Exner's voluminous office, Lee Hartley pulled a swig from a small silver flask as he waited for Alan to seat himself behind his majestic desk. The Canadian NABS control leaned forward, elbows firmly planted on the desk, hands folded, and palms down.

"Let's have it, Lee; leave nothing out."

Upon hearing Lee's detailed account of the previous night's incident, Exner leaned back in his chair and let out a long, low sigh. "Just what the hell have you gotten yourself into now, Hartley?"

Lee got up from where he was seated and strode over to the desk. He leaned over it until their faces were almost touching and said, "I haven't the slightest," then walked over to the window, staring into space as he continued.

"All I know is this nimrod came from out of nowhere and started taking pot shots; even rammed me a few times. He was driving a dark-colored high performance car. There was no time for that definitive 'Kodak moment.' He's a good driver, damn good, but obviously doesn't know the terrain. That tells me he's not from the area Ex, and it was just too damn dark to get his tag number." Lee turned to face his friend in summary. "That's all I can tell you, man."

Exner had been taking notes. Looking up, he saw the concern on his friend's face. Exner laid down his pen and walked over to the window beside Lee. He gently placed a hand on Lee's shoulder.

"I'll look into it, Lee. In the meantime, watch your six. You're a person of interest to someone, and I intend to find out just who that someone is."

4

The Prodigal Shipwreck

Being a freelance commercial diver had taken Lee Hartley around the world and back again. His underwater work included a myriad of operations: demolition, pier construction, innumerable recoveries for insurance companies and police, underwater investigations, surveys, and photography. He even hosted a few wreck-diving shows between contracts for the Discovery Channel.

In addition, Lee's underwater skills *alma mater* had recruited him to teach a class here and there to aspiring deep sea divers. There was little below the waves that Lee couldn't handle. Diving had been good to him, very good indeed.

But he realized that time was fast becoming his enemy. Against his wishes he was of the opinion that age was ever so slowly sending him behind the far side of the moon. Lee's work seemed to be unconsciously leaning more in the way of underwater consultations nowadays, although he was still up for more adventuresome fare from time to time.

He remained on retainer at the bequest of his friend Alan Exner and NABS since finding and defusing the bomb under the Peace Bridge. As such, Lee was instrumental in reorganizing the Niagara Underwater Recovery Unit into a professional underwater security department for NABS Niagara.

Though far from over the hill, Lee's body still let him know when enough was enough, and that, with increasing frequency.

Later that afternoon, the wounded Sedan de Ville found its way back along the Niagara Parkway and to the Sea Shack outside Fort Erie. Once a failing old hotel, the Sea Shack had undergone new management a few years back. The new owners turned the place into a thriving Wi-Fi café for nautical types, overlooking Lake Erie on Waverly Beach.

Divers, yachtsmen, boaters, fishermen, wind surfers—anyone interested in water-fare came in for a cup of fine coffee in its various derivations, enjoy good food and company, pore over laptops, swap stories, study charts, read, or just soak up the atmosphere.

This was a place of rejuvenation for Lee. Here he met with old friends and made new ones. Not to mention that some of his work came from networking at the "Shack." It was a good place to let your hair down, but as Lee had found out on more than one occasion, not your guard.

Parking the Caddy beside a red Hummer H2 with *Scuba U: Where Diving is Taught in Depth* adorning each of its sides, Lee smiled to himself that there would be at least one patron in attendance that he knew.

Bill Travers, the owner of the Hummer, was a diver from the early days of scuba. Now in his early seventies, he owned a profitable dive shop, the Scuba U. Although he sold the latest and best gear in the business, his real passion was repairing and reconditioning vintage scuba gear from the 1950s and 1960s: old double hose regulators from extinct manufacturers, half-inch valves for early 71.2 steel scuba tanks, old backpacks and gauges; indeed, anything unusual and unique Bill used, collected, reconditioned and sold.

During the formative years of recreational scuba diving, a 1950s TV show called *Sea Hunt* had captivated the interest and imagination of thousands of young Baby Boomers, the generation of which Travers was a part. Starring Lloyd Bridges as underwater investigator Mike Nelson, the weekly half-hour program had become a worldwide phenomenon.

Travers soon discovered that the gear used in *Sea Hunt* was now the Holy Grail of aging divers worldwide, and it commanded handsome sums on eBay. But for many, it wasn't just good enough to just own a piece of dive history; as life support equipment, it had to function safely as well.

Travers was one of the few repair technicians in North America that could do the job. He repaired antique scuba gear from such venerable but extinct scuba manufacturers as Healthways, AMF Voit/ Swimaster, Sportsways, Nemrod, Northill, Dacor, and others, along with US Divers Company, the latter being the only company still in business today.

Such equipment had a huge cult following on eBay. Vintage scuba groups from all over the world sent their antiquated dive gear to Travers to be reconditioned so they could safely dive it with pride.

Lee loved the crusty and eccentric but knowledgeable old diver. Travers was tough, but he was honest, and possessed a heart of gold. But get on the wrong side of him . . .

Although sharing Bill's passion for older gear, Lee preferred the best contemporary equipment if only for the peace of mind such gear afforded, especially at the depths he incurred during the course of his work. He always knew he could depend on any equipment Bill sold, from whom Lee purchased exclusively, and knew that when his gear went in for its annual servicing, you could stake your life on Bill's repairs, as well he had.

The two had known each other for over fifteen years and had shared many underwater adventures together. As with Lee, diving was a way of life to Travers, which is why the two had become such lasting friends over the years.

This passion led Travers to open his own dive shop dubbed the Scuba U, a name most appropriate as, like a high-end learning institution, he had educated literally hundreds of diving enthusiasts *in depth.*

But Lee had been around Travers long enough to know that there was a right way, a wrong way, and Bill's way. When diving with Bill, it was done his way. Regardless, Travers had quickly become one of the most competent and respected charter captains at the eastern end of Lake Erie.

Entrance to the Sea Shack was gained through a genuine WWII British submarine hatch, complete with lockdown wheel. The heavy black steel door groaned open with unbelievable ease due to its unique pulley system. Lee stepped in and was greeted by an inanimate figure fully clad in antique hard hat diving gear. The "diver" held a treasure chest in his arms that displayed the Shack's menu specials on its front.

The Sea Shack had many full-sized imitation palm trees strategically spaced throughout. Two large saltwater aquariums had been placed in tandem in the center of the coffee house to provide a natural semi-private wall. Vibrant and exotic ocean fish inhabited them and were the subject of much conversation and delight among the establishment's patrons.

Looking around the aromatic coffee-scented café filled with patrons, Lee found his old friend sitting with his back to the rear wall. Above Travers' head hung a long fishermen's net adorned not with seashells and the like as is customary, but with old scuba regulators, spearguns, and other undersea equipment from diving's early days. Lee ordered and received his usual three-quarters coffee/one-quarter hot chocolate with a well-toasted everything bagel topped with garlic flavored cream cheese, and then strode over to greet his friend.

"So how are things at the hallowed halls of the Scuba U, William?" Lee smiled as he savored the site of this old weather-beaten white-haired diver before him; without doubt the best antique display piece in the entire establishment.

Bill Travers looked over his reading glasses from the newspaper he was perusing, and at seeing Lee, unceremoniously beckoned him to sit down. A Tilley hat lay on Travers' knee. It was rare not to find it on his head, thought Lee.

Like many of Travers' generation, however, Lee knew that his friend had struggled hard to adapt to an information age that made everything, and everyone, seem increasingly impersonal to him. Nevertheless, Lee was still amazed at the muscle tone his old friend managed to retain.

Making eye contact as soon as Lee sat down in front of him, Travers smiled his trademark "polite" smile, which faded almost as soon as he launched it.

Travers noticed that Lee was not his usual jovial self. "Smile, buddy; I'll pay for the stitches."

"Had a tough night last night," Lee said, and Travers could see that his friend was deeply troubled.

"What, Lee? Give me the 411."

"I was heading up to the Falls along River Road last night when this psycho came out of nowhere and started shooting at me."

"Holy crap! What's with that?"

Lee explained in detail what had transpired the night previous.

"The kicker is, I don't have the foggiest idea who was chasing me, or more importantly, why," Lee summed up.

A silence fell across their table, broken only by the subdued chatter of other patrons and the perpetual bubbling of the aquariums.

"Man, it's a good thing I didn't need your old crate last night after all," Travers said, shaking his head forlornly.

"I wish you had," Lee said. "So how come you didn't need the Caddy anyway?"

"Well, I took the Hummer to the garage to have some new heavy-duty shocks put on. I figured if I have a mean lookin' machine, it needs to perform like one, right? But when I got there the mechanic, Aiden, had ordered the wrong size shocks!" Travers picked the Tilley up and beat his knee with it, then returned it to its perch. "He may be a solid mechanic, but he can be a real knucklehead at times."

Ignoring Travers' good-humored poke at his mechanic, Lee said, "Bill, what time were you at the garage on Thursday night?"

"About six, I think, Lee. I was goin' to leave the Hummer overnight Friday and have Aiden drop me off at your place to pick up your hemi, because as you know, I had a group dive trip planned for the weekend. But turns out I didn't need it."

Travers noticed that his friend was deep in thought. "Yer creepin' me out, Hartley! You keep ponderin' like that, and the smoke detectors are gonna go off!"

Lee was slowly spinning his coffee mug around by its mouth on the table and nearly dumped it. His quick reflexes won out, however, and Travers let out a sigh of relief.

"Bill, maybe the guy in the sports car knew all this somehow. Maybe he was gunning for *you*. There's no reason anyone would be after me."

"Gunning for *me*? Why would someone be gunning for me?"

Lee looked deep into his friend's eyes as he took a sip of coffee. "Bill, is there something you're not telling me here?"

"Lee, as sure as we're sittin' here, I can't think why anyone would be out to get me."

"When did you make your appointment to have the shocks done on the truck?"

Travers thought for a moment then said, "A couple or three days ago, I guess. It was Tuesday. I called you from the garage after puttin' the order in while l thought of it, to see if you could spare the Caddy until my truck was done if I needed it."

"Aiden said he'd have the shocks in by late Thursday. He told me that if I'd bring in the Hummer before closing on Friday, he'd install 'em on Saturday. But no, the knucklehead goes and orders the wrong size, and then tells me he wouldn't have the right ones in until Monday at the earliest."

"Bill," Lee pondered, "can you remember if there was anyone in the garage beside you and Aiden on Tuesday?"

"Not that I can—wait a minute. There *was* a late model black Viper that followed me all the way to the garage on Tuesday. Nice machine, that one. Then this big Indian or Mexican lookin' dude came in. He didn't say anything, just fingered through the magazines while me and Aiden was talkin', like he was waiting to get an estimate or somethin'."

"I don't want to alarm you, Bill, but it sounds like the same car that chased me on the Parkway last night. He must have overheard our conversation about borrowing the Caddy for Friday and thought it was you driving it. He was after *you*, Bill, not me!"

"But why, Lee? I haven't done nothin' to nobody!"

"You may not think so, but it's definitely something Exner will want to mull over," Lee said.

Although the two didn't think either was the intended target of the previous night's attack, Lee had an ever-growing suspicion that once again, his old friend had somewhere, somehow, bit off more than he could chew.

The two ate their bagels in silence. Then Bill's expression suddenly changed to that of excitement. Looking around the room and satisfied that no one was within immediate earshot, Travers leaned toward his pal, this time with a genuine grin.

"I found a wreck off Manitoulin Island in Lake Huron last week, Lee. Didn't want to tell you or anyone else about it until I did some research about her. I know South Baymouth is off limits for divers because of the ferry channel to Tobermory, but the whole area around Tobermory is full of shipwrecks. You know how monstrous the storms can be up there. I figured surely somethin' must have gone down off the largest fresh water island in the world, so sue me."

Lee shook his head in disapproval. He knew that if divers were caught diving the restricted waters off South Baymouth, it would not bode well for the diving fraternity as a whole. And if anyone would be caught at something like this, Lee knew it would be his old buddy.

Undaunted, Travers continued. "Anyway, she's like nothin' I've ever seen in those waters. I mean, this wreck is pristine, Lee! She's upright and perfectly intact, except for the masts that busted off, but she's in only eighty feet of water!"

Looking around again and lowering his voice, he winked at Lee and continued. "From what I've seen, she appears to be from the mid—to late 1600s, and a big one she is. She reminds me of Cap'n Crunch's good ship *Guppy*!"

"The 1600s?" Lee pushed back from the table lowering an elbow to his knee, chin cradled in palm. He became lost in thought, as evidenced by the tapping of a forefinger repeatedly aside of his nose.

"No, it couldn't be from that era, Bill. Most of the ships that went down in that location were from the mid-to-late 1800s. Prior to that there weren't any sizable ships plying the Great Lakes."

Lee directed his gaze at the old wrinkled squints where Travers' eyes were concealed, and knew he had just opened the proverbial can of worms.

"How'd you come to that conclusion, anyway?"

Bill Travers was no fool. Although he came across as a crusty simpleton, he was far wiser than he let on. He loved history and had an extensive library of nautical books and underwater journals that would rival that of the Cousteau Society.

"Lee, sure as I'm lookin' at yer ugly puss, I swear I've found La Salle's *Griffon*! I looked it up; did a *lot* of lookin'. The architecture alone cries out French craftsmanship. She doesn't look like anything I've ever seen that's ever plied the Lakes."

"She looks kinda like a Spanish galleon, but I know she's not one of those; not as big, for one. I *do* know the French of that era patterned *their* trading ships after the galleons of the Dutch. How do I know this, you ask?" Travers smiled smugly. "Among other things, she's got a low draft designed for access to shallow harbors and bays. Plus, the bow is squared. But that's not all . . ."

Lee sat guardedly amazed as Travers continued to enlighten him as to the lost ship's identity. The more Travers spoke, the more convinced Lee was that his friend may be spot on with his assessment of the wreck. If it was indeed the *Griffon*, the discovery would rock the underwater archeological world; it would be a find of true international proportions.

Travers continued. "The clincher for me was the lead caulking between the planks for mortar."

Lee leaned forward, and locked his gaze deep into the eyeless squint of his friend. "So?"

"Sooo, the *Griffon* wasn't built in France," Travers said. "She was built almost right on our doorstep just across the Niagara River at Black Rock, New York. The early explorers had to work with what they had at hand. La Salle's crew didn't have the resources of the French shipbuildin' industry over here, so they improvised: big time."

"Lead was readily available, so that's what they used for caulking. It was heated until molten and then poured as mortar between the planks. Also, Lee, the deckin' looks rougher than bloody hell. In modern vernacular, the ship was a French knock-off."

Lee snorted a smile, then let out a long, low two-toned whistle.

Both men sat in collective silence as each inwardly entertained the ramifications Travers' find would generate if she was indeed La Salle's fabled lost ship, the *Griffon.*

In the mid-1670s, French adventurer Rene Robert Cavalier Sieur de la Salle was sent to New France by King Louis XIV. La Salle had received a land grant near present-day Kingston, Ontario, where Lake Ontario flows into the St. Lawrence River at its easternmost end. It was here that La Salle constructed Fort Frontenac.

Soon thereafter, and with an advance party of eighteen of his countrymen, La Salle left the fort for the Niagara Falls area, whereupon he built a small fleet of ships that were to operate between trading posts on the upper Great Lakes. These ships were to be laden with furs and other goods, and then travel eastward along the St. Lawrence River to what is now Montreal, Quebec, and thence to the Atlantic Ocean, bound for France. At least that was the official plan.

It was during this time that some of La Salle's men under the guidance of Father Louis Hennepin discovered Niagara Falls. Then in early 1679, La Salle's expedition climbed the Niagara Escarpment, traveling south some twelve miles to Cayuga Creek, where construction began on the first sailing vessel to ply the Great Lakes above Niagara Falls.

Christened *Le Griffon* by Henri de Tonti, La Salle's lieutenant and best friend, the ship was named after this mythical animal that possessed the body and legs of a lion but the wings and beak of an eagle. It was a griffon that was emblazoned on the family coat-of-arms of Count Frontenac, La Salle's major sponsor and good friend.

With the increasing hostility of the local Seneca braves in New France, workers rushed to complete construction of the ship. By the summer of 1679, the forty-five-ton *Griffon* was ready to set sail. It took twelve men on the beach using towlines to launch the *Griffon* manually into the swift swirling waters of the Niagara River.

As a precaution against potential Indian sabotage, the *Griffon* was anchored a safe distance off shore for a time, then moved several miles upstream and safely moored off Squaw Island before sailing on its first mission.

Trading posts were quickly established on the shores of the upper Great Lakes, with La Salle sailing back to Niagara laden with beaver pelts. Then a strange thing happened. Within a year of her christening, the *Griffon* mysteriously vanished, crew and all, without a trace. *Le Griffon* thus became a legendary ghost ship of the Great Lakes, her fate unknown and her crew never to be heard from again.

Travers pushed back his chair, got up, and strode behind Lee. Sliding his right arm around Lee's shoulders until they could see each other's face again from the seated man's left side, Bill looked around, then whispered, "I've seen enough spy movies in my day. The walls have ears, my friend. If you want to know more, meet me at the shop in an hour."

With that, Bill Travers gave Lee a few pats on the shoulder, placed his trademark weather-beaten Tilley hat on top of his large pumpkin head, ran a finger across its brim in a mock salute, then sauntered out the door.

Lee sat bewildered. He absentmindedly licked a finger to pick up and eat sesame seeds that had fallen to his plate. From the previous evening's low of nearly being run off River Road to this morning's high at the prospect of exploring a virgin wreck of great historical value, he was lost in conflicting thoughts.

Lee made a mental note to take his friend Alan Exner's advice to proceed with caution. While Exner had NABS unofficially running down leads to the owner of the mystery vehicle, Lee had a gut feeling there was a strange connection between his incident on the Parkway the night previous and something Travers was into.

Lee smiled as he recalled that Travers *had* spun a yarn or two in his day. However, when it came to his passion for wreck diving, he was all business. Lee wasn't exactly sure what to think about the whole thing.

Travers had a habit of getting in over his head, of not counting the cost before jumping into things. More often than not, the old fart had a penchant for leaving his friends to pick up the pieces when things got beyond his control.

Like now, Lee thought as he rose to leave, having consumed the last of the fallen sesame seeds. *The old knucklehead stuck me with the bill—again.*

Having paid the tab, Lee emerged from the Sea Shack and secured the hatch behind him. He gratefully absorbed the heat of the sun as its rays sliced between the leaves of the numerous oak and maple trees surrounding the coffee house while a balmy warm breeze caressed his body.

A beautiful day in the neighborhood, Lee thought, as he watched Travers' Hummer round the winding drive out of the car park.

Just as he went to open the door of the Caddy, he was suckered with a vicious punch to the left kidney from behind that slammed him into the side of the vehicle.

His attacker, in harsh broken English, said, "Keep your nose out of where it does not belong, *señor*!"

The blow would have doubled over a lesser man. But this infuriated Lee more than hurt him. Not waiting for a second helping, Lee Hartley instinctively spun around counterclockwise. He blocked high with his left hand as he did so, just as a vicious overhand right nearly found its mark. Lee immediately countered with two solid knee strikes to the assailant's groin. As the man doubled over in pain, Lee drove him to the ground with a downward elbow strike to the assailant's upper spine.

But there were two of them. The second attacker was thwarted in an attempt to crush Lee's head with a tire iron. Lee connected with a solid spinning back kick to the man's solar plexus. He immediately followed up with a back fist and an uppercut throat thrust, knocking this one hard onto his back, gasping for air. The tire iron clanged harmlessly to the pavement.

A screech of burning rubber drew Lee's immediate attention to the end of the driveway in time to see a black sports car, a Viper, disappearing around the bend. Out of blind fury, Lee broke into a run after the slick vehicle. After a minute of futile, angry pursuit, he came to his senses and walked back to the Cadillac, out of breath and out of answers. The first assailant had run off by the time Lee reached the Caddy, no doubt picked up at a predetermined point by the Viper's driver.

It wasn't the attack, or even the fact that he had lost his keys in the fray; it was the fact that another hand had been won by the mysterious driver of the Dodge Viper that consumed Lee the most.

Adding insult to injury, a crowd of patrons had by now rushed over to Lee, who was resting his head against the driver's side window of the Caddy exhausted and sore, not necessarily in that order. He was not surprised to notice through the mob that the second assailant had also vanished into the woodlands that paralleled the lakeshore beside the Shack.

A quick search revealed his keys under an SUV parked beside Lee's vehicle. People were milling around, expressing their disgust in varying degrees of expletives at the unprovoked attack. Several offered their assistance out of genuine concern. Lee thanked the patrons for their concern as he opened the Caddy's door, clambered in, and roared its ancient engine to life.

Onlookers were still brewing over the incident even as they watched the cloud of dust left in the wake of Lee's damaged old car as it entered the main highway and disappeared from view.

His jaw hard set, Lee's only thought was to get to the bottom of this thing, and the sooner the better.

5

Arson!

Hot coffee is best administered through the mouth in careful sips to achieve its calming effect. To dump said coffee over oneself while driving, however, greatly inhibits that effect in direct proportion to both the temperature of the coffee and the number of protective layers of clothing worn. Wearing shorts during such an incident greatly exacerbates the situation, prompting several obligatory high-pitched profanities from the victim, as evidenced by Lee's startled outcry.

The incident was soon forgotten as Lee pulled into the car park of Bill's dive shop. Travers' Hummer was parked in its usual spot. But the scene before him was one of complete and total incomprehension. Glass littered the parking lot, and he saw that the store's large front display window had been blown out. Smoke swirled from a side entrance, the door blown off its hinges from the blast. The store looked as though it had been a successful training target for the practice of military ordnance.

Screeching to an abrupt halt, car still idling, Lee was out of the Caddy almost before it stopped, in a desperate bid to see if anyone was inside. A stench of burning wood and smoldering wet suit neoprene invaded Lee's nostrils as he stepped cautiously through the frame where the front window had been, calling out as he entered. Lee carefully threaded his way through smoldering debris that was strewn everywhere.

"Bill . . . Bill!" Lee cried out, heart in throat, as he clambered through the hot, smoky remains of the dying Scuba U.

Lee choked his way deeper into the ruins. He penetrated as far as possible, then was forced to retreat to replenish his lungs with fresh, cool air from outside the smoldering building.

Lee cursed himself for going home to clean-up and change following the unexpected attack outside the Sea Shack, then stopping for a coffee in a failed attempt to regain his composure.

He jogged back to the Caddy, grabbed his cell, and dialed 911. He punched the send button then threw it back onto the front seat of the car as he hurried around the side of the building. He knew the on-duty 911 operators would trace the call and automatically dispatch emergency vehicles to the scene if no one responded to their queries.

Lee returned to the smoke-infested shop, going in low as the air was cooler and easier to breathe closer to ground. He grabbed a T-shirt off a rack that had somehow survived unscathed and used it as a handkerchief, but even so, was forced to the windowless frame on several occasions to fill his lungs with fresh air.

As the showroom slowly purged itself of the acrid black smoke, Lee could see that much of the front end of the shop had been destroyed. The inventory of wet suits, masks, fins, and snorkels were reduced to unrecognizable heaps of molten rubber and plastic on the floor below, where they once proudly hung awaiting purchase.

Lee's breath was taken away on several occasions as his throat automatically closed up from the thick stench of superheated smoke inside the building.

"Bill . . . BILL! Where the hell are you?" Lee now crawled on all fours, seeking to get as much cool oxygen as he could at floor level. His passage came to an abrupt end when he came to the buildings' central support pillar, which had collapsed onto the main display case in the center of the store, blocking any further penetration.

Lee backpedalled out into the fresh air once again. He sprinted around to the side entrance this time. Gaining entry, he heard a groan beyond a tangled mess of dry wall and wood intertwined with a heavy rack of dry suits. Kicking much of the debris aside, he struggled until he could squeeze by the rack. This allowed him direct access to the faint groans beyond.

With heavy wisps of smoke impairing Lee's vision, he tripped over something soft. It was an arm. He lost his balance, and propelled headfirst into a supporting wall. His eyes and lungs burned from the smoke and fumes. Bright flashes of light exploded from behind his eyes. Lee had no doubt that if he looked up he'd see a circle of stars swirling around his head as depicted in the cartoons of old.

Kneeling down, he shook his head from side to side in an effort to regain composure and focus. He saw the unconscious figure of a man. He struggled to locate a pulse on the face-down figure. Fortunately there was one, albeit faint.

With increasing concern, Lee also noticed that the man was bleeding from the lower left quadrant of his abdomen. Although he was not moving, the man was at least breathing on his own, though in obvious discomfort.

Lee carefully felt his way up the man's lower back to his neck, searching for possible breaks. Finding none, he gently pulled the man over into a face-up position. From there, Lee managed to get him into a sitting position. Finally, he bear-hugged the distraught man through the side entrance and into the safety of fresh air and afternoon sunshine.

Lee was somewhat relieved to see that the man he had just saved wasn't Travers, but he had never seen this man before. Sirens in the distance grew louder, a good sign, though it did little to abate the exhausted Hartley's concern for his missing friend.

He leaned against the soot-soiled outside wall of the dive shop and struggled to get his own breath. He retched in spite of his best efforts not to. A wave of nausea washed over him and he dropped to the ground, weak and mentally confused. A wave of welcome euphoria enveloped him as he slowly faded to black, and unconsciousness became him.

Two local fire department pumper trucks, two ambulances, and several Ontario Provincial Police cruisers all arrived on the scene simultaneously with a fire rescue vehicle arriving scant seconds later.

Bystanders began to accrue at an alarming rate. Several police officers were quick to channel the traffic around the scene and to establish a perimeter, while others kept the public a safe distance away. A pair of paramedics from each of the two ambulances loaded the injured men into their vehicles for immediate transfer to the local trauma center.

In and through it all, no one noticed the black Dodge Viper that crept to a halt in front of the carnage then was waved on by police.

In a swirl of dust and black rubber smoke, the Viper then rocketed away from the Scuba U in total irreverence to the shock and awe of the scene it left behind.

6

Browbeating The Help

Rolling the end of the *Cohiba* slowly in front of his Zippo lighter, Carlos Rodriguez drew deep on the premium Cuban cigar.

Ahhh, the taste of home, he thought.

Rodriguez was short, balding, and overweight; an ugly little man. It wasn't these features that denoted his ugliness, however. It wasn't even because of a severely pocked face from a nasty *herpes zoster* infection contracted during his teenage years. No, it was his cruel visage. His was the face of a merciless killer. His was the face of a man who was used to getting his own way one way or another.

Rodriguez was reclining on a chaise lounge in front of a large swimming pool. The mirrored surface of the calm water reflected the rays of the sun directly into his face. As if on cue, a shapely bronzed woman wearing the skimpiest of bikinis appeared. She handed him a *mojito* on a silver tray. Rodriguez fondled her derriere for several moments before he gently removed the iced glass from the tray. Observing his discomfort, the woman opened an umbrella situated at the side of the small table beside him to shield his face.

He smiled at her thoughtfulness as he blew a perfect smoke ring up into her face. Amused, she brushed the side of his cheek with the back of her hand and then left.

Life is good in this country, thought Rodriguez. *One can do anything here.* He smiled to himself as he drew on his *Cohiba*, slowly rolling it between his fingers. *Justice was an acquired commodity in Canada, as in any democratic society. A person was free to do as one pleased as long as one had the money to assuage it.*

The Cuban Secret Service paid its foreign intelligence agents well, which was why he was sent to Canada as part of a sleeper op. But Rodriguez was also a member of the Establishment, a shadowy organization principally comprised of rogue DGI operatives with an agenda of their own.

While he didn't know specifics, Establishment members had been made aware that an operation was currently in the workings: one that would parallel that of his government's. Rodriguez' current assignment for the Establishment, if successfully completed, would set him up for life. Despite the stifling afternoon heat, it was this thought that caused him to break into a comfortably cold sweat.

The blonde in the skimpy bikini returned to his side. "There is a man to see you, darling."

"Can you not see that I am busy, sweetheart? Tell him to come back tomorrow." The ugly little man took another sip of his *mojito*. He took a drag off his cigar, then watched the blue smoke curl off its end.

"It is your friend Gino," the blonde said. "He's says he needs to see you right away." She looked down on the balding head.

"That idiot is no friend of mine. We simply have a working relationship. Tell him to get his ass in here. Tell him it had better be good."

At that, the woman left. Rodriguez felt like having her again as he watched her leave. *Three times a charm . . .*

Rodriguez got up and walked the perimeter of the swimming pool. He watched with vacant interest as a sparrow swooped down to perch at one of several bird feeders in the yard.

Gino Vaselino was primarily a lieutenant in Rodriguez's Cuban cell who had little knowledge of the Establishment. He was powerfully built and as rugged as he looked. The antithesis of Rodriguez, Vaselino was painfully handsome, which made Rodriguez jealous. He was reticent to have Vaselino around his women. Vaselino wore his thick jet black hair long and slicked back. His well chiseled smooth body was nearly devoid of hair. Although charming with the ladies, he was not too quick on the uptake.

Gino swaggered into the courtyard. Rodriguez heard the loud, confident click of Gino's expensive Italian shoes as they connected with the hard marble deck surrounding the swimming pool as he approached.

"Tell me it is done." Carlos said without greeting. He continued to watch the bird feeder even though the bird had since taken flight at Gino's approach. Turning abruptly to face his lieutenant, the ugly little man raised the stub of the *Cohiba* and pointed it at Vaselino's face. "Tell me it is done, Gino. For your sake, tell me it is done."

At this, the man who had arrived with all manner of confidence was no longer the same man of a moment ago. He looked down at his feet as he spoke.

"We watched the café, like you said. The old man showed up. We waited for him to leave, as he always goes to his shop from there and so we knew where he'd be. We waited for his friend as planned. When he came out several minutes later, we roughed him up, real good, then caught up with your seller at the shop."

Gino isn't smiling his usual sadistic smile, thought Rodriguez. *He's lying.*

Gino continued, "We went to the diver store, and struck up a conversation with the old fool. But he was on to us and would not talk.

So we softened him up a little. When the old bastard still refused to tell us where it was, we searched the place real good. We didn't find the painting, so we took care of business. We have him at the grotto now, Carlos."

Quiet prevailed for several minutes. In fact, it was deafening. Rodriguez sat patiently as if waiting for the punch line. When it didn't come, he slowly and politely asked, "So where is this man's friend you were sent to pick up?"

Silence.

"You let him get the better of you, didn't you? *Didn't you*?" Rodriguez walked over until they were so close together, Gino could smell Rodriguez' putrid breath.

"Let me tell you what I think happened, Gino," Rodriguez said. "I send three men, *three men,* to pick up the friend and he got the better of you. Tell me, Gino, how is that possible?" The remark was more a statement than a question.

"The friend . . . he is much younger and very fit, Carlos. We did not expect . . ."

"Shut up, you fool," Rodriguez spewed venomously. "I will ask you once again, what did you do?"

Gino Vaselino was a ghost of the once confident man who had come to deliver his report. Vaselino's eyes began to glaze over, signifying anticipatory repercussion. Rodriguez was good at sensing fear. Seeing Vaselino this way pleased him immeasurably.

Vaselino raised his head to signify he still retained some dignity, that he hadn't completely failed. "We did not fail with the old man, Carlos. We burned his place to the ground. He is at the grotto now, awaiting your arrival."

The ugly little man slowly walked around his lieutenant. He circled him several times. This visibly upset Gino as evidenced by the sweat stains expanding beneath his armpits.

"You have said 'I' a lot, Gino. You mean to say, *Javier* and I. Is this not so, Gino?" The circling stopped when they were face to face. Again the smell of the disgusting little man's breath insulted Vaselino's nostrils.

"Carlos, I—that is, *we,* burnt his place to the ground, just as you instructed when he did not tell us where your last painting was." The cockiness was returning. "But he will talk soon. Of this I promise you!"

Again that dreaded silence. "I will ask you once more, my good friend. Where is Javier?" Rodriguez' stare all but bored holes though his lackey's head.

"Javier, he got hurt in the fire, Carlos. Bad. I had to leave him. I grabbed the old man; I had to get out."

"So . . ." Carlos Rodriguez was full of anger, to the point that he had to walk away from his underling's presence. His gaze returned to the bird feeder. The bird had returned and was happily pecking away at the seed within.

"I will ask you a most important question. A question so important, it may determine whether or not you will see tomorrow." The ugly little man returned to face his lieutenant. "So tell me, Gino, tell me that you left no loose ends." Rodriguez put a fatherly arm around his shoulders.

Vaselino knew he was shaking. He couldn't help it. He wondered how he ever allowed himself to get into such a situation with this crazy man.

"No, Carlos, no loose ends. On my mother's grave; no loose ends."

A smile broke out on the ugly little man's face. He reached into the inner pocket of his robe. Gino thought, *this is it! I'm going to die!*

What came out was not the gun Gino envisioned, but a cigar! "Here, my good friend, have a *Cohiba*. Permit me to light it for you . . ."

7

Ms. Shankar

Lee's consciousness returned in a myriad of confusing thoughts. Although aware of being in a hospital room, the *scent* was definitely not standard hospital issue.

Rolling over in his bed to face the room's entrance, Lee saw that the scent was nothing native to the room, but was that of the most beautiful woman he had ever laid eyes on. He wasn't dreaming, as confirmed by several self-inflicted pinches.

She was the embodiment of all things sensually feminine. Resplendent in a light beige halter-topped mini-dress that hung just above her knees, the statuesque forty-something woman of Indo-Caribbean descent had the most delicate feminine curves. Her long athletically-honed delicious legs encased in exquisite mocha-colored pantyhose poised at eye level brought him to rapt attention in more ways than one. Scanning slowly up her body, he allowed his eyes to decompress momentarily at her full and nubile breasts.

Lee used the remote to raise the head of his bed up so he could get a better look at this woman. He stared into her hypnotically beautiful green eyes perfectly framed in long, luscious black hair.

Smiling to herself, she strode closer to the head of his bed and placed a hand on the railing. "Mr. Hartley? Mr. Lee Hartley? My name is Bindhira Shankar. I represent the US Central Security Service, a branch of the NSA, and am currently assigned as liaison to the Niagara control of the North American Bureau of Security. How are you feeling?"

"I've been better, thank you," he coughed for sympathy.

Looking steadfastly into Lee's eyes without once averting her gaze, Bindhira continued. "I have been sent here to speak with you concerning your recent incident as reported by NABS control, Mr. Alan Exner. Mr. Exner has reason to believe that you may be a person of interest under surveillance by a faction involved in a plot that could affect the national security of both our countries."

At this, Lee sat up, adjusted the pillow so he could comfortably see to speak to this gorgeous creature, and smoothed his hair back with the fingers of both hands. She never took her eyes off his. He found it hard to take his eyes off of her, but in spite of this "handicap" said, "Alan sent you here? So he finally believes me now? Have you located the driver of the Viper? Do you know where Bill is? Just what *the hell* is going on, Ms. Shankar?"

"Please, Mr. Hartley," the young woman said calmly. "I know you have been through a lot. In fact, from the police reports it seems you are a hero, saving that man's life at the scuba facility fire. We are currently in the process of putting this puzzle together. When we do, we will have the answers to these and other questions you may have, but first we need your help."

"We need to know exactly what happened, your observations, your insights, anything that can help piece this together. There does seem to be a correlation between what happened to you on the Parkway and what happened at your friend's establishment. It is therefore in everyone's best interests that we find those responsible as soon as possible."

Bindhira Shankar lightly skimmed her fingers along the top of the bed rail. Looking past him out the window, she remarked, "My, what a beautiful view you have here, Mr. Hartley."

Indeed he had, for those luscious legs were all but in his face again. It was as though she was aware of this, perhaps a form of therapy she hoped would bring him around.

"Yeah, it's the best view I've had in a long time; I mean, it definitely is conducive to making one feel better." *Stop babbling, you idiot,* Lee thought to himself, *don't be a fool; play it cool.*

Looking down at him, Bindhira's smile faded as she reached into her purse. "Perhaps this is not a good time to talk, Mr. Hartley. Here is my card." Placing it on the small table beside him, she produced a pen and scribbled on the back of the card. "I am staying in Niagara-On-The-Lake at this hotel. The doctor says you will probably be discharged by tomorrow. We could talk then, if you please. In the meantime, keep well, Mr. Hartley."

As Lee rolled to pick up the card, Bindhira playfully scooped it up. Her eyes again met his as she handed it over to him. It was as though the card was electrically charged, for when their hands touched, Lee suddenly felt very alive in his nether regions. Both held the card until Lee's gentle tug freed it from her grip.

"Call me Lee, please," he said. "This 'mister' stuff makes me feel old."

Bindhira smiled a wonderful smile, her brilliant white teeth and dimples magnifying it a hundredfold. As she walked to the door, she said over her shoulder, "There is much to discuss, for your life and that of your friend may be in peril. I await your call, Mr. Hartley."

And with that she was gone, leaving her scent behind for him to savor.

Lee plopped his head back on the pillow. He was perplexed, yes; aroused, yes; but his attention turned to his friend. What had happened to Bill Travers?

His mind didn't have time to mull things over, however, as the charge nurse came in just then. She smiled, rolled him over, and injected a muscle relaxant into his butt cheek that soon put him into a deep sleep—and a much-needed one at that.

8

An Infatuation

By noon the next day, Lee was discharged by his doctor with a clean bill of health. The smoke he inhaled had done no permanent damage, although it had temporarily impaired his body's ability to absorb oxygen. He was admonished to abstain from diving for a few days, and to lightly exercise a minimum of three times per week to bring his cardio-respiratory system back up to par.

As he left the front lobby of the hospital and into the bright rays of the noonday sun, he was greeted by a series of loud oscillating strobelike beeps. Looking to his left, he saw a strange vehicle. It seemed to be a form of concept car. A curious cross between what appeared to be part '57 Chevy Bel Air and part '66 Ford Mustang Fastback, though in an updated and more streamlined package that really caught the eye. Although the vehicle was an eye-stopper, it was the driver that drew his greatest admiration.

Another unique blast from the futuristic vehicle and a woman's voice called to him by name.

“Ms. Shankar, what a surprise!” Lee’s admiration of the car faded as he looked down into the open driver’s window and into this fabulously gorgeous female creature’s eyes.

“I’ve just been discharged . . .”

“Hence my arrival, Mr. Hartley. Please get in. I need to speak with you, and time, as they say, is of the essence.”

Without being asked twice, Lee hopped into the passenger side cockpit of the curious vehicle. “Only if you promise to call me by my first name, and it isn’t ‘mister.’”

Bindhira looked over at him, while transferring her long, jet black hair over to her left shoulder so as to better take in Lee’s rugged features.

“Very well then Mr.—I mean, Lee. My close friends and associates call me Bindhi.” At this, she pulled out and away from the curb, the powerful engine barely audible.

Without missing a beat, Lee immediately seized the opportunity to secure a place in that envied category. He looked straight into those lovely eyes and said, “Bindhi it is then. By the way, thanks for the lift. My car’s . . .”

“. . . not my concern at this point, Lee Hartley. Your missing friend, however, is.” She looked back to the road in time to expertly navigate around a cyclist who had more than his share of the road in front of them, then continued. “Mr. Travers may have latched onto something that could prove deadly in the wrong hands. It is our belief that is why he has gone . . . missing. We also have reason to believe that both your incident on the Parkway and the explosion at the dive shop were interconnected.”

Lee never tired of the natural beauty along the Niagara Boulevard, and he renewed this feeling again as they wound their way to Niagara-On-The-Lake, several miles below the escarpment. Traffic was light at this time of day, the scenery beautiful as always. Lee turned to face his stunning chauffeur, then pulled out his little flask for a swig of his precious liquid before replacing it with a smile.

Bindhira's above-the-knee navy blue dress with matching pantyhose notwithstanding (although duly noted), Lee's demeanor changed to one of grave concern.

"What am I missing here, Bindhi? What aren't you telling me? And don't tell me Bill's a CSS asset. He's definitely not the cloak-and-dagger type. Whatever you've got going on, I know the guy well enough that he'd spill any information he had for a cup of coffee. But I also know that if he did know something of value, no bad guy could beat it out of him. He's just that kind of guy."

Bindhira Shankar looked to Lee and scanned his visage. She trusted his statement based on the facial indicators he displayed. It was good intelligence for future reference.

"Your friend William Travers is not one of our agents, Lee, but he *has* gotten himself involved in something that could jeopardize international security. It is therefore imperative that we concentrate our efforts into finding Mr. Travers before any irrevocable harm is done."

Bindhira, conscious of Lee's eyes absentmindedly enjoying the sun's rays as they reflected off the blue nylon covering her legs, tugged her skirt a little farther south.

As if on cue, Lee refocused his gaze to the Niagara River. What had Travers gotten himself into this time? He inwardly rephrased that question to include himself.

The two traveled on in silence. Bindhira looked discreetly over at Lee from time to time, and drank in his rugged good looks. Wearing a white short-sleeved dress shirt with the top two buttons open at the neck, military-style shorts, and leather sandals, his proximity made her tingle. Lee's long hair tousled in the wind as his wise brown eyes unconsciously scanned the surrounding territory.

Bindhira knew that Lee was an experienced man of the world. She pegged him as intelligent and strong, but felt he also possessed a sensitive side as well. She also knew that he was not one to mess with. The CSS agent had read Lee's file, a file he wasn't aware that NABS had on him.

Lee was an expert underwater, but he was also an expert at *Ichido Ryu Karate* as well, and had earned black belt status within the eclectic system. It was a formidable fighting system that incorporated essential elements of Japanese *jiu jitsu* and *aikido*.

Lee didn't merely practice karate techniques, he *became* them. Once while conducting a contract diving job off the coast of North Carolina, three men boarded his boat and tried to commandeer it. One had a rifle, one a machete, while the third was unarmed.

According to the NABS report, Lee permanently dispatched the two armed men and nearly drowned the third. In a bizarre coincidence in Lee's favor, if it hadn't been for the testimony of a nearby passing trawler's first mate, who just happened to witness the whole thing through his binoculars, Lee could very easily have gone to jail.

In court, the mate testified that it was as if they were filming a "Bruce Lee movie" on Lee's boat. Feet and fists were flying in every direction, and it happened so fast, the mate thought the whole thing was staged. But when he saw Hartley throw one of the men over the side of the pitching boat, he knew this was no movie.

The trawler's captain was informed, the US Coast Guard summoned, and Lee arrested. Luckily, they fished the semiconscious man out of the water. Lee was eventually exonerated as it was found that he acted under threat of his life. A lesser man would never have lived to tell the tale.

It was subsequently revealed that these same three pirates had murdered over a dozen boaters over the course of several months, and had plundered and sunk their boats all within that same vicinity. Not only had Lee walked away a free man, he was also personally awarded a civic medal of honor by the governor of North Carolina in gratitude for eliminating the piracy threat in his jurisdiction.

There were other incidents in his records, with Lee apparently in the wrong place at the wrong time and with the wrong people. One of the diver's greatest weaknesses was that he never backed down from anything or anyone. But it was clear from Lee's file that he could be a very dangerous man if need be, but a good man to have on your side when the chips were down.

Bindhira was counting on it.

9

The TaZeR

Pulling into a rest area along the upper Niagara River, Bindhira brought the powerful vehicle to a graceful stop. They climbed out and stood together in front of the car with the river before them. A sudden cool breeze brought merciful relief from the heat of the day as they took in the magnificent view. The leaves of the birch and maple trees along the shoreline danced in time with the breeze along the water's edge, which did much to soothe their spirits. Reeds along the riverbank gracefully undulated in perfect unison as if in harmony with a full orchestra.

Neither sensed the need to engage the other in conversation. After a few minutes, Lee asked, "What kind of car *is* this anyway? I've never seen anything like her."

Bindhira's sensuous green eyes met Lee's gaze head on, then smiled deliciously. "It is an UMI TaZeR to be exact. There are few in existence, so I am not surprised you have not heard of it. It is what you would call a functional prototype. The TaZeR had been under development for many years, and only recently delivered to Controls in each of North America's ten NABS sections."

"I wasn't aware that United Motors International was into the spy business, but I suppose everybody is nowadays."

Lee's masculine interest in the TaZeR was met with Bindhira's subtle bemusement. She was grateful that the supercar was taking Lee's mind off Travers' plight if only for the moment. But Bindhira saw both concern in his face and fatigue in his gait. His interest in the car came as a welcome respite, but she knew his mind was on the welfare of his friend.

"As you know Lee," she said, "a few years ago, the top three North American car companies merged in an effort to pool their resources to stave off declining sales due to the influx of inexpensive Chinese imports that were flooding the market. UMI was successful in their endeavor, providing not only more affordable vehicles, but much more innovative and safer ones as well."

"I see you are an aficionado of older automobiles, Lee. The TaZeR *was* patterned after the 1957 Chevrolet Bel Air and the 1966 Ford Mustang fastback. These two vehicles were chosen for the prototype as they were considered the most iconic of their period. However, the TaZeR model is much safer, and comes with several innovations not available during the era of the originals."

Bindhira could see she had his undivided attention. Lee almost lovingly ran his hand along the TaZeR's right rear tail fin. She caught herself feeling a little jealous at the affection he poured over the machine. This handsome new acquaintance stirred her emotions more than she cared to admit.

"Innovative isn't the word," Lee said. "UMI could *bury* the rest of the competition if they went public with this baby!" Lee looked up into her face rather abruptly. This caught her off guard, for he saw that she was admiring *him*. It was now Lee's turn to inwardly smile as the Indo-Caribbean woman blushed uncontrollably.

It was becoming increasingly apparent that chemistry was developing between the two—a chemistry Lee felt would not have time to develop in light of the circumstances in which they currently found themselves.

Bindhira's long dark hair wisped tantalizingly around her radiant face in the intermittent breeze as she continued. "I was not talking merely about the machine's looks, Lee. The TaZeR has access to the world's third most powerful supercomputer. Dubbed the *Sequoia*, this computer system is a petascale Blue Gene/Q supercomputer, originally constructed by IBM for the US National Nuclear Security Administration."

Although Lee could navigate around computers in relative comfort, he didn't have a clue what she was talking about. But he could see she was now in her element, and he just enjoyed listening to her British accent. "Pretty impressive, Bindhi," he said, not really sure why.

"The IBM Blue Gene technology exceeds twenty *petaflops*," she continued, "or one quadrillion floating operations per second. That is fifteen times faster than the previous most powerful supercomputer in the world, Lee. That equates to more processing power than the *entire list* of the top 500 supercomputers currently in operation today."

Lee put his hand up. "Excuse me, teacher, but what exactly is a petaflop?"

Bindhira smiled at his unabashed innocence. "A petaflop is the speed capacity of the computer," she explained. "The Sequoia operates faster than twenty petaflops. Simply put, it can perform twenty quadrillion calculations per second."

Lee shook his head and looked skyward in mock frustration. "So it's a pretty fast computer that can do a gazillion things at once. Why didn't you say so?"

"Let me put it this way, Lee. Twenty petaflops equates to every human being on the planet doing three *million* computations each and every second."

"I sure could've used the thing in high school," Lee quipped.

He came over behind Bindhira and hugged her around the waist from behind, and then gave her a soft kiss on the neck. She placed both of her hands over the top of his and laid her head against his chest. They stayed in this position for several minutes until Bindhira gently pulled away and strode the short distance to the river's edge. Lee was still within earshot.

Without turning to face him, she continued her explanation. "Originally designed to ensure the safety and reliability of the nuclear weapons stockpile of the United States, a portion of the Sequoia system has been assigned to other military and counterintelligence purposes, which is why NABS is permitted access to it."

This visibly piqued Lee's interest, as evidenced by his raised eyebrows and low whistle. Bindhira paused a moment to gather her thoughts.

"Sequoia uses 1.6 million IBM power processors and 1.6 petabytes of memory. The system is housed in dozens of refrigerator sized racks, and occupies over 3,000 square feet in a warehouse-sized laboratory somewhere in Northern California."

It was obvious to Bindhira that she now had Lee's undivided attention. "Sequoia runs on the Linux operating system, and deploys a revolutionary switching infrastructure that takes full advantage of every advanced fiber optic technology in use today. Lee, it is the equivalent of having over two million laptops all rolled into one!"

"Ah, excuse me, Ms. Spock, but . . . uh, you're not planning on giving me a test on any of this, are you?"

The look of feigned worry caused Bindhira to break out into the warmest, most feminine laughter Lee had ever experienced. He realized that this woman had bewitched him, and it was at this moment he realized that pleasing her greatly pleased him. It would be a moment forever etched in his mind.

"No tests, Lee, but only because I know you are a quick study. Am I right?"

Lee just nodded and smiled.

"In the field, all TaZeRs are equipped with Sequoia HMIs, or human machine interface terminals, which allow all our systems to respond in micro-mini seconds. Among its many amenities, the vehicle has crystal clear infrared digital 3D video cameras front and back, military special ops-grade GPS capabilities that can pinpoint an object to within three feet and from several miles away, voice recognition activated controls, which I won't bore you with here, and a computerized tracking system that can launch a homing projectile into any vehicle within a twenty-foot radius of the TaZeR. This provides the monitoring sections of the various agencies with almost unlimited tracking Intel."

"In addition, by interfacing the Sequoia with four military-grade satellites in geostationary orbits using advanced extremely high frequency or AEHF technology operating at a 44 GHz uplink on the EHF band, and 20 GHZ downlink on the SHF band, the system uses a large number of narrow spot beams directed toward the earth to relay jam-resistant and frequency-hopping communications to and from any Sequoia-Sat terminal in the world."

"Thus the name 'TaZeR,'" Lee deduced. "Nice. Unbelievable, but nice. I suppose you'd need a sizeable mortgage to acquire one, eh?"

"I have no knowledge of the cost of these specially adapted vehicles. A thousand mortgages would probably not cover it, Lee. No expense was spared in the development of these systems following the 9/11 New York terrorist attacks. To that end, I do not feel it too great a price." She smiled her beautiful smile.

Lee caught himself staring hungrily into Bindhira's delicious green eyes, which she patiently endured. Lee could see that she was waiting for him to say something. "Forgive me, Bindhi, but your eyes are so breast—uh, *breath*-taking."

Bindhira awarded him another of her testosterone-inducing smiles. Her beautiful dimples added their authenticity to it. "Lee, you are such a boob!"

They both laughed at her unexpected play on words, which served to strengthen the weak-knee syndrome he experienced whenever she was in close proximity. Lee smiled to himself. He now knew how Superman must have felt when exposed to Kryptonite. But Lee was at a greater disadvantage than the Man of Steel, for his kryptonite was a hot-blooded sensuous woman.

Bindhira sauntered back to where Lee was standing in front of the TaZeR. Once again the two stood side by side in silence, simply enjoying the warmth of the sunshine and the magnificent view of the Niagara River with Navy Island in the distance. The gentle rustle of leaves in the wind, along with the fact that they were totally alone completed the romantic, picturesque setting.

The grass beneath them was soft and lush enough that Lee clutched her hands and gently pulled her down to the ground to sit beside him. He had to know more of this beautiful creature.

"So, Ms. Bindhira Shankar, you seem to know a lot about me. Isn't it time for me to know a little about you?" A curious mix of timidity, weakness, uncertainty, and almost fear crossed her visage at the innocent request. Lee smiled in spite of himself at seeing the smooth olive skin of her face and neck blush once again.

She looked meditatively down at her lap for a few moments, and then directed her gaze back to the river coursing by. She was careful not to look at him when she began to speak.

"Lee, it is not an unusual request to want to know something about those you work with, about those you care about."

She looked fully into his face, illuminated by that exquisitely beautiful smile. Lee returned it and then said, "The ball's in your court, my dear." He folded his arms as if patiently waiting for her to speak.

"Right. I was born in a small village on the southwestern coast of Trinidad called Claxton Bay," she began. "It is a beautiful little village actually. Lee, the whole island is beautiful. It is alive with a pulchritude not found anywhere else in the world."

Lee could listen to her all day. That enticing British accent, the calming warmth of her voice, and the love she still harbored for her native country endeared her all the more to him.

"I thought you had some East Indian in you," he interjected in approval. She turned to face him.

Lee saw genuine affection for him in her eyes. They spoke inaudible volumes to him. They told him now that what he had just said was not taken as idle flattery, but born of true appreciation.

"*East Indian*." Bindhira smiled at the term. "I haven't heard that used in a long time. The people in my region are now considered to be of *Indo-Caribbean* descent."

"I knew that," Lee said in obvious ignorance, "yes, it's a changing world."

It was her turn to see Lee blush at his *faux pas*. He remained silent, but acknowledged her with a shrug of his shoulders and a boyish smile. She was drawn to his smile. It made him seem less macho and much more attractive.

"My father, Nizam, served in the National Security office of Trinidad for many years. He had great insight and was wise in many things. His consul was highly regarded in our government. In due time, he was honored with a post in New York to represent Trinidad at the United Nations just after it had been accepted as a full member nation on September 18, 1962. Our family moved there the following year. This excited him very much; not so my mother. It was hard for her to adapt to the undisciplined lifestyle of the United States."

"What was your mother's name, Bindhi?" Lee asked.

"Shaliza. Her name was Shaliza. She was a stenographer in the Red House before she met my father."

"What's the Red House?"

"It is the seat of parliament for the Republic of Trinidad and Tobago. It is located in the central part of the capital city of Port-of-Spain in the northwestern part of the island. The Red House is beautifully ornate and a tourist attraction for many."

"My father-to-be saw my mother-to-be several times each day at the Red House, as his office was on the same floor on which she worked. They looked forward to the daily rides they shared up and down the elevator. Their short but enjoyable conversations on their way up and down led to shared lunches at the Red House, then to dates, then to increasingly more time spent together." Bindhira smiled at the romance of it all.

"My father proposed to my mother on the front steps of the Red House at the end of the day he was given his posting. This endeared him to my mother very much. There were so many people coming and going there. How could she—how could any woman refuse such a humbling proposal? Of course she said yes. They loved each other very much."

Lee could see that Bindhira harbored great affection for her parents and their undying love for one another. It was an enchanting story any woman would love to experience.

"Within a month, they were married," Bindhira said, breathing a sigh of relief, "and three weeks after that, they left their beloved country for the United States of America."

"Wow, talk about a whirlwind courtship," Lee said. "How did they adapt to their new life in America?"

"My mother found much unhappiness in the United States. 'Too much hurry,' she used to say. She did not find New Yorkers very friendly. But she managed to find menial jobs here and there. Then, in 1970, she had a daughter."

"A daughter named Bindhira."

"Yes," she laughed and smiled warmly at him, "a daughter named Bindhira. I was an only child. My father had wanted a son, but mother was unable to conceive after I was born. He became increasingly more involved with his work. Following high school, my father enrolled me at George Washington University in DC. I was accepted into a new program at the Elliot School of International Affairs. It took me five years to earn my master's degree in international policies and practices."

"I'm sure your parents were very proud of you," Lee said. "Was it your idea or your father's to undertake those studies?"

Bindhira got up and walked the few steps to the riverbank, then leaned against a large birch tree, lost in her memories.

"I thought my studies in politics would make Father proud. My mother was happy for me, and encouraged me in my academics. But Father hardly noticed my achievements. His work was more important. After several years at the UN, the government of Trinidad bestowed upon him the Trinity Cross, its highest honor, for his 'significant and positive impact on the twin island republic.' It is now called the Order of the Republic of Trinidad and Tobago. My mother of course was happy for him, but knew right then that she would never return to her beloved Trinidad."

Lee came over beside her as she continued, his arm lightly placed on her shoulder.

"Finances were never an issue for us. My mother converted much money into TTDs, the currency of Trinidad and Tobago. She helped her two sisters and their children through many hard times, and this with my father's blessing. One TTD was worth only a sixth of a US dollar. You can imagine how important it was for her widowed sisters at home to receive this assistance."

"Quite a story, girl," Lee said. "So how'd you end up in the CSS of all places?"

"Again: to please my father. The NSA had been recruiting at GWU for 'intelligence analysts' the last year of my studies. The position they offered was officially listed as the 'process of generating intelligence from data and information derived from foreign signals.'"

"I was readily accepted into the Central Security Service division of the NSA following a comprehensive background check and examination. Although my father denied it, I still believe he had a lot to do with it."

"I was immediately placed in the cryptology department of the CSS, which is basically the go-between agency for the NSA and the cryptology departments of the US armed forces. The fact that I speak several languages and achieved near-perfect scores in the higher levels of my studies at GWU also bode well in my favor."

"Very impressive, Bindhi; I'm sure you made your parents proud."

She suddenly appeared distant to Lee as she watched a small fishing boat struggle upstream against the power of the river current.

"You mention your parents in the past tense, Bindhi. What happened to them?"

He watched as her eyes suddenly became sad and heavy.

"911; their bodies were never recovered," she said softly.

Then in a harsher tone that helped repress her emotions, "We must go now. Time is at a premium."

10

Kidnapped!

The dingy atmosphere was cold and damp, and smelled of musty earth. Bill Travers slowly and painfully picked himself up off the hard, uneven dirt floor. How long he had lain there he did not know.

Where *there* was also remained an enigma. With his luminescent watch missing and no ambient light, Travers had no way of telling time. What he *did* know was that not only did his entire body ache, but his head also felt like it was ripe for an explosion.

Stumbling around his environs, Travers realized that he was in some kind of subterranean room. The walls were moist, slimy, and rough, and hewn out of rock. He estimated the area of his confinement to be approximately ten by twenty feet; the ceiling perhaps even higher. He couldn't touch it even by jumping. There didn't seem to be a point of entrance either, as no doorframe could be felt. Bill Travers was cold, hungry, perplexed, and very alone.

He slid down the wall he was leaning against and sat in deep contemplation of his plight. Yes, it was coming back to him. Three men of Latino descent—no, distinctly *Cuban*, came into his dive shop.

There was an argument, then a scuffle; then smoke . . . and a *fire*! There was a fire, then a fade to black. Travers could only remember losing consciousness, and by the throbbing in his skull, that from a blow to the head. They came in, friendly at first, two of them engaging him in small talk. Obviously they were the diversion as the third man, undoubtedly the "torch bearer," was also the one who gave Travers his "floggin' on the noggin.'"

The fog in his mind began to lift. He remembered that the men were deeply interested in his dealings with the last group of Cuban paintings he recently brought into Canada.

There was also a matter of his diving on a certain shipwreck, the *Cristóbal Colón*, while holidaying near the island nation's former capital city of Santiago de Cuba. They didn't like the fact that he was "snooping" around that particular wreck.

He wasn't sure what he told them, but it obviously wasn't what they wanted to hear. He had a sore body and an ash-strewn dive shop to prove it.

Travers rubbed a wet sticky substance from the corner of his right ear. He noticed a metallic smell to it. Blood, type O. His favorite, considering it was *his*. Even with his eyes now accustomed to the dark, there was nothing but darkness to see anyway. An uneasy and claustrophobic feeling pervaded his being at seeing nothing whether his eyes were open or not.

His shirt was ripped in several places and his pants were wet—hopefully, Bill thought, not from pissing himself. *Funny how your mind conjures up such stupid things in dire situations*, he thought.

Bill Travers slowly slid his back up along the dank wall to a standing position. Once again the old diver felt its surface as he had done several times already, both high and low, in an attempt to locate a slit or a latch, a smooth surface even—*anything* that could indicate an opening or avenue of escape from whatever pit this was.

Of one thing Travers was certain: whoever left him there would return. They would be back to get the information they wanted.

And based on his recent experience with these people, he was sure it wouldn't be very pleasant. He only hoped he had the answers they were looking for. But even if he did give them the information they sought, what then? Would anyone ever find him in this hellhole? Was anyone even *looking* for him?

He slid back down the rock face to the ground, and sat on his left leg, which tilted at a crazy angle. Unconsciousness was once again returning to engulf him. Whatever hope he held came from the knowledge that his old and trusted friend Lee Hartley would find him. He had to. He just had to.

Had he remained conscious a few minutes longer, Travers would have heard a concrete slab sliding open beneath the floor not four feet from where he lay.

11

Trying To Make Sense Of It All

The next morning, it was a grim Alan Exner who sat behind his desk in his office at Niagara-On-The-Lake. He was leaning back in his richly appointed leather desk chair, deep in thought. Lee Hartley stood at ease, looking aimlessly out at Lake Ontario through the huge bulletproof windows that allowed the light of another beautiful sunny day into Exner's office.

The ever-billowing white clouds that passed lazily overhead were mindlessly mesmerizing to Lee. He enjoyed this mental interlude: surreal blue sky, slow-moving majestic clouds, the gently lapping waves of the mighty Great Lake at shore's edge, complete with a scattering of sailboats in the distance, their sails at full mast, silently crossing his line of sight.

"How's the man I pulled out of the Scuba U fire doing, Ex?" Lee asked. "He looked pretty bad, but things usually look worse than they are."

Bindhira stood dutifully beside control, unsure how much information Exner wanted to share with his friend at this point.

There was an uneasy pause as Lee looked expectantly into Exner's face.

"He didn't make it, Lee. He took a bullet at point-blank range."

"Shot?" Lee stood bewildered. "Ex, the guy was overcome from the smoke. I didn't see any evidence of a gunshot wound, didn't even see any blood."

"Under the circumstances, you wouldn't have, Lee," Exner said. "A 9 mm tore into one kidney and lodged into a hip bone on the other side. He bled out internally. In light of the situation, forensics was surprised to find the bullet wound."

"We're trying to determine who he was so we can alert next of kin. Either he wasn't carrying ID or somebody relieved him of it. So at this point, we're not sure whether he was there as a customer or as part of the arson/kidnap team."

Lee turned back to look out the window and placed his hands on the sill beneath.

"They murdered their own guy?" Lee looked down to the sill and shook his head. "This just gets better by the minute."

"Lee, I realize you've been through a lot these past few days," Exner said. "I'm taking a gamble that as a trusted old friend and professional in your own right I can depend on you to keep what I'm about to tell you under wraps. Am I right in so assuming?"

With obvious concern on her beautiful countenance, Bindhira placed a hand on Exner's shoulder. "Sir, what we're dealing with on this case should be kept on a need-to-know basis, and that only for NABS personnel. Once this 'arrow' has been fired, it cannot return."

At this, Hartley spun around and walked over to Exner's desk, eyeing Bindhira with a look of utter disappointment at her comment.

"Alan, really, it's me, Lee, remember?" Taking his glare off Bindhira, Hartley now refocused it with laser precision onto Exner's eyes. "Believe me, Ex, *I* need to know," he said. "And I need to know *now*! All the while we've been engaging in meaningless conversation Bill could be getting farther and farther from help. God only knows if he's even still alive."

Stepping back from the desk, Lee turned again to the window, then took a deep breath with his back to them in an attempt to calm down. "Yes, Alan, I *can* keep your secrets. But you and I both know that despite all the 007 shit at your disposal, *I'm* going to be the only one who'll be of any real help to you on this one, Ms. Shankar here notwithstanding."

Lee turned to face them both, silence bearing witness to the truth at hand. He then threw his arms up, his head forcefully thrust toward them as if a human exclamation point, eyebrows now at their highest peak.

The defense rested.

Exner looked over at Bindhira; her gaze already expectantly trained on him. He leaned forward and pushed himself out and away from the desk. Glancing back at the unique NABS logo laser-etched in clear, heavy acrylic hanging on the wall behind his desk, Exner took in a deep breath knowing full well that what he was about to say could never be reclaimed.

"What if anything, do you know about an organization called the DGI, Lee?"

Each man met the other's gaze, a look of determination mirrored in each of their facial expressions.

"DGI, aka Cuban Secret Intelligence Service, formerly known as G2. Some pundits believe they were in on the assassination of US President John F. Kennedy back in 1963. The jury's still out on that one though. That's about it I guess, Ex."

"Oh believe me, Lee, they're still very much in the running for that rap, although I'm not at liberty to expound any further."

"Nooo, of course not." Lee yawned overtly in an effort to impress upon both Exner and Bindhira that although he didn't expect to be made privy to their top secret drivel, he really didn't give a rat's ass.

Exner came over and gave Lee a sympathetic pat on the shoulder. As much as he wanted to give Lee the full picture, he was constrained by duty not to. Nevertheless, Exner felt he owed Lee at least an abridged explanation in the hope that it would satiate his friend's "need to know."

"Lee, a little history lesson is in order to give you a better picture of what we're up against," Exner began. "The principal intelligence gathering bureau in Cuba is currently the *Dirección General de Inteligencia*, the DGI. There are others, most notably the Ministry of the Interior and the Military Counterintelligence Department of the Ministry of the Revolutionary Armed Forces."

"The DGI was established under the Ministry of the Interior (MININT) in late 1961. This new agency included three 'Liberation' Committees, one each for the Caribbean, Central America, and South America, collectively known as the Liberation Directorate or simply DL. It was the DL that overthrew the government of Zanzibar, Africa in 1963. However, in a more selective revolutionary strategy, the Soviets placed considerable economic pressure on Cuba in 1967-68."

"And you're giving me this history lesson because . . . ," Lee questioned.

Exner ignored the sarcasm and continued. "It was the Soviets' way of forcing *El Commandante* Fidel Castro to develop a new revolutionary strategy that would better embrace the Communist ideals, with the eventual subservience of the DGI to the KGB—"

Lee put his hand up as though still in grade school. "Sooo, *Mr.* Exner, what has all this to do with me in general, Bill in particular?"

"I'm getting to that, Lee," Exner continued. "Having gained control over the DGI, the KGB had Castro replace its chief, Manuel Piñeiro, with one José Méndez Cominches in 1969. From that point on, the DGI focused its efforts on collecting military, political, and *economic* information. Their operational division is now dedicated to political and economic Intelligence, sort of like the FBI and CIA rolled into one.

Sometime within the past year or so, we were surprised to discover a shadowy subsection of the DGI's operational division known as the *Establishment*. This was cause for great concern to us. They don't play by anybody's rules, and 'word on the street' has it they're running an agenda of their own apart from that of their government. It's very hush-hush to the point that little is known about it, or them. What we do know, however, is that your friend Travers has been buying paintings from one of their 'fronts' in Cuba, an art studio, and brings them back here to sell; all above board, of course."

"I don't like where this is going," Lee said. "Sure, Travers dives a lot in Cuba. No secret there. He's bound to make a few friends. So maybe he finds out one or two of them are artists, so he finds a way to help them out. God knows how desperately poor they all are down there. So he buys some of their stuff, brings them back, and makes a few bucks in the process." There's no law against the buying and selling of paintings in this country yet, is there, Ex?"

Silence permeated the room as Alan Exner carefully gathered his thoughts. Bindhira looked from Lee to him. She knew Lee wouldn't like what Exner had to say about his friend.

"Lee," Exner said, "the paintings in and of themselves are mediocre at best, and not the focus of our investigation. What's hidden *beneath* the canvasses is, however. And to put both our minds at ease, Travers seems blissfully ignorant of this."

"Ignorant of what," Lee asked.

Exner looked to Bindhira, who nodded her assent, then continued. "NABS agents have uncovered what appears to be coded top secret

Cuban military directives being sent to subversives in this country. Most disturbing, however, is that some of these directives have been issued in Mandarin."

"On a most top-secret level, a joint task force consisting of the CIA, DHS, CSEC, and our own NABS operatives have all but confirmed that there's a plot afoot that involves both the Chinese *and* the Cubans to destabilize North America. We have our suspicions; we can prove nothing."

At this, Lee threw up his arms. "Now wait just a—"

Exner cut him off in midstream. "It's still my dime, so hear me out." It was Exner's gaze this time that spoke louder than words. Lee took the hint and remained silent.

"In 1982, four aides close to Castro were convicted on charges of smuggling drugs into the United States. In *1988,* a former intelligence aide to Panamanian leader Manuel Noriega provided further evidence concerning Cuba's role in the illegal exportation of drugs into the United States. We know this is still going on today, albeit in a much more subtle and refined manner. Their 'exports' have since expanded to include priceless art, antiquities, and precious metals."

"The United States officially declared Cuba a sponsor of international terrorism when they discovered that the island nation closely aligned itself with Puerto Rican separatists and Latin American terrorist groups. And the DGI is up to its eyeballs in it."

"Oh great," Lee exclaimed, "so now we've gone from Bill being a simple art smuggler to being a mule of the DGI and now an unwitting dupe of the Red Chinese?" He paused to look from Exner to Bindhira then said, "Unbelievable!"

Looking up at the ceiling for a few seconds in an effort to gather his thoughts, Lee said, "I'm not one for red-neck language, Ex, but you two can just piss off right here and right now! This is bullshit served on a—pardon the pun—china platter and you know it! Read my lips, Alan, I KNOW William Edward Travers, and William Edward Travers is no damn secret agent *or* smuggler *or* whatever else for Cuba, for the Chinese, or anyone else, for that matter! Seriously, Alan . . ."

With a previous headache now roiling within his skull, Lee pulled out two extra-strength Aspirin express packs out of his pocket, ripped open the pouches, and downed the powder.

With the men at a stalemate, Bindhira took her cue. Her feminine form and soft, quaint British accent combined to make her a welcome no-man's-land between the two old friends. She walked over to the front of the desk and rested her derriere against it. The pervading silence was broken only by the slight soft swish of her nylon encased legs as she crossed them, arms folded. The men directed their attention to her as she spoke.

"Lee, Alan did not say that your friend Travers was a *willing* agent of the Chinese *or* the Cubans. NABS has proof, however, that he has been used as an unwitting mule and has imported subversive coded documents under the radar into Canada by an organization which may or may not be sanctioned by either the Chinese or Cuban governments."

"Well, thank you for *that*, *Ms.* Shankar," Lee said. "At least we've downgraded Bill from traitor to unwitting *putz—that* I can believe."

Lee let out a huge sigh of relief. At least his old dive buddy wasn't directly involved with the political intrigue of these countries. However, concern for his friend once again enveloped him, and he remained attentive to what Bindhira had to say.

She continued. "The artwork Mr. Travers brings into this country is not cause for concern. Intelligence reports confirm that while his Cuban contacts have 'bilked' him by selling lower grade artwork for rather large sums, he still manages to resell them here for a tidy profit."

"Mr. Travers places his Cuban artwork on consignment in a quaint though popular art gallery in Tobermory called the Little Tub Gallery," she explained. "Within a day or so of display, the pieces are sold despite the hefty price tag affixed to them. By monitoring the traffic in and out of the studio, NABS learned that the 'buyers' are Establishment operatives."

"As Tobermory is a popular tourist destination for Chinese visitors, using their agents as buyers is a good move on the part of the Establishment. To throw anyone off the scent, however, they have also used Spanish buyers. It is not a coincidence that no other ethnicity has been involved."

"How would they know if someone outside the network but still part of those 'ethnicities' doesn't just saunter into the gallery and scoop up a few before their marks pick them up?" Lee asked.

"As we mentioned, Lee," Bindhira said, "the prices your Mr. Travers pays for the paintings in Cuba are quite high. So in order to deter ordinary people from purchasing them, the Cubans charge him a hefty fee. But he does not mind because here he doubles the price and has no problem selling them. He has sold every one of them to date. Thus the chances of the average tourist walking into the gallery and purchasing one outside of the network would be fairly remote."

"Establishment operatives are also monitoring the gallery, Lee," Exner said. "They can't just scoop the paintings as soon as they're put on display. That would arouse too much suspicion all the way around, so they leave them there for a few days and then pick them up."

"Do you think the gallery proprietor is involved in all this?" Lee asked.

"We have no evidence at this time, nor do we believe that the owner of the gallery is involved at this end," Bindhira said, pulling a wisp of long hair away from her eye. "And we cannot just walk in and make arrests until we know just what it is this organization is up to."

"From the Establishment's perspective," Bindhira added, "it is pretty safe to conduct their transfers in Tobermory. The village is remote, there is only a satellite police office up there, and as the tiny town is an international tourist destination, trying to trace the paintings after purchase would prove difficult at best."

"Mr. Travers' buyers are 'sleepers,'" Bindhira said, "whose mandate is to secure the paintings and hence the documents with as little attention as possible. They then disseminate the encoded information to various cell operatives who have been embedded in the area. We do not yet know what the scope of these directives is at this point."

Lee said nothing. The whole affair was much bigger than even he had envisioned. He remained silent as Bindhira continued.

"As you know, no flights are permitted between Cuba and the United States," Exner said. "But Canadian airlines conduct regular flights down there and back. Cuba makes good money off Canadian tourists. It's business as usual for us up here. So no suspicions are aroused when tourists return home with souvenirs and keepsakes."

Lee looked over to Exner, then to Bindhira. Through all his hot-headedness over the accusations made against Travers, Lee realized the agents were simply reporting the facts as given them. His visage softened markedly as Exner continued.

"Lee, these Cuban operatives have been using Bill for some time. We've amassed a growing file on his flight frequency, travel habits, and out-of-country acquisitions."

"Reports confirm the Establishment has operatives in regular contact with him both in Cuba and in Canada. That's how Travers appeared on our radar. Again, we don't know at this point who the Establishment is working for, which puts NABS in a double jeopardy."

If brainwaves could generate smoke, the detector in Exner's office would have gone off. Lee's face churned with a curious mixture of both incredulity and confused anger.

"Come on, guys. So Bill Travers, the guy we all know and love, is an integral part of a three-way intelligence sting?"

The NABS control smiled wryly then dropped his head as though checking his shoes. Exner replied quietly, "The facts speak for themselves, Lee. What more can I tell you?"

Lee Hartley looked out over the lake with a blank stare. He didn't know where this was going, and he didn't like it. A silent emotional thunderstorm was erupting in Lee's head. Several moments passed before Lee replied, "Does Travers know about all this?"

Exner took a few moments before replying. "Up until his abduction, I really don't think he did, Lee."

Lee knew Alan Exner just as he *knew* Bill Travers. He couldn't discount what Exner was telling him. Lee's former school chum was never one to play games, while Travers on the other hand was one to get caught up *in* them. The old diver's simplistic innocence and honesty seemed to get him into more trouble than it got him out of.

Lee softened the hold his eyes had on Exner, and came to the realization that Exner should get the benefit of the doubt. After all, Exner *was* in the intelligence business.

Exner took Lee's silence as an invitation to continue. "If it wasn't for *my* intervention the *last* time he came back, Lee, Travers would be rotting in a cell as we speak. I pulled his fat out of the fire after the last excursion before he even smelled the smoke!"

Bindhira caught Lee's attention then picked up where Exner had left off. "Mr. Exner and his agency can only do so much, Lee."

"We *know* the Establishment keeps Travers under surveillance," Exner said. "We *know* they have dealings with the Red Chinese. We *know* that they have allowed him to leave Cuba with artwork that normally would be confiscated as per their laws, yet he has not been apprehended. Just *knowing* these things, Lee, sends up proverbial warning flags."

Lee absentmindedly dug the dirt out of a fingernail as he spoke. "I've seen some of the pictures he's brought back. I've seen a few in his shop, and quite frankly, they're far from Rembrandts. I didn't even know he was moonlighting as an art dealer."

Exner walked over to the left of the window that took up much of the north face of his office. Lee gravitated to the right. Bindhira sat down behind the desk in resignation to the fact that this was going to be a long day.

"Well, to sum things up, here's what we've got," Exner continued. "We've got one William Travers who has made more than his share of trips to Cuba over the past two years. No crime there. However, on one occasion a random search of his luggage at Toronto's Pearson Airport turned up a total of five undeclared paintings stashed in a very large 'sports' bag. That raised a few flags."

"On his very next reentry into Canada from Cuba, he had about half the Cuban National Art Gallery in a large hard case. The only reason we didn't bust his ass then, Hartley, is that we're after the bigger fish in a pond too big even for you to swim in!"

Bindhira now took the lead as she looked over into Hartley's face with those beautiful eyes now full of empathy. "As you may or may not know, Lee, certain pieces of artwork are allowed to leave Cuban soil. But the government has strict limitations concerning the type and size of artwork leaving the country."

"So where exactly do the Chinese fit into all of this?" Lee asked, crossing his arms.

"Would you care to field that one, Bindhira?" Exner turned the floor over to her.

"As you know, Lee, the Russians dumped Cuba literally overnight back in the early nineties. Since then the DGI has scrambled to conduct external intelligence operations in an effort to gain access to technologies required to improve the Cuban economy."

"It seems the Chinese have lent a listening ear to the Cubans and have embraced them much as the Russians did back then. The Chinese no doubt have their own agenda in the 'marriage', but they have been more than willing to pick up where the Russians left off, lending Cuba aid for all manner of infrastructure projects not developed since the 1990s."

"A sizeable influx of US currency has been pouring into Fidel's off-shore accounts, with all fingers pointing to the Chinese as his primary benefactor. Last year's estimate of the Castro brothers' net worth was in the area of eight hundred million dollars. Sources have since indicated their net worth now to be in the vicinity of three *billion* dollars! In one year, how is this so? Obviously, the Chinese are up to something down there."

Bindhira continued to look out the window as she spoke. "A sizeable portion of the funds have been channeled to a Cuban 'trust fund' called the Sierra Maestra Foundation to be bequeathed to the Cuban government and purportedly earmarked for substantial upgrades in the areas of health, education and welfare upon the deaths of both Fidel and his brother, Raul. The foundation is, of course, nothing more than a front for terrorist funding which may involve the Chinese, and a bankroll as payoff to the Castro's."

"Lee," Exner chimed in, "the Cuban Missile Crisis of the early 1960s is small potatoes compared to what could happen down there should China obtain a foothold ninety miles south of the United States coastline! The final 'in your face' to the United States; compliments of the *Revolución*."

Lee strode over to the padded leather chair in front of Exner's desk and plunked down, head in his hands. "Holy crap! The greed just never ends, does it? Political arenas everywhere are nothing more than smoke and mirrors set up to assuage the mass of stupid cattle that we, the people, are. The capitalist ideal of democracy we all know and love truly ends the moment we drop our ballots into the voting box, doesn't it?" he ranted.

"The big corporations that really run the world take over from there, don't they?" He paused in reflection of the impact of his statements. "The corporations of the world have sold us out. Just about every damn thing we buy now comes from China. Not to mention the fact that China literally *owns* one-third of the United States! Can you imagine the chaos that would ensue if they decided to call in that debt *and* have a foothold in Cuba?"

Bindhira strode to another window. The sound of swishing nylon aroused Lee as she passed. "For the most part you are correct in your assumptions, Lee," she said. "You mentioned how it seems everything we buy now comes from China. That is, of course, true. Chinese merchant ships are indeed sailing to most major ports of the world with wares, including Cuba. This is an accepted worldwide fact." She paused to wave off a fly.

"A few more Chinese cargo ships sailing to Cuba in today's world would bring no undue suspicion from anyone," Exner said. "Our great concern, though, is what exactly *are* they sending down there? Based on past experience, the Cubans wouldn't be so careless as to allow them to send weapons of mass destruction down there with today's spy satellites and the probability of a coast guard search and seizure."

"But a new weapon, one that is small and portable, would get through, and that's entirely possible in this day and age."

"Key components of which could be sandwiched in behind legally imported paintings," Lee mused.

"Whatever they're planning," Exner said, "it's to be constructed in North America; assembled and readied for implementation according to someone's timetable."

Bindhira softly squeezed Lee's hand as she sauntered by him lost in thought, swishing her way to the far window. No one spoke for several minutes. The mood was very somber among them.

It was Exner who finally broke the silence. "We've no idea how long this has been going on. As far as we know, Travers has been the sole mule in all this. That leads us to believe that the operation is a relatively small one."

"Very bad things can come in very small packages," Bindhira philosophized.

Speaking through hands now covering his face, Lee said, "I can see how Bill bumbled his way into all this. My question is what the hell do they want with me?"

"Lee, questions concerning this whole nasty affair are legion," Exner explained. "Now you can see how I can't have you going around killing off our leads. This goes far beyond you, far beyond Bill Travers. So far the situation appears to be confined to southern Ontario. But it could lead to huge ramifications for the rest of the free world as well."

Exner walked over to his desk and picked up the phone receiver. "That's all for now. Both of you are free to leave. Sorry, but this call is 'ears only.'"

On their way out, Lee overheard Exner as he spoke into the instrument: "This is NABS Niagara Control Alan Exner, Station 5, 148802. Get me the office of the president of the United States, optimum scramble . . ."

12

In Peril

Consciousness was cruelly restored when a pail of very cold water sloshed over Bill Travers' very sore head. Too weak to offer any resistance, two burly men dead-lifted him up off the floor of the prison, conversing in Spanish. They brought him over to an old wooden chair that had seen better days, and unceremoniously dumped him into it.

There was a large table in front of him. The table itself looked quite old, and seemed to have been handmade out of a hardwood, oak perhaps. It had been crudely carved into the unnecessarily heavy monstrosity it was. There appeared to be heavy gouge marks on its dark-stained surface, as if it had once served as a butcher table. Travers truly hoped it was no longer used for such purposes.

The room was now well lit. It took some time for his eyes to acclimate to the brightness. Where he was, how deep he was, and what lay beyond was at present unknown. The cave held the kind of moldy odor that just wouldn't go away—not a good place to find yourself in if you had breathing problems, he thought.

As his eyes slowly adjusted, Travers stared into the faces of his captors, who stood over him in silent anticipation—of *what* he did not know and was in no real hurry to find out.

Then to his rear, a grating sound, and as he turned to see what it was, one of the strongmen roughly grasped his shoulders from behind to keep him firmly in place while the other man walked over behind them to address the peculiar sound.

Another sound, this time footsteps ascending a stone or concrete staircase—for it was a dense sound, not hollow as if made of wood. A grating sound again, then he could hear a hushed conversation in Spanish between the lead thug and this new entry. Bill deduced that the man holding him in place must be the lackey of the three.

Moments passed in apparent silent appraisal of their captive, perhaps a psychological ploy to increase Travers' nervousness, and to further generate fear of the uncertain fate that lay before him. If that was the case, it was damn well working.

It was several minutes before he heard two pairs of footsteps quietly, almost reverently, crunching their way over the gravelly floor to stand in front of him.

"Now comes the time to meet without the masks, Mr. Travers. I trust my men have been . . . how you say . . . '*cordial,*' in my absence?"

Bill Travers studied the newest man's features with growing recognition. Short of stature, long, thin nose; pockmarked face; soulless black eyes; curly, graying hair receding through the slack tide of advanced years, a scar across his left jugular vein—that scar!

"It's you! You bastard! Carlos Rodriguez!" Travers spit out. "What are *you* doing in Canada? What, you've found it more lucrative to conduct kidnappings in Canada than sell artwork out of your gallery in Cuba?"

"Greetings, *Señor* Travers," Rodriguez said too politiely for Travers' liking. "It is good to see you again, my friend."

"Tell this stun-tard behind me to back off, Rodriguez," Travers shouted. "What are you *doing*, man? What are you, part of the Cuban mafia? Hey, I don't owe you nothin'!"

A sudden surge of adrenaline coursed throughout the aging diver, and he almost broke free. But the man holding him was far stronger. His vice-like grip clamped down on Travers' arms to the point of cutting off the circulation to them.

"Patience, as they say, is a virtue, Mr. Travers." Rodriguez then leaned in so close their noses almost touched, then hissed, "a virtue you would do well to practice if you wish to walk out of here alive!" Then, as suddenly, he reverted back to a kinder, gentler voice. "My friend, what happened to the last painting you brought back?"

"You've gone to all this trouble for a friggin' painting? What'd ya do, forget to sign it or something? Geez, Rodriguez, what the—"

"There are some things about our dealings that are of no concern of yours, *Señor* Travers. Things that would bring fear to your heart," Rodriguez interjected.

Travers smiled in spite of himself. "What could *possibly* bring me more fear than this, Carlos? I was your friend and you've betrayed me. We had a good thing goin', man."

Rodriguez replied with an evil grin.

The Canadian made a vain attempt to pull free, but the ruffian who held his arms cuffed him smartly along the side of his head. Travers took it in stride, then stared menacingly at Rodriguez.

"I thought you and me were *amigos*, Rodriguez. I trusted you." Travers was breathing heavily now. "You and me, we made good money off those paintings. Just what are you trying to pull here?"

The Cuban slowly circled his captive as he spoke. "Gino here thought he had you the other night on the river road. How you managed to elude us in your friend's large automobile the other night, I do not know. I do not care to know. But what I *do* care to know is where that painting ended up. It never reached its intended destination."

Travers did his best to follow Rodriguez as the Cuban continually circled him, but as he wasn't an owl, he was forced to give up. "How the devil should I know? Once I get home, I place 'em on consignment at my dealer's gallery. I haven't the foggiest where they end up, nor do I care. What's it to you anyway?"

Rodriguez stopped in front of Travers, placed his hands on each arm of the chair, and then said, "Fool! You know nothing! We have no interest in your stinking money. It just made our 'transactions' more credible. We watch you, *amigo*. Yes, we watch you in your own country until the paintings end up back in the hands of our people here in Canada."

Travers gave Rodriguez his evil eye squint. "What do you mean by 'your people'? They're sold through my dealer's gallery to whoever can afford them."

Rodriguez smiled a patient smile. "Yes, my simple friend, you sell the paintings, but not just to anyone. But somehow the last group of paintings managed to be acquired by someone outside our cell. Of the three, we are only interested in the largest of them. We simply need to know from you who they were sold to and how we can locate them. Then, you are free to go."

"Free to go, just like that!"

"Ah, Mr. Travers." Rodriguez' smile was devoid of pleasantness. "The less you know the better for you. Suffice it to say that you have been doing us an invaluable service."

Bill Travers liked to think he was no one's fool. But he *had* been played. He had been played by this man and his cronies for reasons unknown, and it angered him greatly.

"Listen, Rodriguez, just let me go. I don't *know* who buys your shit. I don't *care* who buys your shit. I simply make a few bucks off them depending on how much you screw me over for. You get your money, and eventually I get mine. End of story."

Rodriguez studied Travers' face for several moments, as if to decide now just what to do with his captive, then, "Indeed, you *will* get yours, my friend." The Cuban punched Travers so hard in the chest that he almost knocked over the chair he was on.

"Money, all you North Americans think about, care about, is your precious money. Fool! Do you actually believe I sold those worthless paintings to you merely for *money*?" Rodriguez changed up once again and spoke softly to his captive, "My friend, whether you like it or not, you are now up to your yellow eyeballs in a traitorous conspiracy against your country, so I would choose my words and actions very carefully from now on."

At this, Bill drew up and spit into his kidnapper's face; a good one, he thought: a long, thick phlegm-laden missile of contempt.

With unexpected swiftness, Rodriguez immediately backhanded Travers so hard, it was a wonder his head was still attached to his neck. The old diver sat limp, held up solely by the thug who still held his shoulders in a powerful grip. At a nod from Rodriguez, the man relaxed his grip and shoved Travers forward with such force that Travers smashed his head heavily down onto the hardwood table in front of him.

Once more, it was a starry, starry night for William Travers. While he had a few virtues to be sure, keeping his mouth shut was not one of them.

13

Searching Amid The Rubble

The scene in front of Bill Travers' Scuba U Dive Shop was one of seeming total disarray. Two fire trucks, a fire marshal SUV, two Ontario Provincial Police cruisers, and several other unmarked law enforcement vehicles were parked at crazy angles in the car park; there were fire hoses, charred wood, scorched shells of furniture, and blobs of melted neoprene scattered all around.

The blobs had once been wet suits—one of the first products affected by the intense heat of the blast. The acrid smell of incinerated wood aromatically infused with burning rubber and plastics, combined with a plethora of unknowns, permeated the air. Although the fire proper had long ago been extinguished, there were still wisps of black smoke emanating from within the charred building. Inside the shop, the pungent smell was in much greater concentration.

It was into this mess that Lee Hartley, Alan Exner, and Bindhira Shankar found themselves the next day. After considerable private debate between the two agents, it was decided they would fully take Lee into their confidence.

Walking into the shop was hard for Lee. He had spent countless hours here in the past, meeting up with old friends, helping teach countless eager novices, talking diving, planning trips, having great after-dive get-togethers, and going over the new equipment that Travers frequently brought in. Lee was honored to be Travers' unofficial "test" diver for the Scuba U.

Travers' dive shop was like a barber shop of old. It was a place to "shoot the breeze" with like-minded scuba enthusiasts, exchanging stories and ideas, learning about new dive spots, or just hanging out for something to do. You didn't have to spend money to come to the Scuba U. Bill genuinely loved his customers, *all* of them. It didn't matter what you were there for; if you liked to talk diving, you were welcome. The volume of sales more than tripled since Bill had taken over the shop five years ago. Bill Travers was a people person.

He had the gift of gab, unlike the previous owner who was just there to make money. The former owner was a "no freebies, no small talk, just get your shit and get out" kind of guy. Due to simple cause and effect, it came as no surprise that his business was drying up.

Then along came Bill, who entered into negotiations for it almost as soon as the "For Sale" sign went up. Bill used up much of his life savings and bought into the shop simply because he loved diving. At first he didn't give much thought to the business of diving. But his charming and knowledgeable demeanor had developed a large and loyal clientele over the years. They loved Travers and he loved them.

Divers came to the shop in trickles at first, then in droves from near and far to do business with the loveable, albeit quirky "professor of diving."

At the entrance to the charred remains, Exner produced his NABS ID and presented it to an OPP officer stationed there, who allowed them to proceed. OPP officers and local fire officials went about their work inside scouring the ruins for clues to the death and apparent arson. NABS was entrusted solely with the kidnapping of the shop's owner, and the identity of the dead man.

Once inside, Lee, Bindhira, and Exner were amazed at the damage. Whatever caused the fire all but destroyed the entire building. It came as a great comfort to know that the firemen found no further bodies in the charred remains.

"Where did Bill keep his office, Lee?" Exner asked over his shoulder as he presented his NABS ID to another OPP officer who was combing the showroom for clues.

Bindhira pulled a bandana out of her small clutch purse, folded it into a neat square, and then covered her nose and mouth. She carefully stepped over a rack that once displayed buoyancy compensators, jacket-like devices used to keep divers neutrally buoyant while underwater.

"Through here, Alan," Lee said as he sidestepped the remains of the main counter cabinet, leading his associates into the inner sanctums of the Scuba U. The light from the bright summer day was not strong enough to permeate as far into the building as they went, and it grew increasingly difficult to see much further.

"My kingdom for a flashlight . . ." Exner was about to turn around to retrieve one from his vehicle when Lee grabbed his arm by the elbow. Then he stooped down not far from where Exner was standing, crouched down, felt through the debris, and came up with something in his hand.

In a moment, there was a blinding light of incredible intensity flashing before them. "I bet you'd get a good deal on this demo model." Lee was amazed the underwater light still functioned despite the fact that its handle had been reduced to a melted gnarl of plastic due to the intense heat of the fire. Surprisingly, its functionality had not been compromised.

Turning, Lee pointed. "Here we are. Mind your step." Lee stayed at the threshold to the office and held the light into the room as the two agents brushed past him.

Remaining at the room's entrance, Lee said, "A lot of memories here, Alan. I don't know what you're looking for, but I don't think you're going to find much in this mess."

Charred remains of books, magazines, binders, and files littered the office floor. Chairs had been upended, the desk stood at an unnatural angle in the room, its drawers strewn across the floor. There were pieces of gear lying everywhere—regulators with melted hoses, a melted stapler, a blob that was once a computer tower, consumed pens and pencils, and items unrecognizable. Portions of blackened posters still hung on the walls in mute defiance against the surrounding carnage.

"What a mess," Exner said. "No fire did this. This place was ripped apart!" He stooped down to inspect the computer tower, pushing the cindered box around with one of the melted pens beside it.

"I wonder if they found what they were looking for," Lee questioned.

"Doubt it," Exner said. "If they had, Travers' body would be among the debris. Whatever they were after, it was important enough for them to commit murder, kidnapping, and arson simultaneously."

Bindhira looked to the desk. A regulator was on it. She pulled a small brush out of her clutch and used its handle to lift the regulator's first stage up, cocking her head as she did so. "Lee, would you shine a little light on the subject here, please?"

Lee shone the powerful beam onto the desk's surface. "What is this object?" she asked.

"It's a regulator, Bindhi," he said. "The first stage, the heavy thing you're holding up, connects to the valve of a scuba tank. The second stage, the round can on the other end of the hose, is held in the diver's mouth by the mouthpiece that's attached to it, or was attached to it." Lee saw that both the hose and the mouthpiece had been melted beyond functionality.

Setting the unit back down, Bindhira joined the others as they searched the office for any clues it may hold.

"This room was ransacked before the place burned down, Alan," she said. "When a fire occurs, objects don't go flying around the room. Yet everything here is in disarray. Almost everything is out of place."

Bindhira returned to the desk. "But this piece of equipment has been carefully placed on the desk. Why?" She beckoned Lee over with his light to illuminate the regulator. She bent down for a closer look.

"And this," she said, pointing to the yoke of the regulator's first stage, "looks like blood."

At this, Exner came over to see for himself. "Well, I'll be damned," he said as he leaned in. "Looks like someone might have used this as a weapon! I've never heard of a scuba regulator being used as a deadly weapon before, but it's heavy enough to do the job!"

"True, that," Lee said. "With a pretty hefty swing, you could kill someone if you hit them hard enough . . ." Lee's voice trailed off. He didn't want to entertain the ramifications of his hypothesis.

Lee and Exner looked to each other as if on cue, neither wanting to take it upon themselves to speak the worst. "Bindhi," Exner said, "bag that and take it to the lab for testing. This is priority one. Get back to me with the results. Oh, and inform the director general. This thing's getting out of hand. Hartley and I will stay behind and see what else we can come up with."

"Right sir." And with that, Bindhira, led back to the entrance by Lee illuminating her way, squeezed his arm and said, "We will do everything possible to get your friend back, Lee. I promise."

Lee looked into those mesmerizing eyes and deep into her soul. "I know you will."

He put his hands firmly on her shoulders, planted a soft kiss on her forehead, then turned and navigated his way back to where Exner was waiting for him. He coughed at the horrible stench, and fear enveloped his mind.

Lee realized that this was not the work of incompetent amateurs. It was well conceived, well-orchestrated, and well covered up. Someone wanted something very bad. So far, the only lead they had was the blood on the regulator. The stakes were getting higher at every turn. Something had to break, and Lee hoped, soon.

14

Never Let 'Em See You Sweat

A short-circuited confusion coursed throughout the synapses of Bill Travers' brain as he groggily regained consciousness. Before him stood the two men as before, the man named Rodriguez leaning across the ancient table to peer directly into his captive's face.

Unflinchingly, Bill Travers looked up into the soulless eyes that bored through to the back of his skull for what seemed an indeterminate time. Rodriguez then broke the contest, hissing, "If I had *half* a mind, I would kill you right here, right now!"

Travers tried to speak, but found it difficult to open his mouth. Blood had oozed out of his nose, which had forged his lips shut with stickiness. He felt like the tin man in the *Wizard of Oz* who asked Dorothy to "oil me" when she met him for the first time.

Finally, he worked his lips free of their crimson bonds and muttered, "Don't flatter yourself. I doubt you even have that!" he grinned groggily.

Rodriguez flashed a brief evil grin then said, "I have little time to waste. Soon you will be nothing more than a piece of stinking meat left to rot in the afternoon sun. You have cost me a great deal and a good part of my reputation, amigo, for which you will pay dearly."

"I must have that painting. We know it is not at the gallery. If you do not know—and I am inclined to believe you, *Señor* Travers—then may I ask where you *think* it would be?"

"Don't know, don't care." Travers, still dazed, then added disjointedly, "You know something, Rodriguez? You're one ugly bastard, but I'm sure you already know that."

Travers was tired, hungry, and despondent. The ensuing silence was anything but golden to Rodriguez, who nodded to the man standing behind the chair.

The man nodded in kind. He lifted the captive out of his chair like a rag doll and slammed him down hard, onto the table's rough surface. Then he heard a distinctive click. Before he knew it, Travers felt a knife point at his throat, all but piercing it.

"That will do for now, Gino," Rodriguez said politely. Gino reluctantly backed away from the table, but remained close at hand.

"Your life," Carlos threw a hand over his head into the air, "it means nothing to me—and that of your friend *Señor* Hartley, even less. We can burn down his abode; we can even kill him at any time. But one way or another, we *will* find that canvas."

"Life or death; death or life. It is a fine line is it not, *señor*? If you will tell me what I wish to know, you live. Refuse and Gino here will have some much-needed fun." He looked over at Vaselino, whose smile devolved into an evil, toothy grin.

A sudden quietness descended upon the grotto. Then, in a loud snarling tone, Rodriguez said, "You waste my time, *señor*; you do not know with whom you are dealing. Those paintings must be located and returned to the people they were intended for. You sold them to pigeons, fool!"

Rodriguez paused, and then again, that quieter and gentler tone. "I will know what I must know, as you shall see. No one gets in my way!" Rodriguez wagged a menacing forefinger in front of his captive's face, laughing maniacally at the thought of the displeasure soon to be experienced by his prisoner.

Rodriguez suddenly broke into a smile. He put a hand on Gino Vaselino's shoulder and said, "Come, Gino, I have been summoned elsewhere." To the other he said, "Our distinguished guest from the Orient awaits and I must be present on his arrival."

Then in a darker tone, "Osvaldo, no one gets in or out until our return. If you fail in this, I will personally cut your heart out and have it for my evening meal!"

With that, the two left. Once again Travers heard the grating noise behind him. Within a minute, the grating had stopped. Only Osvaldo remained.

The old diver was now solely at the mercy of the remaining Cuban. He walked over to Travers and playfully slapped him on the side of his face a few times. Then in one lightning move, drew and stabbed a large knife into the table's surface. Osvaldo then leaned down and kicked the chair across from Travers a little farther from the table. He then walked around to it, and using the knife handle as a support, he slowly sat down. The strong Cuban stared at Travers as he did so, then smiled evilly and closed his eyes.

Travers was already thinking of ways to ensure they stayed that way.

15

Up Close And Personal

Another beautiful August morning found Lee Hartley in his private fenced-in backyard performing karate *kata*.

With the promise of another hot, humid day in the city, the morning's breezy coolness found him working out solely in a pair of men's blue Combat Nike tights and lightweight sparring shoes. It took him nearly an hour to go through the many *kata* he had studied and practiced over the years. This was a daily routine for Lee and one that he looked forward to and seldom missed. The powerful isometric movements had provided him with a well-chiseled body.

Regular *kata* performance was also a good way of clearing his mind. He found it helped develop an internal calmness that prepared him for the rigors of the day.

Bindhira Shankar, upon getting no response in answer to ringing Lee's doorbell at the front of the house, went around back to see if he was there. She was dressed in bright orange short-shorts that beautifully accented her long athletic legs, and a tight beige cap-sleeved peasant girl blouse that showcased the cleavage of her fine upper feminine assets.

The door to the rear gate of his backyard was ajar, and Bindhira stood there and watched in silent admiration as Lee performed his moves with the speed, power, and ferocity of a tiger. Sweat tore from his body as he punched, kicked, and jumped his way through the various routines.

Bindhira's heart skipped a few beats. Lee's well-developed chest, arms, tight derriere, and muscular legs totally captivated her as she watched.

Then much to her chagrin, she inadvertently dropped her car keys! The clatter upon hitting the pavement outside the gate caught Lee's immediate attention, and he ran over to investigate. He couldn't help but notice the tautness of her breasts, their stiff nipples beckoning him to release them of their bonds.

"Well, what a pleasant surprise!" Lee was going to give her a hug then thought better of it as he felt the perspiration dripping off his chin.

Bindhira, upset that her clumsiness prematurely ended the show replied, "Yes, more than you will know . . ."

A clumsy silence ensued, and Lee, looking down at his tights got the point.

"Uh, come on in while I grab a shower and get dressed. I'll put some coffee on if you'd like."

"You do not have to put on *anything* if you do not wish to . . ." The words came out before Bindhira could consciously restrain them.

Lee noted that a deepening facial hue of redness gave away her embarrassment—no, excitement—at seeing him like this. He beckoned her to follow as he walked from the deck through the backdoor, which lead into the kitchen of his modest bungalow.

Bindhira followed closely at his heels, eyes glued to Lee's tight derriere perfectly defined through his tights.

Knowing that Lee's secret admirer was excited at having witnessed his grueling workout became the catalyst that ignited their roiling chemistries to boil over; her arousal fuelling his.

As Lee turned to face her, she smiled. It was her turn to witness an involuntary emotive response as evidenced by his engorged groin. They stood there silently staring into each other's eyes in a mutual communication that was felt rather than spoken.

She drew him closer and rubbed him to newer heights. Lee held her as one would a long lost lover. Their lips pressed together; their tongues delved into the deepness of fresh mutual passion. Lee's perspiration became hers as they slumped down onto the expensive black and white marble-tiled kitchen floor in a tight embrace.

He lay lightly on top of her, kissing and caressing, caressing and kissing. Bindhira squeezed his derriere, then smiled deliciously. Her suspicions were confirmed. He wore no underwear beneath the tights.

In the moments that followed, the speed and dexterity with which each tore off the other's clothes would have an observer believe the two were a tag team in contention for an Olympic gold medal in the doubles stripping event. The raw lust each exuded toward the other had overflowed to the point of no return.

"Lee Hartley, you have the ass of an Adonis," Bindhira whispered as he kissed her neck up and down seductively.

"Bummer," was all he could get out before she hungrily sought out his lips.

Bindhira became a poster child of wantonness. She gyrated underneath in anticipation of sharing what they both wanted, what they both needed. As Lee delicately nibbled and massaged her nipples to stiff attention, her wetness below revealed a readiness for further exploration.

The two lovers wrestled as one until Lee could contain it no longer and exploded his love deep into her very soul. Bindhira arched upward in ecstasy at the feel of the unusual amount of hot passion entering her, then convulsed repeatedly in powerful waves of her own rapture as Lee's muscular body collapsed, his energy spent. He withdrew then lay beside her. Hot, wet, and exhausted, the two lay there on the floor of the kitchen.

"You know, Lee Hartley," she panted, "there was a time in my country that we would have been stoned after this act."

"You know, Bindhi," Lee mimicked with deliberate ignorance, "back in the day in *my* country, we'd be stoned *before* this act."

The only thing made for brunch that morning was a main dish of passionate love, followed by a side slumber of blissful satiation, followed by a tight mutual embrace for dessert.

16

Deductive Reasoning

Alan Exner grew increasingly impatient as he tried for the umpteenth time to reach Bindhira Shankar's cell. It was unusual for her not to have checked in by now.

His mind unconsciously registered the fact that the heat of the noonday sun had produced barely visible heat waves outside his windows. He had just put his phone down from trying to reach Lee Hartley once again when the NABS secretary stationed outside his office buzzed to inform him that he had two visitors.

"Where the *hell* have you two been?" It was obvious from Exner's tone that he'd been both worried and peeved, and not necessarily in that order. He got up from his desk and met them as they walked into his office. The furrowed brow and intent gaze clearly etched on his face told them in no uncertain terms that Alan Exner demanded an answer and it had better be good.

It was Lee that broke the chill. "Ex, it's not Bindhi's fault. I was working out, and well, something came up. I didn't really think you needed us as early as Bindhi had said." Then, in an effort to reinforce the truth of his lie, "We would've been here sooner if she'd have put out a little more, ah, effort . . . to help me . . . get my stuff caught up, that is . . ."

Bindhira gave Lee a withering look and walked over to the office windows in an effort to conceal both her facial flush and his lame lie. She took in the sunshine glittering off the lake as she spoke.

"Alan, we arrived here as soon as Lee was . . . finished with the chores at his place." She turned from the window, shot Lee a sharp glance, then quickly changed the subject. "Have there been any further developments on the search for Mr. Travers or the shop fire?"

Exner grabbed a file folder off the desktop. Plopping his butt onto the far corner of its mahogany surface, he read quietly from it briefly before replying.

"As a matter of fact yes; several. According to the fire marshal's office, there was one fire set, followed by an explosion that occurred in the upstairs apartment washroom."

Lee and Bindhira took up a position on each side of him.

"There must have been more than one visitor at the time of the explosion," Bindhira said.

"Sooo this tells us . . . ?" Lee's tone rose at the end of his statement.

"Elementary, my dear Hartley," Exner said. "It tells us that a professional team may have come into the shop for information or for something that belonged to them, or both. It tells us that the fire was probably a diversion until the upstairs explosion blew the walls off the place, either to leave no evidence of their visit or," he drew a long breath, "in retaliation for something Travers did to them." He paused, the others still silent. "Finally, it tells us that there's more to this whole sordid affair than meets the eye."

Exner unceremoniously tossed the file folder back onto the desk, which Bindhira picked up as he continued. "It's my guess there were at *least* three individuals who came into the shop. One engaged Travers in conversation, one set the diversionary fire, while a third planted semtex in the toilet tank of the bathroom upstairs after he ransacked the place."

Bindhira: "Plastic explosives?"

Lee: "Toilet tank?"

"A sure indicator of Cuban involvement," Exner stated. "This was a signature technique of the Cuban secret police. Such techniques have kept Castro in fearful control since his *Revolución* of 1959.

"Lends a whole new meaning to the phrase 'shit happens,'" Lee said without humor.

Exner continued. "The upstairs bathroom is the central-most room in the building. The explosion there brought the floor down with it. One flip of the handle and *kaboom*! At least that was the plan."

A silence ensued as Exner walked over to the windows. Lee and Bindhira followed in true pied-piper fashion. Bindhira handed Lee the folder on the way. The two stood looking out over the lake, one at each end window, with Exner in the middle.

"This is how I think it went down," Exner projected. "Perpetrator number one strikes up a conversation with our boy. Perp number two sets a fire in the storage area just past the office, while perpetrator number three sneaks up to Travers' apartment, where he plants explosives in the toilet tank and ransacks the place looking for whatever."

"By this time Travers, smelling fire, realizes two men have left the shop, and not by the front door. He leaves the first man at the counter, goes back to his office, and finds number three rummaging through the drawers. A struggle ensues."

"The fire, in the meantime, begins to take hold. By this time, numbers one and two rush into the office to help a sorry ass number three, if we know Travers as we do. Seeing perp number three having a hard time with Travers, one of the others quickly ends the fight by grabbing the regulator on Bill's desk, swings it by the hose and knocks Bill unconscious. Numbers one and two trash the office in a desperate bid to find whatever it is they were looking for before the place goes up. Unsuccessful, they snatch Travers and flee. That in itself tells us that he at least was alive when they left."

"Some comfort you are, Buddy," Lee said half-jokingly.

"As the fight was not in their script," Bindhira continues, "their escape was delayed, and the semtex goes off, albeit prematurely," Bindhira said. "A hastily placed explosive always does."

"Two of them carried Travers out," Lee speculates, "but the third guy got trapped when the central supporting pillar collapsed by the side exit door which blocked it. When the others couldn't free their man, they killed him."

"Dead men tell no tales," Exner concluded ruefully.

Lee reached into a back pocket, produced his flask, took a small sip, and then replaced it. "Who the hell does that—leaves one of their own behind?"

Exner was pleased at the plausible scenario they had constructed together.

"Sounds credible to me," Bindhira assented. "As your report states Alan, forensics discovered that it *was* Bill Travers' blood on the first stage of the regulator we found in the office."

As they stood looking out over the lake in quiet solemnity, Alan Exner touched each of their arms in unison, returned to his desk, pulled out a drawer, and extracted an evidence bag. "That's not all. Police found this near the building's side exit."

Inside the clear plastic bag was the brass casing of a 9mm caliber bullet.

17

Hope

Bill Travers was a hurting unit. Regaining painful consciousness, he was surprised to find a plate of warm food and a bottle of opened expensive wine on the table in front of him. Though only fish and chips, Travers downed the meal without even using the fork placed there for his use.

Their motives unclear, he was grateful nevertheless for the strength the unexpected meal gave him. For now he *was* alone, and the bottle of red Spanish Solaz Shiraz-Tempranillo did much to both ease his pain and restore his consciousness.

It wasn't until after he finished the food that he realized to his horror and dismay that perhaps they had poisoned him, which was why they left him alone. Suddenly, the meal didn't sit too well with him.

An hour went by however, and Travers thanked his lucky stars that the meal hadn't been tampered with after all. He was still imprisoned though, and that in itself was bad enough. When they came back,

Travers knew that they *would* discover he knew nothing, and had no doubt that his past fear would become a present reality.

He was puzzled by the unexpected change-up in tactics. Unfettered, wined, and dined, he got up slowly, painfully, from the uncomfortable rough-hewn wooden chair and stumbled around in an attempt to regain both circulation and mobility.

The cavern was scantily illuminated by two large candles, one at each end of the table. He wasted no time in scouring his confines for a way out. Remembering the scraping sounds behind him as he sat at the table when the others had first appeared, he focused his attention on the floor. Grabbing a candle, he placed it down behind the chair.

Bending down behind it, he saw that there was nothing unusual about the porous limestone surface. However, when he got down on all fours, he noticed a straight line. Knowing that in nature there was no such thing as a straight line, he traced his finger along it. Pulling the candle over for better lighting, he found that it connected to another at a ninety-degree angle, then another, then another. It was a three-foot by three-foot square cut scored into the floor of the cavern!

Travers pulled himself up and grabbed the fork that lay on the table. He returned to the floor and used its handle to score the lines outlining the square several times. Interestingly, he noticed that some of the powder he had created by scraping the soft rock had disappeared into the crack.

He couldn't find a handle or pull-tab or anything else that remotely resembled a latch to open it, however. He stood up again, placed his hands over his kidneys and stretched backward in an effort to loosen his spine. Once again, candle in hand, Travers reinspected the walls for signs of another means of entry. None could be found.

As he stood there in the dimness of his prison, Travers thought he could hear a deep blast from what sounded like a transport truck horn; no, there it was again. It was a foghorn or the horn of a ship. He must be on a waterfront!

This was the first sound that had permeated the cavern since his arrival. It was obviously a very loud, very strong horn. He discounted a stationary foghorn as they sounded at regular intervals. Could it be a passing freighter? Maybe, but wait! There it was again! Three distinct, albeit faint blasts filtered through the rock. Scanning his memory banks, he came to a single conclusion. It had to be a ferry of sorts. If that was the case, he must be close to a ferry dock, as a ferry would sound three blasts on its proximity to dockside.

Tobermory. That was his first thought. He must be in Tobermory, formerly a small fishing village-come-diving haven at the tip of the Bruce Peninsula in Ontario. Yes, there *was* a car ferry there! The MS *Chi-Cheemaun*—Ojibwa for "Big Canoe", that had been in service there since 1974!

If this was indeed where he was incarcerated, then he had friends here. But how could he get word to them of his plight?

Travers was sure his captors had no knowledge of the couple who bought the canvas for the stateroom of their yacht. If they had, he'd be dead already.

He remembered the older couple at the *Little Tub Gallery* quite by accident the day Mrs. Braithwaite, the elderly gallery owner, put it out on display. It was a painting they simply had to have, one from his last consignment. Would they still be in the area?

What was so important about one particular painting that his captors were willing to kidnap and kill for it?

18

Impromptu Workout

Bindhira had dropped Lee off at his home where he tended to his damaged Cadillac, if only to keep his mind occupied. *What a mess,* Lee thought as he sat in the drivers' seat with the door fully open, one foot on the ground. Grabbing the outside top of the roof with his left hand to get out of the car, Lee's foot slipped when he attempted to get out. He nearly fell. *What the* . . . ?

Hanging onto the car's roof with both hands now, Lee pushed himself up, out, and away from the vehicle. Looking underneath the vehicle to locate the source of his slip, he noticed an opaque liquid dripping slowly to the ground. He knelt down and rubbed some of the liquid between his fingers. It was brake fluid!

Pulling himself under the Caddy, Lee discovered that the leak was not a broken line as he had surmised. One of the narrow metal brake lines had been neatly *sawed* in two! Anger welled deep within. Things were getting personal again. Someone was definitely playing for keeps. Whose buttons had he pushed to warrant this?

A quick request to Alan Exner, and Lee was behind the wheel of Travers' H3 Hummer within the hour. One of Exner's operatives had dropped it off for Lee to use once forensics had finished with it.

Lee determined it was finally time to have his beloved Cadillac Coupe de Ville towed to the local auto recycling shop. He had enjoyed it immensely over the years, but the venerable old steed was now at the point of too much expense for too diminishing a return. It had suffered much over the past few days and needed to be put to its final rest.

For now at least he would use the Hummer with the fervent hope he could return it to its rightful owner very, very soon.

On a whim, Lee decided to drive the Hummer back to the Scuba U to see what was happening there. Lee enjoyed the drive with the windows and sun roof open, taking in the refreshing breeze and sunshine as he drove along the Lake Erie shoreline to Travers' dive shop. It was a cloudless day and the sun was starting to set as he drew near. Lee could see the burnt hulk of the building on his way through the narrow woodland lining the roadway.

Lee immediately hit the brakes when his attention turned to the driveway. It was the black Viper! Lee slammed the transmission into reverse and pulled the Hummer around the bend he had just rounded, where it would not be seen from the end of the car park. Fortunately there was no traffic at this point. He quickly jumped out and headed through the woodland to the shop.

From the protection of the trees and foliage bordering the property, Lee observed the shop without risk of being seen. The Viper was the only vehicle in the car park. There was no activity around the building.

Several minutes later, two men came out the side entrance of the building. They were locked in conversation as they rounded the back corner of the shop.

Ten minutes went by, and the men hadn't returned. There were few trees in the clearing around the property. Lee decided to investigate.

But there was no cover for about thirty feet from the car park to the side entrance. He broke cover at full throttle and reached the building unchallenged. He shot a cursory glance into the darkness of the open doorway and headed to the corner of the building the two men had disappeared around.

Suddenly he was seized from behind by a man who came out moments after Lee had passed the doorway. The man pinned his arms to his sides and called out. A short, stocky man came around the corner and planted a vicious uppercut into Lee's ribcage.

Lee buckled from the crushing blow, but the frustration of the past few days fuelled his counterattack. Using the rear man as a brace, Lee launched a vicious neck-snapping outside crescent kick to the face of the attacker in front, which spun him full circle and dropped him to the ground. The same foot retracted backward and up into a gonad-atomizing heel kick. This was followed by an agonizing stomp to the man's instep.

The third man came around the corner by this time and rushed him with a hunting knife. A lightning-fast rising snap kick knocked the knife painfully out of the assailant's hand. Blinded by sheer fury at the cowardly attack, Lee continued his defense with twin "bear paw" strikes to the man's ears, which imploded the assailant's eardrums. The attack ended abruptly when Lee launched a trachea-crushing throat thrust. The man fell. There was no further movement.

Hearing a war whoop from behind, Lee turned in time to block an iron pipe directed at his face by the man who had held him. He immediately wrapped his left arm around the assailant's descending right, around and above the elbow, effectively trapping the weapon hand. A head butt and several vicious knee strikes brought the man to his knees. Lee then came down hard, very hard, onto the base of the man's neck with a jumping, descending elbow strike. The man catapulted facedown as a lifeless puppet whose strings had suddenly been severed.

Exhausted, hurt, and pumped with adrenaline, Lee stormed the building, no longer concerned for his safety. "Come out," Lee shouted.

"Come out, you cowards!" Lee rushed into the side entrance and nearly fell numerous times as he recklessly plodded through the extensively damaged building looking for someone to tell him what he needed to know. But there was no one; for Lee Hartley had killed them all.

19

Getting Nowhere Fast

An indeterminate period of time had elapsed since the men left Bill Travers alone in his prison cave. He was feeling physically better now, but the candles had nearly expired. It was the first time that he began to worry about his future. He'd given up all hope of finding his way out of this damp, dingy dungeon. Maybe they were just going to leave him to die here.

It was a waiting game however one looked at it. Travers knew he wouldn't be able to take much more punishment from the vicious cutthroats. He could only string them along for a short while, and when they grew tired of him . . . well, he didn't want to go there.

Travers suddenly heard the faint sound of muffled footsteps as they came up a stairway from beneath. The muffled footfalls became more pronounced as they came nearer to the trapdoor. *What to do?*

The familiar grating noise began, and within a few minutes he saw an increasing amount of light emanating from the enigmatic trapdoor as it slowly opened. Through some sort of ingenious electronic motor and pulley system, it automatically slid down and back from view beneath the floor.

Travers moved back from the light that began to flood his confines. When a man's head cleared the opening in the floor, he lashed out with his foot then stepped back into the shadows as the man groaned, then was thrown back and down the stairwell.

Stupid move, Travers, stupid, stupid move, he thought.

He was waiting for the muzzle of a gun to rise through the floor and put an end to his problems, but that didn't happen. The man had been alone!

Cautiously peering down through the opening, he saw a brightly lit stairway landing about four feet below, with no one in sight. He sat on the brink, then jumped through and hurried down the stone staircase. It was two flights before the captive found his captor. He lay sprawled in an unnatural position on the lower landing. Blood oozed from both mouth and right ear. The man lay dead.

Bill could see that it was Osvaldo, that towering hunk of muscle that nearly broke Travers' back when the Cuban body-slammed him onto the table.

"I may be old, but I'm still a force to be reckoned with," Travers muttered over his shoulder as he jumped over the body in a desperate flight for freedom.

At first he was elated to see he'd stumbled upon a dock at the far end of the cavern. He could swim out! But his heart sank immediately thereafter when he saw that freedom would not be so easily achieved. He'd reached a dead end at a small unoccupied dock in front of two tightly shut heavy-gauge steel bay doors.

Large enough to permit a small pleasure craft, Travers thought, they must be locked via a remote transmitter onboard whatever craft this place called home. No doubt the doors extended close to the bottom of the waterway inside the cavern. Still, the man had entered by some route, but from where?

Travers shuddered. All he'd succeeded in doing was move from one room to another in the prison. Oh, and killing a man in the process. Once again that familiar wave of hopelessness washed over him. Dropping down onto the hard, wet stone floor, head in hands, his mind entertained but a single thought: *They're gonna be pissed when they get back: they're gonna be real pissed . . .*

20

An Interloper

NABS investigators were all over the Viper at the dive shop. A forensics team from NABS was all over the three bodies. And a certain NABS control was all over Lee Hartley, towering over him as the latter sat on the curb beside the Viper's right rear wheel.

"*What the hell* were you thinking, Lee? Have you *any* bloody idea what a mess you've put me in, not to mention YOU? Here we have—had, three, count 'em, *three* solid leads on this whole twisted affair, and *you* friggin' take them all out. *What the hell*, Lee? Read my lips, Hartley," Exner continued. "There will be no more killing on my watch! You may have just signed Bill Travers' death warrant. And you, *you* are in deep feces my friend!"

During the height of his tirade, Exner spilled his cup of café mocha all over his shirt and tie. Normally this would be cause for a series of expletives, but in light of the situation, he thought it best to keep his tongue in check.

Regardless, three potentially viable sources of information lay dead, their knowledge taken with them to the grave. Lee Hartley was once again in the eye of the hurricane. Fortunately, however, the Viper was here along with any clues that may lead them to the whereabouts of Bill Travers. He hoped against hope his team would turn up something, anything.

Lee pulled a small flask from his back pocket, opened it, and took a gulp of its contents. He swirled it around his mouth for a second, downed it, and then replaced the cap on the flask, and replaced it.

"Alan, I just came back here to collect my thoughts. I didn't know those clowns were here, and I *sure* didn't expect the welcome I received."

Lee spoke in a broken voice that was almost foreign to Exner. "Bill and I . . ." his voice choked, "we had a lot of good times here. I helped him get this dump in shape to make the Scuba U what he'd envisioned it to be. He got the place for a song, and you know how *he* sings. Man, we had a lot of fun, a lot of laughs here."

"Damn it, Alan! Find out who's behind all this!" He sat with clenched fists at the curb. Then in a much quieter voice, Lee muttered to himself, "Where the hell have they taken you, buddy?"

Out of the assembly of bystanders that had gathered at seeing police, fire, and government vehicles in front of the burned out shell stood a disheveled little girl. She was a skinny little thing about ten or eleven years old, and wore a simple faded red smock and well-worn flip-flops. Her flaxen hair was a long, dirty, tangled mess, but there was something strangely unique about her eyes. They were a vibrant greenish-blue, full of life, and full of wisdom beyond her years. She was alone and missed by no one.

Somehow she had managed to slip through the police barricade. She skirted along the ruins and around the front left corner of the building. She was hidden from view by a large old trawler's fish bin close to the building that Travers brought out each morning loaded up with used scuba equipment for sale.

One member of the forensics team unconsciously smiled at her as he walked from the building to a crime scene van. He would have challenged her, but with his heavy forensics kit and his mind on the task at hand, her presence registered only fleetingly in his mind.

The little girl seemed happy, and hummed a sweet little melody as she sat at the edge of the side car park. She played with her tattered little brown and yellow thinly stuffed teddy bear she was holding. He had lost an eye, perhaps from too much loving. Then, apparently satisfied that her bear had had enough excitement for the day, the child abruptly popped up. She stooped down and uprooted a little yellow flower growing all by itself beside the building. She let her bear smell it, and then danced merrily off into the woods, dangling her anemic furry friend by one of its threadbare arms.

Exner vacantly watched the forensics team scouring the car for clues as he spoke. "I've sent Ms. Shankar back to the office to run the Viper tags and update all branches from the situation room. This case is going to crack wide open real soon. I'm sure of it."

He knew Lee wouldn't have killed those men unless his life was in danger. He noticed that his friend was getting too close to the edge. Still, three men lay dead, and the truth was still out there. But they *had* the Viper. Something was sure to turn up—fingerprints, DNA, records, something.

Changing tact, Exner dropped down to sit curbside with Lee despite wearing his most expensive dark blue suit. "You always were good at kicking ass, Lee, I give you that." Exner put his hand on Lee's shoulder.

"But you can't keep taking the bad guys out, Lee. It's not good for business. You can't be doing this, *all right*? You've really put me on the spot this time. You're not even one of my agents, for frig's sake. You're a consultant, Lee. Consultants don't kill suspects. Consultants don't kill, period. Do you hear what I'm saying? I can't keep covering your sorry ass. We've got three dead bodies and little else."

Lee looked up at his old friend. The diver's normally clear brown eyes were unfocused and distant. "Alan," he said looking down at the stones of the driveway, "during the past several days I have been chased, I have been shot at, I have been viciously attacked by three thugs. The Caddie's been shot up. Then, for good measure, someone cut its brake lines. My friend's home, his place of business, and his livelihood have all been taken away; his life as well, for all we know."

"I'm tired, I'm sore, and I wish to hell I knew where he is. Do what you have to, Ex, but rest assured, I *will* find the bastards who are behind all this, and I *will* deal with them."

Exner knew better than to argue with his friend when he was like this. He rose from where he sat on the dirty curb, brushed the dirt from the rear of his suit pants, and placed a firm hand on his friend's shoulder.

"All this," Exner let out a huge sigh and stretched out an arm at the carnage before them, "all this is bigger than the both of us. Lee. Listen, I want you to go home. I want you to stay there. When I hear anything from any of my departments, anything at all, I promise I'll call. This is a non-negotiable deal, Lee, my final answer. I mean it. Go home and stay there. I've enough on my plate as it is without having to corral a loose cannon at every turn."

"Sir, excuse me, sir?" It was Lewis Mataeo, chief of forensics at NABS Niagara and one of Exner's senior staff. Mataeo walked over to where the two had been locked in conversation. "You might want to come and take a look at this."

They followed Mataeo as he went around to the other side of the car. Inside the driver's side door pouch was a 9 mm Glock 17 black polymer auto-loading pistol with a seventeen-round magazine. Carefully dropping the magazine with latex gloves, it was clearly evident that several rounds were missing.

21

A Most Bizarre Rescue

Bill Travers was desperate, and knew this would be his only chance at escape. *They sent the bastard back to kill me,* he thought, as he walked the length of the rickety wooden dock to its end. The boathouse doors didn't appear old as no rust was evident, at least above the waterline. A thick patina of algae lay crusted where the doors extended below the waterline. Hairlike green tendrils of seaweed gently feathered out and back from the ebb and flow of water seeping in and out from under the doors that opened into the bay.

Travers saw that this natural little "boathouse" must be the only entrance to the grotto, no doubt carved out of the soft limestone rock when the Laurentide ice sheet receded during the end of the last ice age some 10,000 years ago. It was the scouring action of the receding glacier that had carved out the entire Great Lakes system, the largest body of fresh water in the world.

Suddenly the eerie sound of a fog horn reverberated dully within the hollows of the little cave once again. It was becoming increasingly evident that he was held somewhere around Georgian Bay, an extension of the northeastern area of Lake Huron at the tip of the Bruce Peninsula in south-central Ontario.

Georgian Bay was actually a misnomer, for this large body of fresh water reached a depth of 540 feet near the main channel leading into Lake Huron proper. Not far from this channel lay the sleepy little fishing village of Tobermory.

There it was again, another blast. It was definitely the passenger-vehicle ferry, MS *Chi Cheemaun*. The "Big Canoe" was signaling its arrival to Tobermory from Manitoulin Island. If he could just find a way out, he knew that help was only a short distance away. But it seemed a big "if."

Then, unexpectedly, he thought he heard the sound of a small girl's voice. *I must be going mad, he* thought. *No, there it is again!* He distinctly heard the muffled sound of a child singing! A little girl must be playing along the shoreline by the entrance. *Maybe she's not alone*!

"Hey; hey, little girl! Little girl, can you hear me? Help! *Help*," he screamed. "Sweetie, I'm trapped in here! Can you hear me? Please, please don't leave. I'm trapped." Travers' voice was starting to crackle and fade; he'd never screamed so loud in his life. He realized that his cries were probably muffled by the sound of the waves that crashed to shore from passing motorboats.

He walked back the length of the dock to where the voice seemed strongest. *The rock must be thinnest at this point*, he thought. He faced the rough-hewn wall and placed his hands against it, his right ear pressed to the cold, musty surface.

At first there was nothing, and his heart skipped a beat as he realized he may never have another chance at freedom. Suddenly he heard that soft, sweet little voice again! It was indiscernible, but there nonetheless. He couldn't make it out. He'd heard the singing because it was higher pitched. Her little voice wasn't strong enough to permeate through the thickness of the rock without a tune to carry it more clearly though the limestone.

There came another blast of the foghorn. Had it scared the little girl? No, he heard more mumbling! She was still on the other side. She must have heard his cries for help!

"Little girl, I can hear you, but I don't know what you're saying. I can hear you!" Travers beat his fists against the rock in frustration, beads of sweat pouring off his brow. He butted his head repeatedly against the wall where he stood. "I'm still here. Please go and get help! I'm trapped . . . trapped. Can you hear me?"

Silence. The worst sound to hear when trapped and alone. There was nothing but complete and utter silence. Several minutes passed. Travers turned with his back against the rock wall and slid down, one leg beneath him, head back against the wall, eyes closed. He began to drift into a deep sleep, a sleep brought on both by exhaustion and hopeless despair. His head flopped down on his chest. He welcomed the darkness.

I'm hearing voices. I'm gonna die in this God-forsaken hole. So what? If this is all there is to dying, bring it on.

Suddenly he heard a loud grinding, grating noise from somewhere on the other side of the darkness.

What the . . . ? Travers awoke with such a start that he almost knocked himself out when his head reared back, striking the hard rock behind. He didn't even feel the trickle of warm blood oozing out from the abrasion his head just suffered. Red liquid dripped down onto the collar of his shirt.

He got up, staggering as he did so. The leg that was underneath him was numb and reluctant to come alive as quickly as the rest of his body. He heard the snapping of twigs, and a creaking, grating noise of metal on metal. It sounded like hinges that hadn't been in service since the Dark Ages, groaning in protest at being awakened.

The sounds were coming from the far corner of the cavern, furthest from the dock. He hadn't been able to see that far back in the cavern, for the area lay beyond the range of the single low-watt bulb that illuminated the end of the stairway to the dock.

He followed the muffled sound as best he could. Just around a slight bend, he was dumbfounded to see several cracks of light reflecting off the rock wall! As he drew nearer, he saw that it came from a natural narrow passage leading from the grotto directly through the rock face. Travers pinched himself to make sure he wasn't dreaming as he stumbled toward the light.

It *was* sunlight, and it seeped through a very old and very heavy wooden door with ancient iron hinges that had been anchored into the rock face many, many years ago. The intensity of the unexpected bright light that seeped through the slats of the decaying door assailed his eyes with such intensity that it instinctively compelled him to turn from the entranceway to shield his eyes in the crook of his arm. Slowly, very slowly, he lowered his arm from his face, and looked back at the thick rough-hewn partially open portal.

The narrow passageway was barely large enough for a man to navigate. He now understood why he hadn't heard Osvaldo entering the cavern, as the distance from the tunnel to the stairway along with the heavy stone floor trapdoor at the top of the stairs had occluded the groaning and grinding of the rusted iron hinges of the ancient door.

He lost no time in reaching the door and pulling himself through the pinched opening and out into the sunlight. *He was free!* He saw how the door had been concealed over the years by bramble bush and several small trees, well hidden from view of the water's edge several yards away.

Once out he instinctively crouched down and ran for the cover of a majestic blue spruce tree near the tunnel entrance. He looked warily around to ensure he hadn't been observed by anyone watching the entrance. He stood facing the tree and bent over, hands on knees, both to catch his breath and plot his next move.

Suddenly he raised his head with a jolt. *The child! Where was the girl?* Realizing that she too could be in danger, he scanned the woodland back of the bay for any signs of his carefree little benefactor.

It was she who had stumbled upon his place of imprisonment. It was she who had discovered the small but heavy wooden door. And it was she who had opened it as far as her little frame would allow, far enough to enable him to hear the cracking and snapping of twigs and branches around the entrance and the creaking of the hinges while doing so. He owed her his life.

He scanned the area, but it was apparent that she had left. Oh to have the carefree spirit of a child again!

Confident that he had been undetected, Travers retraced his steps and continued through the tight bramble to the water's edge. He felt faint and the trek was arduous. He looked over his shoulder for one final glance back to the place of his intended demise. But when he did so, he lost his balance and nearly fell when he slipped on a soft damp object underfoot.

What the . . . ? Travers cursed as he nearly broke his ankle when he slipped on something underfoot. Bending down to see what it was, he smiled in spite of himself as he bent down to pick up a tattered and dirty little brown and yellow thinly stuffed one-eyed teddy bear.

22

History Repeats Itself

The black rubber Zodiac inflatable boat zipped through the water under the cloak of darkness. Gino Vaselino was at the helm. Carlos Rodriguez sat in the rear, spray hitting him hard in the face as they raced over the white-capped swells. "Slow down, you fool! I am soaked, thanks to your horrid seamanship!"

Vaselino throttled back on the 150 HP Evinrude motor and the inflatable immediately lowered in the water and came to a crawl. This only served to allow the water behind them to catch up, which flooded the rear of the boat. "You stupid dolt! Give me one good reason I don't shoot you in the balls right now!"

Vaselino was inwardly overjoyed at seeing Rodriguez uncomfortably wet. However, he didn't want to incur his superior's infamous wrath for so little an infraction. "Here, Carlos, take my shirt to wipe off with. I am sorry." He pulled his sleeveless T-shirt up and over his crossed elbows, and in one streamlined motion tossed it back to the sputtering Rodriguez. The older Cuban caught the shirt, wiped his face and arms with it and tossed it overboard.

This angered Vaselino. There was a stiff offshore breeze that caused both men to shiver. At least Rodriguez had some protection from the wind. Now bare-chested, Gino had none, which caused goose bumps to appear all over his arms.

"Well, what are you waiting for? Get us to the cave!" Rodriguez snapped without the dignity of looking at his hireling.

Rodriguez was sloshing around with his hands in the water at the bottom of the boat, trying to find something to bail with, but gave up. It was pitch-black now. He was wet and irritable, and just wanted to get back to the grotto.

Gino throttled up, gently now, and slow enough that the swells didn't hammer the bottom of the rubber boat as they made their way in the dark. He was given strict instructions not to use lights of any kind. When a boat came anywhere remotely near, Gino would vector off in the distance until he was sure their wake would not be detected, then resume their original course.

When they reached the hidden entrance, Gino hit a button on the dash-mounted remote, and the facade of the rock face slowly split in two, revealing a narrow canal just large enough for the small craft to enter. The twin doors ground shut behind them as they closed, and the tiny boat disappeared into the inky blackness beyond; the grotto sealed.

Although the old cavern had been carved out centuries ago, it had only recently been discovered a few months back by an elderly fisherman who struck up a conversation at the Dive Inn in the heart of Tobermory with Osvaldo and Javier, Rodriguez' men, who happened to be at the right place at the right time.

It was the very evening the fisherman had discovered it. The two bought him a few drinks and even his meal that night. Assured that the old man hadn't had time to tell anyone of the cavern's existence, Javier excused himself in the middle of the meal, telling the others he suddenly felt "ill."

The fisherman was killed in a car accident that night when his brakes "failed" on a hairpin turn on the King's Highway 6 on his way south to Owen Sound and home—insurance that the secret location of the cavern remained secret.

Very early the next morning, members of the cell discovered the hidden cavern just as the overly friendly fisherman had described it, at the end of Big Tub Road, which ended at Georgian Bay. Using a canoe, Rodriguez and Osvaldo had inspected it and were surprised to discover that it was comprised of a perfect dock area and two dry chambers. With a little work, it would make a perfect lair from which to operate.

Within a week, the foreign agents had constructed double bay doors to better conceal the cavern's entrance and to provide a viable secret entrance by water. The rock face was high, with a sheer drop thirty feet to the bay, but the men had ingeniously devised the bay doors with a stone facade at the entrance to the grotto in the event that the dense foliage at its entrance failed to conceal them from prying eyes.

It had been hard work, but under cover of darkness each night for two weeks, they managed to complete their project. It had been Javier's idea to utilize two heavy-duty garage-door-opening motors and a unique pulley system to operate the large doors. But they were constantly in need of lubrication due to the elevated humidity inside the cavern.

They would have to do without Javier's ingenuity now as it was he who had to be silenced at the dive shop explosion in Fort Erie. The Cubans had tried to extricate the man, but his leg was hopelessly pinned and the intensity of the fire too great. A single bullet served two purposes. It not only put Javier out of his misery, but also ensured he couldn't talk in the remote chance of rescue.

Mooring the boat, Gino helped the wet Rodriguez out of the back of the Zodiac. "Empty the damn thing of water," Rodriguez scolded. He started to head for the inner entrance when on a thought he turned to point a finger at him and said, "And, Gino, this will not happen again. I cannot get sick now. Is this understood?"

Gino looked up just enough to acknowledge his superior. "It will be as you wish, Carlos," he shivered. Gino was colder and wetter than Carlos. It was at that moment that Vaselino determined he had to get out from under this heartless bastard, and soon.

As Rodriguez entered the inner sanctuary of the cavern, the first thing he noticed was the utter solitude of the place. He had expected echoes of Osvaldo's voice, or at the very least, cries of agony from their captive. Something was not right.

The ringmaster of the Cuban sleeper cell withdrew a compact SIG SAUER .380 caliber pistol from its brown leather waistband holster. Surprisingly, the weapon was dry and even warm to the touch. The weapon had been in its holster under his shirt and close to his body.

Rodriguez cycled a round into the SIG's chamber from a full six-round magazine. Cautiously, he proceeded to the stairway at the far end of the grotto. He crouched low as he rounded a corner where the staircase descended from the upper inner chamber.

What Rodriguez saw next held him spellbound. There on the lower landing lay Osvaldo, his head twisted in a grossly unnatural position as if someone had deliberately tried to screw it off then left it hanging over the landing. There was little blood, save for a discharge of bloody froth that had oozed out from his nose and mouth. A straw-colored liquid had leaked from Osvaldo's right ear and pooled on the step below his overhanging head.

Enraged, Rodriguez vaulted over the corpse and charged up the staircase, gun at the ready. He noticed that the trapdoor was open up above him. Tossing caution to the wind, he held the pistol between his teeth and pulled himself up and into the upper chamber yelling, "You are one dead asshole. Dead!"

One of the candles had burned out and the other nearly extinguished. Rodriguez pulled a small flashlight from his pocket and rushed over to the far corner by a small alcove. Flattening himself against the wall, he dropped down and rushed around it. It was empty.

He scoured the whole upper chamber looking for something, anything that would give him a clue as to what had happened in his absence. He went around the room again in disbelief. He cursed, swore, yelled, and screamed obscenity after obscenity in Spanish, essentially to have Travers' balls on a platter.

But his angry tirade was for naught. Carlos Rodriguez stood alone in the chamber. He heard Gino's footsteps coming at his cry, then heard them stop abruptly, obviously at the sight of Osvaldo lying dead on the staircase landing.

Rodriguez dropped through the opening and clambered down to meet Vaselino on the lower landing, who was looking for vital signs on the dead body. "Leave him," he said, kicking the limp figure before him. "He is no longer of any use to us. We must leave now. The prisoner has escaped, and with him the location of the cavern. This base of operations has been compromised."

Without further word, the two left their hideout for the last time, and returned to the Zodiac.

23

Lost And Found

"Dive shop kidnap victim located near Tobermory. Suspend and secure all search operations for same. Agents previously assigned to this case are ordered to stand by for specifics concerning persons of interest. Control will issue updates as they develop. Control out."

Alan Exner returned the cordless microphone to its cradle beside the powerful Sequoia-mediated satellite transceiver under the dash of the TaZeR. The message would be received by all senior NABS personnel assigned to the case via their seq-pods, satellite cell phone devices capable of crystal clarity anywhere in the world.

A husband and wife who were hiking in the heavily wooded area near the grotto had heard human cries of pain and came to investigate. They discovered Travers sitting against a tree, with his shoe and sock off, in a lot of pain. Travers was lucky; it was only a badly sprained ankle.

The couple wanted to help but was afraid to move him too far at the time for fear of aggravating his condition. As they had no cell phone, the decision was made for the wife to leave Travers and her husband to seek help alone at the little fishing village three miles from their location.

The woman made it.

It was early the next morning when an ambulance and NABS team arrived in Tobermory at the end of the large drop-off leading down to the water's edge off the King's Highway 6.

OPP officers cordoned off the end of the only highway that runs into Tobermory. NABS operatives combed the surrounding woodlands and private residences in search of clues to Travers' captors.

Meanwhile, paramedics scaled down the rock face at waterside and poured over Travers, who had managed to make it that far with the man's help. They took his blood pressure, tended to his badly sprained ankle, listened to his breathing, and generally did everything that paramedics do best under the worst conditions. Once stabilized, they hoisted their charge up by gurney to cliff top.

The faces of the two paramedics were strained as they pulled the stretcher-bound Travers up the craggy side of the steep rock face and safety. Lee and Exner both came over by their friend's side. The paramedics unsecured Travers from the stretcher and guided him over to sit on the flat protruding rear bumper of the ambulance.

Unspoken words sometimes speak volumes. Such was the case as Exner looked into the face of the old diver for several silent moments. "To say you had us worried is the grossest of understatements," he said, then added, "welcome back, Bill. You're one lucky SOB, and tough as nails."

"Tough as nails, not," Travers said ruefully, and then added, "I'm sure glad to see your ugly pusses again though."

The two men were engrossed with Bill Travers' bizarre tale of capture and miraculous escape. ". . . and if it wasn't for the kid and that hikin' couple, I'd still be there."

Having received Travers' account, Exner returned to the TaZeR and grabbed the microphone to request a team to infiltrate the grotto that had been Travers' prison. It was his thought that perhaps the captors may have returned.

In the meantime, the paramedics, satisfied at having stabilized Travers and seeing he suffered no residual effects from his trauma, began to pack up their kits.

"He's all yours, sir," one of the paramedics said to Exner. To Travers he said, "It's a good thing you're as sturdy as you look. But if you're sure you're okay, we'll head out."

"Yeah, I'm good," Travers said as best he could without wincing. "Thanks, fellas." Pointing to Exner and Lee he said, "these guys'll get me home. If they don't, I'll give you a call." At this, everyone chuckled.

The paramedics packed up their kits and headed to their ambulance. Lee and Exner helped their friend up and off the bumper. As the driver of the ambulance put his vehicle in gear, he waved at them through the side mirror before pulling away.

Looking from Lee to Travers, Exner said, "Seems neither one of you have made many friends of late. Bill, are there any more men involved in your abduction other than the three you mentioned?"

Travers' knee buckled. Exner grabbed his elbow for support. Travers said, "I just saw three of the bastards. I don't think any other names were mentioned. One of 'em's dead, though; had a bad accident of sorts." Travers looked at Lee and gave him the squint. Looking at Exner he said, "All spoke with Spanish accents. I know one of 'em."

This surprised Exner. "You *know* one? Who? How do you know him?"

"Name's Carlos Rodriguez. He ran the art studio I did business with in Cuba. The other guy's name is Gene . . . Gino Vaseline, somethin' like that. The other miscreant's name was Osvaldo. He's the one that doesn't look so good and won't cause any further trouble. I didn't get his last name though, probably couldn't pronounce it if I did. Probably somethin' lame as in *Lee Harvey Osvaldo*." The men had a chuckle at Travers' ramblings.

"The Osvaldo character was the guy who roughed me up real good. He wasn't breathing when I got out of that hellhole, and if I had to do it all over again, I'd have made the guy suffer more."

Travers explained the desperate manner in which he had dispatched Osvaldo and how he managed to escape with assistance from, of all things, a child.

"A child," Exner asked. "What the blazes would a child be doing down there? It's treacherous enough around these parts for an adult, let alone a child!"

Travers looked from one of his friends to the other. "Hey, Ex, I just calls 'em as I sees 'em. All I can tell ya is that I heard a kid outside, a little girl. She was singing—didn't get a chance to talk to her. I tried, but she couldn't hear me. But I followed her voice and it led to the old tunnel. Out I scampered, and with some much-needed help, here I am."

Both Exner and Lee could see that Bill Travers was visibly agitated at the thought of the whole ordeal. They could only guess the horror at being captured and beaten with the promise of torture, and no hope of being found.

"Do you know why they kidnapped you, Bill?" Exner asked.

"They said they wanted the last consignment of canvasses—no, canvas, one. They were interested in only one of the three paintings I last dropped off up here at the gallery," Travers said. "They didn't say why. They *did* let slip though that the buyers of my paintings were preordained and part of their group, if that makes any sense."

"It's beginning to, Bill, and that concerns me," Exner replied. "As to the girl, there are agents combing the area as we speak. If she's lost somewhere out there, they'll find her."

Exner led Travers over to a cement pad that served as the base for a "new" old-fashioned streetlight. It was low enough and had room enough for Travers to hang a butt cheek off. As he did, Exner said, "So why take you prisoner at all, Bill? If you've successfully done business with these guys before, why did they feel the need to kidnap you?"

Travers looked out over the water of Big Tub Harbor. Whenever he found himself beset by problems, even as a young boy, he found great solace by coming and sitting by the lake. The sight and sound of the white-capped waves crashing on the shore always had a peaceful, calming effect on him. Even now, the lakeside was his personal retreat from the cares and pressures of life, and brought great solace to his soul.

"Bill?" Lee asked.

"Huh?"

"Bill, why do you think they kidnapped you?" Exner repeated. He put a hand on Travers' shoulder.

"One of the last paintings I brought back was real important to them for some weird reason. They thought I was holding out on 'em. Rodriguez just kept yammering on about the last bunch of paintings," Travers stated. "They said I didn't sell 'em to the 'right' guys. Geez. They're mine to do with as I want, I said. I bought and paid for 'em all. Why would they come all the way up here and want only one painting back? I didn't think Cubans were even able to leave their island." He scratched his head in confusion.

This spoke volumes to Exner. It was evident from his statement that Bill Travers truly had no knowledge of what or with whom he was dealing. *Just a guy out to make a quick buck*, Exner thought. Lee had been right all along. Bill might be a little eccentric, but he was solid.

"Apparently, Ex, Bill *has* been an unwitting mule, but exactly of what still remains a mystery," Lee said. He looked at Travers, shook his head, and looked out over the beautiful clear blue waters of Big Tub Harbor and the many islands far out in the pristine bay.

Exner noticed he had a loose shoelace. He bent down to retie it before he rose and continued. "Those paintings of yours aren't worth much at face value, Bill. Now I don't want to sound all cloak-and-dagger, but what's *behind* them may be of infinite importance to these men, and we've got to find out why."

Exner noticed a look of incredulity as it crossed the old diver's face. He continued. "We believe the Chinese are in bed with the Cubans on whatever's about to go down here."

Bill Travers looked down and shook his head. "Holy crap! Holy friggin' crap! Well, there's one thing the bastards didn't get out of me." Travers looked at them with his patented pirate squint.

"What's that, Bill?" Lee asked.

"I happened to be in the gallery the day an older white couple came in and bought my last painting. I didn't get involved in the transaction though. Didn't want to get into a big discussion as to, you know, the history, the artists, what part of the country inspired the paintings, yadda, yadda, yadda. You know how it is. When people shell out a lot of dough for these things, they usually want the whole enchilada."

"Yeah," he continued, "these people were retirees, a real nice couple," he recalled. "They were quite pleased that the paintings came all the way from Cuba. The woman said the artwork was perfect for their yacht," Travers said.

"Their yacht," Exner asked. "Bill, do you know if they received a receipt for those purchases?"

"Hey, I only deal with reputable people. Of course they got a receipt," Travers said indignantly. "I think . . ."

"Hmmm," Exner said, "somehow this couple fell through the cracks and managed to acquire the last painting before the cell contacts moved in for the purchase."

"Way to go, 'mule.' That's Travers, '20 Mule Team' all the way!" Lee couldn't resist. He got the rise out of Travers he was looking for as Bill "winched" up a middle finger and delivered it with his patented one-eyed squinty 'death' stare.

Suddenly, there was an intermittent high and low sonic pitch emanating from Exner's personal Seqpod. "Incoming message, guys; I have to take this," Exner said. Removing it from his belt, he walked away as he responded to it.

He was in deep discussion for several minutes. The men remained silent, trying to pick up anything they could from Exner's side of the conversation, but the waves crashing against the rocks below made it impossible to do so.

Lee looked over to Bill, and so as not to be accused of eavesdropping, he hastily said, "Oh, and remind me to tell you about the 'roid rage' they left for you in the bathroom back at the shop!"

"Lee," Travers said, "how's the Scuba U?"

Lee stumbled around for the right words. "Not good, I'm afraid," he said, stumbling for words.

Exner saved the day when he returned a moment later. As he re-holstered his Seqpod, he said, "Sorry, guys, I've been summoned back to HQ. Lee, you good here?" he asked.

"No worries, Ex. I'll take care of the old fart," Lee said as he looked over and smiled at Travers.

Travers gave Hartley a "wounded" look, and then, palm in, vertically raised the second, third, and fourth fingers of his right hand. "Read between the lines, Hartley, read between the lines."

24

The *Cristóbal Colón*

The next day, the two divers returned to Fort Erie in Travers' red Hummer. Lee had explained the horrific fire that reduced Travers' Scuba U and apartment to ashes in detail. It was a shock, but not the unexpected one that Lee had anticipated.

Bill Travers had seen much of the harsher side of life and had the innate ability to take everything in stride, even this. Even so, with Travers' livelihood and lodgings literally up in smoke, Lee offered to takc his friend in until he got his affairs in order.

They drove the five hour drive to Niagara-On-The-Lake so Travers could fill out official NABS reports on the explosion at his shop, his kidnapping, the death of the man in the grotto, and what he had heard and seen while in captivity there.

Afterward, the two were down the bottom of the gorge at the Niagara Whirlpool munching on fried chicken. Lee was wearing a khaki ribbed sleeveless T-shirt with the imprint of a deep sea diver's helmet on the front, cut-off jeans, Adidas Army TR water-resistant running shoes, and carried a small backpack. Travers wore his Tilley hat, a red Scuba U T-shirt, cargo shorts, and a pair of Doc Marten hiking boots.

The sun was successfully stimulating their endorphins, evoking a euphoric sensation made complete by the perpetual balmy breeze coming off the whirlpool. The water of the Niagara River churned feverishly in a clockwise motion before it spun out of its bowl and catapulted down the rapids leading into the lowest of the Great Lakes, Lake Ontario.

This was a spot of mighty solitude, a place where the fury of the Niagara River, having raged over the mighty cataract a mile or so back, was now rushing to a declining demise. It was a place where Lee often came by himself to clear his head, to think, to ponder, and now to devise a plan.

Travers had much on his mind, but Lee could see that his recent experience at the hands of his captors had definitely affected him. His speech had slowed. He took longer before speaking. He seemed troubled. But, Lee thought, who wouldn't be affected after going through what he did?

"What's eating you, Bill?" Lee finally asked.

"Worms."

Encouraged by the light-hearted response, Lee tried another approach at opening him up.

"Man, I love this chicken. It'll kill you, but what a way to go."

"It won't kill ya if ya don't eat it every stinkin' day, Lee," Bill said as he looked up from under the brim of his beige Tilley hat. He tossed his chicken bones into the roiling froth of the whirlpool.

From under the brim of the Tilley, Lee heard, "Lee, I didn't get the chance to tell ya. I was gonna when ya got back to the shop, but that was before I was rudely interrupted. I told ya about the *Griffon*, and that's cool and all, but what I *really* wanted to tell ya about was the wreck in Cuba where I found this." He removed a medallion from around his neck and handed it to Lee. The medallion, apparently of solid gold, contained a deep red ruby in its center.

Lee wiped his hands on his jeans, and delicately took the valuable object from his friend as though the old diver had handed him the Holy Grail itself.

The medallion had a Spanish inscription on it. The thick gold chain it was suspended from was heavy. The neck chain was obviously a man's, a man of great stature and importance.

"It's beautiful," Lee said as he held it reverently in his hands. "Where'd you find it?" He turned the medallion over and over again, the chain draped over the top of his right hand.

"*This* little trinket was found inside the *Cristóbal Colón*, flagship of the Spanish navy back in the 1890s. The wreck isn't far from Santiago de Cuba, the old capital city. She went down off the coast there in 1898 during the Spanish-American war."

Travers reached over and scooped it up from Lee's grasp, who feigned a hurt look as he did so. "For the several months, I've been diving wrecks around this area of Cuba. The Cuban divemasters are quite reluctant to take you out on this one. It's a long way from the resorts, and about as remote as it gets."

"Makes sense," Lee said as he continued with his chicken dinner. He uncovered a little wishbone on a piece of chicken, unconsciously motioned Travers to grab one end, and made a wish. The bone snapped off in Lee's favor. He pondered a second, and then tossed it into the whirlpool. "What's the Spanish inscription on it say?"

"It says, '*Pride of the Spanish Navy*.'" Travers dropped his brim to look at the medallion as he continued. "The sailor who wore this must have served on the *Cristóbal Colón*, an officer perhaps. It's not something the everyday rank-and-file sailor would have worn. I found it in eighty feet of water inside of what must have been an officer's quarters."

In 1898, the newly minted armored cruiser *Cristóbal Colón* was the flagship of the Spanish Navy. Following the outbreak of war between Spain and the United States on April 25, 1898, the Spanish government sent out a fleet of six ships, including the *Cristóbal Colón*, to defend their interests in Cuba. The *Colón* had been hastily pressed into service even though her primary armament of ten-inch guns hadn't yet been installed. Regardless, and in hopes that a show of force might intimidate the US North Atlantic Squadron, she arrived at the Cuban capital city Santiago de Cuba in late May.

The battle proved to be both a decisive win for the US and an embarrassing and humiliating defeat for Spain.

The real fighting began in July. Admiral Pascual Cervera onboard the Spanish warship *Infanta Maria Teresa* opened fire on the USS *Brooklyn*. The Americans quickly rallied with battleships *Texas, Indiana, Iowa,* and *Oregon*. It was the USS *Iowa* that hit the *Maria Teresa* first with two twelve-inch shells. Mortally wounded and on fire, the *Maria Teresa* was ordered by Admiral Cervera to run aground. The rest of the fleet raced for open water.

Unfortunately for the Spanish, their ships had consumed all the hard premium coal on the race over from Spain, only to have inferior, quicker burning coal remaining in their bunkers. To make matters worse, studies conducted long after the battle off the southwestern Cuban shore estimate that as high as 85 percent of the Spanish ammunition was defective as well. Not a good way to ensure victory in any battle.

After more than an hour of intensive fighting, all but the *Cristóbal Colón* had been put out of commission. When she turned tail along the coastline, the battleship USS *Oregon* chased her down, opened fire, and forced her aground.

The *Cristóbal Colón* burned to the waterline. During various storms over the years, she pulled away and slipped into deeper waters off the coast, where she lay undisturbed for many years until its fairly recent discovery.

The battle off Santiago de Cuba marked the end of heavy naval operations during the Spanish-American war. The battle had been a mismatch from the start. When the smoke settled after the skirmish, the Americans had lost one sailor and suffered ten wounded. The Spanish suffered the loss of all six of their ships, 323 sailors, and had 151 wounded.

In addition, seventy Spanish officers, including Admiral Cervera, along with 1,500 men were taken prisoner. With the Spanish Navy reluctant to dispatch any further ships to Cuban waters, the island's garrison was cut off, ultimately forcing them to surrender.

Both men sat mesmerized by the sound and speed of the water as it rushed by them. Bill carefully returned the medallion to his pocket. Lee reached into his backpack, extruded his little flask of fluid, pulled a sip, and then returned it.

"When you're up to it and all this is behind us, I'd like to go back with you to dive the *Colón,"* Lee said, lightly punching Travers's arm.

They took in both the heat of the sun and the cool spray of river water as it coursed by them for a time, then Lee put a hand on his friend's shoulder and said, "So, Bill, how are you really?"

Bill Travers raised the brim of his Tilley to look his friend in the face. "I'll tell ya, Lee. I was never so scared in my whole life. I thought a lot about life, all the while hopin' I'd see ya blast yer way in and take out those losers. I know how tough ya are and all. Of course that never happened, but I know you would've if you knew where I was."

"It wasn't for lack of trying, Bill, believe me."

Travers continued. "But it got to the point that I was kinda resigned to it. What I didn't get was the time I came to and there was that warm meal set out for me. I still can't figure that one out. But the mind games these guys played, Lee, these guys mean business. They're tough *hombres*, cutthroats in every sense of the word. If Exner goes lookin' for 'em, he'd better have a SWAT team or somethin' better with him."

Lee could see that just talking about his ordeal sent shivers down his friend's spine. Travers had gone through what few men have, let alone someone his age. Talk about tough.

They sat quietly and once again were awed by the majesty, the roar, the spectacle of thousands of tons of water coursing not four feet from where they stood on the riverbank, until Lee spoke. "Bill, I don't know how best to break this to you, but the NABS investigators never found any sign of a little girl anywhere near that cavern. They looked, believe me, they looked. No sign of anyone, let alone a child."

Bill Travers was visibly upset at this. "No little girl? Well, how'd I get out then? Answer me that, Lee. And while yer at it, what about that stupid bear, the one I just about slipped and broke my neck on? They must have at least found that, didn't they?"

"Nothing turned up, Bill, not a thing."

Travers walked over and leaned against a lone pine tree that had defiantly rooted itself as close as possible to the riverbank. He had a perplexed look on his face.

"You mean to tell me that Exner's super-government-agent-spy guys couldn't find a stupid bear, an old dumb-ass lookin' stuffed bear that was right out in the open?"

Lee only smiled helplessly. It didn't happen often, but he was really at a loss for words.

Mercifully, Lee's cell rang. Travers looked on expectantly. Lee could barely hear the voice at the other end from the roar of the fast-moving water. "Lee, Exner. Find Travers and meet me at the agency. Clean up as much as possible; get here as soon as possible." At this the phone went dead.

Turning to his friend, Lee said, "We've just been RSVPed to NABS, sounds important." Without another word, the two began the arduous trek back up the side of the Niagara gorge at double time.

25

Alphabet Soup

Exner's office was vacant when the two men arrived an hour later. But his private secretary spotted them and informed them a meeting was taking place in the situation room and that they were expected. She pinned them both with visitor tags and then beckoned them to follow her shapely figure.

The situation room held a veritable alphabet soup of agencies. Delegations from nearly every major agency—NSA/CSS, CSIS, CIA, CESC, BEST, DHS, and of course NABS—were in attendance. Also present was a Canadian general and his attaché from Joint Task Force 2, Canada's ultra-secret Terrorist Response Unit.

If anyone didn't fit in at the meeting, it was the odd couple of Lee Hartley and Bill Travers. They had stopped at Lee's place on the way. Lee changed into a respectable yellow dress shirt, dark blue slacks, and brown leather loafers. Bill, on the other hand, being a few inches shorter and a few inches wider, had little choice but to wear the same clothes he had on, Tilley hat and all.

Travers looked down at his Visitor's ID badge. "Will ya look at that, we're what ya call 'official consultants.'" Lee hadn't bothered looking at the mandatory IDs given them. But sure enough, they were classified as "Official Field Consultants-NABS." It was a catchy title that meant little, but had nevertheless been authenticated by control himself.

"Welcome, ladies and gentlemen; please find a seat. Thank you."

The speaker identified himself as Scott Culp, CIA sub-director, out of Langley, Virginia. Lee smiled to himself at the stereotypical upper management CIA desk jockey: mid-sixtyish; narrow, beady eyes; overweight; and red-faced, with a rim of white hair and a case of self-importance. Culp wore an expensive three-piece navy blue suit, white dress shirt, and red tie, complete with a small American flag on the left lapel.

"Right," he began. "This is currently what we've got and what we're working with. A recent series of seemingly unrelated events has raised eyebrows in local Canadian intelligence, which has prompted NABS to alert the CIA. We in turn felt that every agency represented here needed to be included in the loop as well."

"We have strong reason to believe a terrorist cell is currently operating in Ontario. Its members are primarily Cuban with ties to the People's Republic of China. Their goal could well be for China to get a foothold in the Western Hemisphere via Cuba to advance the causes of both countries, which at this point are not crystal. It has all the makings of a do-or-die drama for the brothers Castro." Culp paused to scan his Sequoia terminal pod.

Lee looked over at Travers then gave him a smack on the shoulder, pointing up at Bill's head. Taking the hint, Travers removed his Tilley. Lee shook his head, produced his little flask, took a swig, replaced its top, stared at it absentmindedly for a minute, then returned it to his pocket.

"A short while ago," Culp continued, "the RCMP and CSIS entered into a top secret joint project codenamed Sidewinder. Its purpose was to assess the threat posed by the acquisition and control of Canadian companies by either members or associates of Chinese Triads with direct affiliations to the ChIS, Red Chinese Intelligence Service."

Culp paused to take a sip of water. He spent several moments working up information on his Sequoia terminal amid the buzz of the agents in the room. Looking back up at his audience, the CIA man loudly cleared his throat to draw everyone's attention back to himself.

"The deeper they got into this investigation, the more disturbed they became, and with good reason." Culp was forced to pause as a young red-headed woman in the middle of the gathering had a violent coughing episode. The man sitting next to her thumped her back a few times. This seemed to alleviate the condition. When she finally got things under control, she sheepishly raised her hand slightly in apology to everyone and to signify she was okay.

Upon seeing her hand, Culp continued. "There are several indicators based on the findings of CSIS that Canada faces a multipronged threat to her national security. A conservative estimate is that currently, over 300 Canadian companies are under the direct or indirect control of the Red Chinese."

He took another pause for dramatic effect. "The scope of their findings has evolved to include 'legal' Chinese corporate, industrial, and technological acquisitions within the United States as well." Culp paused to glance at his Sequoia terminal as he jingled loose change in his pants pocket. "Not content at stopping there, the Chinese are now looking to Cuba to further their interests, thereby clandestinely establishing a base in the Western Hemisphere at the same time. That, ladies and gentlemen, is very disturbing, and partly why you are here."

Lee craned his neck to see more of Bindhira. She was barely visible, sitting up near the front on his side of the room. Looking over at Travers, he gave him a little nudge as he was on the verge of nodding off. Straightening himself with a jolt, Travers reached into a pocket and pulled out a stick of gum. Lee just shook his head as the aroma of strawberry-kiwi permeated their environs moments later.

"In 2001, China was accepted into the World Trade Organization. As a result of this gesture, she has risen to become the third largest foreign market for US goods. But the Red Chinese are involved in an extensive web of discriminatory policies, and maintain foreign ownership restrictions in over 100 business sectors."

The senior CIA analyst took a sip from his water bottle. He spent several moments studying the information on his desk terminal to ensure his presentation remained accurate.

"China has gone through many legal hoops to get where she is today on the global market. She has used this as a front, ladies and gentlemen, to get at our most innermost technological and military secrets. There have been several incidents in both the US and Canada where they have been caught red-handed in corporate and industrial espionage."

"Recently, trade secrets were nearly acquired by two Chinese nationals at a plant in Kansas City. In another instance, one of our national chemical corporations went through litigation with a similar firm in China for conspiring to steal its trade secrets. A superconductor company in Massachusetts had trade documents stolen by an employee and sold to a Chinese wind turbine company for $1.5 million. On and on it goes."

The agents in attendance listened with rapt attention to every word that Culp said. The usual sounds of crowd rustling were at a bare minimum, with many leaning forward, careful not to miss a single word.

"These incidents are merely the tip of the iceberg. In every instance, the refrain was the same from the American industry officials. One high-ranking company official put it succinctly, 'The persistent and increasingly complex cyber-attacks from China attempting to steal trade secrets, as well as spies within our companies selling us out, has put a costly drain on our resources. It is very difficult to defend against such constant threats.'"

"Now our intel reports an abnormal increase in shipping traffic from China to Cuba with many of the incoming crates quickly spirited off in army trucks. There are few heavy industries on the island, and fewer still that have the capital for costly purchases of any sizeable amount. Just what the hell they're hoarding is what, collectively, we must find out."

"We're currently faced with a joint Chinese-Cuban operation that is clandestinely importing materials into this country to be disseminated to persons unknown for purposes unknown. Although there've been scattered reports concerning the potentiality of such a cell in existence here over the past year or so, there's been no concrete proof revealing an active operation."

"Through an extensive interrogation of dive shop owner Mr. Travers here," Culp extended an arm in Travers' direction, "we have discovered that an organized network has been using him to import works of art for legal resale into Canada."

Lee nudged Travers, who stood up so everyone could see him, then reclaimed his chair.

Culp paused to take a sip from his bottled water. He pulled a tissue out of his suit pocket, dabbed his mouth, then continued. "Mr. Travers is a Canadian citizen who annually conducts several scuba diving trips to Cuba. A few months ago he met the 'owner' of an art studio in old Havana in a well-known local bar, La Bodequita Del Medio. The bar was frequented by Ernest Hemmingway in the 1950s and is reputedly the birthplace of the mojito cocktail, but I digress." Several in attendance chuckled at the aside. Culp continued.

"Mr. Travers struck up a conversation with this man on several occasions and they became friends. This led to a business proposal, whereby Mr. Travers would purchase several of his studio's pieces for legal resale into Canada. The paintings are average works of art. Mr. Travers places them on consignment in a small art gallery called the Little Tub Gallery in a small lakeside town in central Ontario called Tobermory."

"We've recently discovered that virtually every one of these paintings has been snapped up by either Chinese or Spanish 'tourists.' We have strong reason to believe that these buyers are part of a now activated sleeper cell, which is retrieving coded information contained beneath the canvasses to provide direction and methodology to them. At this point we don't know specifics, but they don't know, as yet, that we've 'made' them."

"Cuba has apparently learned from past mistakes. She has become much more clandestine. There are several Chinese 'dignitaries' that have been on Cuban soil for some time now, and have been very careful not to attract undue attention to themselves. This is cause for concern in itself."

"Laser satellite intel has revealed that the materials sent to Cuba from China appear to be nothing more sinister than lab equipment and supplies. And that's not unusual, as Cuba conducts outstanding medical research. However, this sudden influx, along with an increase in Chinese nationals entering the country, *is* definite cause for concern. The kicker: some of these men have been identified as top-ranking biochemical scientists. If they are planning some type of bioterrorist attack in Canada, it could also spell serious trouble for the United States as well."

"We, that is, the United States, do not wish to be caught in some damned pincer movement with our pants down. I must emphasize, however, that we have the full cooperation and participation of the Canadian government."

Looking over at Exner then Lee and Travers, he went on. "NABS agents have completed a thorough investigation of both the arson scene in Fort Erie and the vehicle left behind on site. In addition to a foreign casualty of the fire, a 9 mm Glock handgun, and several prints off the rental car found at the scene, we are hopeful that the forensics team at NABS will lead us to widening our knowledge base of a potential international incident afoot."

Culp looked down at his Sequoia terminal for a rather indeterminate period of time then said, "Several documents in Spanish,

Mandarin, and code found stuffed behind an interior backseat panel of the Viper found at the arson scene were of greater interest to us." He paused again to look down at his satellite pod.

There was a hush among the crowd. Whispers began to sweep the room. It was obvious this was big, really big, and something that could not be allowed to fester in this country.

Lee noticed several people among the crowd he recognized, people he was sure he'd seen in other places, at other times. People he didn't know were agents. He was relieved when an overly rotund man two seats up and three over left for the restroom. Now he had a clear line of sight at Bindhi. She was resplendent in a short black velvet dress with a low square neckline, and carried a small white clutch with a looping gold-colored chain in front. Her hair was in a tight bun, which showcased the delicate Indo-Caribbean features of her face and neck. As if on cue, she looked back as he spotted her, and smiled wantonly.

Their gaze remained fixed on each other's for several moments until Travers knocked over his bottle of unopened water into the lap of the JTF2 general he was sitting beside. He was clumsily in the process of mopping up the general's lap with an already soaked napkin, much to the chagrin of the general.

Noticing the look on the embarrassed general's face as the aide pushed the old diver away, Travers immediately ceased and desisted. It was a disruptive incident, but one which brought much-needed comic relief to this most serious of meetings, as those around them broke out into hearty laughter, much to the chagrin of the general.

Culp, stone-faced, continued. "The documents were very telling, to say the least. What I'm about to relate here goes no farther than these walls, under penalty of immediate termination without pension. Do I make myself clear?"

He surveyed the room, observed nods of assent, then took another dramatic pause to underline the seriousness of what he was about to say. Satisfied, he continued. "The papers uncovered in the vehicle at the scene appear to be authentic DGI documents, originally 'eyes only' for the Castro brothers. In them were found alarming parallels to a plan hauntingly similar to what the Soviets devised that led to the Cuban Missile Crisis of October, 1962. The difference this time is that the Chinese want a kick at the can.

Culp's aide, who had been standing along the wall at the front of the room behind him, replaced his cell phone into his pocket, came over to Culp and whispered into his ear for several minutes. There was a brief hushed verbal exchange between them. Culp meditated on the conversation for a few moments, and then nodded his agreement. The aide returned to his previous position.

"The president has just given his approval to reveal the contents of those documents to you at this time." He looked more serious than ever now. "China has indeed entered into an agreement with Cuba to use the island nation as a base from which to develop and deploy an as yet unknown weapons system. There *is* an established sleeper cell currently active in the vicinity of Southern and Central Ontario as I speak. Their principal means of communication dissemination *is* through coded document transference."

A collective gasp filled the situation room during the revelation of this update.

"We've not been aware of any direct or encoded satellite communication between China and Cuba, which in itself is cause for great concern. The operation they are planning is still disturbingly off our radar. We've been most fortunate to have uncovered these documents when we did."

Culp looked down to Exner, Lee, and Travers with a nod. "For its efforts to aid China in this endeavor, Cuba is to receive the funding, supplies, and resources she desperately needs to rebuild and refortify her crumbling infrastructure, which had abruptly ceased upon the dissolution of the Eastern Bloc in the early nineties. As determined from documents uncovered in the vehicle at the arson scene, whose code was fairly easy to break, a joint Chinese-Cuban scientific project has developed a new weapon, codenamed *Vector*, which will have the potential to wreak enormous physical and economic disaster in North America."

"If the Chinese were to neutralize the US dollar, they'd literally have a monopoly on world commerce. They would emerge a superpower and certainly not be one to embrace democracy and the way of life we have all come to know and love."

At this point, an agent patiently stood up, waiting for Culp to acknowledge her, which he did with a nod.

"Sir, regarding Vector, have you any ideas as to just what it entails?"

The svelte middle-aged brunette wore a tailored black pantsuit, with her hair braided in a sensuously long ponytail. She rather nervously adjusted her eyewear as she remained standing for his reply.

CIA sub-director Culp appeared a little bumfuddled as to how best to answer the question. He spent a few frantic minutes tapping on his Sequoia terminal, studied its screen, and then casually raised his head to scan the audience before he spoke.

"*Vector*, if taken literally, can mean a number of things, all definitely of concern, and all potentially lethal. The word *Vector* can refer to a course or compass bearing of an airplane. Innocuous? Remember 9/11."

"Another type of vector is a quantity that has direction and magnitude represented by a line segment, where the length represents the magnitude, and whose orientation in space would represent direction. Some form of laser *Star Wars* technology perhaps?"

"*Vector* is also a term used to describe the means through which an insect or similar organism is capable of transmitting a pathogen to an infinite number of hosts through an injection or bite, causing malaria, yellow fever, tularemia, dengue fever, and the like."

"*Vector* could also refer to an agent such as a virus, which carries recombinant DNA or a modified genetic material used to introduce externally produced genes into the genome or genetic material of an organism, which causes genetic mutations. If that was the case, it would be of a deliberate nature."

Then he paused, looked carefully over his audience, and added seriously, "And if anyone wants me to repeat all that, you'll be fired on the spot!" At this everyone laughed, though the bulk of laughter carried a nervous energy about it. The brunette sat back down during the brief period of levity.

"As you can see, any one of these explanations for a vector is cause for serious concern. At this point, we simply don't know what form this *vector* is going to assume. It's up to each one of you, your departments, and your agencies. The prime directive here is to prevent and resolve."

Culp paused to raise his right arm at eye level to get a reading from the Rolex President chronometer on his wrist, and then continued without losing stride. "Aside from all things *vector*, the Sleeping Giant is sleeping no more. China has overtly beefed up her military for no apparent reason, and has recently completed the construction of a nuclear aircraft carrier, with more on the drawing board. To tide them over, she has acquired another carrier from the Ukraine, refitted to her specifications."

"Currently, the United States has eleven aircraft carriers. Most countries have only one, if that. China is indeed going to be a pain in our ass for some time to come. She is also close to perfecting her own version of the stealth fighter called the J-20, which by our estimates may be in service as early as next year. Its true capabilities remain unknown as to range, types of sensors, radar-absorbing coatings, and the like."

Culp paused. He was a man not used to playing number two, and the expression on his face belied his determination that China was not going to one-up the United States in military technology.

"Preliminary intel suggests the Chinese J-20 fighter has less sophisticated radar-blocking devices and is powered by a weaker engine than our stealth birds, for whatever consolation that gives. But it doesn't end there. The Chinese military, with an estimated working budget of over $100 billion per year, is concurrently developing *another* stealth fighter, the J-31. This fighter, though currently still on the drawing board, is designed to be more mobile than the J-20, and equipped with landing gear that will enable it to be carrier-launched. The icing on this cake, ladies and gentlemen, is that China plans to sell J-31s to her allies, allies such as Pakistan. They're pulling out all the stops and," he looked down, shaking his head, "thanks to domestic corporate greed and the selling out of our companies, banks, jobs, and technologies to them, the Reds are already capable of replacing the United States as the next unilateral economic and military superpower."

The air conditioning kicked in with an unexpected high-pitched squeal that startled everyone, even the JTF2 general, who at first was annoyed with the aggravating noise, but then relieved that it was nothing more. A woman at the far back and an older man from the front corner of the assembly seized this opportunity to seek out the facilities, excusing themselves to those around them as they did so.

Several minutes passed as Culp worked on the Sequoia, then studied its screen. He surveyed the room, and then went on. "We got lucky in 1962. We want no surprises this time around. Seeking, finding, and destroying weapons of mass destruction are not as easy as in the past. Satellites, even the latest, equipped with advanced extremely high frequency (AEHF) penetration capabilities, are limited in their effectiveness against newly emerging technology to secret such assets"

"Add to this the logistical nightmare we're faced with, as Chinese freighters sail to practically every major port in the world with their wares. Now, with an increase of Chinese 'trade' to Cuba, you begin to understand what we're up against.

"'*Be subtle that you are invisible. Be mysterious that you are intangible. Then you will control your rival's fate.*' These are the words of Chinese general Sun Tzu from his treatise, *The Art of War,* penned in 509 BC. We have been warned."

A silence spread like wildfire in the room. This was beyond anyone's comprehension. Every agent in the room knew that literally the fate of the free world could well depend on what they did or failed to do in the coming days.

Low whistles and expletives of incredulity permeated the room. The room was abuzz as a low monotone of indiscernible speech enveloped the situation room, louder than normal so as to rise above the air conditioning system.

As one of the contingents from the US National Security Agency stood up, the murmurs died down and those in attendance turned in his direction.

"Castro's losing it," the agent said. "He's been there, done that. We've maintained our boycott of his country for decades. What the hell's he really up to?"

Heads now turned in CIA sub-director Culp's direction. He allowed the uncomfortable rustling among those in attendance to die down before allowing himself to speak. "It's no secret that the Castros' are on their way out. And those in the know aren't fooled into believing that Fidel's puppet brother, the first secretary of the Communist Party of Cuba, Raul, is the new *el Commandante* of Cuba."

"But make no mistake about it, the bugger's younger brother still pulls the strings. What we must realize is that the old guard has nothing to lose. They desperately want to see the glory of their *Revolución* continue as long as they do, even if it has to get a boost from Communist China. The CIA has had a number of top assets in Cuba for several months. The Cuban bastards are very secretive and very tight-lipped. But what we *have* found out so far is not good."

"With additional delegations from the Red Chinese government coming to Cuba, things are definitely heating up. We've been fortunate that none of our agents' covers have been blown—yet." Culp paused to look over at the agent who was still standing. "Sorry, what was your name, son?"

"Wickson D. Tripp, NSA, sir," he replied, then sat down.

"What they're doing, WD," Culp continued, "is that they're going double or nothing. What better way of accomplishing this than to attack the United States through Canada? We know much; we can prove nothing. But believe me we have agents, as you well know, working on it day and night." Culp looked over to Alan Exner, who was seated in the rear corner by the west rear window. "If it weren't for the diligence of the NABS Niagara team under Control Exner, we'd still be in the dark on this. Alan?"

Culp waved a hand over to where Exner was sitting. Taking his cue, Exner stood up and gave a subtle bow. Then he said, "Your agencies will be receiving updates as they become available to us." He returned to his seat. A loud round of appreciative applause was given for his efforts.

The man that left the room took this opportunity to return to his seat, excusing himself as he worked his way through the row to sit back down. The woman returned to her seat in similar fashion moments later.

A female representative of US Homeland Security took this slight disturbance as an opportunity to stand up to address the group. Culp looked over to her and gave a slight nod.

"Maegan Blackenthorpe, Department of Homeland Security. We're told history repeats itself. You, sir, tell us that we're not in the dark on this. Truth be told, we weren't in the dark at Pearl Harbor in 1941, nor were we in the dark when 9/11 went down. There are other instances in more recent memory of such knowledge that fell on deaf ears. The botched Cuban invasion at the Bay of Pigs in 1961 resulted in the deaths of more than 100 members of the CIA-sponsored invasion team at the hands of Castro's forces. We sent them in but didn't back them, and on it goes. Based on such a track record, Mr. Culp, this is cause for serious concern." Agent Blackenthorpe surveyed those around her, cleared her throat, and then reclaimed her seat.

A pall enveloped the boardroom. At this point a pin could've been heard if dropped following the Homeland Security agent's candid remarks.

Scott Culp appeared to be at a loss for words. Looking down at his Sequoia terminal, he closed it slowly, almost delicately. Then, looking around the room, he nodded. He nodded to those on his left and repeated the motion to his right. He nodded until the entire group of people in his charge felt included in what he was about to say.

"There were reasons." Then, as if to catch himself, a brief pause. "There *were* reasons. But I can only answer for that which is happening in the here and now. We *are* forewarned, and we *shall* prevail. Ladies and gentlemen, we cannot, we *must not* drop the ball on this one. The economical world is shrinking daily, the stakes are high, and the ramifications of what we do or fail to do could be exponential." With that, he sat down and became locked in conversation with a man seated to his left.

The whispering and murmuring among the agents in the room went on for some time, until Culp stood up once more.

"NABS, under the direction of its control, Alan Exner, will run point both here and on the cell end in Tobermory. His section has the most experience to date on this whole affair."

At this, all eyes were on Exner. Alan Exner, a man of men, blushed profusely, but it wasn't because he was singled out. Here he had been singlehandedly dealt a task that could come back to bury him if he failed. Then again, he thought, if he did fail, he wouldn't be the only one to be buried.

"All involved agencies will receive their protocol by tomorrow morning,' Culp continued. "Some of you will receive domestic assignments. Others will be assigned to China, Cuba, or wherever else this damn affair takes us until we have this thing contained. I must stress most emphatically that there will be no interagency squabbles on this one." Culp paused for dramatic effect as he looked around the room.

"This comes directly from the president. The bad guys are knocking at our backdoor, people. We have to be first-time correct on this one, and that means full cooperation from each agency and from each one of you."

A curt nod from Culp, a "we'll be in touch, thank you," and then the CIA man and his aide left the room amid hushed and hurried whispers.

26

Wu Yang

Wu Yang had never visited Niagara Falls. In fact, the sixty-four-year-old Chinese ChIS agent had no recent memory of vacationing at all. Vacations were for the weak and unfocused.

The Chinese Intelligence operative smiled at the hundreds of people—he thought of them as pigeons, enveloped in the cool white mist of the Falls. They were soaked as they stood along the side of the mighty rushing waters, as six million cubic feet of water per minute cascaded past them over the brink 170 feet below en route to Lake Ontario.

Simple pigeons! If they only knew what he knew; but then, how could they?

Yang appeared the incarnation of the "typical Chinese tourist," complete with a huge Nikon camera hung around his neck. He wore a well-worn gray fedora and black trench coat. In the crook of his left arm he carried an ornate wooden cane topped with a solid gold dragon's head.

There were many of Chinese descent in attendance today as per the norm, and to the casual observer, he fit right in. He was very polite, and his face radiated genuine warmth; a warmth that deceived the best of those who crossed him.

The only thing slightly out of the ordinary about Yang was that he was alone, and that was very rare in a popular tourist environment such as this. He stepped back and away from the spray to remove his sunglasses and dry the lenses with a tissue.

Had a casual observer not been so casual and inspected Yang's camera and cane, they would be surprised to learn of their additional properties, properties not to be found in any store.

His cane sported a lightning-fast, spring-activated, two-inch titanium needle charged with 40 milligrams of tetrodotoxin or TTX. TTX is the deadly neurotoxin found in pufferfish; 100 times deadlier than cyanide, and with no known antidote. Even though 25 milligrams was sufficient to kill an average size human, Wu Yang was always one to err on the side of caution. His cane was capable of delivering three such doses if need be. On several occasions, he had used two charges. But it was comforting to know there was an extra dose, just in case. It seems that no one ever comes unarmed to private parties anymore.

Then there was the camera. From all outside appearances, it was a vintage model Nikon FE 35 mm SLR camera, complete with a Nikon Nikkor-O auto 1:2 35 mm f2.0 wide-angle Nippon Kogaku Pre A1 prime lens. Upon closer inspection, one would curiously note however, that the lens cap was from a Canon camera.

With the telescopic lens extended, the "camera" was capable of decrypting any message sent or received from any source. It could then re-encrypt messages and beam them directly to any Chinese Intelligence Service (ChIS) substation requesting them.

The interesting thing about these encryptions, was that even to a trained CSS monitor they would sound like satellite-beamed 'white noise' and be summarily dismissed.

No, Wu Yang was not here to enjoy the real estate. Although a senior operative in the ChIS, he was also a high-ranking member of the Establishment. His official mission was to coordinate his people with the Cubans on their 'joint venture'. But both he and the Establishment had other plans.

Politely pushing his way through the throngs of tourists vying for a glimpse of the falls, Wu Yang spotted his man. He wore an expensive white silk shirt, dark blue pants, and Yang noticed, very expensive leather shoes from Seville. The man's face was pocked in dozens of small craters, poor devil. But it was the scar across his right jugular vein that impressed Wu Yang the most.

The man had his back against a wall of the Table Rock building, smoking a cigarillo. Upon seeing the stately Chinese gentleman approaching him, he immediately dropped it underfoot.

"Mr. Yang, I presume?"

Wu Yang bowed slightly. "You are very perceptive, Mr. Rodriguez. One may think all Chinese look alike, but not many sport a cane in the crook of their left arm and wear an old gray fedora at the same time, as you were instructed to look for." Then looking into the younger man's cold gray eyes, he said, "You are late, Mr. Rodriguez."

Rodriguez was at first taken aback, then angered at this. "But I am here now, Mr. Yang, in fact—"

"Enough Mr. Rodriguez!" Yang had become impatient. "Time has been wasted; time that can never be reclaimed. I trust you have not been followed, either physically or electronically?"

The Cuban was determined to take the lead from this Chinese agent. "I was here an hour *before* you showed up, Mr. Yang. In that time no one had the slightest interest in either you or me. I made very sure of that."

Wu Yang smiled a genuine smile at this. "You *are* a careful man, Mr. Rodriguez. I like that. I must say though, that four cigars smoked in such a small period of time are not conducive to one's continuing good health. You may wish to reconsider this habit."

Carlos Rodriguez now saw Wu Yang for what he was: a most dangerous man. A man like himself: wary, coldblooded, merciless. He was angry at Wu Yang for filtering him out of the crowd so easily. This old *Palestino* was not to be trusted. He made a mental note never to turn his back on him. The ChIS man was good at his trade, maybe too good.

As irritated as he was, Rodriguez was determined to put aside his feelings for the good of Cuba and get this thing over with; and the sooner, the better.

Wu Yang grasped the elbow of the Cuban and steered him from the crowd. "The last communiqué out of Cuba never reached our people. That information and a certain attached package was essential to detailing where and how we are to proceed." Yang smiled, but the smile was not to signify his pleasure. "Due to this breach, we will have to improvise, and in doing so, mistakes may be made. Costly mistakes, Mr. Rodriguez."

The two walked along the promenade by the mighty cataract as its white mist enveloped them. In unison they picked up their pace to get out from under it, as fast as the milling crowd would allow.

Suddenly, Wu Yang stumbled when his toe caught a crevice in the sidewalk. Rodriguez wanted the old Chinaman to fall, even better, to seriously hurt himself, but his reflexes were faster than his thought processes. He grasped Yang's collar and right arm just as the older man toppled head first into a group of Pakistanis walking toward them.

The cane, still in the crook of his left elbow, canted forward, striking point first into the stomach of the man in the center of the group. In a desperate bid to regain his balance, Yang's grip tightened on the golden dragon head of the cane.

The young Pakistani man immediately went into convulsions, gasping for breath as the tetrodotoxin began to paralyze his diaphragm. Froth emanated from the man's mouth. He writhed in agony and collapsed within seconds of the unintended lethal injection.

Adrenaline poured into the Cuban's veins. Rodriguez grabbed Wu Yang's shoulder and yanked him around the stricken man and through the crowd that grew around him. The fedora of the ChIS man blew from its perch as they lost themselves in the swirling mist ahead.

They ran until the old man could run no more. Putting an arm around the old man's waist, the Cuban half dragged, half carried Wu Yang until they reached Rodriguez' rented Nissan. In a screech of smoldering rubber and smoke, they sped out of the Dufferin Islands' car park as fast as the powerful GT-R would allow.

Rodriguez had much to answer for, but many more were his questions.

27

The Gift

It was late evening when Lee's doorbell rang. He had just emerged from the shower. Pulling a robe over his lithe figure, he loosely tightened the knot of its belt in front and answered its ring. Bindhira Shankar stood there, her beautiful long hair being tussled by the midsummer's eve breeze. She was resplendent in a white knee-length cotton dress with a gold chain around her tiny waist. Her nylon-covered legs were a mocha hue, with high-heeled shoes that closely matched.

"Whatever you're selling, I'm interested," Lee said at seeing her. Bindhira smiled her heart-stopping smile. An obvious look of contentment spread across her face at catching him in his robe.

Seeing her happiness, a wrapped gift, and a bottle of red wine in hand, he grabbed her by the waist and arm and whisked her inside. Lee locked the door, relieved her of her packages, and pulled her close to him. Bindhira wrapped her arms around his thick neck, and then placed her head down onto his powerful chest.

"It is good to see you too, Lee." Her beautiful green eyes rose to focus on his. They held each other for several moments, then ramped-up the closeness with a breath-defying kiss.

Moments later, she gently broke away to arm's length. "I thought your friend was here. I saw his car out front."

Lee went into the dining room and returned with wine glasses and a cork screw. Upon his return he said, "Bill's in a NABS safe house for the time being. Exner's got a few pairs of eyes on him there, so I've commandeered his Hummer."

"I am sure your friend is not too content being babysat by Alan's men," Bindhira said, smiling.

Lee laughed at her appraisal of Travers. He popped the cork and poured the wine. Lee kissed her upraised hand before he gave her a glass. They touched glasses, took a sip, and then sat down on Lee's lavish black leather sofa. He pulled two round cardboard coasters from the drawer of the exquisite mahogany coffee table in front of them and then sat his glass upon one. Bindhira placed her glass upon the other coaster, and then snuggled in under his arm.

They sat silently like this for several minutes, sipped some wine, and enjoyed the warmth of both the closeness and the alcohol. Lee gently pulled away and rose to light both a scented candle and a gas fireplace in the corner of his living room. He returned to the sofa and poured more wine for them both

Bindhira in turn got up and went to the bureau. She returned with the gift she had brought. He pulled her to him, and they resumed their previous posture.

"Open it," she said expectantly. Lee couldn't help but notice that her hormone-infused eyes held the certainty of more to come. He kissed her forehead and relieved her of the package.

"What? No card?"

Quick on the uptake, Bindhira replied, "No, you *are* the card!" She laughed her sensuous laugh.

Lee took his time as he unwrapped the small gift. Relieving the small white box of its wrappings, Lee gently pulled on the red string of the bow and opened the top.

Bindhira watched his eyes light up as only a man of adventure could at such a gift.

"A gold coin, from the *Atocha* no less!" Lee pulled her close and gave her an extended kiss full on the lips. "Is it genuine?"

"Of course, silly," she laughed into his ear.

The *Nuestra Señora de Atocha* was the most famous of a fleet of Spanish ships that sailed between Spanish ports at Porto Bello, Cartagena, and Havana bound for Spain. The ship was named after the Parish of Atocha in Madrid, thus her name, *Our Lady of Atocha*.

The *Atocha* arrived in Veracruz in the summer of 1622 and took onboard a priceless cargo of gold, silver, copper, stunning jewelry, gems, and even tobacco. So immense was the treasure that it took two months to record and load it aboard.

Six weeks behind schedule, she finally left Havana heavily laden with her priceless cargo of treasure.

Two days out from the Cuban port of Havana, the *Atocha* was driven by a severe hurricane near Dry Tortugas, about thirty-five miles west of Key West, Florida. She was mercilessly driven onto the coral reefs whereupon she quickly sank, drowning everyone aboard with the exception of three sailors and two slaves.

It wasn't until 1985 that a former chicken farmer turned underwater treasure hunter, Mel Fisher, stumbled upon her remains in a mere fifty-five feet of water. Several years later, Fisher had extruded over four hundred million dollars of breath-taking jewelry, beautifully crafted gold objects and coins, silver pieces-of-eight, and innumerable gold and silver ingots. He had spent over sixteen years of his life searching for the *Atocha* and was famous for his motto, "Today's the day!"

The *Atocha's* remaining cache of wealth still has yet to be discovered. A few years ago, Fisher's company discovered another find of great worth: an antique emerald ring appraised at an astounding $500,000.

The site is still active. According to the galleon's manifests, it's been estimated that one-half of the total treasure the *Atocha* was carrying has still, as yet, to be uncovered. The silver-dollar-sized gold coin and chain Bindhira gave to Lee hadn't seen the light of day in nearly four hundred years!

"To say 'thank you' seems vulgarly cheap. Bindhi, I-I'm at a total loss for words!"

Seeing his face light up at her gift would forever be etched in Bindhira's mind, a proverbial "Kodak moment." Were those tears welling up in his eyes?

"Then say nothing."

They sat silently content as they held each other's gaze and bodies.

Reaching down, she gently took the coin from his hands, opened the delicate clasp on the chain, and placed it around his neck. She closed it with a kiss.

"I want you to wear this always. Promise me you will wear this always, Lee," she said, almost pleading.

"I promise, my love," he said.

They held each other for an indeterminable time before Lee was able to talk. He gently left her side, strode over to the ornate mahogany grandfather's clock beside the fireplace, and then turned to savor her beauty for a few moments before speaking.

"So what's the word? Has NABS been issued their protocol yet?"

She took a sip of wine and cradled the glass in both hands. "Alan had it within the hour of Mr. Culp's departure. There have been several developments in the meantime."

Lee sipped the rest of his wine and then topped his glass back up. "Care to enlighten me?"

Bindhira rose, glass in hand. She delicately kicked off her shoes by the side of the coffee table, and padded over to stand in front of the fireplace. She took a sip of wine and continued. "The black car, the Viper, was a rental, which incidentally had been rented with a stolen credit card. The signatures on the rental forms were unintelligible, but the manager did recall a few of the customer's features."

She paused to take a sip and watched as Lee did likewise. "The man who rented the vehicle was a large muscular man with a Spanish accent, and apparently very rude. It seemed the manager was relieved just to get him processed and out the door."

"What else?"

"The man you pulled out of Mr. Travers' burning building was also of Spanish descent. His wallet contained a photograph of a middle-aged woman and female child, presumably his wife and daughter. We could not turn up anything at our end, so we sent a Sequoia-enhanced image of it to Interpol in Lyon, France. They were able to get a fix on the subjects in the photo."

Lee walked over to the fireplace. Taking her glass, Lee walked back to the coffee table, grabbed the wine bottle, and topped it up. She took a sip from her glass as soon as he handed it to her, and then placed it on the mantel behind her. She then took his glass and repeated the motion. Her leg slowly nudged its way through both of his, rubbing higher and higher beneath his robe.

The hungry embrace and lengthy kiss that ensued was born of mutual passion. He grasped underneath her leg to steady her as they allowed themselves to fall against the mantelpiece. Bindhira's nylon encased leg was soft, warm, and sensual to his naked skin.

They remained against the mantelpiece in warm embrace. A deep, pleasant ache manifested itself in Lee's engorged groin. Then to his disappointment, Bindhira broke away. She crossed to the other side of the room, concern etched on her face.

"What is it, Bindhi? What's bothering you?" Lee walked over, wine glasses still on the mantelpiece. He took her gently by the shoulders, looked down into her beautiful but sad face, and said again, "Bindhi, what's wrong?"

Looking deep into his eyes, she saw genuine concern. "Lee, Alan needs you and your friend William in Cuba straight away. Your flight leaves at noon tomorrow." She looked down. "The trip is not for pleasure."

"Cuba? Where in bloody Cuba?"

Bindhira went over to the front door, where her clutch sat on the table. She withdrew a tattered photo from it and handed it to Lee.

The black and white photo was of poor quality. It was of a fisherman's boat on the water near the shore. Inside the boat was a little girl, about nine or ten. Standing in the water on each side of the boat was presumably her mother and father. All wore happy, genuine smiles.

He could see that Bindhira was troubled. "This photo was in the wallet of the man you pulled out of the fire, Lee. As you can see it is badly worn, but there is the name of a town scribbled on its back in pencil, with last summer's date. It is a squalid little town called Chivirico. It is about half an hour's drive west of Santiago de Cuba."

"You are to locate the woman there. See what you can find out about the man in the photo and if she knew his purpose for coming to

Canada. An ordinary Cuban citizen would not have been allowed off the island."

Saying nothing, Lee guided Bindhira's hand under his robe. As it fell open, she smoothed the robe off his shoulders and allowed it to fall to the floor. He stood naked and erect before her. "I may have a flight to catch tomorrow," he said, then looked down with a devilish grin, "but this flight leaves tonight."

28

An Uneasy Alliance

"What *the hell* was that all about, Yang?" Rodriguez asked. He took a drag off his fat cigar. The Cuban had had enough of the formal protocol he was ordered to extend to the Chinese Intelligence agent, and he had had enough of Wu Yang.

"How did that man just 'happen' to die in front of us, Yang?" Rodriguez reiterated as he blew a large smoke ring off the windshield between them as they made their way out of the traffic maze past the Horseshoe Falls. Within minutes they had pulled out onto the Queen Elizabeth Highway on their way to Tobermory.

"I was so careful in making sure we would not be noticed," Rodriguez continued. "Then YOU decide to test out some weird-ass Oriental death shit on an innocent right in front of us? You may have compromised the whole operation, Yang!" Rodriguez stared over at Wu Yang. "This will be duly noted in my upcoming report to the Establishment. You are just lucky we got away when we did."

Wu Yang was at total peace, and this unbalanced the Cuban Intelligence agent even more.

"My dear Mr. Rodriguez," he said calmly, "as you know, I tripped quite by accident. That man's death was also an accident as a result of my ineptitude. By necessity I too must be armed, though in a much more efficient manner than you with your crude, impotent Swedish sidearm."

Wu Yang could see that Rodriguez was visibly unsettled at his knowing the type of weapon the Cuban agent carried. This pleased Yang, for an unsettled enemy was an enemy easily destroyed.

"You are the one who will be reported, but to my government, Mr. Rodriguez. Need I remind you that your agency is to be at our complete disposal? That makes you nothing more than a tool, Mr. Rodriguez, a tool that can be cast away should it not function as was originally designed. No, Mr. Rodriguez, you are in no position to ask the questions here."

Wu Yang could see the color drain from the Cuban's face. He will serve his purpose, thought Wu Yang, and just as surely the Cuban will be destroyed once that purpose was fulfilled.

"And please to toss that infernal cigar out the window. I do not wish to suffer your inevitable fate of lung cancer." Wu Yang left a pause for effect as he continued, "I should hate to slip inside our vehicle as my cane is very close to your side."

Yang saw Rodriguez take a look and gasp. Sure enough he could see that, indeed, the heel of the cane was aimed at the Cuban's side as it rested on Yang's lap.

The Cuban had been told in no uncertain terms that Yang was the point man sent by the Chinese government to oversee their mission.

However, within the government sanctioned cell, members of the Establishment were to carry out their orders as required up until the time for the organization to carry out *its* directive. It would be a daring move, but for the members of the Establishment, it would be double or nothing.

And double at this moment seemed pretty good to Carlos Rodriguez, who had grown tired of carrying out the bidding of a government that was run by tired, narrow-minded, and careless old extremists.

For now he would kiss the old Chink's ass, but when this was all over he would personally see to it that Wu Yang would have a "horrible accident." That was his stock in trade, and Rodriguez was good at it. But his gut told him the Chinaman may entertain similar sentiments toward him, thus he would have to remain vigilant around Yang at all times.

The two travelled along in silence. Rodriguez could sense the ever-wary Chinaman looking over at him from time to time. This unnerved the Cuban greatly, and his respect for the ChIS agent was one born solely of fear. Not a good work ethic to have, he thought, especially with so much at stake.

It was Wu Yang who finally broke the uneasy silence. "What is our destination, Mr. Rodriguez?"

Carlos hated it when Yang addressed him as such. But he had quickly grown to hate anything this man did. "We have a five-hour drive ahead of us. We are driving up to a little town at the tip of what's called the Bruce Peninsula, to a little village called Tobermory. It is where our cell has been operating." "I drove all the way down to Niagara Falls to pick you up. It was a needless waste of time, but your instructions were for me to pick you up personally."

"Ah, but precautions are what we must undertake as professionals, Mr. Rodriguez," Wu Yang said. "As you well know, we have a strict timeline that must be followed, and my safe delivery to the cell was entrusted to you. Nothing must be left to chance and no opportunities afforded the enemy. Our timing must be precise if we are to beat our governments to the punch, as they say."

"Well Yang, I might as well tell you now as later," Rodriguez confessed. "Our base of operations has been compromised. The man we used to deliver the final 'package' your people was to have picked up has escaped our custody." He paused in an effort to control his temper. "You left us no time to properly interrogate him, because *you* wanted *me* as your personal chauffeur. How he managed to escape, we do not know. But we lost a man in the process, a good man. The cell had used that base for some time, and to great advantage. But the authorities are no doubt combing the grotto as we speak, so we have been forced to operate out of less efficient quarters."

Wu Yang raised his eyebrows at the candid honesty of the Cuban operative. They drove on in quietude for several minutes. Then with slow, careful diction, Wu Yang spoke. "Well, Mr. Rodriguez, that does throw the proverbial monkey wrench into the mix, does it not? One thing I wish to impress upon you, my friend. You, me; we both stand to lose a considerable amount—our very lives in fact. We must not fail in our quest to finalize the plans our superiors have painstakingly worked out for the mutual outcome both our countries anticipate."

Though not much comfort, the Cuban was somewhat relieved at hearing this. He hadn't considered this angle of the operation. He simply assumed the Cubans would be the expendable ones should any part of this joint venture with the Chinese fail.

It came as a mild epiphany to realize that a vetted, experienced Chinese agent like Yang was also an expendable asset. But was the old bastard telling the truth? Maybe,but probably not. Rodriguez refused to take anything Wu Yang told him at face value. He was determined not to let his guard down, just as he was determined not to fail in his part of the operation.

Much was troubling Rodriguez on the way to Tobermory. One of his operatives *had* failed, but that failure had been taken care of. Of much greater concern was that he had just lost three more men left behind to ensure their tracks were covered. His people seemed to be the weak link in the operation at this point. More reason to fear Wu Yang.

Rodriguez nearly became incontinent at the thought of the authorities discovering their documents. How could he explain the loss of three more men? None of this would bode well with his superiors.

In the meantime, he was still leader of the Cuban contingent, and determined to show Wu Yang just how competent the Cubans could be in spite of such a loss. His mouth suddenly went dry.

"Do not consume valuable energy lamenting the failure of your men, Mr. Rodriguez," Wu Yang said, as if reading the Cuban's mind. "I understand you have recently lost several operatives at the hands of one man who has bungled his way into our activities. This man, Lee Hartley, will be taken care of in a most efficient way, I assure you."

Rodriguez looked over at Wu Yang. Surprisingly, Yang smiled at him. It seemed genuine.

"Yes, it is true," the Cuban said. "This I have just learned. Thank you for your support."

Yang offered a slight bow of his head. "Since you are currently operating at a deficit in manpower, and since the painting must be retrieved at all costs, I will assign a few of my trusted and capable colleagues to assist your men in this quest." Wu Yang paused to emphasize his next point. "It is my humble opinion that no reports need be transmitted by either of us to *any* of our handlers, government or otherwise, Mr. Rodriguez. To do so would only serve to reflect poorly on our mutual competency. Are we agreed on this, Mr. Rodriguez?"

Rodriguez didn't have time to reply. A tractor trailer pulled out in front of them to pass a tank truck ahead of him. He had to jam on the brakes. The two transports travelled side by side for over a mile as neither driver would give way to the other. Rodriguez was forced to remain behind until the passing lane became clear.

The agents drove along in harnessed silence during this act of motoring selfishness. Finally the truck in the passing lane slowly overcame the tanker and sluggishly returned to the driving lane. Rodriguez pushed the accelerator to the floor and the Nissan immediately responded. They pulled out and flew by the two big rigs, leaving them quickly behind.

"Mr. Rodriguez, are we so agreed?" Wu Yang repeated.

Rodriguez gathered his thoughts for a few moments before speaking. "Yes, yes, Wu Yang, I heartily agree. To bring attention to matters we will soon regain control of would not benefit either of us. We must pool our resources and have each other's backs if we are to be successful in this venture."

Wu Yang was pleased to hear this. "Excellent, Mr. Rodriguez, most excellent indeed."

Carlos Rodriguez could see that his associate was genuinely relieved. The Cuban breathed a sigh of relief. Maybe the Chinaman would prove to be a valuable ally after all.

They stopped at a McDonald's outside of Guelph for a burger and bathroom break. Other than small talk, neither spoke much when they went into the restaurant out of seasoned caution in the event someone overheard their conversation. Soon thereafter they left the restaurant, fed the Nissan at a nearby gas station, then continued on the King's Highway 6, which would take them directly to Tobermory.

After a few miles of weaving around slow-moving farm vehicles, delivery trucks, and the like, Wu Yang spoke up. "We must make every effort to eradicate the thorns still in your side, Mr. Rodriguez. That man who escaped your custody and his friend will have to be dealt with most expediently before things begin to spiral out of our control."

Rodriguez couldn't agree more. "You are right in this, Wu Yang. They have taken several of my men out of action and compromised our most excellent base of operations. The painting has somehow slipped through our grid into the hands of party or parties unknown. I had hoped to extract information concerning this from the Canadian Travers. I am not of the belief that he knows anything, but have instructed my man to terminate him if his methods of persuasion fail to bring results."

"Let us hope your man obtains the information we need from this buffoon. But remember, many are the facets of the jewel of misfortune,

Mr. Rodriguez." Yang was careful to observe his driver's face to determine his emotions. He detected anger, fear, and determination. All were good, very good indeed.

Wu Yang was beginning to realize that this Cuban was more efficient than he had originally believed. "We will have this meeting with our underlings at your new location, then set about to flesh out our objectives."

For the remainder of the trip the two refrained from further dialogue, each lost in his own thoughts. But Wu Yang had much more on his mind.

29

All-Expenses Paid Trip For Two

The Skyservice Boeing 747 carrying Lee Hartley and Bill Travers touched down a few minutes past four thirty the next afternoon in Santiago de Cuba, following a four-and-a-half-hour flight from Toronto. The airport terminal at Santiago was very small and lacked climate control. The air was hot, humid, and smelled of disinfectant.

There were several army personnel inside the receiving area, more so than was needed for a terminal of its size. Some were leaned against walls; a few had their backs to countertops, elbows supporting them. They watched the travelers with suspicion as they filed into various lanes, passports in hand. Other personnel conversed quietly among themselves. To Bill Travers, they were like sluggish flies hanging about in the midday heat.

The two divers in turn approached the older female inspector at their wicket to present their passports. She bore the wary scowl of a customs official, as is protocol for customs personnel everywhere. Surviving both her scowl and stock questions, they were admitted entry into the country without incident.

Upon retrieving their luggage, they exited the terminal and flagged down one of the many local taxi drivers. A short amicable cabbie placed their four bags into the trunk of his old Russian-made yellow Lada Niva 2101 four-door and asked for their destination.

Chivirico is a tiny little town, if it can be called a town, about ninety minutes from the airport. Amazed that the ancient little vehicle got them there in record time, the Canadian divers simply had the driver drop them off at the center of town. The driver was ecstatic at the ten-dollar CUC convertible peso tip he received from them. The overly-friendly Cuban driver placed their bags at the curb, waved, and then sped off.

"That was about a month's wages for the guy," Travers said as he picked up his two bags. "He'll probably take next week off."

"I'm sure he deserves it," Hartley said, smiling.

Three young boys were kicking a worn out soccer ball between themselves in the street. They eyed the Westerners with suspicious interest. Lee pulled out his flat little stainless steel flask and drew a few pulls before picking up his bags.

He never ceased to be disgustingly amazed at the squalor the Cuban people had had to endure since Castro's revolutionary forces overcame Batista's regime on New Year's Day 1959. It was like coming out of a time warp when landing in Cuba: ancient automobiles from the fifties in rough condition but still running nonetheless; once proud official buildings that had denigrated to little more than slum dwellings from lack of upkeep; dirty children playing in the streets with little if any adult presence, ill dressed in hand-me-downs donated by visiting tourists. In spite of this, however, most people managed a pleasant smile when greeting them.

Politics stink the world over, thought Lee. The rich few in the wrong places always profit at the expense of the many.

As the two left the corner, the soccer ball slammed into one of Bill Travers' bags, nearly knocking him over from a kick that was too powerful to have been delivered from one of the boys. Looking over, Travers saw that the children had disappeared. In their place was a tall, wiry Cuban standing across the corner, arms crossed and smiling.

He wore an olive green Cuban "Fidel" army cap, a worn black Nike T-shirt, a pair of camouflage khaki shorts, and old leather *chancletas*, a type of flip-flop, on his feet. Sporting a heavy graying beard, he had the appearance of a Fidel clone.

Walking slightly ahead of his friend, Lee was oblivious to the man until he noticed that Travers was no longer behind him. Turning, he too did a double-take at seeing the man on the corner. The interloper waited until Lee walked back to where Travers was standing. As Lee approached his friend, the man came over to them. The three men stood quietly facing each other. Several people passed by and around them, hardly giving them a second glance.

Looking down both streets warily, the Cuban broke the uneasy silence. "*Señors*, permit me to introduce myself. I am Juan Ramon Zayas. Come, I have a small van not far from here. I have been assigned to pick you up."

The Canadians were unsettled at this. "Pick us up? Assigned by whom?" Lee looked at his friend, then to Zayas. "We're not expecting anyone to do anything for us here, *amigo*. We're tourists, here for a good time," he said cautiously.

"Yeah, whatever it is yer sellin', we don't want any," piped up Travers roughly. Then he added, "*Especially* paintings!"

At this, Lee removed his friend's Tilley hat, swatted him on the arm with it, and then stuffed it back on his semi-bald head.

Zayas smiled politely at this. His dark, piercing eyes under-laid with heavy circles were not unlike those of *el Comandante's*.

"Yes, you are right to be cautious here, my friends. *Señor* Exner said to expect you sometime later this afternoon, and here you are, right on time! Come, come." He waved them toward him as walked to his nearby vehicle.

The Canadians shrugged at each other in unspoken agreement to play this out. They had not expected anyone on the inside, nor had anything been said to them about meeting a contact. Still, Zayas had dropped the name of NABS control Alan Exner, not common knowledge on an obscure street in a secluded Cuban village. Lee knew this was a precaution to protect control's assets.

They followed the man to his beat-up old white 1958 Volkswagen Kombi T1 minibus, threw their bags into the side door of the vehicle, and clambered in. Looking around to ensure they were not being watched, Zayas climbed into the derelict van himself, then pulled away, leaving a swirling cloud of dust in their wake.

Although the Canadians weren't sure where they were headed, they were sure things were going to get very interesting, very soon.

The streets of Chivirico were surprisingly well paved, and the late-day sun was still very hot, especially at this time of year. Lee was intrigued by the uniquely constructed tapered stone hydro poles, silent sentinels that had remained in place for over sixty years, still dutifully holding up electrical lines that powered the tiny village of some 16,000 residents.

The people they passed seemed fairly well-dressed, no doubt from the hand-me-downs of sympathetic tourists. The villagers seemed content as they went about their business. Interestingly, no one paid any attention to them as they drove past.

"So just where are we headed, Zayas?" Lee asked.

Juan Zayas looked over at Lee, who was sitting in the front passenger seat beside him, and smiled. "Do not worry *señor.* I am taking you to the woman your friend *Señor* Exner wishes you to see."

"Sooo who is she, Juan-man?" Travers asked from the rear of the bus.

"She is Mercedes de Quesada, *señors.* Her husband is missing. His name is Javier Alvaro Rafael de Quesada. He works the sugarcane fields. Poor Javier. He is never content with his life. He always wants more, much more; but don't we all?" Zayez then laughed lustily.

As they continued on their way, the Canadians noticed with curiosity that several street vendors hawked their wares on anything from pushcarts and wheelbarrows to wagons that looked like the popcorn carts of old. Lee was especially curious at the sight of men who carried a myriad of implements and supplies on their backs for sale, whom he imagined daily held the hope that their loads would be significantly lightened before day's end.

The palm trees lining the roads were indicative of true paradise, thought Lee. But like many Caribbean islands, Cuba was paradise only to the visiting *touristas.* The much welcomed *Revolución* that ousted Batista in 1959 under Fidel Castro merely kept the Cuban people more solidly underfoot. Castro's regime made millions of US dollars off the backs of the repressed populace who worked the sugarcane and coffee fields. The more affluent citizens, the ones who could speak English, worked the tourist resorts and drove taxis.

The time capsule that was Cuba has been out of step with the world for over half a century. Lee had travelled the world and always marveled at the fact that the happiest people were ironically also the poorest. Overall, Cubans were a proud, hard-working people who possessed an almost ethereal elegance about them. They were a simple people who had learned the secret of loving family and friends above possessions. In so doing they had triumphed over the rat race. God bless them all, he thought.

The beauty of the wild scrubland, the spartan huts, the outbuildings—all were quaint in their own right. Small water towers stood as silent sentinels on the corners of rooftops above the little square Caribbean blue dwellings. These assured an adequate supply of water if their inhabitants were careful in its consumption.

Juan said little on the journey inland, and both Lee and Bill Travers silently wondered if they were entering an elaborate trap.

It was another hour or so before their fears were assuaged. Far into the island's interior and heavy foliage, they eventually came to an isolated encampment. No other vehicles were present, but there was evidence of recent human activity.

As the men climbed out of the old VW minibus and stretched their legs, Juan rushed around to grab their bags. "Come, *señors*, come this way," Juan urged them with repeated head nodding toward the makeshift hovel.

The dwelling was constructed of a montage of rusted corrugated steel sheets, cardboard boxes, old tires, garden hoses, and even the hood of an ancient, long forgotten Buick.

Upon gaining entrance to the homemade hovel at Juan's beckoning, Lee and Travers could see that it was vacant. The dwelling was a lot roomier than it appeared from the outside, and definitely had a woman's touch. Even though the floor was of dirt, there were still curtains framing the open rectangles that served as windows. Dishes had been washed and covered to keep the flies off them. Everything had a place and there were no peculiar odors of any kind. Despite the crude structure, it was well cared for. It was home to someone.

Female clothing was neatly folded on an old card table that served as a countertop, and smelled fresh, which suggested that whoever lived here had recently done the laundry. Lee noticed there was no male or children's clothing anywhere to be found. The small dwelling yielded nothing of any real value, but such as they had was valuable to them he knew.

The three men came back out the front entrance as there was no rear exit, and went around the back of the dwelling. The yard surrounding the hovel had materials lying about similar to that of its construction, perhaps for future repair. Large boulders, dry scrub land, and sparse foliage defined the area to the rear. They returned from whence they came and congregated at the minibus.

There was nothing of interest and no one evident as far as the eye could see. The place was well secluded and seemingly devoid of any human presence apart from the three *amigos*.

"Why would anyone want to live in such a God-forsaken place?" Travers asked to no one in particular.

"No one, unless you had something to hide or needed to be hidden," Lee said.

"The woman you seek, she lives here *señors*," said Zayas.

"Where would she be this time of night, Juan?" Lee asked.

"I know nothing, only of where she lives," Zayas said.

The sun had now dropped beyond the western horizon, and a steady chill had already begun to permeate the air.

"We're going to need a place to stay for a while, Juan," Travers said. "Can you find us such a place?"

"Si, Señor." Zayas smiled, pointing to the path leading up to the hovel. "Here, in the little bus. There is room for—"

"Not going to happen, Juan-man," said Lee firmly.

Bill Travers vocalized his thinking. "Lee, we're not far from the Hotel Brisas Sierra Mar. It's only about a half hour's drive from Chivirico. I've stayed there before on a few of my dive trips. Whether or not we can just show up unannounced and get a room is—"

"Exner's problem. Right then, Hotel Brisas it is." Turning to face their Cuban chauffeur, Lee put a hand on his shoulder and said, "Juan, my good man, would you be so kind as to take us there?"

"*Si, si*. I know it well *señors*. But I do not know when this woman will return."

"We'll have to see if she returns tomorrow. It's our best option, and it's nearly dark. We would only succeed in frightening her away if she were to see us waiting for her tonight," Lee said.

The men piled into the ancient vehicle for the return trip to Chivirico, and hopefully, a place to bed down A place that was larger and more comfortable than an old, beat-up, Volkswagen minibus.

30

Caught In A Double Cross

Bindhira Shankar waited patiently in Alan Exner's office the next morning as instructed. She was a little early, as was her custom. While waiting, she inspected the bookcase along the wall of his office to see just what kind of books control read, what kind of man he was. She had known of him, of the tragic loss of his wife, but little else. She had learned early in life that the least you knew about people, the better it was for all involved.

At exactly 9:02 Exner arrived, café mocha in one hand, valise in the other. Through the open threshold he saw her poring over his book collection and smiled.

"Finding anything of interest, Ms. Shankar?" he asked.

She turned abruptly to face him. The door had been open, but she inwardly chided herself that his entrance startled her, took her by surprise, and that bothered her.

"Good morning, Alan. You have some interesting volumes, yes," she said. Then on a more serious note, "Have you heard any news from our men in Cuba?"

Alan Exner came around to sit at his desk. He took a sip of his hot drink, looked into the cup for a moment, then responded. "Our contact down there, Juan Zayas, has already taken them under his wing."

"Hartley and Travers have found their way to the Brisas Hotel outside Santiago. It's a popular resort for travelling Canadians, and NABS operatives have used it often, discreetly of course. From the message received, they were more than a little put out that I 'neglected' to arrange accommodations, but I wasn't sure where they'd end up and didn't want to take a chance on compromising my people down there."

"Hartley said it was definitely preferable to living out of Zayas' beat-up old minibus. A nice little surprise for them, compliments of NABS. I was fairly certain it would only be a matter of time before they'd turn up there given their location."

"The message was Sequoia encoded, was it not?" Bindhira asked with concern.

"SOP, Ms. Shankar, standard operating procedure. Sequoia also provided a photo of the minibus they were in, complete with tag number, thanks to its sat-link." He nonchalantly took another sip of his café mocha.

"Do you not think we should have sent properly trained agents in their place, Alan? I do not wish to question your authority of course, but they could be in grave danger down there."

Exner rose from behind the desk, patted her shoulder, then walked over to take in the window view of Lake Ontario and the glistening city of Toronto beyond.

"That's precisely why I didn't send any of *our* people, Ms. Shankar. Hartley and Travers can handle themselves, and better than most. Plus, they're both frequent travelers to Cuba. For the most part they behave themselves, stay on their resorts, and dive, little else. DGI observers are well aware of their activities down there, and so far haven't drawn any attention from them. The boys are perfect for the job. Not so if we send someone they're not familiar with down there."

Bindhira strode over to the other side of the large bullet-proof office window and said softly, "But Lee Hartley is on NABS retainer for *underwater* investigations and bomb disposal work only, Alan. He is not trained for field operations."

"True, Ms. Shankar, although with what Travers stumbled onto down there, his underwater talents will undoubtedly come in handy."

"I do not understand, Alan," Bindhira said. Exner gently touched her elbow as he walked over to his desk, sat down, and brought up a file on his Sequoia computer terminal. She followed and came around to view the screen.

What he pulled up was the underwater photo of a shiny brass metal box Bill Travers had taken on his last visit to Cuba. The box was about four feet long and two feet wide, and its top was stamped with Chinese characters in one corner. It wasn't a clear shot as the photo was taken deep underwater. To make matters worse, the flash from Travers' inexpensive underwater camera had partially occluded some of the foreign characters.

"This, Ms. Shankar, is the 'get out of jail free card' for Mr. William Travers. While on a dive excursion a few months ago in Cuba, he dived on the *Cristóbal Colón*, a Spanish warship sunk by the American Navy during the Spanish-American war of 1898. He discovered the strange metal box abandoned in one of her holds."

"Up until now, all eyes had been on the art dealings Travers was involved in. My gut tells me this box, strange as it seems, may be tied in somehow to the Cuban art dealings he makes."

"Following the CIA briefing, Travers recalled the box with the Chinese script down there, and ran it by me. It was a curious item to find on an old wreck, shiny and all, so he took a photo of it."

"What would Chinese cargo be doing on a one hundred year old Spanish warship?" Bindhira closely examined the writing on the box as she spoke over Exner's shoulder. "Alan, would you happen to have a magnifying glass by chance?" Rummaging around his top desk drawer, Exner produced one and handed it to her.

She leaned down to study the photo closer. "The container does not look like it has been in the water long. It had to have been recently planted on the *Colón* before William made his dive. The question is, why?"

"I agree," Exner said. "Travers said that something shiny caught his eye when he trained his underwater light in the hold as his group swam over. It was near the end of their dive and he was lagging behind the others. The divemasters down there are quite insistent that their groups stay together, so he was forced to abandon any further exploration. He had time enough to pull out his camera and snap the pic, with the intent of returning alone to check it out later."

"Fortunately, the weather hasn't been conducive to diving the wreck the past few weeks due to unusually high winds, so hopefully it'll remain undisturbed until Hartley and Travers get there."

"The increase in Chinese shipments to Cuba is beginning to make some sense now. The crates that have recently been arriving on their naval docks have been relatively small, and not as sinister as the large cylindrical tarp-covered missiles imported by the Russians in the early sixties."

Exner smiled. "I'll be damned. 'Old' Bill has played the part of the man that piloted the American U2 spy plane reconnaissance that discovered the Russian missile silos in Cuba."

"How do you mean, Alan?" Bindhira asked quizzically. She sat on a corner of his desk, still intently studying the photo on Exner's monitor.

"Before the Cuban Missile Crisis several decades ago, a routine flight was made by an American U2 spy plane flying thousands of feet high in the air over Cuba. The pilot took astonishing photographs of several missile silos and launch sites covertly being erected in the island's interior. Turns out that the Russians had been sending innocuously long crates concealed under tarps aboard their merchant ships to Cuba for some time. It was subsequently discovered that these crates contained intermediate-range intercontinental ballistic missiles capable of carrying thermonuclear warheads."

Exner got up and gestured for her to sit in his chair, then stood beside her as she accepted. "In essence Travers has stumbled onto something eerily similar."

Silence prevailed. Bindhira was intently studying the box through the magnifying glass, and scribbling on a pad beside Exner's computer. When she was done, she just sat and stared at what she had written.

Exner, perplexed by this, startled her back to normalcy when he spoke. "What, Bindhi?" He inwardly rebuked himself for addressing her in this unprofessional fashion; his knee-jerk reaction at seeing her astonishment trumped his personal protocol.

"Alan, this is Mandarin. The characters on the box indicate that there are sensitive entomological and biological components contained within! The unit itself is both waterproof and depth compensated. It is designed to be underwater for a set period of time. My god, Alan, if this is what it appears to be . . ."

Exner's astonishment came from a different front. "You speak *Mandarin*, Ms. Shankar? I didn't notice that little detail in your dossier."

She looked up into his face as the shadow of a slight smile crossed hers. "Alan, I am sure there are several omissions on *your* dossier as well, truth be told." His uncharacteristic blush provided the only answer she needed.

Exner smiled in kind, then directed his gaze at the monitor and image before him. He quietly mulled some thoughts around in his mind, which led him to a disturbing conclusion. "Entomological warfare . . . of course," he began, "that of infecting insects with a pathogen to be used for dispersal over selected enemy targets. EW is much cheaper and more insidious than conventional bombs, yet with no damage to property or possessions."

"Any species of common insect could be infected with practically any type of virus: tularemia, smallpox, brucellosis, typhus, Marburg, equine encephalitis, Q fever, or other viral agents and toxins. Highly infected, these flying little kamikazes could be incubated right in the backyards of enemy population concentrations. Entomological scientists could even condition uninfected insects, like bees, to directly attack an enemy. How do you go about fighting an army of insects?"

Exner got on the hotline to Scott Culp, CIA headquarters, Langley, Virginia. His succinct encoded message included the promise of more information to be forthcoming as it developed. Turning to Bindhira, he said, "Ms. Shankar, what do you know about the current CBW status in China?"

Before she could speak, he raised a finger to her to hold her thoughts as he spoke to his secretary over the interoffice line. He ordered Chinese take-out for them, as a formal lunch date was no longer an option.

As he hung up the phone, he said, "Chinese *is* okay isn't it, Ms. Shankar?"

She rolled her eyes at him. "Very apropos, Alan; yes, it will be fine."

The thought hadn't occurred to him, but even he smiled that all this talk about China had subliminally projected the idea into his mind of ordering Chinese food for the two of them.

"In answer to your question Alan, the status of chemical biological warfare in China is tenuous at best."

She suddenly broke topic and smiled at him. "Alan, you are much too formal. It would be appreciated if you would address me as Bindhi forthwith."

Exner pulled back his suit coat, hitched up his pants, unconsciously tweaked the bulb of his nose with a thumb, and smiled openly. Bindhira revealed her conquering smile to him once again. It was heavenly, and its warm genuineness reminded him of his deceased wife, Marlissa. Oh how he missed her!

"Right then, Ms. Shankar. Forthwith, you shall hereby be forever known as Bindhi, where appropriate of course."

She afforded him a curt nod, and then continued. "China has been improving upon and building up her CBW arsenal for several years. In 1997, pursuant to the Chemical and Biological Weapons Control and Warfare Elimination Act of 1991, the United States imposed strict trade sanctions on five Chinese individuals, two Chinese companies, and one Hong Kong manufacturer for knowingly and materially contributing to Iran's chemical weapons program."

"Both the Nanjing Chemical Industries Group and the Jiangsu Yongli Chemical Engineering and Technology Import/Export Corporation were directly involved in the export of dual-use chemical precursors and/or chemical production equipment and technology."

"*Dual*-use chemical precursors? What the devil is that?"

"It means that while the Chinese exports looked innocent enough and would normally be used for peaceful means, the reality was that Iran was 'beefing up', as you would say, her biological weapons systems with these products, of which China was well aware."

"It sounds like the NSA has versed you quite thoroughly in 'eyes only' Chinese Intel." Exner was obviously impressed and very glad to have her in his corner on this one.

"I have had recent dealings with the ChIS prior to my temporary attachment to NABS," she replied. "Up until now Alan, we were adequately monitoring the situation. In light of our current situation, however, NABS needs to be brought into the loop. It is time for us to make a stand." Bindhira sensed what he was thinking. "Alan, please understand that I am not at liberty to discuss the Chinese-Iranian connection at this time. I am simply here to render all the assistance you may need from the United States on the current Chinese-Cuban affair."

She rose and paced back and forth, head down, along the wall that fronted Exner's bookcase, lost in thought. Then abruptly she stopped pacing and turned to face him. "Alan, that box was purposely planted on that wreck for any one of a number of reasons. It could be so positioned to test the effectiveness of EW on remote Cubans prior to sending the material over here. Or, they may have a plan in place to retaliate in the event of a sell-out. *Or,* it may be a completely separate subversive organization of some sort that is poised to double-cross the Cubans and the Chinese if/when their ultimate goal is achieved."

All were viable possibilities, thought Exner. The whole affair was becoming more and more complicated by the hour. He hoped that sending his friends Lee Hartley and Bill Travers to Cuba was something he would not live to regret.

Bindhira was right, thought Exner. Good divers or not, they may be in too deep already, and whether good or bad, he would be solely responsible.

31

Same Plan, But Different

Rodriguez, Gino Vaselino, Wu Yang, and several of Yang's men met early the next morning in an abandoned run-down motel off the main highway leading into Tobermory. The small establishment had not been in service for many years and was well concealed from the highway by a forest of blue spruce trees engulfing it. A member of the Cuban cell had found the motel quite by accident one day, and it was wisely decided to be kept in mind as an alternate meeting place should the grotto be compromised.

Rodriguez was first to speak. "We have been beleaguered by a number of unfortunate setbacks," he reported. "Four more cell mates lost their lives at the old man's shop, bringing the total to five men we have lost to date."

At this news, a hushed murmur spread throughout the men. Wu Yang was concerned. Such losses were poison to any cell's morale and could seriously jeopardize the mission.

"The old man's friend, Lee Hartley, is a meddlesome diver who has seriously interfered with our plans," continued Rodriguez. "He foiled us from capturing the old man on our first attempt. We then tried to persuade Hartley to stay out of the old man's affairs, but he turned out to be tougher than we expected. But we managed to capture the art vendor, Travers, soon after." Rodriguez' voice turned guttural and his fists became clenched.

"We had the man and held off serious interrogation of him until I returned from a trip to collect Mr. Yang here from Niagara." He looked daggers at Yang. The ChIS operative saw this but his face remained calm. "One of my top operatives guarding Travers was somehow overpowered. The old man managed to escape from the grotto and is still at large. Osvaldo did not survive the escape. Then an opportunity presented itself to sabotage the brakes on Hartley's vehicle to take care of the meddler once and for all, but once again we were unsuccessful." Carlos Rodriguez was visibly angered. "I grow tired of this man."

"At this point," Wu Yang said, "we must find out who slipped through our net and acquired the painting. Concealed beneath the canvas are several very important packets we need to complete the final phase of our operation."

"It is true that we have suffered a number of unfortunate setbacks," said Rodriguez. The men we lost were good men, trained specifically for this operation. But I am most grateful to you and your contingent, Mr. Yang, for agreeing to assist Mr. Vaselino and me to complete our assignment. I am well aware that your men have been entrusted with a different objective." Rodriquez paused, put a hand on Vaselino's shoulder for a moment, and then continued. "We must intensify our activities to fulfill the assignment within the time allotted us." He looked at the men before him before continuing. "I need not remind you of our collective fate should we fail in the quest to carry out our assigned tasks."

Wu Yang nodded his agreement and then added, "Yes, we must work together, and efficiently, if we are to bring the *true* purpose of *Project Vector* to a successful completion, without incurring the combined wrath of our governments."

"Even though the number of cell operatives has diminished, I am confident that each of you will accept the additional responsibilities our deceased brothers have been forced to abandon. I suggest we separate into two teams of three, with the rest in reserve as needed. I shall coordinate from this motel."

"Team one shall consist of Choi Li, Huang Fu, and you, Mr. Rodriguez. This team will return to Niagara to hunt down and liquidate the two dogs that have seriously affected our operation. Team two will consist of Chen Fa, Shing Shen, and Mr. Vaselino. You men shall remain in this area and locate the whereabouts of the last painting Mr. Travers brought back to this country."

Wu Yang paused. He draped his cane over the crook of his left arm, and fondled its gold dragonhead as he continued. "Those in possession of the painting must be liquidated. There can be no loose ends. It is paramount that I have that last piece of art in my possession within the next forty-eight hours."

"Choi Li, you will act as leader of team one and take your team to Niagara. Chen Fa, you will be, as they say, point man for the recovery and extermination team here. Both teams will maintain on-going reports to me. As senior operative in charge of this operation, it is my duty to keep the Establishment informed of our progress. They in turn will report to the governmental hierarchies of both our countries what we wish them to know of our progress."

"Together, we shall achieve what the Soviet Union could not do. History must not repeat itself, gentlemen. It is time to force the West to pass the baton to those who better deserve to carry it, the Peoples' Republic of China," then he shrewdly added, "hand in hand with our Cuban allies, but *under the complete control of the Establishment*, as we have so planned."

"The packets and information we have received from our superiors in Cuba," Vaselino said, defiant as ever, "have provided the groundwork and mapped out our mission. Should we not then fully concentrate our energies on our mission, rather than waste it on retribution?" Vaselino's arms were crossed and he wore sunglasses despite the fact they were inside the motel office.

"I understand that it was wise not to be collectively briefed until our operations were established here in the event of capture, but we waste precious time plugging holes when the whole dam is about to burst!"

"My Cuban friend," Wu Yang replied, "is it not most prudent to take care of the small things before they become big things? In so doing we suffer no dishonor. We must, as they say, 'safely bring the ship into harbor.' Remember, we are all on that ship."

Wu Yang felt the time had come to enlighten his men on the mission they were involved in and its ramifications. This would give him time to take care of doubters should they try to opt out and/or sabotage the mission. He lifted the tip of his cane to inspect it, then slowly lowered it back to the floor before he addressed them.

"Gentlemen, please take a seat." The men all found a chair and quietly seated themselves. Then he continued. "It is imperative that no one discovers the small matchbook packets concealed beneath the artwork we seek. The documents and coated matches contained within are essential components of Project Vector."

"You see gentlemen, the heads of the matches contain a particular strain of pathogen, the properties of which I will not bore you with. Our scientists have collectively developed a stealth weapon specifically designed to thrive in the climate of the Great Lakes region of North America. The pathogen has been genetically modified for maximum virility in this geological zone and its five lakes to ensure a most unique and reliable delivery system."

Rodriguez' temperature was on the rise. He had been led to believe than only a few hundred would be affected by the pathogen. But this region was populated by hundreds of thousands of people. He couldn't see how mass genocide had to be a necessary part of the overall plan.

Still, in all, if Project Vector went according to plan, he would be heralded as a hero to his people if his participation in the Establishment had anything to do with it. The organization's goal was to truly put the power in the hands of the *people*, not their governmental regimes.

Yang looked over at his countrymen appreciatively. He much preferred working with his own kind. Chinese were good soldiers and didn't question orders. It was too bad they too would have to die like the Cuban dogs following the successful completion of the implementation phase. Then he would have to work fast at wresting complete control from the members of the Establishment. Once he made his move, he wouldn't be able to turn back, and there would be nowhere to hide if he failed.

"The method of dissemination is most unique," Wu Yang continued. "'Documents' have been placed beneath the matchbooks in specially designed and hermetically sealed brass boxes designed to resist the effects of the water pressure upon them. These boxes containing the experimental virus are being placed in numerous shipwrecks within the five Great Lakes and at varying depths by a team of expert scuba divers handpicked by top members of the Establishment as we speak."

"We have a specially equipped research vessel not registered in North America that is currently conducting 'oceanographic experiments' in each of the lakes. The vessel is equipped with our latest radar-rerouting ghost imaging array, aptly named the *Ventriloquist*."

"How does this Ventriloquist work?" Rodriguez asked.

"A very good question, Mr. Rodriguez," Wu Yang replied. "This ultra-top-secret system recently designed in China," he beamed proudly, "emits a continuous series of deflecting beams around the vessel. To foreign governmental satellite tracking facilities and the radar installations of enemy navies and coast guards, our vessel will be miles from where their devices detect it. The actual position of the vessel will not show up on conventional radar equipment as long as the array is functioning properly."

"It is akin to a stage ventriloquist who 'throws' his voice to make it appear that his dummy is talking with a voice of its own, thus the name *Ventriloquist.* The Ventriloquist is currently installed in several of our nuclear submarines and will soon be adapted and integrated into our bombers and fighter jets as well."

The men in the room all looked to one another with astonished glances. Such technology seemed the stuff of science fiction. Wu Yang could see a new fear transfiguring each face as they now looked at him with renewed reverence.

"But I digress," Wu Yang said, smiling. "The release mechanisms engineered into each of the boxes are depth compensated. The water pressure that acts upon the brass boxes planted at varying depths will chemically alter the catalyst contained within the fibers of the 'document' paper. The resultant paste will then combine with the chemically treated match heads ripe with Ebola virus."

"The deeper the boxes have been planted, the more virile the 'pulp' will become. Once incubation is complete based on their time submerged and the depths at which they are placed, they become 'live' and ready to be released by remote control. Once the boxes are opened, the liquid paste released will quickly form a gas through interaction with the cold fresh water. The dense molecular gas will remain together and intact as it breaks the surface of the water and spreads inland."

"Only one other high-ranking Establishment member and I will have possession of these devices. As a safety precaution, both devices must be synchronized in order to detonate the release mechanisms of any and all boxes. This action will set off small charges sufficient to blow open the box covers. The sudden decrease in water pressure and exposure to cold fresh water will readily convert the paste into a highly concentrated gas. Once the gas hits the atmosphere, it will not dissipate but float cohesively over the landscape."

"Direct inhalation of the pathogen will reap an immediate terminal effect. However, the true nature of the virus is that it has been genetically engineered to spread and infect the breeding areas of mosquitoes, wasps, and black flies. Several months thereafter, the eggs of these insects will hatch, and they will be natural carriers of the virus, infecting everything they sting—or in the case of black flies, bite—by injecting the concentrated toxin they carry directly into the bloodstreams of thousands of unsuspecting victims."

"So that is why the project has been codenamed *Vector*," observed Gino.

"Very perceptive, Mr. Vaselino," Wu Yang praised with veiled disdain. "Any injection by needle or stinger, in this case, is a vector-induced injection. The media will then release information concerning a 'mystery plague' in a remote Canadian area. Government doctors and scientists will then of course concentrate all their efforts there."

"At that point, we will initiate phase two." Wu Yang saw pangs of incredulity as it crossed the faces of the men. "Our divers are placing such a box in two shipwrecks under each of the five Great Lakes in such a way that their release will not be impeded within the wreck."

"Five lakes; ten shipwrecks; ten containers. He paused for dramatic effect. "And soon thereafter, tens of thousands of casualties! If for some reason we are unable to directly control the release due to the loss or theft of one of our remote controllers," he continued, "the depth compensating mechanisms will automatically trigger the release of their contents at regular intervals, depending on the depths they have been positioned at."

"The shallower the box, the longer the catalyst will take to infuse the match heads and the longer it will take for their release. But they *will* be released one way or the other—another safety feature designed for the success of the mission."

"Once released, there will be no turning back, and there will be nowhere to hide. We will have the Western dogs stumped, perplexed, and totally at our disposal."

Wu Yang smiled evilly, and his eyes glazed over. This put even his countrymen in attendance ill at ease. "Imagine the mass hysteria at having a virulent plague manifesting itself in the most unlikely of places with no way of combating it. North America is just the beginning. Once we have them under our feet, we will subjugate our own respective governments, using their own weapon against them, and giving power to the people, where it belongs. *We*, the members of the Establishment, will rule the world!"

Gino Vaselino spoke up. "Mr. Yang, your plan is sound, but the scientists of North America are not stupid. Do you not believe they will learn of the insect delivery system and quickly devise a way to combat it?"

Wu Yang looked over at Gino and thought, *you simple Cuban cur. When we are finished with you stupid peasants, your people will suffer a deadlier fate. And there will be no one to help you.*

"By the time anyone determines the cause, it will be far too late, my Cuban friend. Our scientists have employed an existing pathogen that will mutate and resist any form of treatment or cure."

"Up to now our brightest scientists have been experimenting with diluted forms of the virus to see if it could withstand the extreme cold and pressure of the deep fresh waters of the Great Lakes. Their experiments were a resounding success."

The boxes that were being planted contained a powerful strain of Ebola, but one that could be compromised given the right set of conditions. This was not a bad thing, Wu Yang explained, as it would give the Americans false hope into thinking their countermeasures were proving effective.

Once the perfected *finalized* strain was introduced in similar fashion, however, its effects would be unalterable, irretrievable, and chronically deadly for years to come. This strain, concealed within the packets beneath the final painting, was the ticket that would guarantee compliance from even the Chinese government. The Establishment would control the world! But these were the packets that had gone missing . . .

It was a heinous plan and one that was textbook Chinese. However, it had been finalized in his country, thought Rodriguez, and that would elevate Cuba to a glory it had never known. Cuba would share in China's glorious victory over the Americans! How he hated the American imperialists.

With the United States short-circuited through the ensuing chaos to come, Cuba would finally have their revenge over them, and he, Carlos Rodriguez, would be the new hero of Cuba! His name would displace that of Fidel Castro's from the history books. Fidel and his cronies lied to their people, raped the country of its wealth, and relegated her citizens to live their lives in ever-descending squalor.

But he, Carlos Rodriguez, would be heralded as being instrumental in liberating Cuba from her heretofore destined eternity of poverty. It was Rodriguez' turn to smile; he was poised to be the new savior of Cuba!

Rodriguez' dreams of vanity misted away for the time being when Wu Yang once again addressed the cell members. "You have your orders. Carry them out quickly."

His final remark chilled even Rodriguez' spine. "Should you fail in your assignments, you would be wise not to return."

32

A Drive In The Country

Drinking Cuban coffee on a Cuban beach at a Cuban resort while watching a Cuban sunrise was living the dream, thought Lee Hartley. Even though he and Travers had been up late the previous evening, they both arose in time to witness a magical sunrise. The ever-present cool breeze coming off the Caribbean Sea, the smell of the salt-laden air, watching seagulls circling the shore for their breakfast—it all felt good. But the Canadians had a strong feeling that this was about as good as it was going to get on this trip.

"Stinkin' Exner, eh, Lee?" Travers remarked as he tore off bits of buttered toast to throw to the gulls. He admired their ability to see small tidbits from so high above and then swoop down with pinpoint accuracy to scoop up their snacks and still maintain their flight path.

"My mind had formed a harsher expletive to describe him than that, Bill," Lee said. "He could have told us about these accommodations; could have told us a lot of things."

"It's probably cloak-and-dagger protocol not to advise *field consultants* what the hell's going on. Anyway, sure beats shackin' up in a crap-ass little bus, don't it?"

"Yeah, true that, Bill. Say, where's Zayas? Did you see him on any of your numerous forages back to the breakfast table?"

"Ouch, and no, I didn't. The poor bastard's probably never eaten and slept in such luxury. We may not see him for some time."

"We've got our work cut out for us today, and waiting around for him is not on that agenda," Lee said ruefully.

Almost as if on cue, Juan Zayas stumbled up the beach to greet them. Disheveled, slightly inebriated, and still not fully awake, he said, "Good morning *Señor* Lee and *Señor* Billiam. It is a great day, is it not?" He swayed as he stood on the sand.

"What's up, Juan?" Travers smiled. "Looks like you're not!"

Zayas looked down at himself. Then he took a deep bow, looked back up at them, smiled, and said, "I am here, am I not? I am awake and ready for your duties."

"Well, for one, Juan, we always make sure we're not wearing our shirts inside-out, and two, we refer to ourselves by our proper names. *Billiam*? Who the hell is that? The name's *William.* W-I-L-L-iam. *Comprendo,* señor?"

Lee had to laugh at both the drunken appearance of their Cuban contact and Travers' unusually well-appointed rebuke.

The Cuban peeled his T-shirt up from his stomach and looked stupidly at it. Lee could see him trying to figure out if it really was inside out. It was.

"These things will never happen again, I assure you, Señor Bill, ah, I mean Señor WILL-iam!" Juan's smile was as bright as the rising sun and as phony as a three-dollar bill.

"Time to blow this pop stand, Juan-nie boy, but there's a slight change of plans today, because I'm drivin'," Bill Travers said matter-of-factly.

Juan was quick to realize no discussion would be forthcoming on the matter. Saying nothing, but visibly hurt at being demoted from pilot to navigator, Juan simply pulled a key out of his faded knee-length khaki cargo shorts and handed it to Travers.

The trio left the Brisas Sierra Mar hotel complex with Travers at the wheel of the minibus. Zayas sat beside him providing directions, and Lee sat in back. The paved streets of Chivirico and its environs soon morphed into mere dust trails. The *tourista* facade quickly faded in the rearview mirror as they began the arduous trek back to the dwelling they had visited the night previous.

Zayas looked over at Travers and smiled. He could see Travers was not proficient at shifting gears on the faltering standard transmission of the VW. Travers caught the Cuban doing his best not to laugh out loud, and grimaced.

Suddenly Lee yelled from the backseat, "Watch out!"

A scrawny herd of cattle had decided to cross the small dirt road not a hundred feet in front of them. Immediately Travers yanked the wheel, throwing them off the road and onto the rutted and rocky scrub brush terrain. The old VW bounced hard several times as it hit the ruts, and several heavy scraping thumps emanated from beneath the old vehicle as it bobbed and weaved for several hundred yards before the old diver was able to regain control and bring the vehicle to a stop.

"*Joder sustantivo!*" Juan Zayas exclaimed as he wiped the sweat off his brow with the bottom of his T-shirt. He sat physically shaken by the incident, but not mentally stirred.

"Shut 'er down Bill," Lee said as he jumped out of the bus. Travers and Zayas followed suit and came over to where he stood at the rear of the bus.

"Good reflexes, sunshine, but let's keep our eyes on the road in the future, shall we?" Lee put a hand on his friend's shoulder with a gentle shake.

The bottom carriage of the vehicle and rear left wheel-well had suffered numerous scrapes and dings, and the muffler pipe had nearly pinched off near the tailpipe. Outside of these, the old VW seemed to have survived the impromptu off-road excursion. Lee made a mental note to pry the pinched muffler pipe open at day's end when they reached their destination and the van had cooled down.

"As Mr. Spock on the original *Star Trek* TV show would say, 'Minimal damage to exterior hull, Captain, shields still holding,'" Travers said in an effort to appear nonchalant even though he, like their Cuban friend, had been shaken-up by the near mishap.

Lee opened the engine access panel at the rear of the vehicle to inspect for potential damage to the engine. "Good thing this old beast has an air-cooled engine," he said to no one in particular. "If she had a rad, we'd be walking the rest of the way. I think we're good to go, boys."

"The jury's still out on that," Travers said, then went around the side of the bus to relieve himself.

Zayas, upon hearing the healthy stream, turned his back to Lee. Within seconds another stream was well on its way. Lee shrugged, dropped his fly, and joined the chorus.

Within minutes they boarded the bus and continued on their way. Both Lee and Travers recognized some of the landmarks they had passed on their way the previous evening. The trip yielded little to the average tourist. Royal palm trees, scrub land, boulders, and a narrow dirt road were the offerings of the day as they neared their port of call.

The VW backfired and spewed out black smoke every once in a while, and its engine began to miss with increasing frequency, but by early afternoon the Kombi T1 minibus transporting the Canadians and their guide arrived without further incident.

"Bill, see those two large bushes up there to your left? I think we can park this thing in between, but I want you to back her in," Lee said, pointing between the front seats as they neared the narrow lane that led to the de Quesada residence.

Travers obediently complied, and the old bus came to rest between the bushes with a few feet to spare on each side. The men exited the vehicle, with Zayas asking, "Why are we parking here Señor Lee, when we still have farther to go up the path?"

"I'm just not comfortable with that Juan," Lee said. "It's the diver in me, I guess. We'll travel the rest of the way on foot, but not on the path. That way, should there be any unwelcome guests they won't find our footprints."

"Splendid idea, Lee. I was just going to suggest that," Travers said, smiling. He took off his Tilley, looked at the sweat-stained band inside, and then replaced it on his noggin.

"Listen!" The others strained to hear the reason for Lee's admonition. The sound of an approaching vehicle could be heard in the faint distance, and grew increasingly louder.

"Juan, is there another route vehicles can take in this area, or would they all pass this way?"

"No Señor Lee, all motor vehicles, donkeys, and bicycles, they must come this way. It is the only way for miles."

"Right then," Lee said. "Everyone get behind the bus. Let's just see what we shall see, shall we?" The men took cover behind their semi-concealed vehicle.

Within several minutes they saw that the approaching vehicle was a decrepit old blue Dodge stake truck. It was apparent that the stakes along the sides of the upper part of the pickup's box were not original equipment and had been replaced, probably several times.

The pickup seemed to be in no hurry as it passed them by. Its tail pipe emanated thick plumes of acrid blue smoke that drifted over in their direction. As it enveloped them, Lee put his nose into the crook of his arm. Travers took off his hat and wafted it before him in a vain attempt at clearing the air around him. Zayas made no effort whatsoever to avoid breathing in the sickening fumes. It was a way of life to the Cuban, and he had apparently developed an immunity to their toxic odor.

The ancient Dodge turned up the dirt lane leading to the de Quesada dwelling. From their position, Lee had to run around the side of the large bush concealing the left side of the bus, and stood tightly beside it to obtain a better vantage point. He could make out three heads inside the truck as they drove up the lane. The middle head was shorter; no doubt a woman between two men. But were they riding with her, or was she their prisoner?

Lee had a gut feeling it was the latter, and if the earlier incident with the cattle was any indication, the day was not going to get any better. His feeling was confirmed when he noticed a gun rack with two rifles in stocks hung outside the cab beneath its rear window.

33

A Close Call

"No, there hasn't been any word yet from our operatives in Cuba." Alan Exner was on the microphone of his scrambled Sequoia satellite transceiver with the secretary of the US Department of Homeland Security while piloting the TaZeR down the Queen Elizabeth Way.

"Yes, they're in Chivirico and will reestablish contact with us once they have further intel on the man Hartley pulled out of the fire." He listened for a few moments as the secretary spoke. "Yes, the liaison from CSS is with me and we're on our way to Tobermory as we speak." There was a lengthy pause. "Yes, and we're following up on a lead at the gallery where William Travers put the paintings up for consignment."

Bindhira flipped down the sun visor and touched up her lipstick.

"We're hoping to locate the people who purchased Travers' last consignment. There's a strong possibility they may lead us to the cell."

Bindhira replaced the sun visor, and then turned to watched Exner as he continued his conversation with the secretary, who was in her Washington, D.C., office.

"That's a distinct possibility, ma'am. Yes, yes, we will. Thank you, ma'am, will do . . . you as well. Exner out." He replaced the microphone on its cradle.

He had to bring the TaZeR to a crawl at a flagman's urging as they entered a construction cone zone up ahead. Two large tandem dump trucks veered across both northbound lanes on which they were travelling to dump their loads of crushed stone.

Now at a dead stop, he said to Bindhira, "Ours is a very delicate operation. One wrong move and the mice will scatter. We can't afford to lose the trail. We may not get another chance to pick it up in time. That was basically the nature of the sat-call, and believe me, I am well aware of it."

As the flagman waved them on through the tar-scented cone zone, Exner continued. "We need to find the people who picked up that last consignment, Bindhi. I want to snoop around in Tobermory and see if there's been anything out of the ordinary, and also check on yachts recently berthed there." Picking up speed, he pulled out to pass a slow moving van. "I'm hoping the cell or a part of it is still active there. We may just get lucky."

"This is changing the subject, Alan," Bindhira said, "but why did you break protocol and send Lee and William to Cuba? You gave them very little to go on but a photograph and a contact of yours to meet them."

Exner looked over to her for a moment, then back at the road. "Agreed, the method and manner I sent Hartley and Travers to Cuba wasn't protocol. Theirs is a potentially dangerous assignment. But the less they know the better, and not being NABS agents, there's a better chance they'll fly under the radar down there.

They're both very resourceful, and Juan Zayas is a good man. He's a *sleeper asset* for NABS. We have a small network of Cuban nationals who assist our people down there from time to time. Don't forget the main reason I sent them down there, Bindhi. Hartley's a good salvage diver, one of the best. I want him on the *Cristóbal Colón*. I want to know what's in that brass box. And if the thing's booby-trapped, well, Hartley can handle it. Travers can be a pain in the ass at times, but I don't want his ass blown up doing our business either."

"For some reason this does not bring much comfort, Alan," Bindhira said, followed by a wry smile. She discreetly tugged her short brown skirt farther south at noticing the bottom seam of her pantyhose showing. "Alan, how will the men get word to you without Cuban Intelligence picking up on it?"

Exner looked over at her as they came out of a rather steep curve. "Not to worry, Bindhi. Juan has access to an encrypted Sequoia sat phone."

Heading up to Tobermory from Niagara-On-The-Lake involved taking numerous highways and roads until they reached the base of the peninsula. After over four hours of continuous driving, Exner guided the TaZeR into a Petro-Canada service center for refueling. As he refueled the vehicle, Bindhira got out and stretched her legs.

"I will be back in a few minutes, Alan," she said. Exner nodded and then turned away to watch the traffic beside the station as it flew by at speeds much faster than the posted limit.

After several minutes of pumping high octane fuel into the tank of the thirsty high-performance vehicle, he returned the hose to its dock and paid the cashier. Following Bindhi's lead, he went into the store to get a washroom key.

He was just coming out as Bindhira was headed for the parked TaZeR. As she started across the wide tarmac between the building and the parked vehicles, Exner noticed a sports car heading directly for her from behind at high speed, wheels spinning, blue smoke billowing in its wake.

"Bindhi, watch out!"

The words had no sooner left his mouth than she immediately dived out of the way of a speeding car. It brushed past her with tires squealing as it rocketed out of the service station lot for the highway.

Dropping the rest room key fob, he ran over to her as fast as he could. She was lying against the side of a white Fiat 500, her skirt up around her waist, right leg bleeding.

"Bindhi!" he yelled. Exner could see she was visibly stunned. As soon as he reached her, he pulled her skirt back down to modest proportions and placed his hands gently on her shoulders. "Bindhi, where are you hurt?"

Waving his concern off, she reached up with both hands. He pulled her up so she could lean against the little car.

"Alan, I am fine."

"Your leg . . ."

". . . is not as bad as it looks. Your warning, though, was most timely and very much appreciated," she said as she bent down, hands on knees, to regain her breath.

"You've got damned good reflexes, girl," was all he managed to get out.

"One needs them in this business, Alan." She looked up and smiled warmly into his face.

"*That* was no damned accident! It was a red sports car, but I didn't get the tag number. Are you sure you're okay?" he asked. His furrowed brow indicated deep concern.

"I will be fine, Alan. I just need to tend to this superficial bleeding on my leg," she said, looking down at it.

"It looked like a late model Nissan GT-R," Exner said. "A car like that's worth over 100 K. Nobody drives a car as recklessly as that unless it was for hire. The damned fool had you dead to rights, Bindhi." Then as an afterthought, "Who in their right mind would want to run over a 'supermodel' like you anyway?" Exner caught himself too late. It didn't happen often, but Exner hated blushing. Once the process started however, it was impossible to restrain. He could feel the heat mounting in his ears and he knew they'd be as red as a beet.

Bindhira straightened herself up and smiled at him once again, mercifully without comment. He was impressed both with the calm demeanor she exhibited and the efficient manner in which she had professionally thrown herself out of harm's way. There was much more to this woman than met the eye, he thought, and he was glad to have her on his side.

Bindhira had lost one of her high-heeled shoes; the other had lost its spike. Her pantyhose had runs in several places, and blood continued to ooze out of the lacerations on her lower right thigh. Her right upper arm had an ugly, dirty red scuff mark, no doubt suffered when she shoulder-rolled away from the murderous vehicle.

Trail mix was strewn over the immediate vicinity, and one of the water bottles she carried had ruptured and its contents had leaked out of a split in its side as it lay against the Fiat's rear wheel.

Exner assisted her to the rest room. The key was still where he had dropped it. He went into the men's side with her and locked the door. When they came out she had shed her bloody pantyhose. Her wounds were indeed superficial, and they had removed the blood and dirt around her scrapes and wounds. Upon exiting the rest room, she leaned on him as she walked barefoot beside him to the TaZeR.

Helping her into the vehicle, he said, "Stay here, Bindhi. I'm going in to see if I can get copies of the past hour's transactions, and a look at the security footage. He came from the rear of the building, so I'll start at the businesses there. If he paid cash, we're sunk, but it's worth a try."

Within half an hour he climbed into the TaZeR and handed Bindhi a few receipts. The TaZeR was on the highway at speed within seconds. He pushed a button on the console. A small screen automatically revealed itself as the satellite radio revolved backward.

"Get these off to headquarters would you please, Bindhi?"

Bindhira stacked the receipts into a small pile and then placed them on a tray beneath the center of the dashboard. She then punched a series of buttons to activate the scanner, let out a small sigh, then sat back against the leather bucket seat. "The printouts should be there by now, Alan. It is a long shot, but a shot nonetheless."

Exner looked over and smiled. "As soon as we reach the next town, our first order of business is to get you into a new outfit, compliments of NABS."

34

Little Shop Of Horrors

"Chinese drivers are the worst!" Gino Vaselino exclaimed as the red GT-R rounded Bay Street, the main road into Tobermory. He had been nattering away at Chen Fa, leader of team two and driver of the car he, Fa, and Shing Shen had been riding in. "That NABS car we had been tailing had their control in it as well. Why did you not wait to take him out instead? Wu Yang will not be impressed with your actions this day,"

Vaselino chuckled out loud. "So much for taking care of loose ends. Seems like screw-ups aren't confined to Cubans in our little group, are they, Chen Fa?"

"Enough, Round Eye!" snarled Chen Fa. "Another chance will avail itself. The American woman, like her compatriots, will all be taken care of in good time."

Chen Fa directed his attention to finding a parking spot close to the Little Tub Gallery. When he did, he neatly parallel parked the sports car perfectly between two larger vehicles quickly and without correction of any kind. Shing Shen, sitting in the backseat behind Chen Fa, patted his compatriot on the shoulder. Gino Vaselino grimaced in his direction. The speed and precision of the maneuver impressed even him.

The three men exited the vehicle, stretched a bit, then made the fairly long walk from the parking area to the winding cobblestone pathway of the gallery. The walkway was framed by medium-sized spruce trees. The aromatic scent of pine heavily permeated the area.

Apparently the little gallery was not air-conditioned, for the door was open in an attempt to offset the hot, humid air of the day. Two large, thick blue spruce trees offered a welcome provision of cool shade at the gallery's front entrance.

The three men took up their positions. Shing Shen stood outside near the entrance and lit up a small filtered cigar. Chen Fa, upon entering the little gallery, drifted to the rear entrance of the building to seemingly engross himself in several local works of nature. Gino Vaselino browsed near the cash register, and as expected, was the first to be approached by the scholarly-looking aged female attendant.

"May I help you, sir?" she asked pleasantly. The astute elderly lady wore an ankle-length skirt and wore flat black shoes. Her blouse was dated and had a frilly square neck outlined with silver sequins. She had a pearl necklace in triplicate around her neck to complete the picture of a long retired university professor or librarian.

"I am most hopeful that you can, my dear," Gino said, smiling as he looked deep into her eyes. She blushed and placed a hand on the countertop as if to steady herself in the presence of this tall, handsome young man complete with an intriguing Spanish accent.

Vaselino smiled at the way his charm had swayed her so quickly. "My dear, I am here concerning a painting from my country that has just recently been purchased from this fine gallery. Do you keep records of your purchases?"

"Why yes, yes, of course," she beamed at her competence before him. Their conversation was interrupted when a middle-aged couple decked out in yachting apparel meandered in through the front door.

"Do excuse me a moment, won't you?" the proprietor requested. A slight regal bow from the Cuban granted her the freedom to address her new customers.

Vaselino looked out the front entrance and verified Shen's presence. He saw him at the end of the walkway looking out across Bay Street and Little Tub Harbor. The small harbor was full of yachts and dive charter boats of varying sizes and states of condition.

There was a rather large volume of traffic passing by on the one-way street in front, which led up a hill to various shops, motels, and restaurants beyond. He looked to the rear of the gallery and saw Chen Fa leaning in for a view of the private back room and exit beyond. Good. Everyone was in place.

The middle-aged nautical couple was interested in a single piece of artwork that depicted a large sloop riding the crest of a huge wave in the midst of a roiling mid-lake storm. *Time bandits,* Gino thought—*capitalistic well-to-dos who waste this woman's time only to buy nothing.* They seemed enthralled by the painting. They inquired about the artist, the artist's family, if the artist owned a sailing vessel, yadda, yadda, yadda.

Finally the couple took a gallery business card with the promise to return, and left the gallery. *Like that's going to happen,* Gino smiled derisively.

The proprietor returned to address him. "I'm sorry," she said. "You were interested in a painting we recently sold? Which one?"

"Actually, my dear, I need to find the whereabouts of the people who purchased it; a painting from the last consignment left here by a Mr. William Travers," he said. "It is very important to my country."

"Oh my," she said with genuine concern. "It sounds important. I would love to help you." She smiled and placed her hand on the showcase. "But you see we have a policy about not releasing personal information regarding our buyers or sellers. Some of them are—well, some of them are very affluent and influential, and it wouldn't do for us to give out that sort of information." The elderly woman retreated behind the relative safety of her showcase and cash register. "I'm sure you understand."

Chen Fa now came up just behind the woman where she couldn't see him, as if interested in some murals mounted on the wall behind her.

"But this is most important," Vaselino pressed. "You see, I am from the Cuban embassy in your Ottawa. That particular painting has been stolen from our country and must be returned at once. Your silly 'policy' is delaying a very delicate international matter." Then he added, "I am sure you understand."

The elderly proprietor was obviously at a loss. Nervously she asked, "Do you have a card, sir?"

The Cuban looked perplexed. "A what?"

"A card; you know, a business card with your name, embassy logo, and phone number that I could see for verification?" The woman was nervously insistent now and determined to hold her ground.

The Cuban was quick to reply. "Si, yes, but regrettably not on my person at this time," he said, then quickly changed the subject. "I need only inspect your records to determine where I may locate the paintings in question. I assure you that your clients will be more than fairly recompensed for their inconvenience, and we would not divulge how we obtained their private information."

He saw that the woman was pondering it, so to seal the deal he added, "As I stated, it is most important that I return to Cuba with that painting. It would take but a short moment of your time to check your files. Please, I am prepared to pay you for your trouble."

Warning bells went off in her head. The elderly proprietor could see that the man was getting bolder now, almost imploring. "Please permit me to make a phone call. I'm sure it will be all right, but I must get authorization."

"Authorization?" Vaselino shouted. "*Authorization?* I just want to look at your damned records. Where are they? Show them to me now, and I assure you no harm will come to you."

"No," she hissed. "No, I can't. I won't. Please leave the gallery now. Please," she whimpered. Seeing the fire in his eyes, she turned to run, only to crash into Chen Fa, who was blocking her only avenue of escape.

Vaselino ran to the front door to summon Shing Shen. On the way he heard a sudden, sickening crack. Fa had quickly and cleanly snapped her neck. The Cuban looked over his shoulder in time to see the woman slump to the floor as Chen Fa released her. Vaselino stood momentarily transfixed. He stared at the Chinese agent, who stared murderously back at him. The Cuban called out from where he was standing. Within seconds Shing Shen came into the little shop.

"Shing Shen, lock the door. Let no one in," barked Chen Fa. "Mr. Vaselino, please assist me in locating the gallery's ledger of sales. We must move now, and quickly."

Vaselino began pulling things out of the drawers below the cash register. The body of the woman before him impeded his search, so he gently nudged her small frame with his foot until she was clear of the lower drawer. Shing Shen did as instructed and then flipped the "open" sign over at the front door to show its "closed" side to the road. He pulled the venetian blind down behind the window of the front door and peered through the slats.

Chen Fa, in the meantime, went into the backroom. Inside, one wall was lined with several cardboard business boxes with dates on them. Most of the contents were copies of estimates, inquires of various sorts, and utility receipts, but nothing of interest to him.

Going through the final drawer of the front desk, Vaselino looked down and barely saw the dead woman lying at his feet for the papers and books he had thrown over her during the search. Turning, he curiously noticed that the narrow bookcase behind the front desk against the wall was not square with it. He began checking the spines of the books, looking for anything that could be construed as a record of receipts.

After several minutes of unsuccessful searching amongst the books, he pushed the bookcase back to square it up against the wall. As he did so he heard a *click*, and to his astonishment it receded partway into the wall! He pushed the bookcase further in to reveal a small room behind. Inside the room were several works of art, no doubt high-end pieces. There was also a desk, tabletop computer, TV, and last but not least, a large floor-mounted safe.

"Hey, Chen, come here!" he shouted. "It must be in here!" Both Shing Shen and Chen Fa ran over to where Vaselino was standing inside the doorway of the concealed room.

"Can you do it, Shing Shen?" Chen Fa asked his compatriot.

"Yes, but I will need my kit," Shen replied.

Suddenly the doorknob of the front door turned violently one way and then the other. Whoever was on the other side was determined to gain entrance to the gallery. Instinctively, Chen Fa said, "Everyone inside, quickly!" There was a handle on the other side of the bookcase. He pushed the bookcase closed.

After a short period of time, the rattling of the doorknob ceased, and the men inside the secret room all breathed a sigh of relief.

"This must be where the transaction book is kept. Shing Shen, you must go and get your kit to open the safe. Mr. Vaselino, we must get rid of this body." Chen Fa made sure his team knew who was in charge.

As Shen started out the back entrance, Vaselino followed him. "Where do you think you're going Mr. Vaselino," Chen Fa asked.

The Cuban turned and said, "We need a boat to get this carcass out of here. You got a problem with that?" At this, Chen Fa said nothing. The two went out, leaving Chen Fa alone in the secret room.

On leaving the gallery, Shen walked back behind the rear of an adjoining building before doubling back to their vehicle. Vaselino walked directly back through the small wooded area behind the gallery until he came back out to the highway, then walked the short distance back to the village's main road that led to the marina.

Vaselino walked between the slips, looking for a boat large enough and with cover sufficient enough to conceal a body. There were vessels of various types and descriptions floating in the small marina of Little Tub Harbor, from mid-sized open fishing boats to scuba diving charter boats to high-end yachts. Gino noticed that few people were visible on the decks of the larger boats, and not many people around the slips. He knew he had to act quickly to secure a boat before it got any busier.

At the end of the last slip and only a few hundred yards from the gallery, Vaselino found a twenty-three-foot Baha Cruiser 230 Sport Fisherman single inboard/outboard duo-prop outdrive. It was perfect for their needs.

Meanwhile, Shen returned to the gallery with his kit and began work on the safe. Chen Fa kept lookout through the slats of the closed venetian blinds at the front entrance. Once in a while a couple would amble partially up the short cobblestone pathway leading up to the gallery, but upon seeing the blinds down and the closed sign between window and blinds, none ventured all the way to the door.

Soon a loud audible metallic *click* permeated the quiet of the gallery. Shen triumphantly opened the door to the safe. "Well done, Shen!" Chen Fa said, coming back and into the little room. Going through the safe he found bundled bank notes in varying denominations, several accounting ledgers, mortgage documents, and several legal papers. On the bottom shelf, in a back corner, Chen Fa pulled out a well-worn brown leather-bound journal.

Inside Fa found names, postal codes, dates, dollar amounts, and even the time of day transactions had been made at the gallery. The old woman had indeed been the efficient record keeper she had said she was. He smiled to himself and looked up at Shing Shen. He too was elated. They were one step closer to recovering the missing painting.

Within a half hour, Vaselino returned through the rear entrance. "Ready?" he asked.

"Ready," said Chen Fa. Then, "help Shen with this."

Vaselino looked to the floor at a rolled-up carpet by his feet. "What do we want with this?" he asked.

Chen Fa looked at him with disdain. "The body's inside. Just do as you are told."

Vaselino looked down again at the carpet. It had been rolled and folded over and secured with binder twine at each end. It seemed far too short to have stuffed the small woman inside. Gino noticed that the carpet was the one that had been in the corner behind the desk in the hidden room.

"We had to break her legs to make her fit. The bundle will now draw no suspicion," Chen Fa said.

This disturbed even Vaselino. They had killed the woman for basically nothing, and now this, he thought. He prided himself at being a professional, but did not like killing if it could be avoided. But the Chinese seemed to relish in it, he thought.

Soon they had the carpeting out of the gallery and had just thrown it into the small fishing boat Vaselino had commandeered, when a pair of fishermen stopped to chat on the slip beside their boat. They were bewhiskered and both sported advanced beer bellies. They wore black faded Harley Davidson T shirts, khaki cargo shorts, and work boots.

What North Americans would refer to as 'red neck twins', the Cuban thought. He smiled derisively.

"I hope you're not planning on dumping that out there, are you, fellas?" One of the men joked and pointed out on the open lake.

Gino was fast on the uptake. He smiled congenially and said, "You kidding? This is going in my cottage on that island over there, see?" He pointed to an island way in the distance directly out from the harbor.

"Lucky stiffs," the other fisherman said. "Wish we were going with you!"

At this, the enemy agents laughed. "The next few days are strictly a work party for us," Vaselino said.

"Then let me rephrase that," the man said. "It sucks to be you guys—for the next few days, anyway." Everyone laughed and the fishermen continued on their way.

Watching the men make their way off the dock and into their truck, Chen Fa said, "Well played, Mr. Vaselino. Let's shove off so we can dump this garbage. We have what we need here."

35

Confrontation

Following the old stake truck at a distance, with Lee Hartley in the lead, Bill Travers and Juan Zayas jogged up the winding dusty path leading to the makeshift dwelling where Mercedes de Quesada made her home. The men were careful to use what cover they could. Trees were sparse, but several huge boulders were scattered in the field along the path, which made for ideal cover.

When they arrived at the little hovel, they could see that the cab of the truck was empty. So was the gun rack beneath its rear window. Voices could be heard from within the little structure but were hard to distinguish. The Canadians turned to Zayas for insight as neither spoke Spanish.

"It is hard to tell, señors," Zayas said, "but the men, they are unhappy with Mercedes. They are asking her about something and she is not replying." He strained to listen more closely.

The trio edged ever closer to the dwelling until they had reached the rear of the truck. The front door of the hovel was only about fifteen feet away. A loud slap and a startled cry emanated from the open front door. Hartley made a move to rush in, but both Travers and Zayas held him back.

"No, wait Lee," Travers said. "We aren't in a position to save the day just yet. Don't forget about those rifles. Let's hang back as long as we can and see if anything comes of it." Lee thought the better of it and lightly slapped Travers on the shoulder.

"Yeah, you're right. But if they hurt her—"

"Shhh," Zayas said.

The voices inside became louder. With Zayas translating when possible, it was evident the men were trying to find out where her husband, Javier, had been all this time. The men were evidently not going to leave until she told them where he was.

More harsh words and then another slap, louder than the previous one, emanated from the hovel. As Travers once again restrained Hartley, Zayas said, "Señors, there is much more to this than meets the eye. They have the daughter! Her name is Maela. It seems they have had her for some time and will kill her if *Señorita* de Quesada does not tell them where her husband is."

"What? That's it, I'm going in whether you guys are coming or not," Lee said.

"No Lee, don't," Travers said. "They've got the girl. Yeah, we could probably take these pukes out now, but we won't find out where the girl is, and I highly doubt we could beat it out of them."

The men were still standing behind the truck. Lee said, "We've got to secure better cover. If they come out we're sitting ducks here." He pointed to heavy brush near the far corner of the hovel.

"Over there."

Travers and Zayas started to go, but Travers saw that Hartley wasn't moving. "Coming," the old diver asked.

"In a minute," Lee said. As he shooed Travers in the direction of the brush, Lee pulled himself under the truck.

They could hear the women jabbering a mile a minute, as though giving her captors a thorough scolding. Now closer to the hovel, Zayas could better hear what they were saying. As the dialogue continued inside the dwelling Lee stealthily appeared behind his friends.

"I hate it when you do that," Travers said.

"These men, they are very bad," Zayas interrupted. "They are DGI. They are going to take Mercedes with them. *Señors*, they say she will never see the light of day again. If these men say this, this they will mean."

Suddenly one of the men came out. He was in his mid-thirties, tall, thin, and wiry. He had a rifle stuck under an arm, and stopped in front so he could light the cigar that hung from his mouth.

Within seconds, Mercedes was propelled out the entrance. She almost lost her balance. The other man followed close behind, a rifle slung over his shoulder. Pork barrel-chested and wearing a solid green uniform complete with trademark Ché Guevara black beret, he was the obvious leader of the two.

Mercedes looked tired and beaten. Dried blood had crusted beneath her nose, and her dress was ripped below her left armpit, showing part of a bared breast. She wore no shoes. Pork Barrel shoved her toward the truck. This angered her. Summoning what strength she had, she kicked him in the testicles. The man doubled over, cursing obscenities. The other man tossed his cigar to the ground and came over to help contain the belligerent woman.

At this, Lee pounced. He swept the leg of the doubled over big man, which dropped him to the ground. At the same time, he reached out and grabbed the barrel of the rifle the other man was bringing into play. Taken by complete surprise, the man only had time to feel the pain as Lee spun to the inside of the man, and still holding the barrel of the rifle aimed at the sky, broke it from the man's grip and shoved its butt several times into the man's stomach.

The wiry man had almost brought his rifle to bear on Lee, but Lee already had a bead on him. "No, *señor*, no," Lee said, walking closer to the man. By now Travers had run over to relieve Pork Barrel of his weapon. The stout Cuban ambled to his feet and raised both hands in surrender.

Zayas was quite impressed with the actions of the Canadians. "Bravo, *señors*, bravo!"

"Juan, tell these two not to try anything. We want to know where the girl is and now, or I'll shoot them both where they stand," Lee said, and meant it.

The middle-aged woman didn't know what to make of all this. "Who are you? Why have you come here?" she asked.

"You speak English. That's good. Name's Lee Hartley, Ms. De Quesada. That's Bill Travers with the rifle, and our good friend, Juan Zayas. We're here to get your daughter back," Lee said.

Expecting hearty thanks for a good job well done, she rebuked them instead. "Fools!" she said. "They have my daughter and were going to bring me to her. Now what you have done will get her killed!"

"Relax, Ms. de Quesada. If there's going to be any killing, I'll be doing it," Lee said.

Pork Barrel smiled evilly. "This bitch, she is right, *señor*. The child, she is as good as dead, and all of you," he said, waving his arm at the three of them, "will not be far behind."

"Shut yer cakehole, fatso! Don't make me use this!" Travers said, taking aim at the man's head in grim determination. "I've had enough kidnappers for one bloody lifetime." Travers looked from one Cuban to the other with his patented one-eyed death stare.

Even though he hadn't killed anything, let alone anyone, Travers was convincing enough. Pork Barrel came over and stood silently beside his comrade, hands still in the air.

Unexpectedly, the de Quesada woman came over and pummeled the surprised Lee Hartley's chest with her fists. "You bastards! You have no idea what you have done!"

At this, the wiry man shot a knife-hand blow into the neck of the startled Hartley who had lowered his weapon at Mercedes surprise attack, stunning him. Pork Barrel seized this opportunity to swipe Travers' gun barrel to the side, and a desperate struggle for the rifle ensued. Zayas grabbed Mercedes by the arm and ran for cover.

The wiry man ran to the truck, threw himself in, and attempted to start it. He tried unsuccessfully several times, but the engine failed to start. In fact, it wouldn't even turn over. By this time, Travers had kicked Pork Barrel in the shin and slugged him on the side of the jaw. The large Cuban was bent over once again, this time trying to get his breath. Travers regained the rifle and trained it on his pudgy assailant.

In desperation, the wiry man looked up from behind the wheel. Through the dusty windshield he saw Lee Hartley, whose rifle rested on top of the hood, leveled at his face. The Canadian tossed a battery cable up against the windshield.

"Go ahead," Lee said grimly, "make my friggin' day."

36

Big Crime In A Small Town

It was early evening when the TaZeR pulled into Tobermory. Alan Exner guided the fancy vehicle into a parking spot behind the Dive Inn. The TaZeR drew a crowd wherever it went, and as Exner could see from the balcony above the restaurant, it even extended to a place as remote as Tobermory.

Bindhira looked fetching in long white blouse, skintight blue leggings, and brown leather Rieker sandals as she extracted herself from the vehicle. Exner had stopped in Owen Sound on their way into Tobermory so she could pick up a few things, as well as a decent meal and a little walk afterward to take their mind off the near mishap earlier in the day.

They went in and sat down. It was a rustic medium-sized room. It looked to Exner as if the walls were supported by the dozens of maps, charts, scuba ads, and posters adorning them. Each ordered a Guiness draught, the unofficial brew of Tobermory. There were a growing number of patrons present at this time of the evening and customarily by dusk the place would be full of hungry divers and water sportsmen.

Taking their first sip, both Exner and Bindhira tuned in to the buzz of the night. Apparently someone had gone missing, there was a burglary in a local shop, and an expensive fishing whaler was missing—all in one day! Listening closer, they discovered that the robbery had taken place at one of the local art galleries and the proprietor had gone missing. Seemed like a cut-and-dried case at cursory glance, thought Exner.

He pulled their waitress aside and asked for the manager of the establishment. Concerned that something was wrong with her service, the red-faced attractive young college-aged waitress inquired if there was something she could do to better accommodate him.

"It's nothing to do with you," Exner said, "but we need to speak with your manager."

She smiled and nodded. "No worries, I'll get him for you." With that she left.

"What can I do for you folks," asked the young manager who had come over from the bar to their table moments later. He too was of college age and sported a shaved head. His face bore the efforts of a sparse summer-long beard. What struck Exner most was that the young fellow had no tattoos and no piercings of any visible kind. The only evidence of youthful rebellion was his shaved head. He smiled. The boy had to fit in somehow. "Eric, Manager" was on the name tag he wore on the restaurant-issue blue T-shirt.

Exner produced his credentials and asked if the boy could provide any further details on the strange events that had taken place earlier.

"Yeah, man, it's pretty bizarre. Town talk aside, the cops, I mean the police, talked to pretty much all of us, you know, the managers of the shops and restaurants along the strip here. Of course, none of us had seen anything; we were all in our respective places of business." He laughed nervously. "But I guess cops have to do what cops have to do."

"Eric, can you tell us anything at all about the gallery, its proprietor, and the boat that was stolen?" Exner asked.

"Well, the Little Tub Gallery has been here a long time," Eric said. "Old Mrs. Braithwaite, Agnes, was the owner/operator. She prided herself in dealing with only expensive stuff. Nothing I could afford, that's for sure." He laughed nervously. "The gallery was closed earlier than usual for some reason this afternoon, or so the sign on the front door said. Somebody noticed that the door was open a crack. They looked in and called out. That's when they saw a huge mess around the cash register and did the 911 thing."

"What do you mean by a mess?" asked Bindhira, who had been studying his body language.

"You know, stuff had been pulled out of drawers like someone was looking for something. You know, business papers, invoices, catalogs; stuff. Then someone said the old lady had a 'secret room.' Damned if she didn't! The door to the concealed room was ajar and an open floor safe had been opened. More stuff was scattered around."

"Tell us about the boat, Eric," Bindhira asked.

"Oh yeah, the boat. It's owned by a local guy by the name of Jim McDooner. An old dude, you know, about fiftyish."

Exner smiled and looked over to Bindhira. She acknowledged in kind.

The lad continued. "Not a cheap boat. It was a fancy outrigger. Mr. McDooner took rich dudes out to fish. He knows the water here like the back of his hand. I guess he was some pissed when he found out his boat was scarfed."

"So there's a gallery proprietor missing along with a boat," Bindhira summed up. "What are the chances Mrs. Braithwaite stole something from her own store, made it look like a robbery, stole the boat, and made off for parts unknown?"

"Lady, you gotta be joking. I mean, no disrespect here, but the woman's a fossil. She doesn't even drive a car." Eric had a good chuckle at that one.

"Eric thanks very much for your time," Exner said. "You've been most helpful. Could you have our waitress bring the bill?"

"No worries, guys." As he turned away, a thought hit him and he came back to their table. "Just wondering mister. How'd you know my name?" he asked.

Exner looked again to Bindhira and smiled. They both looked up at the name tag on his ketchup stained shirt. "You know, Eric. Cops do what cops do," Bindhira said.

Eric smiled and shook an index finger their way. "Yeah—damn you guys are good."

Leaving the Dive Inn, Exner and Bindhira walked around the corner on Bay Street and soon came upon the Little Tub Gallery. There was an OPP cruiser in front and police tape across the cobblestone pathway leading to the gallery. It was dusk now and the scene was lit up like a football stadium with portable halogen spot lights.

They were met by an officer at roadside. Exner produced his NABS credentials; Bindhira, her CSS ones. The officer shouted up to another officer who was stationed at the door. "Hey, Johnny: federal agents for the detective." He pointed them in Johnny's direction.

When they got to the gallery entrance, Johnny escorted them over to where a female officer was writing notes in her duty log. "This is Detective Sergeant Jane Hardcastle, folks. Detective Hardcastle, Mr. Exner here is with NABS and the lady is . . ."

". . . with me," Exner said, smiling. Leaving it at that, the officer returned to his duties.

Detective Hardcastle was an attractive petite woman in her late fifties. The natural blonde wore a navy blue pantsuit and white blouse. Once again Exner and Bindhira produced their credentials to assuage any suspicions the detective may have concerning them.

Detective Hardcastle swept back her long blonde hair to get a better look at them. “This must be pretty important for you people to come all the way up here. How may I be of assistance?” she asked.

“Detective, we’re currently working on an international case that has led us here and to this gallery. What do you make of all this?” Exner asked.

“In a word, it’s a quandary,” Detective Hardcastle replied. “For starters the proprietor, seventy-nine-year-old Agnes Braithwaite, has been missing for several hours now.”

“What leads you to that conclusion, Detective?” asked Bindhira.

Detective Hardcastle finished jotting down a few more notes, then gave Bindhira her undivided attention. “A couple of prospective customers came up to the door and were about to leave at seeing the ‘closed’ sign in the shop window. Then one of them noticed the door was ajar. As they entered, they called out. That’s when they saw that the place had been ransacked with no one in attendance, and called police.”

“We made inquiries as to Mrs. Braithwaite’s whereabouts. She isn’t home, nor is she anywhere in town. Evidently she’s a very meticulous person, and not one to leave her gallery unlocked, and certainly not in a mess such as this. This has all the makings of a burglary, but I’m not convinced that it was,” she concluded enigmatically.

“Why not detective?” Bindhira asked as she scanned the area around her.

“Well, a lot of people pour into Tobey this time of year. It’s a scuba diving Mecca,” she said, tossing her hair back again. “The water has excellent visibility, it’s deep, and there are lots of wrecks up here; lots. Dozens and dozens of people mill around Bay Street all day every day throughout the summer. Pulling a heist in broad daylight would be pretty risky, not to mention just plain stupid.” The detective was noticeably not one to mince words. “There’s definitely more to this than meets the eye.”

The detective nodded toward the cash register. The agents followed her lead. She then led them to the small floor-to-ceiling bookcase/ secret doorway behind the counter and took them inside the hidden room. Both Exner and Bindhira were surprised that a small gallery would have need for such a room. Inside the little den much was askew. Documents, paintings, a copier, even a broken computer monitor littered the floor.

Looking into the safe, Bindhira exclaimed, "Alan, look at this." She pulled a pair of pink latex gloves from her purse and donned them. She then picked up two large bundles of new Canadian polymer one-hundred—and fifty-dollar bills. "So much for a robbery," she exclaimed.

"That's what's so intriguing," Detective Hardcastle said. "There doesn't appear to be anything of value missing. There are no bare spots on the display walls, and as you can see, the easels are occupied. Paintings, money; it's all still here."

"I'm not so sure about that, Detective," Exner said. "I see a monitor on the floor, but no tower. Whoever hit this place wasn't interested in art or profit, they were interested in information." He turned his attention to Bindhira. "Bindhi, they were probably looking for a list of recent purchases. This could be the work of an Establishment team. They probably found what they were looking for and made good their escape."

"Always one step ahead of us," Bindhira said. "What I don't understand is whether or not this Establishment is merely an advance team or a separate entity with its own ambi . . ."

While she was speaking, something caught her eye behind and to the side of Exner. Walking around him, she knelt down just outside the den's entrance and below the cash register. Picking up an object, both Exner and Detective Hardcastle could see that it was a small oval pendant made of gold. The clasp of its gold necklace had been broken.

“There may have been a struggle here,” the detective said, scanning the showcase and floor trim for blood splatter. None was evident. “No blood, that’s a good sign.”

“Yes,” Exner said, “in which case we no longer have a missing person but an abducted one. Detective Hardcastle, I would suggest you involve the RCMP. They have greater resources for this sort of thing than do your Ontario Provincial Police.”

“I understand, sir,” she said.

“Very good,” Exner said. “Please keep us in the loop, would you, Detective?”

“Right sir,” Detective Hardcastle replied.

Bindhira smiled respectfully and handed the broken pendant to the detective. With that, the agents left.

Bindhira had wryly noticed that the pendant was of Saint Barbara, patron saint for protection from harm. Saint Barbara was beheaded as a martyr in 235 AD.

Saint Barbara hadn’t done a very good job protecting the old woman either.

37

Dumping The Evidence

The kidnappers were successful in making a clean getaway. No one had suspected anything suspicious, and except for the friendly fishermen, no one had challenged them. It was dark now and Gino Vaselino, who was piloting the boat, knew they would have to put in soon.

Shing Shen managed to extract the hard drive out of the computer tower they had taken from the gallery office. He threw the tower over the side. Resourcefully, he located a plastic waterproof first aid box under the dashboard of the sport fisherman. He dumped its contents over the side. Shen was pleased that the small leather-bound journal and computer hard drive fit nicely inside. He placed the box into a pouch attached to the side of his seat.

The men had traveled for about twenty minutes when Chen Fa said, "Kill the motor, Mr. Vaselino."

The Cuban powered down the craft. The men remained in their seats until the tail wave caught up and surged beneath them.

"Assist me," Chen Fa commanded.

Even though the dead woman was compressed into a small package, it was difficult to maneuver her up to the gunwale of the rolling boat. They almost had the bundled carpet up high enough to shove it over the side when the entire boat nearly flipped over in the process.

"You idiots!" Chen Fa sputtered. "Shing Shen, go stand on the opposite side for counterbalance. Mr. Vaselino, lift her up higher so I can roll her over the side of the boat."

After much struggling against the action of the swells, maintaining their balance while standing, and finally managing to get the dead woman up and over the top of the high gunwale, Vaselino and Chen Fa plopped in unison to the floor of the boat, both out of breath.

Waves lapped affectionately against the bottom of the boat, and darkness was in full bloom around them. However, a partial waning moon soon revealed itself when a lazy dark cloud drifted by high overhead.

"Uh, Chen Fa?" Shing Shen said, looking over the side of the boat. Chen and Vaselino were still recovering from their struggles.

"What is it, Shen?" Chen Fa asked without looking up.

"We, uh, have a problem."

The men reluctantly came over to where Shing Shen was looking over the side of the boat. There, in the faint light of the moon, the men watched as a tightly bound bundle of carpeting meandered sluggishly away from the boat.

"Arrrraugh!" Chen Fa was livid. "Vaselino, that damned woman's carcass is still floating! Didn't you weight her down?"

"You were there when we wrapped her up, Fa. How come you didn't think of it then? You had no problems thinking about breaking the old woman's legs to stuff her into the damned rug for frig's sakes," Vaselino replied defensively.

"The matter we must concern ourselves with now," Chen Fa said, "is to make sure this woman does not impede us any further!" He was careful not to allow his welling anger at the Cuban to cloud his judgment. Anger caused mistakes, and mistakes were usually terminal in this business.

Vaselino said nothing more. He started the motor and they putted slowly over to the floating roll of carpeting. Shing Shen drew it closer to the side of the boat with a grappling hook.

"Now what?" Gino asked.

"Now, Mr. Vaselino, we must lash it to the side of the boat, troll over to a nearby island, and place a sufficient number of rocks inside so it'll sink for good. Then, we head out to deep water and cut it loose. Get it?"

"Got it."

"Good."

The three men in the stolen Bahia Cruiser trolled for twenty minutes before they reached a small uninhabited island in the middle of Georgian Bay. The shore surrounding the island was littered with thousands of limestone rocks and pebbles of various weights and sizes. It took the three of them nearly an hour to disassemble, load, and repack the carpet coffin of the dead woman for a more weighty burial at sea.

Lashing their heavily laden package securely along the side of the boat, the three headed back out into deep water, where Agnes Braithwaite could trouble them no further.

38

Contact Established

The three men, their two prisoners, and the woman stood outside the hovel. Travers trussed up the two Cubans and sat them down with their backs against the rusted corrugated tin front of the de Quesada residence. Hartley, Travers, and Zayas had taken turns guarding their captives throughout the night while the others slept.

Juan Zayas had driven the minibus up to the hovel and had been working on its bent exhaust pipe as best he could with what he had since early morning.

Mercedes de Quesada sat on her porch shaking, and in tears. Lee Hartley had broken the news of her husband's death in Canada to her and why they were in Cuba—at least as much as she needed to know.

He was careful to leave her with a good memory of her husband. Both Mercedes and Zayas had painted the picture of a man who worked hard and loved his family. Lee didn't see any point in shattering that image and telling her about the terrorist he had become however noble his intentions were for his family. He simply told her that her husband, Javier, had been killed instantly in a car accident in Canada a week ago, not that he had been trapped in a burning building with a bullet in his head while in the midst of a mission to kill thousands of innocent people.

The distraught woman wept silently but with increasing intensity as he spoke.

When he had finished, Lee pulled his wallet out, fumbled through it briefly, then handed the woman the worn photo of her family Exner had given him. He patiently waited until she cried herself out, then continued. "Mercedes, what else can you tell me about Javier? When did you find out that your husband was no longer working the fields?" Lee asked.

"Javier was always good to Maela and me—." Mercedes stopped at the thought of her daughter, then hugged the photo close to her bosom. It took her several moments before she was able to regain control of her emotions. "But he wanted more for us. He wanted so much to work in the resort hotels, but his English was not good enough. If you do not work at the resorts at the bar or in the shops, you are treated very poorly. Javier would never have lasted long in any of those positions. He was a proud man," again a pause as she sobbed, "and I loved him very much."

Lee Hartley was a strong man. He was tougher than most. But even to him this was heart-breaking. Losing a husband, let alone a sole provider, would be devastating for a family in a repressed country such as Cuba. Now she stood to lose even what little she had.

"Did you not know he had left the country?" Lee asked as he gently touched her arm for support.

"No, Señor Lee. One evening several weeks ago, a man came to our home. Javier went outside with him and I saw them walk down to the road. They were gone for over an hour. When they returned and the man left, Javier came in to me. He was so happy. He said we would soon be able to find another home, a nicer home. But he had to go away first. I could tell it would be as hard for him as it would be for me. But I supported his decision. He had never made love to me like he did that night. It was wonderful."

She had the far-away memory-laden gaze of a woman who had been very much in love as she looked out over the desolate field. It was evident that she and Javier had had a very special bond between them. Lee felt deep down that Javier's involvement in all of this was borne of the love for his family and not politically motivated. Still in all, he reasoned, that didn't make it right.

"Do you remember anything about the man that visited you that night? His name: anything?" Lee was hoping the woman could give him a much-needed lead.

"He wore a very nice suit," she began, "so I thought he must be a government man. It frightened me when he came to the door, but Javier was happy to see him and that made me feel less nervous. But still I did not like him. I did not trust him even though he was very nice to me. I could not follow all of their conversation from inside our home. But I could make out bits and pieces of it. They were out by the man's car. It was a fancy newer car. The man must have been very rich. "Javier called him . . ." Mercedes pulled back a lock of long black hair from her eye. "He called him . . . Alberto. Yes, Alberto."

Lee made a mental note. He pulled his flask out and took a pull before returning it to the waistband of his shorts. "Mercedes, did Javier give you any timeframe as to when he would be coming back," he asked.

"No, *Señor* Lee. He only said that he would come home as soon as he could, but not to be worried if he was gone for a long while. He told me that we would be living a lot better once he came back, and that being poor would soon be all behind us. But without my beloved Javier, without my lovely Maela, I have no need to live, *Señor* Lee," she sobbed.

"Mercedes, you mustn't think these things," Lee said consolingly. "We can't help Javier, but we'll do our best to find your daughter and bring to justice those who brought this terrible grief upon you."

Her daughter Maela had been kidnapped, her husband killed. Lee could only imagine what Mercedes de Quesada was going through. There was no need to muddy the waters any further by telling her the truth. He determined in his heart to do his best to find the poor woman's daughter. That would at least restore some sunlight to the woman's troubled soul.

Mercedes suddenly drew close to Lee and embraced him. She sobbed quietly on his shoulder. Big, tough, commercial diver, black belt—in spite of all this, Lee Hartley came very close to tears himself. He gently broke free of her embrace, grasped her by an elbow, and walked with her to a low-lying flat-topped boulder, where he helped her to sit down.

Zayas came over to them. He had grease on his face, arms, and clothes. "The bus, it is fixed now, *señor*," he exclaimed proudly. "I must go back into town. Word must reach your superiors in Canada that you and *Señor* Travers are up here."

"Not a good idea from my perspective, Juan," Lee said warily. "We can't afford to lose you now. You know the countryside and how we got here. Besides, that just leaves Travers and me to handle the two monkeys," he said, and pointed over his shoulder to where Travers held them under his watchful squinty eye and the barrel of his rifle.

Zayas looked to Lee as if a thought had just come to him. "Oh. *Señor* Exner told me when you got established here to let him know and to give you a special radio. With it you can talk to him."

Lee was waiting for Juan Zayas to say something, but he remained silent.

"Sooo, what's the skinny on the radio, Juan?"

Zayas looked down at his feet for a few seconds, saw a stone, and kicked it away before he confessed. "Forgive me, but I forgot to bring the radio with me, *Señor* Hartley." Then he added optimistically, "But I will bring it back when I return. There are spies everywhere in this area, *señor*, and if I do not return very soon they will come to look for me. This bus, it is not mine. It belongs to someone I know, and he will wonder where I have gone with it so long."

"What do you mean by 'spies everywhere,' Juan?" Lee said with growing concern.

"*El Comandante*, he has men everywhere, especially at the resorts. They watch everyone that comes into Cuba. They especially watch the people who work at such places. His brother Raul, he runs our country now, or so they say. But it does not matter who runs our country, they trust no one."

"So, Juan, do you think anyone followed us up here? Is that why these men returned with Mercedes, because they were looking for us?" Lee asked, a troubled look crossing his face.

"I do not think so, *señor*, but I cannot be for sure. I need to get back to my comrades who will assist us if we should need their help. But if I do not return very soon, there will be many questions about where I went with the bus and why."

Lee looked over to Travers. It was a funny sight, if the situation wasn't so potentially dangerous. Travers hadn't moved since he and the woman had come out of the house. He was facing the two men, sitting on an old upside-down metal pail, rifle at the ready. He never took his eyes off his prisoners.

"Okay, Juan. Do what you must, but do it quickly. We'll remain here until tomorrow. Bring our scuba gear and grab some extra tanks from the resort dive shop. Make sure you get word to Exner, and then get your buns back here as soon as you can."

Juan was pleased to be of such service to the Canadian agents. "Yes, Señor Lee. I will also bring some trusted men back to help when I return tomorrow." He started to leave for the minibus.

"Oh, and Juan?" Lee asked.

"Si, señor?"

"The radio. Don't forget the damned radio."

"Oh, *si*. I will bring the radio for you as well," Juan said importantly with a big grin. He saluted Lee, then headed for the bus.

The ancient horseless chariot fired up with a shimmy, a loud bang, and several seconds of black smoke before Juan was able to put it in gear. As he backed around to head down the trail, Lee saw him wave. He watched the little bus rumble down the lane until the trailing dust enveloped it completely. He suddenly felt very alone, and if truth be told, a little nervous.

39

Identity Confirmed

The twenty-three-foot Bahia cruiser carrying the three enemy agents made Manitoulin Island by dawn the next day. They had finally been successful in sending Agnes Braithwaite to a watery grave at the bottom of Georgian Bay.

Manitoulin is a large island that lies at the top of Georgian Bay and Lake Huron where the Niagara Escarpment meets the Canadian Shield. It is sparsely populated, but a more direct gateway to Northern Ontario.

Hundreds of vehicles leave Tobermory each summer via the large ferry MS *Chi-Cheemaun* for the two-hour, thirty-mile passage across the Main Channel to the island. The ferry provides a shortcut to and from northern Ontario, alleviating a long drive around Georgian Bay by allowing motorists to drive through the island and exit by bridge at its northernmost tip.

Their goal was to make land in a small inlet a few miles northeast of the South Baymouth ferry landing. They were careful to avoid any marinas in the likely event that the stolen outrigger had been reported.

A good plan, were it not for the fact that they ran out of gas a mile or so from the island.

"Mr. Vaselino," said Chen Fa in a carefully measured even tone. "You stole a boat without checking to see if it carried an adequate fuel supply?"

The Cuban had had enough. "Look, Fa, we are lucky to have the damned thing at all. Need I remind you that I 'acquired' it from a busy marina in the heart of one of the most popular tourist areas in all of Ontario?"

"Vaselino, you and Shen start paddling. I require time to think," Chen Fa said. The look he gave the Cuban was enough to keep him silent.

Not long afterward, dawn began to break. They saw the island and picked up their pace. It had taken over ninety minutes to get as far as they had. Both Vaselino and Shing Shen were exhausted by this time.

To their horror and dismay, upon drawing closer to the island they discovered they were landing exactly where they were trying to avoid—the ferry dock! Undaunted, the two rowers found renewed energy within themselves, and picked up their pace. Suddenly, a bullhorn blared.

"Ahoy, the fishing boat. This is a restricted area. You are unauthorized to dock here and must withdraw immediately!"

Chen Fa looked to the sky, hands in the air. "Vaselino, this trip just keeps getting better with you aboard. So much for stealth, *you fool!*"

"Shut up, Fa, and put your friggin' hands down! We're not fugitives yet. YOU finish rowing with Shing," Vaselino yelled.

Within minutes a Zodiac with two men on board zipped out from the fortified dock area and pulled alongside their boat. When the terrorists explained their plight, the Zodiac returned to base, and within minutes came back to them with a small red plastic fuel container.

The man at the bow of the Zodiac said, "Get this thing out of here now! The ferry will be here in minutes! You've lucky we don't report you to the coast guard!"

Chen Fa took the one-gallon container and handed it to Vaselino who took it and filled their gas tank with its contents. "Thank you, so sorry," Fa said, as he handed back the empty container.

With that, the Zodiac zipped back to its berth. The three men saw the huge hulk of the *Chi-Cheemaun* bearing down on them. Within minutes it would be docking

Vaselino tried several times to engage the engine. Finally the twin Volvo Penta V8s sputtered to life, and he pushed the throttle all the way forward just as the ferry issued several loud warning blasts of its horn. The Bahia cruiser left a huge wake as it roared back out from the sheltered bay of the ferry dock and into open water.

Within minutes, Vaselino found a small uninhabited inlet large enough to accommodate the cruiser. Pulling in, he ran it aground into the sand. There was a sudden heavy grating sound and hard lurch forward as its bottom impacted the sand, sending Chen Fa and Shing Shen to the floor of the vessel. The Cuban maintained his balance only because he had been holding onto the top of the windshield.

Several expletives were exchanged as the men struggled to regain their balance. Vaselino laughed inwardly at his two passengers.

"Quickly. Get your belongings and get out," Chen Fa said. "We must operate on the premise that the men at the ferry dock have radioed in our description and actions to the coast guard. They will discover that ours is the stolen boat and will come to investigate. We have little time."

They tossed their gear out and jumped from the boat and ran for the security of the small woodland bordering the shore. Once safely concealed within, Shing Shen produced the waterproof first aid kit and handed it to Chen Fa.

"Thank you, Shing Shen. You have done well." Turning to Vaselino he said, "And you also, Mr. Vaselino. In spite of yourself, you managed to deliver us out of harm's way, for now."

The others watched intently as Chen Fa placed the small first aid kit on the flat spot of a nearby boulder, and opened it. He extracted the gallery journal and went down the list of names, postal codes, and item descriptions of all major gallery transactions made over the past two months.

Scanning the last several pages, Fa noticed five consignment packages that had Travers' name attached to them. "Recognize any of the purchasers, Mr. Vaselino?"

The Cuban perused the pages. "I can account for only two of them, Fa. They are Cuban buyers the Establishment had in place for pick up." He pointed them out to the Chinese man.

"Hmmm," Chen Fa said. "I myself can account for two more. One is a Chinese national staying with 'relatives' in Toronto. The other is from the same part of China as Huang Fu; a most trustworthy agent indeed."

"That leaves this couple: a Mr. and Mrs. Applegate." Vaselino studied the entry for a few moments. "Hey, Fa, look at this. Their address is listed as *Forever Young*."

"What kind of address is this, Mr. Vaselino?" Shing Shen asked.

"That address, Mr. Shen, just happens to be the name of the large sail boat that was three berths up and one across from the one I commandeered our boat from. It is still in town!" Vaselino proudly explained. "If that boat is still berthed in Tobermory, we have our painting!"

"And the finalized viral agent!" exclaimed Chen Fa.

"We were so close; bad luck has followed us at every turn," Vaselino said. "Well, we cannot risk returning in this boat to Tobermory, Fa." he said. "Anyway, there's not enough fuel left in the tank even if we wanted to."

Shing Shen spoke up. "No, but as you recall, the ferry has just come in. I noticed on the posted schedule at the dock that the vessel does not go out for another two hours due to refueling."

"You are an observant agent, one worthy of your country and position, Shing Shen. Well done!" Chen Fa smiled broadly as he patted the man's shoulder in triumph. Shing Shen beamed proudly.

"Gather up what you need," Fa said. "Leave the rest. We must get back to the dock at once!" Chen Fa said, tucking the journal into the rear of his pants.

40

Project Vector

Wu Yang took a leisurely stroll down Little Cove Road the next morning to the Bay of the same name, the omnipresent cane at his side. In his line of business, one never knew when a dose of tetrodotoxin would come in handy against unexpected miscreants.

Yang loved to walk. It gave him time to meditate, to think, to plan. The road he had taken for his walk was less travelled, and lined with green coniferous trees of various denominations: Douglas firs, blue spruce, and various cedars. He loved the pine scent of the distinctly scented resin these trees secreted to protect them against insect infestations and fungal infections.

Choi Li had reported that his team was unable to locate either William Travers or Lee Hartley in the Niagara region. On the northern front, Wu Yang had yet to receive any communication from Chen Fa. But he was not worried. Chen Fa was one of his most trusted agents, and unlike the bungling Cubans, could be thoroughly trusted to successfully execute his mission.

He was glad to split up Rodriguez and Vaselino. The Cubans had already lost several of their team. Without Chinese assistance, there was no doubt in his mind they would have compromised the whole operation.

It would be preferable to eliminate the whole populace of Cuba and replenish it with obedient Chinese subjects, thought Wu Yang. Then China would have a firmly entrenched base in the Western Hemisphere. Cuba was such a beautiful place. But of course this was wishful, albeit entertaining thinking.

That old bastard Fidel and his "yes man" puppet brother Raul had had their day. For over forty years, *ten* different US administrations had tried without success to liquidate the now physically faltering iron-willed dictator and topple his regime.

Upon Fidel's death, China knew, the fool Raul would soon cave to the Americans. Almost immediately there would be a McDonald's on every corner, and condominiums would litter every beach front. Raul was already loosening the reins somewhat to that effect.

Cubans would fare just as poorly under the Americans as under the Castros, he mused. Americans weren't even able to take care of their own people. Hurricane Katrina and the New Orleans fiasco of 2005 were proof enough of that. No, they would just do what Americans were loved to be hated for the world over: invade, conquer, and exploit. Even Wu Yang grimaced at the thought.

Wind gusts today were sudden and strong as Wu Yang walked along the gravel road. A lesser person would simply have turned around and gone home. He was glad he practiced the Yang style Tai Chi short form before his walk. It served to strengthen his *chi*, the internal strength accrued from assiduous practice over the years.

Wu Yang was caught up in thought. *Project Vector* was his ticket to immortality. When it was all over, China would emerge as the sole superpower of the world—without firing a missile.

Yang smiled to himself. Except for some temporary glitches, he gloated over their achievements so far. Several *Establishment* operatives were already in place around the Great Lakes Region, the heartland of North America, preparing the area for *Project Vector*. Upon successful completion of phase one, phase two would be automatically initiated soon thereafter.

The use of an innocent dupe like Travers smuggling their wares and correspondence into Canada was a novel way of throwing authorities off the scent. A frequent flier to Cuba, with no police record, and no affiliation to any form of organized crime, the old fool easily enabled the Establishment to breach North American security defenses.

Unlike the stupidly arrogant Middle Eastern terrorists who had the egomaniacal desire to take credit for their amateurish and cowardly acts of indiscriminate mayhem, members of the ChIS, together with like-minded agents of the DGI who were aligned with the Establishment, had managed to accomplish far more behind the scenes. It made the others look like the rank amateurs they were.

Industrial accidents, "unexplained" gas explosions in governmental field corporation fronts, massive oil rig spills, cruise ship "mishaps," airline disappearances . . . on and on it went. It was all carefully orchestrated to make the West and their greedy capitalistic exploits look foolishly dangerous before the world, while furthering Chinese causes in the West. ChIS agents were even suspected of being largely responsible for the near financial collapse of the European Union. Even the in-fighting between its member countries was no coincidence.

Project Vector, Wu Yang hoped, would be instrumental in pitting the United States and Canada against each other for petty ineptitudes, as engineered by the Chinese and perfected in Europe.

If all went according to plan, the United States would be financially ruined by Vector. Major installations and corporations along the freshwater coastlines would be among the first to be affected with waves of sickness and death via the dissemination of the deadly Ebola virus hybrid. There would be no one to man the facilities once it became evident that people were dying from a mysterious virus in their midst.

China would of course stand ready to lend financial assistance by acquiring such "high risk" facilities "legally," then milking them of their technology despite the "inherent danger" carefully contrived within the affected compounds.

Yes, thought Wu Yang, this has been a good walk. He smiled smugly to himself. He had reason to. For far too many years, China had been the laughing stock of the world. She had always been considered a backward country with infinite possibilities, the Sleeping Giant of old, far removed from the complexities of modern society.

Well China was no longer the Sleeping Giant. The world would soon see China for what she had aspired to be—a dragon, the next and final superpower to achieve world domination!

The National People's Congress of the People's Republic of China, the highest organ of state power in China, had done a remarkable job of establishing a complex and impenetrable array of smoke and mirrors within the world's major corporate and political structures over the past several years.

Wu Yang was proud to have played a part in this. The aging ChIS agent would soon be taking a major share of glory for his contribution to China's coming world domination. But it would be a China run not by a political party, but by a true party of the people, ruled by himself and select members of the Establishment as chosen by him.

Wu Yang played out the plan in his mind once again for which he had contributed a significant part. It was to be his crowning success, his gift to the People's Republic of China.

Project Vector was borne of excruciatingly complex planning and considerable cost. To freeze-dry and impregnate simple biodegradable booklets of matches with a modified viral strain was cutting-edge and ingenious.

Water pressure at varying depths would prime them much like fuses for time-release into the atmosphere, unless triggered remotely. Those planted closest to the surface would take much longer to mature before those placed deeper in the lakes.

Gases generated when their compression phase was complete would easily override the calibrated spring of their brass "coffins," which would pop the top off the boxes, sending the deadly virus to the surface should the boxes be prevented from detonating manually. Within days, the airborne virus would infect hundreds—thousands of people, most of whom would die gruesome deaths.

The fresh water of Georgian Bay was to be the first "launch site." With a lower specific gravity than sea water, release settings were slightly lower for freshwater installations. One atmosphere of saltwater was twice the pressure of air at sea level, 29.4 psi, which equated to a depth of thirty-three feet. Lesser dense freshwater required thirty-four feet of water to equal the same pressure. For each additional thirty-four feet of fresh water depth, an additional 14.7 psi was added to the total pressure at which an object was subjected to. Such calculations were critical when requiring a longer cure rate.

True viral compression was possible in laboratories, but the plan devised was nothing short of genius, and one that required little in the way of cumbersome equipment, which could easily be detected.

Having divers submerge hundreds of matchbooks in several sealed brass boxes in shipwrecks off the coastlines of major ports along the Great Lakes would not only prime them according to depth, but also conceal them from any means of surface detection. The boxes would protect their contents from the effects of current, sea life, and metal detection once divers had carefully deposited them as instructed.

The beauty of this type of dissemination was that there were literally hundreds of such wrecks in the Great Lakes. Attempting to locate the actual ships containing the viral boxes would prove an impossible and fruitless task even if the plan were to be discovered.

Once phase one was initiated, phase two became an automatic extension of the operation, which was infecting the breeding grounds of mosquitoes, wasps, and black flies where they matured and multiplied. There were untold thousands of wetlands, ponds, and areas of standing water around the Great Lakes region. The insects would spread the Ebola farther inland, affecting thousands more. The results would be catastrophic and North America would be ripe for the picking.

Once Vector became fully operational, the Cuban cell members would be eliminated. The People's Republic of China could not afford to have their Cuban friends sabotage their efforts once they realized their own homeland was slated to suffer the same blight.

The Cubans had their place in the grand scheme of things, but once they had served their purpose, even the greedy Castro regime was earmarked for extinction. The two old fools wouldn't know what hit them. The vehicle of their destruction already lay dormant off their shores, waiting for the appropriate time. One could not be too careful, thought Wu Yang, or it would fail to be a foolproof plan.

He arrived at the beach, inhaled a fresh, deep breath of lake air, and admired its beauty. Little Cove Beach was bowl shaped and covered with smooth rounded limestone rocks, which added to its quaintness. Being small, rocky, and remote prevented the masses from covering the beach with semi-nude bodies in August when summer was at its hottest.

Indeed, this was a beautiful place here in the middle of nowhere. Yes, thought Wu Yang, what better place for the beginnings of a carefully engineered world catastrophe?

41

What Goes Around Comes Around

Juan Zayas was true to his word. Exner received confirmation from his Cuban contact the following morning that his men Lee Hartley and Bill Travers had arrived safely, and informed him of their current status. What Zayas failed to mention was that Hartley intended to rescue the de Quesada girl which wasn't part of the plan.

Zayas, a senior lieutenant in the Cuban Underground Freedom Movement, was hopeful that when this was all over and the Chinese left as the Russians had some twenty years ago, his beloved Cuba would be free at last, even of the Castro regime.

He had spent most of his adult life working underground resistance in the bid to live in a free Cuba. He wanted, as did his compatriots, to live in a country free of dictators and free of countries that sought to use them like Russia, like China. He would also work to free her from the Americans if it came to that.

But freedom from the Castros would be the best freedom of all. Over fifty years of oppression, of deprivation, of loss of dignity for many. The time has come for these things to end once and for all.

Several of his brothers within the movement had disappeared over the years, never to be seen again. Others had been tortured, several killed. It was dangerous business opposing *el Comandante's Revolución* government to be sure, but many were tired of the poverty and empty promises of the Castro regime, and were determined to undermine it at every opportunity.

Pedro Rey Ramirez and Luis Perez Sosa were loyal to the cause and had worked with Zayas on several occasions. Ramirez was in charge of the Chivirico unit. Both he and Sosa were efficient and well-trusted within the movement. They had been commandos in Castro's army and were very good at what they did. Both were eager to meet the Canadians and assist them in any way possible. Their knowledge of troop movements and patrol boat patterns around the island would no doubt come in handy.

Pedro Ramirez left Chivirico in a black 1958 Series II Land Rover that he had acquired from one of their safe house locations and proceeded to Hotel Brisas Sierra Mar, where he picked up Luis Sosa with the Canadians' belongings and dive gear.

The dive shop manager at the hotel had also included four fully charged scuba tanks, two weight belts, and several other items he thought they might need. The manager had worked for them before and would be well paid for this service.

They then picked up Zayas outside the resort when they refueled the Rover before the arduous trek up the mountains.

They knew that Castro had eyes everywhere; and to do everything as inconspicuously as possible would mean they would live to see another day. Each member of the unit had been well trained to avoid detection in all of their dealings, which included not being tailed at any time.

Zayas learned that the Chinese had had divers in the water near the vicinities of several shipwrecks around the island nation. He was hoping that the Canadian divers would have an idea why. For now, he had to get back to Hartley with the Seqpod satellite radio.

Lee Hartley removed the restraints of their two captives under the watchful eye, and rifle, of Bill Travers. Their captives needed a good stretch and something to eat. As they ate, Lee asked Pork Barrel, "I'm only going to ask you once, because I have absolutely no use for piss-ants like you who use little girls as leverage. Where is she? Where is the de Quesada girl?"

The large Cuban had his mouth full of scrambled eggs that Mercedes had grudgingly made for them. The fat man looked up from the can that housed his brunch, looked up at Lee, then turned, and forcefully spit the food out.

"You come to our country and you get involved in our affairs, involved in things of which you know nothing about. This does not bode well for either of you, *señor*."

He looked over at his thin comrade. "Miguel and I, we are prepared to die." He laughed up at Lee and included Travers in the gesture. Travers slammed the stock of the rifle against the side of their jeering captive's face. The Cuban let out a grunt, turning his head in the direction of the blow so as to minimize its effects.

It seemed to loosen him up somewhat. "The girl was our insurance that de Quesada would be a good soldier when he left Cuba," he offered reluctantly. "But then he got himself killed in your country." The Cuban paused and then looked down to the ground. "The girl was of no further use to us, except for—"

In midsentence Lee grabbed the man by the throat and threw him to the ground. The surprised man staggered back to his feet, choking. Pork Barrel swung a haymaker at Lee who easily dodged the lumbering limb, then struck a powerful blow to the exposed kidney of his attacker.

The surprised Cuban wobbled back, huffing and puffing. Meanwhile, Travers had the thin man with his face to the wall, legs spread apart. He enjoyed watching Lee slapping Pork Barrel around.

The fat man came in once again, this time low, in an attempt to take Lee to the ground. As the man dived into Lee, Hartley leapt up into a double knee strike that caught the man squarely under the chin. He fell flat onto his back, unconscious.

"Don't tell me you killed him, Lee," Travers said.

Suddenly Miguel threw a heel kick up and into Travers' groin. Travers doubled over, lowering his rifle to the ground. The Cuban wrestled over the rifle with Travers, but the older man was stronger and heavier than his attacker. A single punch on the chin with his non-gun hand spun the slight man around and down to the ground.

The Canadians waited until the two slowly pulled themselves up to a standing position. Lee took the rifle from Travers, cocked the carbine, and leveled it at Pork Barrel's chest.

Mercedes was dumbfounded at everything she had seen and heard. She rested her head against the doorframe and began to cry convulsively.

Feeling her sense of hopelessness, Lee turned back to the fat man. "You're not going to tell me anything, are you?"

"Go to hell, you bastard!" With that he spat in Lee's face.

"Montoya!" Miguel shouted.

Lee calmly looked the man in the eye. "You really shouldn't have done that." He smiled faintly and looked down. He then raised his eyes up to meet the Cuban's, and without taking his eyes off the man's face, fired a round into Pork Barrel's left foot. Lee then wiped the spit off his face with the bottom of his shirt.

This took the piss and vinegar out of Pork Barrel. He howled and hobbled and howled some more. He sat down, he stood up, and he cursed and carried on, until finally Travers had had enough and pushed him against the side of the hovel, denting its corrugated steel in the process. The big man slid to the ground clutching his wounded foot.

Miguel was both shocked and surprised at this unexpected turn of events. He was led to believe that Canadians were peaceful people. Travers trussed him up again, and motioned him over to sit beside his wounded comrade.

Lee checked the foot wound. "Bullet went right through. We'll clean it up and get it bandaged *after* you tell us where we can find the girl."

The man was in a lot of pain. His breathing was heavy and erratic. Pork Barrel, aka Montoya, looked up at Lee Hartley with all the contempt he could muster.

Silence. It was a showdown. Lee aimed the rifle at the man's other foot. "I'll bet I have more bullets in this rifle than you have guts, my friend," he said. Lee cocked the carbine again for dramatic effect. A cartridge ejected and hit Miguel square on the nose. He wasn't impressed.

"All right; *all right!*" Pork Barrel wasn't as tough as he looked. "She is in a safe house. Raul said no harm was to befall her, that she would be okay."

"Raul, as in Raul *Castro*?" Travers asked. The man nodded dejectedly.

Miguel spoke in rapid-fire Spanish to Pork Barrel. He obviously wasn't well versed in English. All the Canadians got out of the impassioned one-way conversation was that Montoya mustn't give in.

The big man, Montoya, fired back a reply to Miguel. His words sounded defeated but resolute, to which no response came from the thin man.

Lee went to Mercedes who had remained in the doorway, her back still turned away from them. Together they went into the hovel. Coming out moments later, Mercedes carried a small bowl of water and a towel. Lee had a clean pair of socks and a knife. He cleaned the man's bloodied foot up and bandaged it by wrapping the socks around the wound using an old piece of string to tie it off.

"What kind of op are you running here, anyway?" Lee asked, raising his rifle to the man's groin.

Mercedes left them and soon returned with a moistened facecloth. She placed it on Montoya's forehead, then backed away and ran back into the house.

"DGI is working with the Chinese Secret Service on a plan that cannot fail, and one in which you will not live to see executed," Montoya said derisively.

"What plan is that, Montoya?" Lee asked.

"We will bring the United States of America to her knees. We will succeed where others have failed!"

Travers came over and stood beside Lee. He looked down at Montoya and said, "You're all a bunch of screw-ups, Montoya. Your leaders couldn't *handle* running the world; shit, they can't even run this stinkin' little island."

This angered Montoya, who tried to get up but the pain was too great. Miguel looked over at Montoya and said something no doubt derogatory in Spanish to them, then looked down in defeat.

"Well, Montoya," said Lee, looking at the both of them. "You're going to take us to this 'safe-house,' and we're going to return Mercedes' daughter to her. Then you're going to tell us everything you know and more about this 'plan' of yours. He placed the rifle barrel against Montoya's forehead where he sat.

"You Canadians are supposed to be *peacekeepers*," Montoya moaned.

"Underestimating Canadians is your first mistake," Lee said. "We don't take kindly to terrorists, much less child abusers. If we get Maela back," he continued, "you have my word that we'll let you and your sidekick go."

"If we don't or if we find out she's dead, you'll see how many *pieces* of you we decide to *keep* and how many we throw to the sharks."

42

Forever Young

Tobermory is a picture-postcard village in late summer. The bowl-shaped Little Tub Harbor was surrounded by quaint little shops, galleries, and restaurants. The boardwalk was a popular meeting place for scuba divers and yachtsmen. Its long expanse overlooked the numerous dive charter boats, tour boats, and lengthy expensive yachts resting in their berths within the Tub.

Alan Exner had just come out of the small satellite OPP station. Bindhira was at the wheel of the TaZeR. As Exner got in and buckled up, she asked, "What do they know so far, Alan?"

"Take us to the marina, Bindhi. We have a name and a place. The OPP were advised by CSEC to stand down until we got there."

Without word, she engaged the powerful engine and left the station in a cloud of dust as they headed toward the center of town.

On the way, a wry smile crossed Exner's face. "We've a good lead, Bindhi. There was an older couple, a man and wife, who came to the gallery a day or so ago. They were interested in several pieces at the gallery. The couple said there were three men in the gallery while they were there. The woman said they made her feel nervous, and that they seemed pretty shifty. Two of the men were Chinese. They seemed anxious for them to leave."

Bindhira pulled the TaZeR into one of the last available parking spots in front of Little Tub Harbor. As they got out, she said, "That's it? That's your lead?"

Exner led her down a slip where several large sailing yachts were moored. He stopped to look at her. "Turns out they know of a Caucasian couple who recently bought a Cuban painting from the gallery!"

"You're joking," she said. Were it not for Exner grabbing her by the arm, she would have fallen into the water when her high heel caught on a mooring rope tightly bound to its cleat.

He smiled at her, and she nervously smiled back. "I spend too much time saving you to be joking," he replied.

They stopped for a few moments so Bindhira could regain her composure. Exner could see that she enjoyed the nautical atmosphere of the marina.

He continued. "The gallery couple met the art purchasers, Stuart and Patricia Applegate, up here. Turns out both couples own sizeable yachts and have put into Tobermory here and there throughout the summer."

"No priors on the Applegates. Seems like the stereotypical retired couple. Mr. Applegate made his fortune in the insurance business. Now they sail the seven seas, and uh, the five Great Lakes. The couple from the gallery said the name of the vessel we're looking for is . . . ," and with a sweep of his hand, directed Bindhira's gaze to the stern of the vessel they were approaching. Its name was the '*Forever Young*'."

The vessel appeared unoccupied. The two agents called out but received no reply. With a mutual glance, Exner assisted Bindhira up the small gangplank and onto the deck of the vessel. In well-trained fashion, Exner silently circled his finger for Bindhira to check around the main deck while he went below.

After several minutes, she came down the gangway to find Exner studying the wall of the main stateroom. To the right of the queen-sized bed was displayed a large over-framed painting of a sizeable sailing vessel rounding a point protected by a stately lighthouse. Several gulls circled the air above the cutter, and whitecaps broke around the bow of the ship, which indicated she was well underway. The sky was picture-perfect blue, with a radiant sun partially masked by large, fluffy cumulus clouds. Exner could see why they bought it for their stateroom.

Bindhira lifted the painting off the wall. Exner remained by the door. Laying the painting face-down on the bed, she stepped back to cover the door while Exner came over and, using his razor-sharp pocket knife, cleanly cut around the wrapping behind the artwork.

He extracted several small packets and several sheets of letter-sized paper. Lifting them aloft to Bindhira in triumph, they broke out into smiles.

"Well done, Sherlock," Bindhira said.

"Actually it's elementary, Watson. Methinks the game's afoot," Exner exclaimed in his best impression of Sherlock Holmes.

Looking around the room, Exner located a gym bag that sported a Fitness Revolution gym logo on it. Removing a pair of navy blue leggings, white sports bra, and pink Nike athletic shoes from the bag, Exner found it ideal to house their findings.

Carefully opening one of the packets with his pocket knife, Exner found a few dozen or so smaller packets of what appeared to be regular-sized matchbooks, the complimentary kind from a bygone era that used to be found in glass bowls for patrons at bars, hotels, and the like. The documents were in both Spanish and Chinese. These would need to be translated.

He shoved the gym items under the bed, and then carefully placed the documents, packets, and matchbooks into the gym bag.

Bindhira carefully replaced the painting back on the wall while Exner cleaned up the portions of wrappings he had peeled off the back of the painting. "No sense leaving a mess and alarming our hosts," said Exner.

The two came up on deck, making sure beforehand that no one was near the vessel before they departed down the slip, precious cargo in hand.

As they walked to the parking area, Exner grabbed Bindhira's arm. "Bindhi, look: the red Nissan that nearly ran you down!"

The agents sprinted to the sports car. Exner approached from the front, Bindhira from the rear, weapons drawn. No one was inside or anywhere near the vehicle. Exner felt the hood. "Hmmm, hood's cold. It's been here for some time," he said holstering his weapon.

They scanned the perimeter to see if anyone paid any undue attention to them. No one had. Exner motioned Bindhira to follow him to the TaZeR.

Once inside, Exner swung the dashboard clock around, revealing a series of buttons. Bindhira climbed into the passenger seat beside him. He pushed a button, and the onboard computer screen in the middle of the dashboard illuminated. Punching in a series of coordinates brought an aerial view of the parking lot over the TaZeR into view. He fine-tuned the image down until the little "ants" on the ground were revealed as people that milled around the car park going about their business.

He then punched in the timeframe he wanted to observe and hit another button. A different screen came up. This one began to fast-forward images on the screen. Exner watched as the time stamp in the bottom-right corner of the screen began to advance quicker and quicker.

"Nothing out of the ordinary here, Bindhi," he said.

He entered another time parameter, hit another button. Setting the system to scan, they watched the screen intently for several minutes.

Suddenly Bindhira called out, "There! Back up a few frames, Alan. More . . . more. That's it! That's *him*! That's the man who tried to run me over, Alan," she cried out.

The video showed the red GT-R wheeling into the car park. Almost before it stopped, a thin, well-dressed Oriental man emerged from the driver's side. Another man of similar ethnicity exited from the backseat. A third man, taller and stockier than the others and of unknown ethnicity, emerged from the forward passenger side. They crossed the street.

Exner and Bindhira watched as the three men casually walked up the cobblestone pathway that led to the front door of the art gallery. One positioned himself at the entrance of the gallery, the other two went inside.

After a few minutes Exner said, "Look at this!" He fine-tuned the picture quality. They watched as a middle-aged couple came up the walk and into the gallery. "These must be the 'nautical people,'" Bindhira said.

They watched with increasing incredulity. They saw the couple as they left empty-handed. Ten minutes later in real time, they watched as one of the men left and quickly walked behind the rear of an adjoining building before doubling back to the Nissan. He grabbed something out of the trunk. It was a silver metal carry-on case, probably aluminum. He returned to the gallery with it, this time through the front door.

Another period of time went by. Soon the same man exited with the case. He retraced his steps and returned it to the trunk of the sports car.

Fast forwarding another half hour or so, they watched with rapt attention as the taller man came from out of nowhere, appearing from the bottom of the screen, along the sidewalk that led to the marina.

"How did he get out? I did not see him exit the building with the first man, did you, Alan?" Bindhira questioned.

"No," Alan paused, his mind in high gear. "He must have exited from the rear of the building. If he came from the marina he would have had a fair walk through the brush at the back of the gallery until he came to the highway, then would've had to double back down the main drag to the water."

They continued to watch the footage. Soon thereafter, the three men in question filed out of the gallery entrance. Two of them struggled as they carried a rolled-up rug between them.

The men came directly down the cobblestone pathway towards the main village car park. They paused at the curb for a few moments as several cars passed by on the upwardly curving road to the higher part of town, then crossed the street.

"My god Alan, they must be carrying the Braithwaite woman's body inside that carpet roll!" Eyes glued to the screen she added, "Surely she can't be *that* small, Alan."

"I can't see it either," Alan agreed. "But she must be in there; that's why they're struggling. The question now is where have they taken it?"

As the two watched the drama unfold off the TaZeR's satellite-beamed Sequoia recordings, they followed the three men down to the last slip, where they unceremoniously tossed the carpet wrapped body of Mrs. Braithwaite into the bottom of a fishing boat.

One man jumped into the boat and started the inboard motors while the other two tossed in the bow and stern mooring lines before hopping into the boat themselves. Moments later they were gone, taking with them the broken body of poor old Mrs. Braithwaite.

"Can you track them out in the bay?" Bindhira asked as Alan pushed more buttons and fine-tuned more dials.

"The Sequoia sat-trac is only designed to recall recorded land-based, close-proximity activity wherever the TaZeR is currently located. As cool as that is, it's only capable of tracking a square-mile radius at that, Bindhi," Exner explained, obviously frustrated.

"At least we partially solved the mystery of the missing Mrs. Braithwaite," Bindhira said.

"We also know," Exner added, "that they were heading north-northwest when they left the dock. That would take them to Manitoulin Island, some thirty miles from here. The ferry makes several trips a day from Tobermory to Manitoulin loaded with vehicles as a shortcut to the north as an alternative to having to drive all around the bay."

"As to why they were headed there . . ."

43

La Revolución Revisited

A tall, frail old man looked out over the seascape spread before him from the second floor balcony of his favorite villa. His hands were characteristically clasped behind him, and the brisk Caribbean Sea breeze blew through his thin gray hair. He never ceased to enjoy listening to the rustling leaves of the royal palm trees that framed the villa as the perpetual breeze coming off the ocean gently massaged their fronds.

He had done much in his life and had no regrets. However, the stress of his profession had taken its toll on his eighty-eight year old body. He moved slowly when he walked now, and used the chairs and tables around the villa to support him as he navigated through.

The perpetual comfort he had derived from smoking his favorite cigars had long since been forsaken and all but forgotten at his doctor's urgent admonitions. He still missed smoking a *Cohiba* now and then, but he knew they had been slowly killing him, so he quit smoking several years ago to slow the process down, if even a little.

"Another *fantastico* day my dear brother," he said to the other person sitting on a patio deck chair. "The years, they have come and they have gone so quickly." He gripped the railing with both hands, both to steady himself and to lean over to conceal the tiny tear that oozed from his left eye.

"Indeed they have, my brother. But we have done well, you and I," the other man said. The other man was a little shorter and looked much younger than the eighty-three-year-old that he was. "The Americans, they could not touch us. All these years they have tried. *Si*," he reflected, "they have tried. But we are still here and they are still there, where they belong. You have managed to keep Cuba free of its enemies, and I am proud to have been a part of your success."

"My success," the frail older man said, "lies in the fact that I have surrounded myself with good people. People I could trust, people who would, who have, laid down their lives for me and for our *Revolución*."

"*Viva la Revolución*!" said the younger of the two.

"*Si*; *viva la Revolución*!" The older man looked back to his brother and smiled. "Those days, they were good. Dangerous but good, my dear brother. We have seen much, and we have done much together."

"You have made Cuba the great country it is today, my brother," said the seated man.

"*Si*, it *is* a wonderful country. I only hope, my brother, that what we have done will not be lost to the newer generations. I have fears about this, Raul. I harbor deep fears of this in my heart."

"But why, Fidel? You have seen how the Russian dogs let us down. The millions of dollars they were going to provide Cuba as payment to set up their bases. Comrades we trusted, comrades who were going to help get our country back on its feet. But for all intents and purposes, they left us in the cold; the much-needed infrastructure projects they started were suddenly abandoned, and at a time we depended so much on them."

Raul Castro took a sip of his rum and pulled a drag off his long *Bolivar* cigar. "The Chinese have not been the thorn in America's side the way the Russians were," he said. "They are much more diplomatic and subtle. Diplomacy is the political tool necessary in these times to sneak in under the enemy's radar. The Russians, they were too arrogant and bullheaded."

"The Chinese on the other hand, not so. Our people will benefit greatly from their assistance; of this I am convinced, Fidel. Once the Project Vector affair has been successfully carried out, we shall reap the revenge we have waited so long for." Even Raul thought it too good to be true.

Fidel looked at his brother and smiled. "What they wish to do can only help perpetuate our cause, Raul. You know as well as I that once the Castro influence leaves Cuba, the American dogs will rape our country blind. They will not be able to do this thing if the Chinese are allied with us and this Project Vector is as good as they say!"

"I only hope you are right. You always were the practical one, Raul," Fidel Castro said. "Coming from the world's longest serving defense minister, such assurances bring much comfort to my tired old soul." He smiled lovingly at his brother.

Raul looked down to the courtyard below in thought. Memories deeply embedded in his mind came to the fore. He pondered a few moments, then looked to Fidel as he spoke.

"I know you hate the mention of them, Fidel, but I have been *your* Bobby Kennedy, your confidant. You and I have had many discussions as brothers-in-arms, as did they. Together we held off not only the Kennedys, but American influence altogether for over fifty years! The titles you have given me have been appreciated, Fidel, but they mean little . . . that you have taken my counsel seriously all these years, *that* means a great deal."

"Soon Cuba will be a force to be reckoned with on the world stage, and that because of you; because of *you*, Fidel!" Raul reached down to the little table beside him and sat his cigar in the open coconut shell he used as an ashtray, then rose up to put a hand on his brother's shoulder.

"Because of my actions the world may have ceased to exist many years ago, my brother," the older man said. "I could not totally blame the Americans. If that damned Khrushchev had listened to me, *listened-to-me!* I did not *want* their missiles of destruction here, but he was very persuasive. He promised me, us, *Cuba,* much money for infrastructure improvements. All he wanted he said, was a few missile bases established here ninety miles from their country, because the Americans had missiles in Turkey, right on their very border—much too close for comfort by any standards."

"I told Nikita not to bring those missiles secretly into Cuba. We had a sovereign *right* to receive anything from anyone overtly, including the Soviets. There were no laws, international or otherwise, to keep us from obtaining them. But that stupid Communist *cochino* insisted on sailing them openly into Cuba."

"Nothing is conducted in secret when done on the American doorstep. I warned Nikita that this would tip our hand to the imperialists, that a sudden influx of Soviet ships bound for Cuba would be monitored and investigated. But that pompous fool would not listen. If Khrushchev hadn't taken Kennedy seriously, the Americans would have initiated a first strike on Russia, destroying half of the world. Then Niki would have destroyed *our* half of the world without thought for Cuba." Fidel raised his fist into the air, shaking it violently.

"That was then, this is now, dear brother," Raul said, gently squeezing Fidel's shoulder, prompting him to lower his fist and calming the fiery man down. "You did well," Raul continued. "We all did as well as we could back then. But we must not dwell on the past. *Si,* the Russians, they let us down again in the early nineties. But we have taken their bitter pill for the last time. Fidel, we are still here. We still run our beloved Cuba. Where are your accusers? The American *cochinos* have gone thorough ten presidents; the Russians many leaders as well. Remember brother, the Russia we knew is gone. But Cuba is still here, and Cuba will rise to its proper place in world affairs. I can feel it in my old bones, Fidel!"

"With the assistance of the People's Republic of China, this time we will succeed. *Viva la Revolución!*" Raul turned his elder brother around by the shoulders so they could look each other in the eyes. "Fidel, you and me, we are still here and together we can still lead our country to greatness. We have this one more chance, Fidel!"

The frail man looked into the eyes of his younger brother. They looked at each other for several unspoken moments. Fidel could see the fire that was still in Raul's soul. That same fire he had seen in the eyes of all his men when they battled Batista's army in the mountains of the Sierra Maestra so many years ago.

"Yes, my brother, this time we will not fail," Fidel relented. The truth was he was too old and too tired to care much anymore about anything. But to keep the dream alive in his brother, he continued. "The Chinese are our new brothers now. They are not like the Russians. I know they will fulfill their promise to rebuild Cuba in the face of the American imperialists. Our Argentinean brother Ché would have been proud of us, Raul. I feel his spirit with us now! *El Movimiento de 26 de Julio* still lives on. And Ché is just as much a part of the coming greatness of the new Cuba as we are."

In a surprise move, Fidel turned and leaned down to the little table. He picked up Raul's now extinguished cigar, fired it up, then drew slowly, deeply. Raul watched his brother's eyes close. He watched as *el Comandante*, the great Fidel Castro, savored old memories the deeply inhaled cigar vividly restored to his aged mind.

After several minutes, Fidel reluctantly handed the cigar to its rightful owner. He gave Raul a hearty slap him on the back and a big smile crossed his weathered old face.

"Yes, my brother; v*iva la Revolución!*"

44

Reinforcements

Neither Lee nor Travers managed to extract any further information from their two captives. It was obvious that their fear of the DGI, Castro's secret police, was far greater than their fear of them. To be fair, Lee thought, the poor bastards' families were no doubt always in the sights of the DGI, and any failure on their part could be catastrophic for them. Such was the peril of government agents in flunky regimes like this the world over.

Lee had seen it firsthand travelling the world as he had, and it stank. He had plied his trade as a commercial diver in many such countries and saw how their people were repressed and desperate, living hand to mouth under fear for their lives while their bureaucrats wallowed in luxury, indifference, and narcissism.

The next day was typical paradise in the mountains of the Sierra Maestra: hot and dry, with the ever-present breeze bringing much needed respite from the heat. Unfortunately, few clouds traversed the sky to bring relief from the incessantly hot radiation of the sun.

From Lee's vantage point he could see for miles, although the road was greatly occluded as it wound between large boulders, trees, and natural depressions in the landscape. On the up side, he thought, it should be fairly easy to hear any loud, lumbering vehicles if they strained to climb the mountainside. He pulled his little flask from the waistband of his cargo shorts and took a hearty swig, swishing it around his mouth to savor the flavor.

One thing that Lee appreciated about Cuba was the fact that the island nation had no natural predators or poisonous creatures to cause harm to either the native inhabitants or visitors. As was usually the case in such banana republics, the greatest danger to man were the dictators and the lackeys they employed to keep the masses mercilessly underfoot and in constant fear.

Mercedes was in her kitchen making a brunch for the group consisting of rice, beans, banana bread, and papaya juice. The Cuban commandos under Travers' armed watchful care were each having a cigarette, their backs against a large boulder to the west of the hovel, which provided a cool respite from the searing heat. Lee was ever-vigilant as he kept a sun-shielding hand over his eyes to see down the road from the hovel. He was not one for surprises.

Suddenly he heard the faint roar of a vehicle's engine coming up the mountainside. He figured it was about five minutes out. Fearing the worst, he yelled to Travers, who ushered the prisoners to the rear of the building and behind a series of tall palm trees. It took longer than expected as Pork Barrel, still in pain from the shot to his foot, limped slowly. Lee ran into the hovel and grabbed Mercedes by the hand to lead her out behind the structure, but not before hiding the meal she had prepared so it would appear vacant.

They waited for several minutes. The roar of an old engine grew increasingly louder. Lee held his breath, hoping the vehicle would simply pass on by. But no, he could hear it slowing down. He knew whoever it was would be upon them in a few minutes. Looking at Travers, he then turned to Mercedes and said, "Mercedes, tell these men here that their lives depend on their silence, and so help me, if they so much as cough I'll slit their throats!" He softly shoved her over to where the men stood under the cover of Bill and his old rifle. She spoke to them. When she finished, Pork Barrel looked over at him and grudgingly nodded. They would give him no trouble.

From the paltry cover of the palm trees behind the corner of the hovel, they watched as a blue and white 1957 Ford Crown Victoria pulled in. Its solid chrome bumper reflected a painful glare from the sun that temporarily blinded Lee as it came to a squealing halt.

Still not able to see clearly, Lee heard a car door creak open and then slam shut. A few moments later, another door slammed shut. To his trained ears, the time lapse of the second door that slammed meant that someone else must have gotten out from the backseat of the two-door sedan.

Bill Travers never took his eyes off his captives, rifle at the ready to shoot either or both on a moment's notice if need be. He wisely kept his distance from them. He let Lee do all the peeking, leaving him to determine their next course of action.

His eyesight finally restored from the glare, Lee heard them inside the hovel, no doubt checking to see if anyone was inside.

Then a man came around each corner of the rear of the house simultaneously. They appeared unarmed, but were dressed well by Cuban standards. As they came together behind the rear of the building, one man removed his straw hat to wipe the perspiration from his brow. They were now peering around to the front of the building. Lee saw his chance and pounced on them like a vicious tiger defending her young. The two went down, Lee with them. They tousled around on the ground, yet no one was able to get a solid punch in.

Travers pulled Mercedes behind him, motioning his captives to go ahead of him to where the men were sprawled on top of each other like a grade school goose pile. Then another man appeared. It was Juan! He pulled a cigar from his shirt pocket and rolled it slowly between his lips. Seeing Travers with Mercedes and the two captives, he smiled at them, then at the three on the ground. He shook his head.

Juan shouted over to the three wrestling men, "Señors, when you are done with your play, please to get up so I can introduce you more civilly. *Señor Lee*!"

"Wha—?" Lee pushed one of the men off him. The other had already disengaged and pulled himself to his feet. "Juan!" Lee said, looking warily over at the two men as he got to his feet.

"*Señor* Lee, allow me to introduce my comrades from the Cuban Underground Freedom Movement," Juan said, still smiling at what he had just witnessed. "The man on your left, *Señor* Lee, is my right hand man, Pedro Rey Ramirez, who has been in contact with your Alan Exner. The other gentleman is Luis Perez Sosa, a man who has been very sympathetic to our cause for the past several years."

Lee shook hands with the two and said, "Sorry about that, fellas. No hard feelings intended."

"None taken *Señor* Hartley. You were a football player once, *sí*?" Sosa asked, smiling.

"No, just a little over-cautious, Luis," Lee said.

"One can never be too cautious in Cuba, *Señor* Lee," said Ramirez sternly. "I understand completely, although I hope you will not greet us in this manner every time," he joked.

The three shook hands, then they turned to Travers, Mercedes, and the two captives.

"I see you still have our prisoners, *Señor* Billiam," said Juan Zayas, "although a little worse for wear, no?"

"Yeah well, we had to dust 'em off a little when they tried to take advantage of us 'peacekeeping' Canadians," Travers said, shaking the hands of the three visitors.

Lee whispered to Mercedes, who excused herself and went around to the front of the hovel.

"Did you get the stuff, Juan?" Lee asked.

"We ran into some trouble a few miles out of the Sierra Mar Hotel, *Señor* Lee," Zayas said seriously. "There were men waiting for us at a roadblock. They must have been undercover DGI as they wore suits and drove a fancy *coche*," Zayas said, pointing around the side of the hovel. "They asked where we were going," he continued, "and wanted to see what we had in the back of the Defender."

"If they saw your scuba gear, we would have gotten into serious trouble. There were three of them and three of us. We all got out. As I opened the rear gate, two of them pushed me aside and looked in. I slammed the gate as hard as I could, which caught them by surprise and took the wind out of them. Luis gutted the other who had us at gunpoint. Luis is very fast, very good with his knife," Zayas said.

Sosa beamed proudly at this recognition before the Canadians. Travers inwardly shuddered. Lee maintained a poker face, but was glad the man was on their side.

"I slapped the others around pretty good," Zayas continued. "They had not expected any resistance from us. Then we grabbed your gear from the Defender and placed the three men inside it. We then set it on fire and pushed it over the cliff across the road where they had stopped us. It was quite a pleasing explosion at the bottom of the canyon, I assure you, *señors*," Zayas said.

Lee looked over to Travers, who smiled at these valiant men and their recent accomplishment. These were men who had families and cared for them very much, men who wanted a better life for their loved ones, even at the cost of their own; men who had seen their share of violence but were coldly efficient when necessary for the sake of the cause they believed in.

Lee knew they had seen good men, women, and sometimes even children tortured and mutilated. Or they had simply vanished with no trace, because they were suspected of being "disloyal" to the *Revolución*. Lee wondered when the "ship" would finally come in for the beautiful people of Cuba. *What is life without freedom?*

Mercedes came out with the brunch she had prepared. The newcomers thanked her heartily. “So you have our gear, eh?” Travers asked. “Good. But the radio, did you bring the radio, Juan?”

“Yes, the radio, she is in the Ford along with your gear,” Zayas said.

“You’re a good man, Juan.” Lee’s smile embraced all three men.

Turning to the captives, Ramirez said over his shoulder to Lee, “These men, they have been questioned *señor,* no?”

“They have been questioned, yes,” Lee said. “We are trying to find the child of the woman whose home this is. The child is eleven years old. Her name is Maela. From what we’ve gathered, the girl was abducted by the DGI soon after her father, Javier de Quesada, left for Canada a few months ago as insurance he would not defect. I pulled him out of a burning building, but he died a few days later.”

Lee lowered his voice so Mercedes could not hear. “Someone at our end shot him. Thing is, we don’t know if the bastards that have the girl are aware of this.” Then he added, loudly enough for the rest to hear, “and she better be alive for their sakes.” He looked over to the captives.

Turning to Pedro, Lee then said, “I need that radio. Mercedes said that a man named Alberto came to their house and talked with Javier just before he was sent to Canada.”

“*Alberto?*” Pedro Ramirez was obviously shocked at hearing the name.

“You *know* this man, *señor*?” asked Mercedes hopefully.

Lee turned to Mercedes in a bid to change the subject. “Your food is excellent, Mercedes. It doesn’t get more delightfully Cuban than this. Thank you for your thoughtfulness.” Then he said to Sosa, “Luis, could you please help Mercedes clean up in the kitchen?”

“But . . . but, *señors* . . . ,” Mercedes sputtered.

"Luis, please . . . ," Lee softly prodded.

At this, Luis nodded and gently took the woman by the arm and led her back to the hovel.

When they were out of earshot, Lee turned to Pedro and said, "Pedro, Mercedes told us that a man named Alberto came to speak with her husband in private just before he left the island. Who is this man?"

Zayas looked to his comrade, then back to Lee. Pedro eyeballed the two captives, still carefully guarded by Travers.

"Alberto is station chief of the DGI in the Santiago de Cuba district, and a very wicked man, *Señor* Lee," Pedro said. "These two here," he said as he pointed, "they are muscle for him. Alberto has eyes everywhere." Pedro raised his hands and pointed his index fingers several times toward his eyes to reinforce what he had just said. "He recruits men where they work and where they live to spy on others. Any hint of discontent, any careless words spoken against the *Revolución*, and Alberto's men come and take peoples away."

He ran his fingers through his heavy, thick black hair. "These peoples, sometimes they come back, sometimes they do not. The ones that come back are usually scarred for life." He paused as if remembering some of the faces. "They rarely talk about anything once Alberto has had them for a time."

Montoya, "Pork Barrel," heard every word that Pedro said and laughed, which unsettled Travers. In response, he gently placed the rifle barrel deep into the furrowed brow of his prisoner.

"And guess what, fatso; yer gonna take us to him, aren't you?" he said. "And not only that, yer gonna help us bring the lady's girl back."

Out of the corner of his eye, Travers saw Miguel positioning himself as if to pounce. In one sweeping gesture, rifle still on Montoya, Travers threw a low side kick into Miguel's face as he attempted to rush the old diver, which slammed him back against the building.

It would have been funny were it not for the seriousness of the situation.

"Right, Pedro, the Seqpod radio now," Lee said. Turning to Zayas, he said, "Juan, I want you and Luis to take the prisoners in their truck." Then to his friend, "Bill, tell Mercedes to throw some things together. We've got to get out of here. DGI will soon be looking for their men and the Crown Vic."

He then walked over and picked up the battery cable on the ground in front of the truck. He raised the hood and replaced it. Going back around to the cab of the old Dodge, he pumped the accelerator and turned the ignition. After several tries and with great reluctance, the old Dodge came to life in a plume of defiant black smoke.

Travers shook his head at Lee, then handed his rifle to Luis, who took it with relish. Juan double-checked the bonds of the two captives and then marched them over and into the back of the pick-up. They were positioned at the tailgate. Luis sat behind the cab with the rifle leveled at them. Juan jumped into the passenger seat awaiting Pedro.

Lee followed Pedro to the Ford, where they unloaded the Canadians' luggage and equipment and threw it into the trunk of the Crown Victoria.

Taking the Seqpod from Pedro, Lee gently shook the man's shoulder with a confident assurance that brought a smile to the Cuban's face. It was the first smile he had seen cross Pedro's face since they met.

With his back to the door of the old Ford, Lee punched in the numbering sequence required to authenticate access to the supercomputer system used by NABS. Within seconds he was conversing not with Alan Exner, but CIA sub-director Scott Culp!

"Sorry, Mr. Culp," Lee said. "I thought I'd accessed our NABS office in Niagara, not Langley."

"You did, son," was the terse reply. "What's your status down there?

Perplexed, Lee nevertheless explained everything that happened to them since arriving on the island. Culp said little.

"Duly noted. Yes Hartley, we'll look into this Alberto, his ties with DGI, and what his unit is doing down there in Santiago. There's an increase in Chinese presence and activity on the island. Whatever they're planning, it seems they're stepping it up."

"Right sir. I, uh—is Control onsite? I'd like a word with him," Lee stammered. He had not expected the CIA agent manning Control's office.

"Not possible, Hartley."

"Sir?"

"I've been called in because your control and the NSA woman have vanished without trace."

45

Meeting The Applegates'

Chen Fa, Shing Shen, and Gino Vaselino returned on the last ferry to Tobermory and got some much-needed rest. They decided against returning to the abandoned motel where Wu Yang was staying. As he mentioned, Yang did not want to see them until they had recovered the paintings. So the men opted to stay at a little motel off the beaten path on the other side of the village.

The morning got off to a promising start with the rising sun and a sky devoid of clouds. The men showered, and by midmorning walked the short distance into town and the Dive Inn for breakfast. A waitress led them to a table in the middle of the room. Vaselino would have none of this. They needed a more remote location in the large, well-appointed restaurant. As all the corners were taken, it was apparent the waitress could not accommodate them.

There were many patrons in the restaurant, as brunches were very popular in the little town. There were always more people in Tobermory in the high season than restaurants.

Vaselino became indignant to the shocked waitress. Chen Fa quietly grasped him in a vice-like grip above the elbow and pulled him gently back and away from her, smiling to her as he did so.

"Thank you, miss," Fa said politely. "We will wait until one of your corner tables becomes available." The college-aged young woman nodded, then left, her face flushed.

Turning to Vaselino, Chen Fa whispered, "You would do well to control your hot-blooded Cuban temper, my friend. The last thing we need in this place is to draw unwelcome attention to ourselves."

One look at Fa's mesmerizing murderous gaze was enough to corral any inclination on Vaselino's part to argue. Chen Fa relaxed his grip on Vaselino's arm. The latter yanked it away.

As the three men stood silently by the window awaiting a suitable table, they could not help but overhear a conversation taking place at the table to their right, which was situated along the wall.

An older man and woman were on the last lap of their pancake-and-egg breakfast. The couple was the type drawn to little villages such as this, enjoying all that the quaint environs had to offer, free from the bonds of schedules and work constraints those not retired were still forced to endure.

"Isn't it terrible about that elderly woman at the gallery, Stuart? Why, we were only there about a short while ago. I hope nothing bad has happened to her."

"I wouldn't worry about her too much, Pat. She's old; probably wandered off in a 'senior moment.'" He smiled at her. "I'm sure the old woman'll turn up soon enough."

"Stuart Applegate, shame on you! She's not that much older than we are," the woman said. "Come on; finish up so we can get back to the *Forever Young* and change. I'd like to walk the trail today."

The three foreign agents stood there dumbfounded at what they had just heard. Here were the very people they were looking for! Luck had finally come their way! These were the owners of the *Forever Young*, the very people who'd managed to slip through the cracks of their operation. The men hoped for a quick retrieval that would greatly please Wu Yang.

As the Applegates' were finishing up the last morsels of their brunch, the attractive young waitress came over and placed their check on the table. Turning to the three men, she said, "I'll be with you in a minute."

"Don't bother, we're leaving. Thanks for nothing." Vaselino instantly regretted his crass comment as Chen Fa briskly cuffed the man on the back of his head. They left just as the Applegate couple rose to pay for their brunch.

The three started to walk down to the dock when they saw the couple coming out of the Dive Inn. The men stopped to "sight-see" and allowed the couple to overtake and pass them on the wooden boardwalk that led to the vessels that were berthed inside the little harbor.

Once the couple dropped down into the *Forever Young*, the men set to work. After a few people passed by the ship's berth, Shing Shen positioned himself at the gangway, while Vaselino and Chen Fa dropped down onto the deck of the yacht. The couple had already gone below.

Going below, Chen Fa gently tried the handle to the closed door of the stateroom and found it was locked. Turning to Vaselino, he motioned the Cuban to kick the door in, then to remain outside the room.

In one fluid moment, and to the Applegates' utter shock and astonishment, the door to their stateroom was violently kicked in. They held each other and cringed at this foreign man who stood at the threshold staring at them. Horribly frightened, the woman opened her mouth to scream. Vaselino rushed in and gave her a violent backhand, which knocked her unconscious onto the bed. Enraged, Stewart Applegate attempted to wrestle with the large wiry Cuban.

Vaselino effortlessly caught the man's weak punch in midflight and strong-armed him to his knees. Seeing that the fight had already left the man, Vaselino leaned down and said, "We are not here to hurt either of you. We come only for one painting. It is an irreplaceable work of art that has been stolen from our country," he lied. Looking around, he saw a large painting hanging beside their bed. "This is it, *sí?*"

He grabbed the man's weak arm and pulled him up. Struggling with all his might, Vaselino pushed the man over to his dazed wife.

Chen Fa walked over. "You will not waste our time. Surrender the paintings to us and we will permit you to live. I think that is a fair trade, no?"

The man was consoling his wife, who was softly sobbing, her head buried in a pillow. Turning to Chen Fa, Stuart said, "The painting on the wall over there is our most recent acquisition. Take it; take whatever you want, only please don't harm us. We won't tell anyone. We have no desire to get involved with you. Please take it and just leave us alone."

Vaselino sneered at them. Chen Fa simply stared at the old man with his mesmerizing gaze. *Typical rich bastards*, Vaselino thought. *So accustomed to letting their money do the talking for them. They're totally out of their element, their world, when their wealth can't help them. Fidel was right on one thing. Our way of life is much superior to this ungrateful, decadent, and excessive lifestyle. Let them squirm.*

Chen Fa ripped the large marine painting from its mount. He handed it to Vaselino. "Check the back of the painting. There should be something beneath the paper backing."

Vaselino looked at the majestic seascape for a brief moment. Then turning it over, he shouted to Chen Fa, "There is nothing here, Fa. Whatever was here has already been taken. See for yourself."

Leaving the man to tend to his wife, Chen Fa came over to inspect the painting. The backing had been torn away and whatever was there had been removed, then the backing hastily replaced.

Looking up at Vaselino, Fa then walked around the foot of the bed to where the husband was sitting beside his wife and said simply, "Where is it?"

No answer.

In one fluid movement, Chen Fa had pulled the man off the bed, spun him around, and trapped both of his arms. Their faces were inches apart. "I asked you a question, and I do not repeat myself," Fa hissed.

"I-I don't know what you're talking about. It's . . . just a painting. You don't treat a valued piece of art like that. Please; who are you people?"

Weary of his pathetic pleas, Chen Fa spun the man back around with such force and blinding speed that he landed face down and diagonally across his stunned wife.

Vaselino stood in awe at the speed and technique of the Chinese man, and determined he would never underestimate the man at any cost.

"Tie them up," Chen Fa ordered. "We must leave. Someone has beaten us to the painting and must be found!"

Vaselino left the stateroom to find rope with which to tie the couple up. It wasn't hard to find rope suitable for the job on a yacht this size. Within minutes, he returned with a small diameter hemp rope and tightly trussed the couple back to back, gagged them, and left them sitting on a corner of the bed. He then went out to effect a quick repair on the door. It was not as badly damaged as he had initially thought.

Before exiting the stateroom, Chen Fa took the precaution to close and lock all the windows. He unscrewed the handles off each of them and put them in his pocket. Then he located the TV remote and turned the large screen unit on, volume up high. Exiting the room, he managed to wedge the door tight shut from the outside. Before leaving, he broke the inside door handle off for good measure.

"It is a small town," Chen Fa said. "We will leave no stone unturned until we find that for which we seek. Come, for we have much work ahead. We must not fail Wu Yang."

The three then disembarked the *Forever Young*, walked down the slip to their vehicle, and left the town with a bitter sense of failure in their hearts.

46

NABed

Alan Exner came to, nauseated and unable to move. He found that he was lying on a stainless steel table, his wrists and ankles shackled. He groggily surveyed his environs. It was a large wood-paneled and well-appointed room. The wall to his right was lined with books of various sizes, thicknesses, and colors. To his left looked like a nineteenth-century roll-top desk in perfect condition. There was a teakwood door directly across the room from him that was closed and probably locked. A small window on the wall above the desk was covered by a heavy curtain, so he couldn't determine if it was night or day. There were no clocks in the room, his Rolex Submariner watch was missing, and he had no idea how long he'd been out.

He was woozy, but his faculties were slowly returning. His head was spinning. No, his head *wasn't* spinning. He could feel a gentle side to side sway. As his mind continued to clear, it became evident that he was on a boat, a ship of some sort. Tied up yes, but definitely on the water somewhere, but where?

Bindhira: where was Bindhira? He called out several times in the hope he could at least hear her voice elsewhere in the room.

His mind was coming into focus now, and he began to remember. He remembered how the two of them located a hidden cache of innocent-looking paper matchbooks concealed behind a painting that Travers had brought back from Cuba. He and Bindhira had located the painting in a stateroom aboard a yacht christened the *Forever Young*. Exner realized the room he was currently in was far too large to be aboard that yacht.

Desperately trying to reconstruct the events that led to his present predicament, he closed his eyes to try to recall his recent past.

He and Bindhira had just stepped off the private dock at Little Tub. An elderly Chinese man had engaged them in conversation as they headed back to the car park. Yes, now it was coming back! The man, in his pleasant quaintness, told them he had come up alone to catch the ferry to Manitoulin Island to visit some friends but arrived too late to secure his ticket.

The old gentleman seemed rather excited, as though he had never been to such a beautiful little lakeside village before. In his charming quaint little way, the elderly Chinese man asked if he could take a photo of them with his new camera, which they could not help but agree to. At this, Exner remembered setting the gym bag containing the packets down on the concrete bumper at dock's end to accommodate the elderly Chinese gentleman's request.

Exner thought nothing of it at the time, but in retrospect he considered it odd that the gentleman's expensive Nikon camera employed a blue flash. Strange also was the fact that the flash was not the usual single quick white "pop" of a conventional unit, but rather an irritating series of increasingly brighter pulses that radiated ever-intensifying shades of blue over a period of several seconds before exploding into the semblance of a normal photo flash.

The man then insisted on treating them to a quick drink at the Dive Inn. Small talk ensued, but after his second drink Exner began *to feel very weak, very tired. With Bindhira's help, the Chinese* gentleman managed to get Exner down the stairs of the open-air second floor bar area of the Dive Inn.

Exner recalled that they had gotten him as far as the car park. Then he remembered that Bindhira had clutched at her stomach. Then he blacked out.

The mysterious man must have brought them here and placed them in restraints. But where *was* Bindhi and who did this enigmatic person work for?

Exner strained to hear sound, any sound, human or otherwise. He faintly detected the gentle lapping of water as it burbled against the hull of the boat. He struggled against his restraints in a test to see if he could break free. This, however, proved nothing more than an exercise in futility.

The effort of straining against the plastic zip ties that held his wrists and ankles proved too much for him, and he faded once again into a troubled unconsciousness.

He came to at the sudden sound of a woman's scream. He heard a struggle, a loud slap, and then feet being dragged across the floor. Then a one-sided muffled conversation.

Suddenly a key rattled in the lock of the door, and a man stood at the threshold. It was difficult for Exner to focus on the man's face because of two bright electric lanterns that shone off each corner of the upper casement of the door.

Exner feigned unconsciousness, hoping to draw the person closer to determine whether he was friend or foe. The man remained where he was for several moments, as if deciding on what action to take. Seeing Exner unconscious, the person approached.

"Ah, Mr. Alan Exner," the male voice said. The man slapped him lightly about the face. In spite of himself, Exner opened his eyes. "We have met before, as you may well recall, but this time without the masks."

Exner strained to peer into the face of the man who stood at the foot of the table. His eyes cleared sufficiently that he was able to see the man clearly.

"My name is Wu Yang," the elderly ChIS operative said, sitting down on a chair beside Exner. He cupped his hands over the top of his cane and laid his chin on them. "Forgive me for this most unsettling means of procuring you and your lovely assistant. I am in the employ of the Chinese Secret Service. I tell you this because you will not live to make use of this information, and only because a worthy fellow agent, though an enemy one, deserves to know these things before he dies."

"What did you do to us, Yang?"

"Ah; the disrupter strobe. A most unique Chinese development indeed, Mr. Exner. The strobe consists of waves of controlled naturally occurring potassium 40 radioisotopes, generated in the form of gamma infused ultraviolet rays, which have been found to induce narcolepsy in the normal human brain." Exner noticed that the man was enjoying this way too much.

Yang continued. "The pulsating intensity of the ultraviolet strobe combined with potassium 40 gamma emissions induces the brain's synapses to convulse, effectively disrupting the recipient. Unlike an epileptic's uncontrollable bodily convulsions that occur when their brain is subjected to bright light or fast-changing scenes, such as those found in the movies these days, disrupter strobe convulsions are confined solely and temporarily to the brain. The intensity of these emissions can be significantly increased or decreased by the simple manual adjustment of a focusing ring on the camera lens."

"The nausea you experienced was the result of a larger than necessary dose, for which I apologize. I regret I am not as yet proficient with this particular feature of the agency issue camera. I was quite elated by the fact that my ineptness did not kill you. Your friend became much sicker than you, but she is recovering as well as can be expected."

"So what happens if you use this thing on an epileptic?" Exner really didn't want to know but he was stalling for time to think of a way out of all this.

Wu Yang looked down at his captive. "Mr. Exner, you should be more concerned about your own wellbeing than that of your companion at this moment. The answer to your question, however, is that it invariably results in a very excruciating, very violent death."

"Unfortunately, the convulsions in an epileptic exposed to the disrupter strobe do not subside as they would a natural bout, which results in the muscles slowly knotting up to the point of cutting off all circulation and oxygen to the organism. The victim is reduced to nothing more than a hardened ball of curled up meat within minutes." He paused, then added, "How fortunate for you and your assistant that neither of you are epileptics, Mr. Exner."

Exner was horrified at this. He doubted that any of the Western intelligence agencies had any knowledge of such a weapon. What else did these devils have up their sleeves?

The NABS control had to find a way out. But for now, he needed to get as much intel as he could in the event they escaped from this madman. "What's your plan, Yang? You expect me to talk? If you do, I don't know anything. If I could, would you really expect me to?"

"Mr. Exner," Yang said, "any intelligence you think you may have is but old news to us." Wu Yang laughed Exner's bravado off with a wave of his hand. "Regrettably, I only expect you and your female friend to die. You see, your only crime has been being in the right place at the wrong time."

"You harm the girl," Exner said, "and so help me Yang, you will die as excruciatingly as humanly possible! You have no idea with whom you're dealing!" Exner cursed himself that Yang had captured them so pathetically easily.

"Please, Mr. Control of NABS, please. Who you are, who the girl is does not concern me. What does concern me is that you and your people have gotten too close to exposing a plan the Establishment has been developing for months under utmost secrecy. An endeavor even the Chinese and Cuban governments have no knowledge of, at least not yet. But soon enough they will, I assure you."

"Yang, our people know what you're about. You're not as sly as you'd like to think."

"Mr. Exner, your organization only knows what we wish them to know," Wu Yang lied. "I truly regret that such a capable pair of agents such as you and Ms. Shankar have to die, but such are the hazards of our profession, is this not so?" He removed his chin and hands from the cane, stood up, and then lifted its bottom up to inspect the tip.

"I have men out to dispose of Mr. Travers and Mr. Hartley, no doubt two of your best agents, however disguised their respective covers."

Exner dismissed the error of the statement and its content and said, "The girl, Yang. What have you done with Bindhira?" Exner felt he was a step away from insanity.

"She is alive, for the moment. Unfortunately, I cannot say the same for you." Wu Yang raised the cane and placed its tip to Exner's neck.

"Vector, Project Vector!" Exner called out breathlessly.

At this Wu Yang withdrew the tip and calmly returned to his seat. "What knowledge of Project Vector, if anything, do you possess, Mr. Exner?" Wu Yang asked the question with unnerving politeness.

Exner struggled to get a better look at his kidnapper. Yang was good at keeping his prey at a disadvantage, and remained just out of Exner's peripheral vision; a technique no doubt borne of experience. Exner knew that the interrogation techniques of the ChIS could be cruelly barbaric, and that this was only a precursor. Keeping Bindhira's status from him was the cruelest torture of all.

"First, I need to know the woman is alive, Yang." Exner cursed himself for the crackle in his voice, which indicated nervous fear.

"Do not waste my time, Mr. Exner," Yang said sinisterly. "Imagine my surprise at so unexpectedly running into both of you up here." Yang now came into full view, stood over his victim, and ran the tip of his cane along Exner's chest and neck.

"You as control of NABS could be of great use to me, Mr. Exner, truth be known. But I digress. You will now answer the question!"

Yang shoved the tip of the cane under the soft palate of Exner's chin, but for the first time Exner knew he had struck a chord with his captor.

"Ah yes; the young woman." Wu Yang had recovered quickly. "She has been secured in another area of the ship. I assure you no harm has come to her—yet. She will soon recover from the effects of the disrupter strobe as you have."

The Chinese agent leaned over, and their faces were so close that Exner could feel the uncomfortable heat of his sour breath. "One last time: what do your people know concerning this Project Vector?"

Exner's brain was in overdrive. Had Yang not inspected the gym bag they had brought off the *Forever Young*? Was he not aware of the people who owned the painting and its latent secrets? And if *he* didn't have the bag, was it still at the end of the dock where they took Yang's photo? Most disturbingly of all, had the bag been picked up by person or persons forever unknown?

"Where are we, Yang? Are we out to sea?" Exner stalled for time to allow his razor-sharp mind to formulate a plan while he actively engaged his enemy in conversation.

Wu Yang rose from his seat. He looked down at Exner, then without a word, left the room, closed the door behind him and locked it.

At this, Exner breathed a huge sigh of relief. But he cursed the fact that he had been relieved of his Rolex. The top of the watch bezel had a spring-loaded razor sharp blade that could easily have cut through the nylon restraints of his wrists.

Wu Yang was very thorough, and he discovered, very deadly. The chances that he and Bindhira would walk away from this situation seemed slim to none.

The futility of the situation created an anger that Exner channeled to his wrists. He pulled, he twisted, and he strained, and pulsed against the nylon restraints. It was only when he yanked downward with all his might out of sheer frustration that he detected a faint hint of slack.

The constant heat generated by the friction of his rubbing the bands against the steel table had slightly expanded the plastic of his restraints. This, along with the twisting motions of his wrists, had caused the ties to partially loosen, sufficiently enough to provide additional room to pull and twist, which loosened the bonds even more.

His wrists bloodied and raw, Exner managed to break his left wrist free. Desperately looking around, he noticed a pair of pliers among other small implements, no doubt there for his torture, on a small table beside him.

With great effort, he managed to stretch over far enough to grasp them. The agent was then able to free his right wrist by twisting the lock on the cable tie with the pliers in his left hand until it snapped loose. Wasting no time, he quickly freed his left arm. Within minutes he released his ankles, had jumped off the table, and was in search of anything that could be used as a weapon against his captors.

47

Destination Breached

Hartley and company broke camp in the mountains of the Sierra Maestra. After Lee relayed the disturbing news of the disappearances of Alan Exner and Bindhira Shankar to his allies, he, Travers, and their newfound Cuban friends did their best to cover their tracks at the de Quesada residence before they parted company.

"We will take these men to a place where we can better interrogate them, *Señor* Hartley," Pedro said.

Lee nodded and shook the man's hand. "Good. We have some unfinished business of our own to take care of Pedro," Lee said.

Travers helped the Cuban woman into the Crown Victoria with her belongings.

The two captives remained quiet in the box of the open pick-up truck. Luis kept a sharp eye on them. Ramirez nodded as he popped into the driver's seat of the old Dodge beside Zayas. Looking back to Lee through the open cab window he said, "be sure to dump that old tub as soon as possible, *señors*. You would not want to be found driving a DGI vehicle without the DGI agents that came with it, I assure you."

"Thanks for the tip, my friend," Lee said.

Juan shouted back to the Canadians through his open window. "I will return for you in a day or two, *señors*. I know the area you will be diving. Tread carefully. Castro informants are everywhere."

"Thanks, Juan. Be safe," Lee said. With that, the old pick-up lumbered away in a trail of dust down the little lane that led to the main road.

"Mercedes," Lee said, "do you have everything? We may not be back for some time."

"Everything but my daughter, *Señor* Lee," she said sadly.

"Juan and his associates will find her Mercedes," Lee said through the open driver's side door. "But for now you must stay focused and diligent." He and Travers got into the car. Looking over at his old friend, he said, "Do we have all our gear aboard?"

Travers turned to Lee with a squinty eye. "Truly we do, *Señor Lee*." He then looked back at Mercedes with a wink, which brought a reassuring smile to her face.

Without further ado, Lee fired up the venerable old Ford Crown Victoria. Smoke billowed from its ancient exhaust pipe until the engine came back down to an idle. He backed the vehicle up and then headed down the lane, bound for the base of the mountains and the Caribbean Sea.

The perilous trek down the mountain was difficult at best in the big Ford. The shocks of the ancient vehicle were all but non-existent, which made the ride very bumpy and uncomfortable in the rugged terrain. The heat of the day removed any comfort that remained.

The road had been washed out in several spots, and on several occasions Lee had to slow the vehicle to a near standstill from time to time as they navigated over large, deep potholes in the road. As they neared the coast, the men were awestruck by one of the most beautiful seascapes Cuba had to offer.

The midday sun reflected off a surreal teal colored ocean. White caps sporadically covered its surface to complete the beautiful oceanside tapestry. Billowy white clouds passed lazily overhead, and their shadows swallowed the old Ford from time to time as they floated by on their eastward trek. Seagulls high overhead cried out to one another on their insatiable quest for food.

Travers stuck his head out his open window and marveled as some of the birds seemed to hang suspended in the sky as if on pause mode despite the wind's best efforts to dethrone them from their lofty perches.

An unexpected encounter with a huge pothole nearly knocked Travers out the window. Lee looked over at his chum with a hunch of the shoulders and a sorry expression on his face. Travers took his hat off and cuffed his friend on the shoulder with it. A sweet laughter came from the backseat. This caused the men to laugh as well, which brought a welcome release from the tension they all felt.

The landscape was barren, save for small patches of palm trees here and there, and for the ever-present boulders that dotted the roadside for miles.

When they finally reached the base of the mountains and the shoreline, Lee came to a junction at this point as the road now went either right or left, with the ocean directly in front. He brought the vehicle to a stop. "Which way, William?" Lee asked, and looked over to his copilot.

"The *Cristóbal Colón* is west of here, Lee," Travers said, "so hang a left. There're no other roads leading to the ocean along the way, and it's very narrow along the base of the mountain. Make sure you give a wide berth around corners. Drivers down here don't value their lives like we do," Travers kidded, but Lee knew all too well he was essentially correct.

"How far from here, Bill?" Lee asked.

Travers leaned forward and scanned the area through the scratched and pitted windshield. "I'd say at least an hour or so, Lee. When you come upon the wreck site, you'd never know it unless you've been there a few times. There's nothing to mark the wreck's presence from the shore."

"Left it is," Lee said as he turned left along the mountain. They noticed with discomfort huge boulders suspended high above the narrow road along the mountainside as though lying in wait for the right victim to drop upon. On the right however, a Caribbean seascape brought delight to their eyes; a breathtaking living canvas of sky above blending seamlessly into the surface of the glistening water below.

Looking at the fuel gauge, Lee said, "I hope we have enough gas to make it. We've got about a quarter tank left. If we do make it, we'll have to find a place to ditch this pig far out of sight. Hopefully, after the dive we'll be able to hitch a ride into one of the towns on a hay wagon or something."

Travers watched Lee reach into his pocket. Once again his friend produced his little flask and took one last deep pull from it. Lee shook the remaining drops in his mouth then tossed it out the window in disgust.

"I've been dying to ask you this for some time, Lee," Bill said innocently, "and now's as good a time as any. I know you don't drink to any considerable extent, so what is that gooch you've been swizzling all this time?"

Lee looked over at Travers and said, "It's something I've been hooked on, and my little dark secret."

"Why does that not answer my question?" Bill pursued.

"You probably won't understand, but here it goes anyway. What I kept in the flask was Paul Newman's parmesan and roasted garlic salad dressing. I love it. My name's Lee Hartley and I am an addict, so sue me." He smiled. "Plus, I wanted to help old Paul out."

For an indeterminate time Travers just sat there and looked at him. "'*Old Paul*' has been dead for several years now," Travers said. "So how could you possibly help him?"

"Bill," Lee said, "Paul Newman and his daughter have donated over $340 million to various worthwhile charities through the sales of their products for several years. The Newman's have taken no profits from the sales of their salad dressings. But the stuff is awesome and simply the best in the world, bar none!" He then added by way of confession, "I've found a little swig now and then gives me a boost."

"With that said, *amigo*," Travers said, "how is it that we're in the mountains of the Sierra Maestra, in Cuba no less, and you're still suckin' the stuff back? And what happened to the salad part of the equation?"

"I brought a stash down here," Lee replied. "And yes, I like it on salads too." He could see his friend was enjoying this. "You should give it a try, Bill."

"No, no, I don't do drugs."

"It's not a drug, but I do enjoy its *off label* benefits. Anyway, give me a break. I don't *drink* it; I *sip* it in minute quantities."

Bill Travers squirmed a bit in his seat, then said, "How long have you been doing this, Lee?"

Lee replied, "I dunno. A year or so, why?"

"*A year or so?* Hey; acknowledging your addiction is the first step they say." Then with a squinty eye locked onto his friend's face, he added smugly, "Somewhere out there, there's probably an SDA, Salad

Dressing Anonymous group or something we can get you into when we get back," Bill joked.

"Let him without sin cast the first stone," Lee quoted from the Bible.

"Great. I have friend with a serious salad dressing fetish," Travers mused.

"Bill?" Lee looked over at him with eyes that belied all the seriousness he possessed. "As I'm obviously quite busy keeping this pig on the road, would you be so kind as to winch up your middle finger and take a good look at it for me?"

The two men broke out in laughter. Travers looked behind Lee to Mercedes, who chuckled along with them. Mercedes enjoyed the light banter between the men, and it did much to lift her spirits, if only somewhat. She had been quiet for most of the time, however. The woman had much on her mind, not the least of which was getting her daughter back alive.

The winding road was very treacherous in spots, yet the Cuban woman greatly admired Lee's driving expertise as he expertly navigated over and around washouts, potholes, and boulders along the way.

The road tracing the bottom of the Sierra Maestra mountain range proved to be a perilous route for miles. A cement bridge had its back broken, no doubt by a hurricane that had gone through the area. At one point well onto the bridge, Lee wasn't even sure its surface was sturdy enough to support their heavy vehicle due to a center span that had all but collapsed. Sizeable chunks of the decaying bridge littered the small canyon below.

Evidence was everywhere of the abruptness of work stoppages along the mountainside road—work abandoned by the Russians when they withdrew their support in the early 1990s.

At one point Lee had to back up several hundred feet on one of the many bridges to permit a large stake truck crowded to overflowing with sugarcane workers to continue unhindered as it made its way to towns and villages farther east.

After a few more miles, Travers spoke. "Hold up partner, hold up. I think we're here. I think it's time to lose this old crate."

Lee had been too preoccupied myopically navigating around huge stones and small boulders, washed out spans of roadway, and treacherous curves to notice two military jeeps and a small tourist-type bus about a quarter mile up the road parked on the beach side.

Instinctively he brought the vehicle to a dead stop and slammed the transmission into reverse. He hugged the mountain and prayed there would be no traffic bearing down on them from the blind curve behind. He sped backward as fast as he dared without bringing unwanted attention from the seaside group.

Travers pulled out a pair of binoculars. The men left the vehicle and trotted up to the bend in the road for a better view. After Travers observed the activity for a time, he handed them to Lee.

Several men were milling around the side of the bus. They pulled out a large, obviously heavy crate from the cargo compartment. At the water's edge they also spotted four or five others looking out to sea.

Seeing enough, the men ran back and climbed into the Ford. Mercedes squealed in fear as Lee reversed the heavily bouncing and vibrating Crown Vic until he found an open area carved out of the mountainside that was largely concealed by tall shrubs. There was just enough room for him to run the Crown Vic into the shrubs and out of sight of the mountain road.

Cautiously the three exited the car and returned to the bend in the road where they could observe without being observed. Travers adjusted the lens of the binoculars until he clearly saw the activities at the beach.

"This is the place, Lee, no doubt about it. This is the beach we dive off to reach the *Cristóbal Colón.*" Travers was silent as he scanned the beach and small crowd with curious interest before handing the spy-glasses to Lee. "What do you make of all this?"

Lee adjusted the glasses to accommodate his visual acuity and watched for several minutes before he made his assessment. "I see several Cuban military officials." Fine-tuning the binoculars a little further, he then said, "Chinese! By my count, there's four, no, five; there's five Chinese men."

"Nothing wrong with your count Lee, that's what I got. And just because they're not in some kind of uniform doesn't mean they're not military."

Mercedes could not restrain herself any longer. "What does this all mean, *señors*?"

Ignoring the question, Lee asked of her a more pertinent one. "Mercedes, do you know this place?"

"No *Señor* Lee. I have no reason to come this way."

Looking to Travers, Lee said, "I have bad vibes of getting caught and never seeing the light of day again. On the plus side, it doesn't look like they saw us. Everyone is still going about their business."

Lee lowered the glasses and faced Travers and the woman. "Let's grab our gear out of the car. We'll stash it away from the vehicle to be safe and stand down until they leave."

The trio extruded their belongings and scuba gear. There wasn't much ground between where they parked the Ford and the base of the mountain. It was Mercedes who located another hollow area concealed by brush and boulder not fifty feet from where the car was positioned. Not big enough for them to hide in, but perfect to conceal their equipment until needed.

Lee grabbed a night-vision monocular from his pack. Though it was still light, the monocular would prove its worth once darkness fell.

There was a thin veil of brush that skirted the beach-side of the road, sufficient enough to provide good cover for them to move unobserved. They crept slowly toward the men and vehicles on the beach.

After about fifteen minutes, Mercedes whispered, "*Señors*! Look down there. A good spot to hide—no?"

There below them, where the edge of the vegetation gave way to a slope of rock and more beaches beyond was indeed a small grotto. It would be more than adequate for them to rest without being detected.

Bill caught Lee's attention, pointed to his eyes, then silently trotted off to his left for several hundred feet. He came to a curved point where an outcropping of rocks jutted out into the sea. It would provide a natural barrier from prying eyes on the other side.

Mercedes stood beside Lee. Through the lens of his monocular, he saw Travers drop to the ground, binoculars in hand. He lay motionless, and for several minutes continued to observe the action further down the beach with intense interest. Then he looked back and motioned for Lee to come.

"Stay here Mercedes," Lee instructed. "We'll signal you when it's safe." She looked into his eyes and unexpectedly grabbed him around the neck and planted a sensuous kiss on his mouth.

"Please be careful *Señor* Lee. I will wait here as you say."

Caught off guard, Lee gently lifted her chin. "I will. Thank you, Mercedes." He then trotted off to his friend's position.

Lee noticed with curiosity that Travers hadn't taken his eyes off his target all the while Lee was running over to him. When he arrived Travers said, "It looks like they've doing something on the wreck, Lee. Have a look; Chinese and Cubans. And from what I've seen, the Chinese civilians seem to be calling the shots."

Lee took up a position slightly further down range for a better vantage point. Although he could hear them talking, Lee cursed the wind and the surf that prevented him from understanding what they were saying, not that he understood Spanish *or* Chinese.

"I wonder what they're doin' down there," Travers questioned, more to himself than anyone else.

"From what you've told me," Lee said, "the *Cristóbal Colón* is a pretty large wreck, Bill. I don't think it prudent to dive right now, no matter how careful we think we are. Better to wait until they leave."

They continued to watch for nearly an hour. Lee was just about to head back when Travers, who still had his binoculars trained on the men, said, "Lee, wait! Divers returning!"

Lee fine-tuned his monocular. "How many in the water?"

"Two by my count, Lee," Travers replied. "They're definitely professionals, and their gear looks pretty technical. Not anything you'd normally find down here."

"'*Normally*' being the key word," Lee said grimly.

Lee returned to his vantage point. He, too, watched as the divers struggled to get through the heavy surf and undertow as the crashing waves receded from the beach.

Two of the Cuban military men removed their boots and waded out to assist them. One of the soldiers fell and was under for several seconds before he reappeared.

"Gets deep out there fast, Lee," Travers said, by way of commentary. "There's a lot of deep-ass 'soup bowls' carved out from the rip tides around these parts."

As the men regained their balance in the surge, the divers set about removing their gear with the help of the others.

Then the Canadians heard chatter on the jeep radios. One of the soldiers standing beside a jeep reached in and grabbed a microphone. He listened for several minutes, then responded into the mic. With a circular swirl of an upraised arm, he shouted to the men. Everyone moved at double time.

The men packed their equipment and themselves into the vehicles, then the caravan unceremoniously vacated the beach. The Canadians, backs against a high outcropping, hugged the rocks tight in order to avoid detection as they whizzed past, black smoke spewing from the tailpipes of the three vehicles. "So much for the environment," Travers muttered to himself.

As they returned to the grotto and a waiting Mercedes, a disturbing thought crossed Lee's mind: *what had happened to Exner and Bindhira?*

Travers snapped Lee out of his reflections when they reached the grotto. "Care to check out the underwater environs, *señor*?"

"Let's get wet," Lee returned grimly. "I'm curious to see what these guys were up to."

48

An Unusual Intervention

The sunset in Tobermory was surreal. The last vestiges of the sun's light reflected off the underbellies of passing clouds in the most beautiful hues of deep red, orange, and yellow above a deep blue lake as the large orange ball slowly disappeared below the western horizon.

Many tourists, tired from the activities of the day, visited the many and varied little shops and dive centers around town, or found their way to the platform at the "Tugs," where they watched divers suit up on this eastern side of the outer mouth of Little Tub Harbor.

Here, four little tugboats lost their lives either through fire or having run aground in the early years of the twentieth century. The area provided a popular shallow and safe wreck-diving experience for divers of all levels, and was an ideal spot for a night dive.

The large platform also provided an unparalleled view of beautiful Georgian Bay, the lighthouse that guarded the entrance to Big Tub Harbor, and tonight, the sunset beyond. No one is ever disappointed at the spectacular view that soothes the soul here on a warm, clear summer's night.

As the tourists made their way to the lower western part of the town where the action was at night, no one paid any attention to a happy little girl who walked along the dock. She wore a simple faded red smock and inexpensive flip-flops. She was alone save for a one-eyed brown and yellow emaciated looking teddy bear clutched under her arm. She was a pleasant little thing who hummed and hopped as she passed the shops, stores, and washroom facilities on the west side of town. At this time of day, the sun dropped behind the building tops here, and quickly plunged everything below into an ever-cooling shadow as the gloaming set in.

The child seemed content by herself. She stooped down now and then to pick up a coin or some other small but useless item abandoned by its owner, and put them into the pocket of her little smock.

As she neared the end of the dock, she stopped when she witnessed a man and woman being wrestled, as if lifeless, into the trunk of a car by an elderly foreign man with a cane. The man looked her way but apparently didn't see her, because he didn't smile, nor did he ask her why she was there all alone.

No one else witnessed the event, as it took place behind a small harbor dumpster. The man then slammed the trunk of the car, threw his cane onto the passenger seat, climbed in, and sped off.

In his haste, and perhaps due to the encroaching darkness, the man must have failed to see the small bag that was left at dock's end. Pedestrian traffic is low along this particular area of the dock at night, as only owners and visitors of the various yachts and sailboats moored there were permitted access then.

The child watched as the man's car disappeared around the corner from Bay Street as it headed south and away from the tiny village. She looked down at the small bag emblazoned with a Fitness Revolution gym logo. She removed the teddy from under her arm and held him with both hands at arms' length in front of her so he could see her face at eye level with his single eye. She smiled at him and then patted his threadbare head before returning him back under her arm.

The child stooped down to pick up the bag. It was awkward for her but she managed, in spite of the fact that she almost dropped her bear in the process. She slid her little arm through the straps of the gym bag and held it tight to her body, like a woman would clutch a large purse.

Innocently oblivious to oncoming traffic, she crossed the road as she hummed and skipped her way into the woodlands behind the Little Tub Art Gallery.

49

Confusion

Darkness now cloaked the little village of Tobermory. Three men of Wu Yang's team two had spent the past hour at the Dive Inn. Each had their hunger satiated by the inn's famous fish and chips platter, with a few pints of Guiness to wash it down. The talk around their table was sparse, for each man feared what their master, Wu Yang, would do to them if they returned empty-handed.

"Fa, I'm surprised you let those rich old fools live. You should have killed the dogs. Now we risk identification and capture. Whatever were you thinking?" Gino Vaselino asked the team leader.

"Fool!" Chen Fa said. "There has already been one death in this village at our hands. Two more would be sure to bring federal law enforcement down on us. We do not want that." Chen Fa looked at the two men across the table. "Someone has beaten us to the painting. We must find out who that someone is," he said as he summoned their waitress.

The young woman noticed his raised hand and came over to their table. The petite young brunette wore short blue terry cotton shorts and a thin long-sleeved beige T-shirt tied off at the waist, sleeves rolled up to her elbows.

"Tell me," Chen Fa said to the young woman, "did anyone come in here with an unusual package?" Then as if to allay suspicion at this rather peculiar request, he smiled and continued. "We are looking for some friends who were to bring us some urgent medical supplies, but we somehow missed them." His countenance lightened somewhat. "How could we miss someone in this little village?" Chen Fa smiled disarmingly, and held up a twenty-dollar bill.

The young girl, different from the one they had encountered earlier, thought meditatively for a moment as she looked among the three. "Let's see," she said as she took the twenty and stuffed it deep into the ample cleavage beneath her shirt. "People come in here with packages all the time. You know, with all the shops and stuff, but they're like, ordinary people. I mean, well, you know, touristy types. Not like you guys, I mean . . ."

Shing Shen came to her rescue, "Yes, we know what you mean. But did anyone come in here with an *unusual* package?"

Vaselino dropped his head, supporting it on one hand between thumb and forefinger above his brows, elbow on table, slowly shaking his head from side to side.

"Well," she began, "two men and a woman came in a few hours ago. She carried one of those old fashioned gym bags, not the usual type of bag you'd carry around here." The girl smiled sheepishly.

Silence ensued as Chen Fa carefully considered her story. He looked intently into her eyes, which disconcerted her somewhat.

Finally he said, "Is there anything else you can tell us about these people? Did you hear where they were heading, or what exactly was in the bag?"

The girl, relieved that the man was not mad at her—for that was how she had initially read him, said, "One was an elderly Chinese man.

I remember he walked with a cane." At this the three were taken aback. The girl continued. "It looked like the other man was ill, because the older man and a beautiful looking Indian-looking woman helped him outside. The woman had the bag with her, and that's the last I saw of them."

"I see," Chen Fa said. He looked down at the table as though defeated.

"You have been most helpful, thank you." He reached back and pulled out his wallet, leaving a crisp plastic Canadian one hundred dollar bill on the table in front of him. "This should cover our meal and your help, should it not," he asked innocently.

The girl was ecstatic. "Mister, that's about forty dollars more than your bill!"

"Not enough for someone as attractive and observant as you. Please take it; you have earned it, my dear." At this, Chen Fa rose from the table. Shing Shen and Gino Vaselino followed in kind as Fa headed for the door.

Each man was lost in thought as the three walked along the shore without conversation.

Shing Shen was the first to break the silence. "Chen Fa, do you think it was Wu Yang?"

Chen Fa suddenly stopped walking, which nearly caused Vaselino to fall into him. Ignoring this, Chen Fa looked past him to Shing Shen. "I am most certain of it. Why he came into town and how he knew who had the material is beyond my comprehension. But if *he* has found it, I do not know how we will fare with him."

"So now what, Fa?" Vaselino said uncertainly. "We are doomed no matter how you look at it. Yang told us not to come back if we failed to uncover anything, yet for some unknown reason he has taken the initiative and single-handedly retrieved the material himself. We have no recourse but to return to him."

"And that, my Cuban friend, is exactly what we are going to do," said Chen Fa sternly. "I have witnessed firsthand how Wu Yang deals with deserters. If we value our lives, then facing the music, as they say, is the most logical choice for us."

The men walked along about half a mile before they returned to their vehicle. They reluctantly drove back to the old hotel they used as a replacement base in the stead of the one that Travers had compromised.

The men were relieved on their return to find no one at their hideout. Following a search of the immediate vicinity, Shing Shen said, "This is not like Wu Yang, not like him at all."

"In this you are correct, Shing Shen," Chen Fa said. "And Wu Yang would never allow himself to be captured. I am sure he has his reasons and that he will contact us in the imminent future.

"In the meantime, I am going to get some sleep. I have a feeling we are all going to need it," Vaselino said as he headed upstairs.

"An excellent idea, Mr. Vaselino, for indeed we shall," Chen Fa agreed. He collapsed into a large overstuffed leather chair in the large foyer of the old hotel. Shing Shen found refuge on a well-worn chesterfield in the farthest corner from the door.

Each member of the trio entertained similar thoughts throughout their uneasy night. *What the devil was Wu Yang up to?*

50

Free In Captivity

Alan Exner freed himself from his bonds. He held an ear to the door of the cabin wherein he remained a prisoner. He tried the door. It was locked and tightly secure.

His only other option was to climb out the window. He went over to it and yanked open the curtains. It was a porthole, and thus too small for a man to squeeze through. All Exner saw was pitch blackness beyond.

Without his watch he had no way of telling time, but he knew daybreak had to be soon. He had to find Bindhira immediately and get off the ship, but how?

The only discernible sounds were the droning of the ship's engines and the creaking of its joints. The heaving motions Exner felt told him they were navigating through rough water.

The only thing he could find of any practical use for self-defense was an eighteen-inch steel ruler on the desk. Other than pens, paperclips, and a nearly empty wooden cigar box, there was nothing that would be useful to him. But he did have one thing in his favor: the element of surprise. They wouldn't know he had freed himself from his restraints when they returned. He would be ready for them.

Exner had visibly surprised Wu Yang when he mentioned Project Vector. Perhaps his ruse had worked. Perhaps Wu Yang would bring Bindhira to him in good faith so the Chinese agent could find out just to what extent Vector had been compromised before he killed them both. Another possible scenario, and one he hoped was wrong, was that Bindhira had already caved under torture, told them the little she knew, and had already been summarily executed.

In any event, they would be returning for him.

He was but one against how many crew? Even if, with Bindhira's help, they managed to overpower their captors, what then? Exner had no idea what type of ship they were on or where they were heading. And he didn't like the fact that Wu Yang had shoved off in such haste with them aboard.

He heard footsteps coming down the corridor. They were getting louder. Exner switched off the lights and crouched behind the door, ruler in hand. He heard two men talking but couldn't make out their muffled speech.

A key rattled in the lock. The door opened and the lights were switched on. Exner knew the man would be confused for a few moments at not seeing him still restrained to the table.

It was Exner's cue to act. With his left hand he jerked the first man, Chinese, unexpectedly into the room by the wrist, throwing him off balance. He simultaneously tripped him with his left foot, accentuating the man's sudden loss of balance. The man fell flat on his face.

The second man now stood at the threshold. Exner spun around the door, pulled back one end of the ruler, and let it slap smartly over the man's nose. The recoil of the light steel ruler gave the man quite a start, and his eyes began to water profusely. As expected, the man instinctively put his hands to his nose.

Exner directed a powerful swiping side elbow to the man's jaw as he attempted to lash out. He man fell back, unconscious.

The second man reached behind his back no doubt for a weapon concealed in his belt. A quick and forceful rear heel kick doubled the man over. Exner grabbed him by the collar and sent the man hurling out into the corridor, causing him to sprawl over the first assailant.

Quicker than Exner would have liked, the man rolled, produced a semi auto loading pistol, and sat up aiming the gun through his legs.

The NABS agent instinctively hurled the ruler at the man's face with all his might. An end corner of the instrument caught the man directly in his right eye. Liquid vitreous matter oozed out of his eye socket. The man dropped his gun and clutched at his eye, still positioned on the cold steel deck.

Exner quickly slammed the man's head violently forward and down between his legs, hard, onto the steel floor. The assailant recoiled backward with such force that he smacked the rear of his head onto the floor behind him. He lay prone and motionless.

Exner quickly pulled the man into the room. He came back to the threshold and carefully looked around. With no one in sight, he ran out and quickly recovered the man's weapon from the hallway.

The first man had come to by now and slowly tried to raise himself up. Exner threw a violent backhand strike against the man's temple, which threw him heavily back against the table. He slid like a ragdoll to the floor.

Exner searched them both. He left the room with two sets of keys, two .45 caliber handguns, two combat knives and one VHF radio.

He locked the door with one of their keys then ran down the hall, radio in hand, and listened for any chatter that would clue him in as to what was happening aboard ship.

At the first stairway he came to, he ran up toward the main deck of the ship in the fervent hope that this sudden turn of events would not put Bindhira at further risk. With their lives on the line, it became Exner's sole mission to find her, to free her, and to escape together before a furious Wu Yang discovered their absence.

It was a tall order at best . . .

51

Pandora's Box

The water off the southeastern coast of Cuba was incredibly clear. Lee checked his dive computer for his current underwater status: depth, sixty feet; dive time, thirty minutes; tank pressure, 2,600 psi; gas, air; temperature, 78 °F; heading, SSE. He looked over at his buddy, Bill Travers. He saw without an OK hand signal that his old diving friend was not only all right, he was loving it.

Topside, Mercedes was to observe and report any activities to the Canadians on their return. She didn't know exactly what she would do if anyone approached, but she wasn't about to let them down—they were her only hope of getting her daughter back alive.

Lee had professionally dived in Cuba on several occasions before at the request of the Cuban government, notably Havana Harbor, then on the USS *Maine*, and finally in the *Bahia de Cochinos*, the infamous Bay of Pigs. Bill was his assistant on each one.

But Lee enjoyed diving for *any* reason. It was a passion he had pursued his whole life. From the time he crawled around on his knees in the family backyard, 'diving for treasure' at six years old with twin "tanks" (two large sixty-four-ounce empty tomato juice cans strapped to his back with an old belt of his father's), to many years later, diving 250 feet below the frigid waters of the Atlantic Ocean to the sunken Italian luxury liner *Andrea Doria* as safety diver for a National Geographic exposé, diving was deeply and terminally infused in Lee Hartley's DNA.

He had logged over five thousand dives over the years; Travers, maybe three thousand at best, not counting his innumerable pool sessions and quarry forays with hundreds of aspiring scuba enthusiasts out of his Scuba U dive shop.

The Scuba U. It had to be tough for his good friend. Lee knew that Travers was in a position to retire if and when he so desired, but the old bird loved diving and loved teaching people how to experience the underwater world. He didn't really know what Bill would do when this was all over, but for the time being he seemed content here, in Cuba, with Lee.

Lee was grateful for the little time Travers had to reflect on the bad fortune that had befallen him. He would return to Canada homeless, unemployed, and no doubt emotionally scarred from the trauma of his captivity.

At the ninety-foot mark, Bill signaled for Lee to follow him further out and to the right of their current position. The water was unbelievably warm and clear even at this depth, and Lee could see clearly for about sixty feet in every direction. The standard-issue stubby yellow scuba tanks would give them a good thirty minutes or so at this depth, more than enough time for their mission.

Suddenly, as though an old TV screen came into focus, there lay the ship in all her glory: the *Cristóbal Colón*. The old battle cruiser had not aged well. Saltwater was slowly reducing the once proud ship of the Spanish Navy to a dissolving hunk of rusted metal. Many rivets in the steel plates had perished, and several hull plates had curled outward. Their sharp exposed edges posed a very dangerous threat to the unwary diver.

Travers was a bad one for chronically swimming ahead of his dive buddy, and this dive proved no exception. He was already hanging off the bow, waiting for Lee to catch up.

Once Lee arrived, Travers motioned for him to follow as he swam around the bow to the port side of the ship. He switched on his underwater light and peered down into the holds through the crushed metal. Extensive damage was evident from the relentless barrages it received during the Spanish-American War of 1898 at the hands of the US Navy.

Travers looked back to Lee, then went over and down into an open hatchway. Lee also reached for his light and switched it on. He could see his friend's bubbles as they cascaded up through the gloom from the inner bowels of the ship and through the decayed metal decking on their way to the surface.

Lee checked his computer read-out once again before he pulled himself over the side of the hatchway and descended into the ship. The instrument display told him he had about twenty minutes left of no-decompression time at his current depth of one hundred feet. This window would decrease, however, as he followed Travers' bubbles deeper into the hold.

Lee saw live mortars and several five-round magazines of live rifle ammunition. They were scattered everywhere along the decking. He exhaled deeper to make himself less buoyant, then expertly drifted down to the deck, where he picked up one of the rifle magazines. He flipped the magazine over and peered at the base of the ammunition. The year 1896 was stamped onto the bottom of the brass casings. Lee placed one into a pocket of his BC as a large moray eel darted quickly over his left fin, startled out of its hiding place in a desperate bid to safely locate another.

Within a few minutes he found Bill hovering over a long, shiny brass case. Drifting down, he saw Travers shake his head. When he saw Lee's face, he pointed to his right twenty feet away. There lay a second box!

The brass container Bill discovered on his previous dive to the *Colón* had been much closer to the open hatch and more easily visible from the outside where a large section of plate was missing. The newly installed box was better placed so as not to be observed from outside the wreck. But why would they have planted a second deeper in the same hold? Both men had seen divers pull out a box which they believed was the one Travers had seen earlier.

Jagged steel was everywhere, and a diver's worst nightmare should any part of his gear become entangled or worse yet, cut. Lee was careful that the regulator breathing hose off his right shoulder was pulled in and away from it. He gripped the mouthpiece between his teeth a little tighter.

The brass container was new, and designed to be watertight as well as impervious to the elements. It bore no visible Chinese inscriptions, however. Travers was attempting to lift it when Lee rushed over and pushed him away. At first Travers thought that his friend might have suffered a hit of nitrogen narcosis (a condition of stupor brought on by the increased partial pressure of nitrogen on a diver's brain at deep depths), but then he understood.

He watched as Lee Hartley carefully examined the box for trip wires or any other evidence of booby-trapping that could trigger an explosion if the box was disturbed. As a commercial diver, Lee had been called in by the authorities on numerous occasions and in numerous countries while on other assignments to defuse booby-trapped devices in and around harbors and private yachts.

He found no such device on the box. Lee motioned Travers to grab an end. Together, and with significant effort, they managed to lift it up. The weight was too much for the two of them however, and they had to let it drop back into the silt of the hold.

The only way the other divers could have brought up the original heavy box was to inflate their buoyancy compensators to a dangerously high capacity. But this action would offset the weight of the box so they could more easily bring it to the surface.

But if one of them had lost a handhold with a BC full of air, he would have suffered a certain fatal air embolism due to an extremely fast rate of ascent once he was free of the weight that held him at depth, due to the ever expanding air in his BC as the water pressure suddenly decreased around him.

No: common sense ruled on this one, Lee thought.

Travers motioned Lee through the plume of silt to try again. Lee pointed to his computer. Looking at his, Travers nodded his assent. They had to go; his air pressure had dropped to eight hundred pounds, enough for a comfortably safe ascent but little else.

Travers held up a finger, then took out his knife and tried to get its blade under an edge of the top in an attempt to crack the container open. Lee swam over and worked at the other end with his knife in similar fashion to double the odds.

Suddenly a surge of milky bubbles burst from under the container's top as it sprung wide open. It knocked Lee back, who lost his grip on the container. The resulting cloud of silt that enveloped them when it slipped from Travers' hands temporarily disoriented them both. The container slammed to the deck, upright with its top closed.

What looked like tiny half-dissolved paper booklets about three inches by two inches in size floated gently out of the box and slowly upward. Some didn't make it through the hatchway, but those that did rose lethargically up and through on their way to the surface.

Inside, Travers found several more packets along with a milky fluid that clung to them, as it had to those that now drifted to the surface. The packets looked like nothing more than mere matchbooks, but at this depth and visibility he couldn't be sure.

Lee tugged at his buddy's arm. It was past time to surface safely. He pushed away and headed up toward the open hatchway. Suddenly, he heard an explosion of compressed air pluming above him.

His regulator hose had caught on a jagged edge of twisted metal plating that dangled from a dark corner overhead. The rubber hose ruptured, causing a massive flow of bubbles and rapid loss of breathing air.

Rising to investigate, Travers found Lee struggling to free his air hose from a tangled mass of piping that hung down from the corner of the hatchway. The tangled mess was no doubt unseated from its already precarious position when the container popped open, thereby sending a powerful rush of compressed air up into it. Lee's regulator continued to spew life-giving air dangerously fast from his tank. It would be empty in minutes.

Instinctively, Travers pulled out his backup second stage regulator mouthpiece and jammed it into his friend's mouth. He then shut down Lee's tank to prevent any further loss of air and visibility due to the build-up of silt that now enshrouded them in total darkness.

As Lee held on to the lip of the hatchway, Travers set about freeing his friend from what would have been an underwater fatality. Within minutes, Lee was free. The two pulled themselves up and out of the hatch into crystal clear water. The two headed directly to the surface without a necessary decompression stop. Both men hoped their computers were set conservatively. If so, they'd have a good chance at beating the bends. If *not* . . .

It was a struggle, as always, to fight the strong pull of the surf and surge once on the surface, but experience prevailed and soon they reached the safety of the beach. Lee dropped to his knees and doffed his BC and tank assembly. Travers shrugged his scuba unit off in like manner and came over to check on his friend.

Looking up at Travers Lee said, "I guess I owe you one, buddy."

"*Guess?* You're darned right you do. You ruined a perfectly good regulator!"

Lee smiled. "How much air did you have left, Bill? I didn't think we were going to pull that one off."

"Oh lots—plenty enough to fill a bike tire or two."

Lee gave his friend a hearty pat on the back. They knew that a less experienced dive team would never have made it back to the surface alive under similar circumstances, which was exactly why Exner had sent them in the first place.

"What d'ya make of that other box down there, Lee," Travers queried.

"Don't know," Lee said, "but whatever we do, we're going to have to take a different approach. Whatever came out of that first one is probably in the second. It didn't look too healthy. I don't want to cause a repeat performance."

Their conversation was interrupted as Mercedes ran over to them from the thin veil of trees that separated the beach from the road. "*Señors*", she said, "they have found the car. I could not tell who or how many persons, but they were there for a good while, then left."

"Not a good sign," said Lee more to Travers than Mercedes. "We're going to have to cover our tracks at every turn from now on."

"When will I be able to go back to my home, *Señor* Lee?" Mercedes displayed a face of sad despondency.

"What can I tell you, Mercedes? I really can't say for sure. I think it would be good to wait a week or so for your sake, my dear."

She became visibly agitated at this. "A week? Oh, *Señor* Lee, I cannot wait a week. What about my Maela? She must be found before then. She will be missing her mother and . . ."

Mercedes choked at the thought of being alone without Javier around to take proper care of them. Travers went over to her. She pulled him tightly to her and hugged him with all her might. She cried in pitiful sobs as Travers gently struggled to get his breath from her crushing grasp.

Once she got control of herself, the men grabbed their gear and jogged back and forth from the beach to the grotto to store it safely inside. They were careful to cover the low entrance with branches, driftwood, and brush. They still had two fully charged scuba tanks and regulators hidden among the rest of the gear.

Darkness was descending fast, and they decided to remain at the grotto for the night. The men each took a three-hour watch to ensure no interlopers would surprise them in the dark of night.

Unknown to the divers, many of the 'matchbooks' had managed to reach the surface. The sudden release of pressure, combined with the increased warmth of the surface water, caused the milky substance on the match heads to chemically bond with the virally treated phosphorous sesquisulphide on the match heads. Within minutes of floating on the surface, the slimy paste vaporized, then dissipated into the atmosphere.

For the three on the beach that night, ignorance was bliss as a strong offshore breeze served to carry the now airborne virus out to sea, to wreak certain death on every human being in its path.

Pandora's Box had unwittingly been opened.

52

A Cuban Interpretation

Major Dayana Eveline Torrado of the Eastern Army's Third Armored Division of the Cuban Revolutionary Armed Forces or FAR (*Fuerzas Armadas Revolucionarias),* stationed in the province of Santiago de Cuba, carefully studied the report she had just been handed by her secretary.

FAR had long been the most powerful institution in the island nation. Throughout the 1980s, the tonnage of Soviet military equipment for the Cuban army far exceeded deliveries in any year since the military build-up during the Missile Crisis of 1962.

In 1989, the Cuban government instituted a purge of the armed forces and Ministry of the Interior, resulting in the executions of Maj. Gen. Arnaldo Ochoa, and Ministry of Interior Col. Antonio de le Guardia on charges of corruption and drug trafficking. The judgment pronounced on them was the well-known *Causa 1* (Cause 1).

The army was severely reduced following the executions. The withdrawal of Soviet backing became so severe that the Revolutionary

Armed Forces were reduced to a mere 80,000 troops. It was therefore imperative that those leading the soldiers were top-shelf and totally committed to the ideals of the Castro regime.

The Ministry of the Interior was soon after placed under the direct control of the Revolutionary Armed Forces Chief General, one Raul Castro. One of the Chief General's first tasks was to transfer dozens of trusted army officers, among them Major Torrado, into the Ministry of the Interior.

It was with certain alarm that what Major Torrado now read before her was to be made known to a larger part of the inner circle. The major dropped the sheaf of papers on the steel desktop in front of her. She drummed the fingers of her left hand on the papers as she considered how best to proceed.

Picking up the receiver of her phone, Major Torrado spoke into the instrument with the commanding tone her position afforded. "I have been ordered to conduct a meeting of great importance here at 1300 hours. It will consist of the persons listed on the encoded report we received earlier."

She listened for a few moments and then replied, "Yes, I realize it is short notice." A few more moments of silence ensued as she listened to the party at the other end. "This is at the request of the president of the council of the State of Cuba, Raul Castro, himself."

"I will handle any fallout from pulling DGI personnel from their current duties. That is all." With that, she curtly replaced the handset back onto the receiver of the black heavy ceramic rotary dial telephone in front of her. What little the major knew of Chinese activity in Cuba had just changed dramatically.

On September 14, 2012, a senior Cuban general parlayed an agreement of military cooperation with China during a visit to Beijing. He said that Cuba was willing to "enhance exchanges with the Chinese military and strengthen cooperation in the training of personnel and weapons upgrades."

The reality of it was that Cuba and China had signed a secret pact between them, which was the real reason the good general went to Cuba in the first place. China would infuse millions of US dollars into the country in exchange for using the island nation as a base from which she could better monitor the activities of the Americans. But the pact involved more than that, much more.

Major Dayana Torrado was one of the select few senior officers Raul Castro had entrusted with this knowledge. Raul was especially fond of the major, for she efficiently performed her duties as well as any man, perhaps even better. She routinely outperformed her fellow officers, and Raul was totally convinced of her dedication to the *Revolución*, her unrelenting devotion to the Castros', and her love for her country.

The major had saved the younger Castro brother's life once, taking a bullet for him during a minor uprising in the early months of 2012, which was quickly and decisively quashed.

Torrado had caught a glint of steel in the second row among hundreds of citizens while standing on the platform beside Raul as he spoke early one evening. She dived off the platform and onto a man armed with a revolver, whereupon she was shot in the thigh.

Major Torrado was soon after awarded *el Comandante's* Medal of Highest Bravery for her "unselfish act in the protecting of one of the founding fathers of the *Revolución* from grievous bodily harm."

It was discovered soon after that the shooter was part of a plot to assassinate Raul by dissidents who realized that another Castro at the helm of the country after the surprise resignation of older brother Fidel would only serve to drive the country further into poverty.

Several coconspirators were quickly rounded up and executed, as was the assassin, by firing squad. Others thought to be part of the group were also arrested. These were forced to bury their dead compatriots before being placed in prison for the rest of their lives, based purely on circumstantial evidence.

This was merely another means of infusing fear into the hearts of the people. It also served as an example to others who plotted against the regime, a regime that had brought little but abject misery to the beautiful people of Cuba for more than half a century.

Raul had personally briefed Major Torrado on an ambitious new Cuban-Chinese cooperative endeavor that had developed a groundbreaking biochemical technology that she was to now share with her trusted aides.

The appointed time came. By 1305 hours there were eight people in attendance in the FAR situation room. Two were high-ranking DGI agents, one of whom was a valued confidant to Fidel himself.

Of the other six, three were Chinese secret service operatives. The remaining three were directly responsible to Major Torrado, head of the Special Investigative Unit, an organization of highly trained soldiers that reported directly to the head of the Ministry of the Interior.

The mandate of the SIU was to uncover plots, ferret out dissenters, and ensure every resort had an onsite operative to observe and report both tourist activities on these compounds as well as their relationships with Cubans outside their walls.

As the major entered the room, everyone stood at attention until she motioned them to sit. She looked over the group and said, “Thank you for coming on such short notice.” She allowed a few minutes for those in attendance to finish rustling about and settle down before she commenced.

“A team of Chinese and Cuban scientists working closely together under great secrecy has developed a silent new weapon of lethal consequence. This weapon does not involve destruction of property, and is now operational.”

“We have been tasked with ensuring that the Chinese-issue Ventriloquist units maintain their functional integrity, and continue to redirect US satellite beams currently trained on our research and development facilities, causing them to be interpreted as being located in the more remote areas of the country.”

Major Torrado noticed with pleasure that everyone was on the edge of their seat. The agents in attendance were now quietly abuzz among themselves, until the major overtly cleared her throat. Almost instantly the fervor decelerated to an utter silence.

Major Torrado continued. “Basically the weapon is a genetically modified viral clone of the deadly Ebola pathogen. In essence, the hybrid virus is capable of replicating itself among select insect species.”

“In addition, the ‘brass’ the containers used to house the virus are comprised of, is a unique alloy that will not show up on any metal detection equipment.”

“This is truly the ultimate weapon,” the major said with conviction. “Nuclear warheads are so yesterday,” she continued. This brought several nervous smiles from those in attendance.

“Nukes are much too cumbersome to transport, and way too difficult to conceal in light of today’s laser-guided satellite tracking technology. Our plan is to ‘seed’ the Great Lakes of North America with this strain of Ebola. The virus will remain safely dormant until such time as it’s deemed necessary to unleash it.”

The major continued. “Virtually undetectable, small, and extremely portable, this remarkable new weapon has the power to destroy our enemies by indiscriminately striking at their very heartland, with virtually no warning.”

“Several specific strategic areas in each of the five Great Lakes are to be the epicenters of dissemination. Specially constructed brass boxes containing the pathogen and its catalyst will be placed inside shipwrecks off major port cities at various depths, awaiting their release.”

The major paused. "The time of their release has not yet been determined. Through this new biological weapon, the Cuban and Chinese cooperative will have the power to bring the entire North American enterprise to its knees."

One of the Cuban men, advanced in years but of some obvious esteem, stood up. The major paused to allow him to speak.

"Major, we all know the Americans do not take kindly to threats of any kind. They will not hesitate to retaliate. We have all been down this road before," he said in a tired, condescending tone.

"Threats are merely a ploy on the part of the weak to elicit a false facade of power in the face of the strong," Major Torrado said as the man took his seat. "Comrade, this will not be a threat, I assure you. There will be no time for our activities to be assessed as such."

The major's tone became increasingly vindictive. "Cuba has been denied trade with America for five decades! For over fifty years they have alienated their people from us, and ignored our descent into abject poverty. Following WWII, the Americans even helped rebuild the countries of their former mortal enemies, Germany and Japan."

"Yet when Hurricane Katrina struck the central Gulf Coast of the United States in 2005, Cuba was one of the first countries to offer humanitarian aid. We assembled over 1,500 doctors and twenty-six tons of medicine on standby as a gesture of good will. Do you know how they reacted?" The major paused for effect. "Their State Department *rejected* our offer, while they neglected their own people!"

A pall descended upon the room. Some in attendance had been aware of this; many had not, including representatives of the Chinese government.

"With Chinese support," she continued, "we will wrest control of this half of the hemisphere without firing a shot. We will throw the North American public into a desperate panic that will place incredible pressure on their government to comply with our wishes, even as their people drop like flies. Mercy shall not be shown them, nor shall they ever spit in our faces again!"

She paused in her near-maniacal fervor. There was unbridled surprise on the faces of some, guarded terror on others, but none in attendance dared speak out. "On the Chinese front, for years the American CIA has been undermining the integrity of many of their projects, from offshore oil drilling to industrial sabotage. The time for the People's Republic to assert their presence on the world stage is at hand. They too grow tired of playing second fiddle to the American war machine."

"The Cuban government has graciously offered our Chinese comrades an opportunity to establish a base on our island a mere ninety miles from the coast of Florida. The time to strike is when the iron is hot, comrades. The United States has been all but financially devastated from their foolish unwinnable wars with Iraq, Afghanistan, Iran, and North Korea. Their blind, insatiable thirst for capitalistic gain has brought about their downfall."

"They have been the captains of their own defeat. These wars of attrition have proved to have been the best way of wearing the capitalists down. With the West on the verge of bankruptcy, the European Union already there, we are ripe to take the spoils."

The room was abuzz with hopes, conjectures, fears, and rumor. Most in the room seemed convinced that if ever there was a time for victory against the capitalists it was now.

"As we speak," Major Torrado continued, "several Cuban and Chinese operatives under Wu Yang, a senior ChIS agent assigned to this mission, are already in Canada, specifically the Great Lakes region of Ontario, to carry out a mission codenamed, *Project Vector.*"

"These men have acquired a vessel and have been clandestinely implementing phase one; that of 'seeding' the Great Lakes with viral implants of the modified Ebola pathogen. This particular strain has been adapted primarily for vector transmission."

A thirty-something Chinese man now stood. The major seemed momentarily agitated by the man, but she quickly brought her emotions under control. "Yes?"

The man spoke in broken English. "I have heard of this virus. How effective is its use as a weapon?" He reclaimed his seat without waiting for her reply.

"Viral hemorrhagic Ebola fever has a fatality rate of up to 90 percent," Major Torrado said. "There is no treatment or vaccine available to counteract its effects once a host has been infected, which is why we chose to develop it. Its lethality is second only to the HIV virus, which is the deadliest virus currently known to man."

"Phase one is nearly complete and consists, as I mentioned previously, of a viral release into the atmosphere, where it will remain in concentration as it settles inland. It will present symptoms in human hosts almost immediately before it automatically initiates phase two."

"The second phase of Project Vector will take longer to develop. As the infectious mist settles on colonies of black flies, wasps, and mosquitoes, the virus will then self-perpetuate through vector-borne dissemination—that is, bites and stings on human hosts. This is the most crucial phase of the project. "

"It is the intent of both the Cuban and Chinese governments to create sufficient shock and awe in North America that it will serve to ensure compliance among other countries as well. Our weapon will be unleashed suddenly and without warning. Then, when the time is right, our plan shall be revealed to the world. There will be no shots fired, no armies mobilized. We will paralyze the American war machine with an unstoppable weapon directed at their very heartland."

"Westerners are but simple lemmings who take no action when their elected officials wage war for greedy gain abroad as long as they can remain 'free' to indulge their overtly decadent lifestyle. It will be easy to control any retaliatory actions once their pride has been destroyed as they witness a horrific death toll on a massive scale never before experienced among their citizens."

She paused to take a sip of water from the small flask on the table In front of her. "They will quickly realize that we will not tolerate any deviance from our demands."

Another Chinese agent wearing an old but still respectable suit stood up as Major Torrado set the flask back on the table. Her annoyance at this interruption was evident in the tone of her voice, which, to the man, resembled a repressed dislike for his people.

"Yes?"

The man appeared apprehensive as he spoke. "Major Torrado. How does this Ebola virus present itself in its victims?"

The room was completely devoid of sound as the major took several minutes to leaf through the documents spread before her. "Ah yes, the symptoms. Normal Ebola symptoms normally present within two to twenty-one days. Our strain has been developed to manifest itself within twenty-four hours of exposure, sooner if one's immune system is weak."

"Fever, intense weakness, muscle pain, and headache are the initial indicators. Soon thereafter symptoms will intensify, and others will manifest. Among them: vomiting, diarrhea, bleeding from bodily orifices, compromised livers and kidneys, and severe dehydration. It must be noted that an infected person's bodily secretions are highly contagious and must be avoided at all costs."

At this, the man who had asked the last question, broke in with another question, albeit sheepishly. "Forgive me again, Major, but why this Ebola? Why not, say, anthrax?"

The major propped herself on a corner of the table. She shifted her short khaki skirt a little farther south to better conceal the exposed panty top of her beige hose.

Unabashed, she continued. "The top secret document before me states that this uniquely modified virus will be initially difficult to detect. Anthrax is old school and easy to detect. Ebola however, shares symptoms will many other serious viruses such as malaria, typhoid fever, meningitis, hepatitis, cholera, and leptospirosis, among others. This will confound and confuse their best doctors and scientists."

The major again picked up the sheaf of papers before her and thumbed through them until she found what she was looking for. "Ebola can only be identified through highly specific tests such as antigen detection," she read, "Others, include virus isolation by cell culture which takes time, reverse transcriptase polymerase chain reaction assay, and enzyme-linked immunosorbent assay."

"In other words, accurate diagnosis of our genetically altered form of the virus will thus be difficult, if not impossible, to detect," she gloated.

She continued to have their undivided attention. "I am familiar with some of these things because I graduated as a doctor of immunology before I embarked on an illustrious career with our beloved army." Major Torrado stood up and paced slowly before her audience, then paused to signify a change in direction."

"Her visage darkened. "Once Project Vector is unleashed, there will be no turning back—for any of us." Then she looked deep into the eyes of those cast before her. "I need not remind you of the consequences should any of this information reach beyond these walls."

"You are dismissed."

Major Torrado saw that her final admonition had its desired effect. She noticed by the looks on their faces that each was eager to comply with her wishes. Indeed fear, she reminded herself, was always the best form of compliance.

53

Regrouping

Alan Exner was faced with a seemingly impossible task. The NABS control, used to being surrounded by capable agents and high-tech equipment always at the ready, was now alone, exhausted, and on a mission he could not fail to successfully complete.

The senior NABS operative took stock of the current situation. He was aboard an as yet unidentified vessel with enemy agents en route to carrying out a mission of some sort. He knew they were at sea, but did not know where. Bindhira was still imprisoned somewhere aboard ship, location unknown. He was armed, but knew that time was running out for them both.

It wouldn't take long before the two guards were discovered locked in the cabin from which he escaped. He only hoped that Bindhira was still alive, that he could find her, and that they could get off the ship before being discovered. It was a tall order at best.

Exner came to the end of the hall and crept up a companionway to the next deck. He opened a nearby fire hose box and stuffed the knives and one gun behind the hose, and out of sight, then closed it tight.

The VHF radio was on, but squelched low to avoid detection. He looked from left to right and back again, then trotted off to the right. As he went from cabin to cabin, he paused and put an ear to each door. When no voices or activity were discerned from within, he quickly moved on.

Exner got halfway down the corridor when a door opened outward not fifteen feet from where he was! He quickly tucked the gun in the waistband at the small of his back. He knew if he used it the sound would bring many more into the fray. The door remained ajar just long enough for Exner to stealthily rush up behind it just as someone was exiting.

He rushed around the door, hoping against hope there was only one attacker. Surprisingly, the person at the threshold was prepared. Exner was met with a simultaneous knife-hand strike to the neck and a knee to the groin which dropped him facedown to the deck in excruciating pain. In the brief struggle, the radio fell from his grasp and shattered as it fell to the metal deck.

On all fours now, he looked up to expect the worst, but was met not with a finishing blow but an outstretched hand!

"Bindhi, how the—?" was all he could get out.

"Not now, Alan. I am sorry. I did not know it was you. Are you okay?"

"You were very kind under the circumstances girl," he managed to spit out. "I'm just glad it was you. The question I have, is—are *you* okay?" Exner then noticed two men sprawled on the floor in the far corner of the room, unconscious.

She pulled him to his feet and smiled. "Better than they are," she said. "But we must get off this ship and notify your people. Alan, from the information I have gleaned, they still have not located the materials we found on the *Forever Young*."

"Which means Wu Yang *didn't* grab the bag off the dock," Exner deducted. "I'm really not sure if that's a good thing or not." The wheels that turned in Exner's mind were nearly on overload. "Wu Yang; where is Wu Yang?"

"Alan," she said ignoring him, "what we discovered onboard the *Forever Young* were virus-laced packets in its purest form. This may mean that in their haste to initiate Project Vector they have put a more diluted pathogen into service. I overheard that their target is the whole of the Great Lakes region." She paused at seeing Exner's perplexed face. "The men were not too careful in their discussions around me. They were going to kill me anyway."

"They didn't know with whom they were dealing," Exner smiled, putting a hand on her shoulder.

Bindhira looked into his face with a boyish confidence she rarely revealed. "Wu Yang has been authorized to release a concentrated form of virus in lieu of the 'test batch'. Their problem is, they don't have it as yet."

She inwardly chided herself. Exner could see it in her face as she spoke. "*We* had it, but where is it now?"

"Concentrated virus of what?" Exner looked past her, then grabbed a hand and pulled her around a nearby corner, out of line of sight of the long corridor.

"What are we dealing with here, Bindhi?" Alan saw a look of horror on her face.

"Ebola, Alan. It's a purified, highly virulent form of the already deadly Ebola virus."

"We've got to at least get to the radio room and contact my people at all costs, Bindhi."

"That was my destination before you so rudely interrupted me, Alan," she smiled. "It is just aft of the bridge, and manned by only one operator per shift."

"Right then. Let's be off," he said.

Within minutes the two agents managed to reach the main deck without detection. Looking out from the companionway exit, it took a few minutes for their eyes to acclimate to the bright light of the midday sun.

Suddenly Exner withdrew. He yanked Bindhira by the shoulder as she peered in the opposite direction. "Incoming—two," Exner hissed. Each instinctively crouched on opposite sides of the companionway entrance.

The voices of the men grew louder as they drew closer to their position.

The first man stepped over the raised threshold. Exner threw a crushing left hook to the man's ribs and tripped him when he doubled over in pain. The man lost his balance and tumbled, heavily, down the companionway.

The second man was too slow to react. He started to draw his weapon when he saw the two, but the gun didn't have time to clear its holster. Bindhira attacked his ears with a painful double bear-paw strike. The man dropped his sidearm and held the sides of his head with both hands in an attempt to relieve the pain of two ruptured eardrums.

In support, Exner grabbed a rusty old stainless steel fire extinguisher from its wall mount and drove its bottom deep into the man's gut. A downward elbow strike to the back of the man's head sent him down for the count.

Grabbing the man's ancient 9 mm eight-round German-made Walther P-38 pistol, Exner tossed it to Bindhira, who instinctively caught it. He scrambled down the companionway to where the first man still lay. Exner pulled a black 9 mm Browning hi-power from the man's jacket pocket and raced up the stairs to Bindhira, who was keeping watch at the stairway entrance.

In unison, both dropped the magazines of their respective weapons to inspect the rounds within.

"At least they're both 9-mils. We can share ammo if need be. I'm good to go, you?" Exner asked as he looked over.

"Locked and loaded," she replied, returning the glance.

"Come!" Exner said as he slammed home his magazine. He grabbed Bindhira's hand after she did the same, and the two sprinted to the cabin just abaft the bridge. Exner was in the lead, weapon drawn and ready. The door to the radio room was unlocked. They were surprised to find it unoccupied.

He pulled the .45 automatic from the small of his back and replaced it with the hi-power. He then removed the magazine of the larger caliber weapon and tossed it into one corner, the magazine into another.

"Must be lunchtime," Exner said, "no one home."

The far wall was taken up by an old radio transmitter and receiver array. "Know how to use one of these?" Exner had seen old marine radios such as these in war movies, but didn't know how to operate the low-tech communications equipment.

"Alan, I work for the NSA. We specialize in signals, messages, and codes of all types and configurations. It has been a long time since I have seen one of these though." Bindhira shot him a quick smile and then set about the task at hand.

He locked the door, and from time to time gazed out its porthole window to check for any unwanted guests, especially the radio operator.

The NSA agent carefully looked over the radio equipment. She plunked herself down into the operator's well-worn leather desk chair. More to refresh her memory that educate Exner, she gave him a rundown of the equipment she was dealing with.

"This is an AN/WRT-1 shipboard transmitter. Its operating frequency is between 300 to 1,500 kilo-cycles. Although it does not have any single side band capabilities, the unit can transmit continuous wave, frequency-shift keying, and voice signals."

"Voice signals would be good," Exner said as he peered over her shoulder.

"If we use voice signals, Alan, the range will be appreciably diminished. It's only a medium-range transceiver. Doing so will reduce its 500 watt output to about 125 watts."

"Great. I guess there's no chance of getting a message onto the mainland from here, wherever *here* is. All I know is we're miles from land," he said.

"To clarify Alan, medium range in maritime radio terms is a radius anywhere from 200 to 1,500 miles, Alan." Bindhira paused to look at him reassuringly. "These parameters however, are determined by many things, such as atmospheric conditions, type of frequency used; even the time of the day, month, and year can affect its operating range."

"How come the thing's so massive?" Exner came around beside her and saw a confusing configuration of dials and switches before them.

"This is an old five-tiered unit. The topmost is the radio frequency amplifier. The second unit is the RF oscillator. In the middle is the frequency control group unit. The control tower supply is the fourth one down, and the last is the main power supply unit." Bindhira was pleased that the old technology was coming back to her so easily.

"The AN/WRT-1 transmitter is excellent for long-range communications, especially during nighttime hours. However, during the day, its effective transmitting distance is somewhat compromised."

Various pitches and frequency squeals broke the silence as Bindhira fine-tuned dials, twisted knobs, and flipped switches.

"I am scanning for one of our frequencies, Alan. Once we have that, we can transmit a crude code signal that the Sequoia system will hopefully pick up, translate, and route to a receiver monitored by NABS," she said as she held the radio operator's headphone set to one ear.

"Why don't you simply radio the Canadian Coast Guard?" Exner knew there was probably a good reason she hadn't thought of that.

Bindhira looked over to him. He was gazing out the porthole. "First of all Alan, we do not even know what type of ship we are on. Secondly, the bridge no doubt has a patch to the radio room and they would know that a 'mayday' has come from their own ship. Thirdly, I hope to send a phantom message to redirect them back to their last port of call."

"Well, whatever you do, do it quickly, Bindhi. I'm sure 'Sparks' will be back from his lunch soon."

The NSA agent rose from the operator's chair and began to rummage through a small filing cabinet to her left. The radio room was very clean and efficient despite the old equipment contained within. The operator clearly took pride in his post.

Within a few minutes, she found what she was looking for. "Alan, the ship we are currently on is an oceanographic ship. She is the *Étoile Profonde* and hails from—Haiti!"

"Hmmm," Exner said. "That's French for *deep star*." It took him a few moments before exclaiming, "*Haiti*? How does one of the most poverty-stricken countries in the world acquire funding for oceanographic expeditions? They still haven't recovered from that magnitude 7.0 earthquake that hit them in 2010!"

"Indeed," Bindhira said. "However, Alan, it all comes into perspective when you realize that Haiti is one of the closest neighbors to Cuba, and Cuba as we know, is now in bed with the Chinese. By being registered in Haiti, this ship is free to 'sail under the radar' as it were, giving her free rein to sail the seven seas without suspicion of any kind; much easier than a ship of Cuban registry."

"And as the United States regularly patrols Cuban waters from outside their territorial boundaries, even a Chinese ship sailing to and from Cuba would be suspect."

"Somebody's been doing their homework all right, Ms. Shankar," Exner said ruefully. "What better platform to conduct oceanographic studies in the Great Lakes than a foreign ship of friendly registry?"

All the while Bindhira was working the radio. Finally she obtained a Sequoia scanning frequency. She dialed in a dedicated emergency NABS code as provided by Exner, then transmitted their current GPS coordinates and situation.

Exner, who had been keeping watch through the small window of the radio room door, suddenly said, "You'd better wrap it up quick Bindhi; we've got company!"

He drew his gun, then unlocked the door and crouched behind it.

54

Achilles' Heel

The warmth of the morning Cuban sun was a welcome respite from the cool night that preceded it. Lee stood at the grotto's entrance and looked in at his two friends, still fast asleep even though it was 7:30 a.m. It had been a stressful few days for all of them. Lee had relieved Travers at 4:00 a.m. for the last watch of the night.

It was easy to be lulled into a false sense of security by the peaceful natural beauty of their seaside surroundings. A cool welcoming breeze filtered through an incredibly blue cloudless sky. Then there was the anticipation of a great wreck dive to come.

But Lee knew this peaceful setting could change in a moment. They were sitting on a powder-keg, and he knew they had to bring up the brass box or at least destroy its contents before anyone else happened by.

As his friends continued to enjoy a much deserved rest, Lee pondered the events of the past day. From what he had gathered from the NABS briefing, things didn't seem to add up. Why would Cubans plant viral boxes around their own country if this was to be a plot against North America? Moreover, why had they changed out the box that had initially been planted there?

Lee was beginning to believe that a group of rogue dissidents from *both* countries was at work here with the right clout and opportunity to wrest power from their own governments when the time was ripe. The implications were staggering.

Lee grabbed his kit from out of the grotto and moved outside to an area distant enough not to disturb the others. He pulled the Sequoia sat-phone out of his bag and removed it from its waterproof protective case.

It took several minutes for the signal to bounce off two military satellites before being scrambled by a third that was dedicated to the Sequoia system. Once Sequoia picked up the unit's security frequency, it was directed to NABs headquarters at Niagara-On-The-Lake.

It was a gruff Scott Culp who responded at the other end. "Hartley, what's your status?" The CIA sub-director got straight to the point, Lee had to give him that.

"Between a rock and a hard place, sir." Their signal was drifting in and out, but the conversation remained intelligible.

Lee relayed to Culp the events of the past few days, up to and including their dive on the *Cristóbal Colón*, minus the opening of the box.

"Strange Hartley, but then, this whole affair is strange." Lee could imagine Culp smoothing a hand over his graying hair. "My take on the situation," the CIA agent surmised, "is that that one of the boxes planted down there could be a means of keeping the Cuban government in check by the Chinese. The other may have been planted by the Establishment to circumvent the Chinese for their own reasons. It must have been placed down there without their knowledge."

"At any rate," he sighed, "we now know we're dealing with a highly virulent strain of Ebola virus."

"Remember, the viral agent has not been field-tested to our knowledge. My guess for the two boxes in that wreck, is that one may contain a smaller dose of a weaker strain to be used to test its incubation time and rate. The second probably contains the real deal as insurance if need be."

"Sir," Lee broke in. "I have strong reason to believe that this may *not* be the work of who we think it is, but rather that of a renegade group with their own agenda. This group is going to great lengths to pin this on the Cuban and Chinese governments no doubt with the intent of threatening them with it as well. But I've nothing, as yet, to prove this."

"I've no doubt there are rogue-operatives imbedded in the Cuban DGI," Culp responded, "possibly even in their military. But if the Castros discover a double-cross, well, it could get ugly at best. But when the Chinese find out . . ."

The seq-pod went silent for a time, then Culp said, "You may be on to something Hartley." He paused. "But whatever you do, *do not* allow the contents of those boxes to be exposed to the air. Once the water pressure is reduced around them, the host fabric of the virus will break down quickly when exposed to the atmosphere and release the pathogen into the environment. As long as it's contained inside those pressurized boxes, life is good. Understood?"

Lee heard his associates stirring in the grotto behind him. They conversed quietly among themselves as they stumbled out into the warmth and brightness of the new day's sun.

"Sir," he said, "when we attempted to raise one of the boxes, we inadvertently dropped it and, well, it cracked open when it fell to the decking."

There was an awkward silence on the other end for several moments before Culp spoke. "Damn." He went silent for a few moments more before responding. "Well, you're still alive and that's good. You should thank your lucky stars, Hartley. There must have been an off-shore breeze last night or we wouldn't be having this conversation. I expect things will heat up at your twenty real soon."

There was a dead carrier as Lee keyed his mic to speak, hesitated, then replied, "Sir, there *was* an offshore breeze last night; a southwesterly one. That means the virus would be heading to Jamaica if it continues on its current course."

Travers trotted up to where Lee was standing, a hand on the rock face beside him. He stood patiently and listened to the one-way conversation.

"You've personally seen the means and method of the viral dissemination," Culp continued. "The perpetrators of Vector have stepped up their game. What with our continuing war on global terrorism, the Iranians, and the North Koreans, you can appreciate the fact that our resources are thinning out."

"This thing is not confined to central Ontario as we were initially led to believe. I'm glad we've got NABS running point on this one. The fewer agents we have on this, the better Hartley. 'Loose lips sink ships,' and all that."

"The president is monitoring this *very* carefully. He wants neither mass panic, nor another missile crisis on his hands. At this point viable, effective options are limited. Both the Cuban and Chinese governments officially deny all 'plot or conspiracy' allegations directly by them against Western powers. This whole affair has all the earmarks of a prelude devolution to WWIII."

"What do you need from us down here sir," Lee asked.

"Our top virologists have determined that a massive disruption such as an explosion will neutralize the delicate catalyst surrounding the virus lying dormant in its host fabric. This will drastically alter its chemical makeup, thereby rendering the substance impotent."

"In a sentence, don't bring that shit up. *Blow it up*. Yesterday. Understood?" The seriousness of the situation was etched in the CIA man's voice. "Your cover's still solid, and I need you guys, Hartley. Don't let us down."

"We have NABS contacts down here that will help us to that end, sir," Lee said.

"Good," Culp replied. "I'll inform our station office in Jamaica at once. The cat's out of the bag now. I hope we're wrong about all this, Hartley. *Whatever* you do, do not attempt to raise that second box. Let's just hope our reasoning is solid and that you unleashed the experimental pathogens and not the perfected strain. Regardless, destroy that second box at all costs."

"Copy that sir," Lee said.

Except for some slight static, the radio remained silent for several moments.

Then Culp came back on air. "Oh and Hartley, while I have you, be advised that Exner and Shankar had been imprisoned on a tramp ship kitted out to look like an oceanographic research ship called the *Étoile Profonde.* Somehow they managed to break free and transmit a faint message on an old frequency known only to NABS."

"However, they're still aboard and in hiding. That was all we managed to get before we lost their signal. You're going to have to fend for yourselves for a while, Hartley," he said with concern. "I understand you men aren't trained agents, but I have full confidence in your abilities. You're both damned good divers according to Exner, and that's exactly what we need down there right now."

"Yes sir, and thanks for the update on control and Shankar. Please keep us in the loop regarding their welfare. Hartley out."

As Lee powered down the seq-pod, Travers asked, "What was that all about?"

Lee stowed the unit and looked up at Travers from his kneeling position. "Well, the good news is that Bindhi and Exner have been located. The bad news is—how can I put this, my friend? We—that is, you and I—screwed up: big time."

"Oh, and how's that?"

"The box we cracked open down there shouldn't have been, Bill. We released some pretty toxic shit and it's heading to Jamaica. Had it not been for that brisk southwesterly wind blowing over us last night, our friend Culp congenially informed me we'd have been maggot food today."

Hartley's lightning fast analytical mind was on overdrive. "We've got to get in touch with Juan as soon as possible. Unfortunately, this radio only provides a relayed link to the NABS district office at Niagara-On-The-Lake. Exner obviously didn't want a higher band of high-tech equipment falling into the wrong hands."

Abruptly, Hartley looked around. The suddenness of the move startled Travers.

"Mercedes," Lee said, concern etched in his voice. "Where's Mercedes?"

Travers spun around and trotted the short distance back to the grotto. Rushing in, he emerged a few moments later, hands in the air.

"She's not here, Lee. She's gone!"

55

Consequences

Bindhira hastily signed off on the old marine radio when voices were heard just outside the radio room aboard the *Étoile Profonde*. She dropped down to the side of the desk that was not visible from the doorway. The NSA agent drew her weapon and lay silent, tight, and low beside the desk. Exner held his line of sight, the Browning raised and at the ready.

The men stopped just outside. Though the voices were unintelligible through the thickness of the steel door, Exner discerned they were speaking in English. Their accents however, belied their nationalities as Chinese and Latino. Exner held no doubt the man with the Latino accent was Cuban.

The door opened and a man entered, still looking outside the room as he broke off his conversation with the other.

Exner drew a sigh of relief as the man outside continued on his way. The radio operator closed the door behind him. Alan Exner was on him at once, the hard black barrel of the 9 mm Browning stuck deep between the man's shoulder blades.

"Tell me you speak English or I will shoot you where you stand!" Exner said slowly, softly, but emphatically. He patted him down with the opposite hand as he spoke.

"Yes . . . yes, I speak the English," the man managed to sputter.

"Good, that's very good. You are the radio operator of this vessel, *si*," Exner asked.

The man, already visibly shaken, was even more so when he saw Bindhira pop up from beside the desk. She spun the operator's chair around for him to sit, her P-38 trained on his heart. "Please; have a seat," she admonished politely.

The man looked to Exner. "*Si,* I am the radio operator. You are the prisoners that were brought aboard, no?" The man hunkered down into his chair.

"Smart man. Where's this ship headed?" Exner demanded.

"Sault Saint Marie, *señor*."

"Bullshit. What's your name?"

"My name, it is Enrico. I swear this to you, *señor*, this is where we are going. I am not told much. I am their radio operator, nothing more."

Bindhira spoke up. "Tell me, Enrico. If that is the case, why are we in the middle of Lake Huron? Why not simply sail along Manitoulin Island, hug close to the shoreline, and save fuel to the Sault?"

"*Señorita*, we do this thing so not many peoples will notice this ship. But—" Enrico stopped short as he knew he had already said too much.

"But what, Enrico? What were you going to say?" Bindhira drew a little closer to him, her gun lowered by her side but ready for use if necessary.

Enrico was visibly nervous at passing out this information to the strangers. He spoke in a hurried, fearful tone, his voice broken and high pitched.

"The bridge has just received a message that we are to turn around and sail back to Parry Sound."

Bindhira walked around in front of him and stood by the door as Exner came over, gun lowered as he faced the man. Exner was good at gut feelings, and his gut told him this man would pose little threat. The crew of the *Étoile Profonde* probably wasn't part of Wu Yang's team, but simply merchantmen hired to operate the ship.

Exner looked over to Bindhira, who caught his eye and smiled. Her smile spoke volumes. It told him that she'd been successful at rerouting the ship.

Wu Yang was summoned to the bridge. "What is it, Captain? It had better be good. It appears as though our 'guests' have inexcusably left their berths and are at large somewhere on your ship!"

Captain Celeste turned from the console he was monitoring to face the Chinese agent. "We have just been ordered to return to Parry Sound, Mr. Yang."

Wu Yang looked down to the floor and tapped his cane gently on the deck to gather his thoughts. "From whence did such authorization come, Captain?"

Captain Celeste looked a little puzzled but remained poised. "The request was short. It said we were to immediately return to Parry Sound by order of the Establishment."

"With no explanation," Wu Yang questioned uncertainly.

"No sir, just that we were to proceed back to our last port of call, Parry Sound, sir," the captain replied.

"Captain," Wu Yang said, "I want you to reestablish contact with the Establishment. Tell them Wu Yang requests a confirmation of the last request given; who countermanded our original course, and that we are urgently awaiting their response."

Wu Yang was perplexed. Establishment operatives would not have risked breaking radio silence—unless an unfavorable situation had developed.

Captain Celeste nodded. Things seemed to be going south very quickly aboard the *Étoile Profonde* and for the first time, the captain noticed that Wu Yang was worried.

Then Yang spoke. "Before you transmit that message Captain, please put me on the ship wide intercom." Flipping several switches, the captain handed a microphone to Wu Yang, who ordered his men to search every inch of the ship for their 'guests', and to escort them, alive, to the bridge immediately upon recapture.

Wu Yang handed the captain back his microphone and smiled to himself. He knew the prisoners would have also heard the message and be in fear, and that was good, for fear was a time-honored emotion that made one less cautious, which in turn would ensure a quick capture.

The bow of the ship cut a foamy white swath through the amazingly blue waters of Lake Huron amid moderate swells. On its bridge, four men were ushered onto the ship's bridge at gunpoint by two of Wu Yang's armed men.

Yang knew they were there, but he remained stoic, with his back to them as he continued to enjoy the view from the bridge.

Captain Celeste cleared his throat rather nervously in a bid to get the senior Chinese intelligence operative to turn around and notice them.

It was good that Wu Yang's back faced the men so they were spared the sight of the sadistic smile that crossed his face. He had detected their presence well in advance of the captain.

He could smell nervous fear a long way off.

When Wu Yang finally turned to face the arrivals, he looked deeply into each of their eyes. He took great delight at seeing their fear, and relished the thought of instilling more.

"You men were paid well to secure our guests, were you not?" The tone of Wu Yang's voice was unnervingly congenial.

The man at the far end of the group, himself Chinese, spoke up. "The woman, we did not know she was so . . . resourceful."

"You did not know she was so resourceful," Wu Yang quoted. "You did not *know?* Have you not been trained to *expect* the unexpected? And yet the unexpected took you by surprise. How is that so, comrade?"

The man beside him, a Cuban, spoke up. "The woman spoke so tearfully and so quietly. We could not understand what she was saying during the interrogation. When I leaned closer to better hear what she said, she attacked like a tiger. Somehow she had loosened her bonds and she attacked."

Wu Yang walked up to the man, their faces a mere inch apart. "But there were *two* of you guarding her. Is *this* not so?" He looked back to the first man.

Both fell silent. Wu Yang stepped back and slowly paced before them all, assisted by his cane. He enjoyed playing the part of a weak old man. It never ceased to lower an enemy's defenses.

Yang's two guards posted themselves just behind the four, one on each side of the bridge entranceway, their lightweight Type 79 Chinese-made 7.62 caliber SMGs at the ready.

Wu Yang looked over at Captain Celeste, who looked to him nervously. The captain then walked the short distance to a nearby desk littered with maps and poured over them with an air of forced urgency.

Yang pointed at the two men he was speaking to and directed them to the far corner of the bridge. No one spoke. No one moved except the two men.

"She is *not* a woman," Yang said to them with an almost fatherly affection. "She is an *operative* of the most dangerous kind, and she is now at large on this ship, no doubt with the male, himself a high-ranking NABS agent."

Yang looked at the other two men, then down to the tip of his cane. As he spoke, he pushed a small button below the ornate golden knob. The spring-loaded cap popped off and to the side in one sudden, silent move.

It happened astonishingly fast. A small double-serrated razor-sharp stiletto blade protruded from the top of the cane and clicked into place. With supernatural speed, Wu Yang drove it deep into the left eye of the man closest to him, the Oriental. Maintaining his grip with the stiletto still embedded in the man's eye, Yang spun around under the cane, which turned the stiletto into a spinning drill bit. The man's eye socket expanded from its original size into a gaping hole the diameter of a golf ball. Blood and brain tissue issued profusely from the man's face.

The body fell forward, twitching uncontrollably, and the smell of feces permeated the entire bridge as the unfortunate man's bowels let go.

Wu Yang then calmly withdrew the stiletto in such perfect time that the man fell forward to the floor as he stepped back in a single almost choreographed move. Then with another touch of the button, the bloodied, brain-spattered blade popped up from the top of the cane and fell to the floor, much as the ejected blade of a reusable razor. The gold cap automatically snapped back into place with a solid click.

No one dared move or speak, save one of the guards, who ran off the bridge to relieve his stomach of its contents over the rail. All eyes remained on Wu Yang, who calmly walked over to Captain Celeste, using his cane for balance as if nothing happened.

The captain resumed his original position, which took him further away from Yang. He cringed when he Yang stared directly at him.

"You might want to clean this mess up Captain," Yang said smiling. "After all, it *is* your bridge, is it not?"

Turning to the other men, Yang said, "I am in a good mood today, comrades," he smiled. "I am giving you men a rare two-hour lease on your lives."

"Prove yourselves worthy of remaining in my service. Find the enemy agents and no harm will come to you. Should they not stand before me at the end of that time, your incompetence will be rewarded in a similar manner."

"That gentlemen, is a solemn promise. Good hunting."

56

Ill Winds

A small fishing boat two miles off the Jamaican coast pitched and yawed as it lay idle, two men sitting in front of their outrigger poles. They'd been fishing their spot for many hours, patiently waiting for a few more ten or twenty pound mahi-mahis to embrace their hooks. Although it was late in the season for the fish, they persevered, as mahi-mahi was a great-tasting delicacy for which the resorts paid well.

"Oumar, I have only one more to catch, and then we will each have eight," the younger of the two said in anticipation. The older man, Oumar, had spent many years fishing the waters of the Caribbean Sea off Port Antonio, a small seaside town on the northeastern tip of Jamaica.

Oumar's love of fishing was evidenced by a well-wrinkled over-tanned face and several blotchy areas of untreated squamous cell skin cancer on his arms that had developed from countless static hours fishing off his boat beneath the searing radiation of the hot Jamaican sun.

Oumar had taken young Manuel in several years previous after Manuel's father was murdered when a drug deal went sour. His mother had died of HIV two years previous. In spite of such grievous personal tragedy, the young lad was a good boy who possessed a positive, albeit sensitive, personality. He was good company for the old man who happily shared his daily take with Manuel.

Although Oumar paid Manuel a meager wage for his efforts, he had established a trust fund for the boy with what he felt the young man was really worth. The fisherman added even more to it as he was able, which he felt would go far to keeping the lad out of trouble in the event Oumar faced an untimely demise.

The wind had changed an hour or so previous. The sun began its trek further west, and painted the underside of the few clouds overhead an intriguing blood orange, an indication that another day's work out on the sea had come to an end.

The old man got up, strode to the gunwale, unzipped the fly of his well-worn shorts, and relieved himself.

Manuel could not help smiling each time the old man ambled over to the other side of the boat for a pee. Several occasions came to the boy's memory when a rogue swell hammered the underbelly of the small boat at the precise moment his old friend pissed over the side. Invariably, he'd be thrown backward in midstream which caused him to soak his shorts.

The boy smiled when he heard Oumar curse.

But something wasn't right. Today there were no rogue swells. Puzzled as to why Oumar had cursed, Manuel went over to see the cause of the old man's angst. Looking into the water off the gunwale, Manuel gasped. The old man looked over to his young friend, stunned at the diminishing stream of red urine. The water beside the boat was red, and would no doubt draw in the sharks.

"What happened? What did you do, Oumar," Manuel asked with deep concern on his face.

Turning to look at the boy as he zipped up, Oumar merely smiled and said, "Manuel, secure our fishing poles. We must leave now anyway. It is the end of the day and I do not feel so well."

Obediently the teenager set about dismantling the outriggers and stowing the equipment into its various compartments.

As he completed his tasks, the youth felt a little trickle out of the corner of his nose. Thinking nothing of it, he wiped the drainage with a forefinger. He unconsciously did this several times. It felt warm and tacky.

Looking down, he saw that the sticky fluid on his finger was blood.

57

Welcome Allies

The Canadians conducted a thorough search of the area around the grotto in a futile attempt to locate Mercedes de Quesada. She was nowhere to be found.

"I don't understand it, Lee," Travers said, scratching his head in defeat. "I had just talked with her in the grotto, then came over to see what you were up to."

"I know, I know." Lee quietly gathered his thoughts. "Something doesn't add up, Bill. I know she's gone through an awful lot in a short period of time. Maybe she just isn't thinking rationally, and wandered off."

"If she's picked up by the DGI and squawks," Travers said, "we could find ourselves in a heap o' trouble, my friend."

"True that," Lee said, "but I promised we'd find her daughter. I was with her husband around the time he died. Her life's been turned upside down, and she's got nowhere to go. I owe her that much, Bill."

“To keep perspective Lee, we’ve got a world to save right now,” Travers said.

Lee’s priorities focused in as Travers spoke. “From the information we’ve uncovered today, that’s exactly what we have to do,” he said grimly.

“There’s a lot more going on behind the scenes here than meets the eye, Lee,” Travers said. “Cubans helping the Chinese sabotage their own country? These guys are definitely freelancers.”

“Bill, if I’ve learned anything in life,” Lee said, “it’s that wherever politics are involved you can bet there are deals on the side. With the stakes as high as they are here, it’s a no-brainer.”

“Pretty ballsy of these guys to take on both governments. Talk about high treason; geez,” Travers said.

“We’ve got to give something more concrete to the good guys, Bill,” Lee said. “But right now, we’ve got a more immediate problem on our hands: Mercedes.”

“We can’t be running all around all over the countryside—”

“Listen!” Lee put his hand up to silence his friend. A vehicle was coming their way and at a high rate of speed. “Quick, take cover!”

The vehicle slowed down as if its occupants were searching for something. When it reached the area of the grotto, the vehicle stopped. Lee counted three doors slam shut, then footsteps as they crunched over the pebbly area that led to the beach sand.

Lee looked over to his friend and whispered, “On my mark . . .”

The footsteps became more pronounced as they drew nearer the grotto. Just as the Canadians were about to pounce, one of the men raised his hand in greeting.

“Ah; *señors*!”

It was Juan! The man with him, Pedro Ramirez, smiled in kind.

"You guys are sure a sight for sore eyes," Travers said as he and Lee exited the mouth of the grotto.

As the men spoke, the Canadians were alerted to the presence of another. It was Mercedes!

"What-*the*-hell," Travers said happily as she came into full view.

"We picked her up about half a mile back," Pedro said. "She started to run when she saw us coming. Once she saw who we were, she stopped and thankfully came with us."

"Mercedes; why?" Lee asked.

Her eyes were filled with tears. "Maela, my Maela is dead *señors*, and my husband too." Then she dropped to the ground in a torrent of emotion.

Juan explained that his methods of interrogation effectively convinced Miguel and Montoya to reveal the whereabouts of their safe house. Pedro took a few men, and with little resistance they raided a small building on the outskirts of Palma Soriano to the northwest of Santiago. Inside, they found the child handcuffed to a bed.

Juan's men determined that Maela had been dead for several days. Although there didn't appear to be signs of torture, her bulging eyes, ligature marks about the neck, and cyanotic skin strongly suggested signs of strangulation. It was obvious that the child had also been raped.

When Lee asked what happened, Juan Zayas explained that the girl's father, Javier, had been sent by Alberto, DGI control of the province of Santiago, to assist in the Establishment's cell in Canada.

Javier was a good man who had fallen afoul of the DGI. The Cuban secret service learned that once he returned home he planned to get his little family out of the country once and for all. Javier's knowledge of the Establishment's plans would be dangerous if it fell into the wrong hands for the right price.

Alberto felt he needed to make an example of Javier. It would not look good for him if the man and his family escaped. So he kidnapped the child as insurance.

The DGI leader had also issued orders to his away team that if any member of the Ontario cell was captured, they were to be silenced to protect the integrity of Project Vector. It was not in the script for Javier to have been trapped in the dive shop fire. When the others couldn't extricate their comrade, they had no choice. They had their orders, so one of them reluctantly shot him and they left him for dead.

No longer needing the girl for insurance, and angered at this unexpected turn of events, Alberto left her to the guards to do with as they pleased. Pedro believed Alberto's goons cleared out soon after Maela's death.

Juan continued to explain to the Canadians that Mercedes had panicked and ran off that morning. She was convinced that they had no intention of locating Maela and would in all probability simply complete their mission and leave Cuba without wasting their time on a missing peasant girl.

As ludicrous as it seemed, Mercedes thought she could get back home on foot and somehow locate her daughter on her own. A mother worried sick about her child will oftentimes do the irrational.

"*Señor* Lee, they have the army on the lookout for you and *Señor* Billiam," Juan said. "When DGI discovered you two had not been in your room at the resort for several days, they became suspicious. But when they found out you had taken your luggage and some diving tanks, you became 'persons of interest.' I have no doubt that should you try to leave Cuba you will both be detained at the *aeropuerto*."

""That's another fine mess you've got me into, Hartley," Travers said.

"Now we're even, buddy," Lee said without humor.

Together Lee and Travers helped Mercedes to her feet. She apologized for sneaking away, and hugged them both intensely. It was apparent to the men that Mercedes would need to remain in their protective custody for as long as they were there.

"Come, my friends," Juan said. "We must leave this place. Soon it will be overrun with soldiers combing the area looking for you."

58

False Hope; Real Fear

Enrico offered no resistance as Exner hog-tied the man using a microphone cable. Removing one of the radio operator's shoes, he slipped the man's sock off and gagged him with it. "For your sake, I hope it doesn't stink," Exner said as he rechecked the man's bonds.

Bindhira was standing at the door keeping watch. "Now what?"

"Listen!" Exner said as he ran over to her and peered out the door's view port. "It's a helicopter! Our people are right on time," Exner said and kissed her on the forehead.

The sound of whirling helicopter blades drew increasingly louder as the craft passed by overhead, and then descended onto the middeck of the ship, just aft of the radio room. Although neither agent saw it, they knew the machine had landed by the slowing beat of the chopper's rotors as the pilot powered the craft down to a mere idle.

Exner opened the door with one hand and grabbed Bindhira's with the other. He started out in the direction of the chopper, but then quickly retreated back into the radio room yanking Bindhira with him.

He collided solidly with her on their reentry. It was a *Keystone Cop* moment to be sure, but Exner recovered, and pulled her safely back into the room. In one streamlined movement, he closed and locked the door.

"What the—" was all Bindhira could get out.

"That chopper's not one of ours," Exner said. "Wu Yang's getting into the thing. Two armed guards are assisting him. Damn it! He'll be gone before our guys get here."

Bindhira looked dismayed. "I do not think 'our guys' will be coming to the rescue anytime soon, Alan."

Exner then unlocked the door and peered out just enough to observe undetected as one of the guards slid Yang's door shut, then backed away in a crouch. Within seconds the sleek black craft powered up, and in a maelstrom of swirling dust and loose debris, the helicopter lifted off the deck and disappeared to the southwest. At this, Exner returned and closed the door in dismay.

"What did you mean when you said 'our guys wouldn't be coming', Bindhi?" Exner said, concern etched in his voice.

The female NSA/CSS agent had been monitoring the radio equipment during the time Exner watched the helicopter activities.

She pulled the trussed radio operator, who was on a swivel chair, to a corner of the room. The wheels rolled to a stop, leaving his face to the wall. Enrico almost choked on the sock-gag when he coughed, but managed to get himself under control.

"It appears that our 'order' has been countermanded, Alan," Bindhira explained. "Not only are we *not* returning to Parry Sound, we are heading in a northwesterly direction. If that is the case, it will take our people far longer to locate us. I did not notice this earlier."

"How so," Exner asked in dismay. He spun Enrico around to check on him. Although visibly confused, he was okay. Exner spun him back to face the wall, then came over and stood behind Bindhira.

"It appears that this old radar array has a very modern scrambling device incorporated into it that prevents unauthorized transmissions for being picked up by outsiders." She reached over and yanked out what appeared to be a smaller version of an old transistor radio attached to the side of the transmitting unit.

"This day just keeps getting better, doesn't it?" Exner remarked facetiously. "So we're now on a Northeasterly course, eh? Hmmm," he pondered. "They're probably making a run for it into Michigan.

Things may be getting too hot for them on this side of the border.

Maybe our people *are* in hot pursuit after all."

"Do not get your hopes up, Alan," Bindhira cautioned.

"We've got to get off this ship, and soon," Exner said.

Going over to the door, Exner peered out its window. Seeing no one, he opened the door and motioned her to follow. Closing the door behind her, Bindhira stayed in step with Exner, both with gun in hand.

The two managed to get behind the wheelhouse undetected. *Strange that no one is patrolling the deck looking for us,* Exner thought.

Motioning the female agent to stay close behind, Exner yanked open the port side wheelhouse door and then barged in. He panned the bridge with his weapon.

Bindhira was appalled at the sight that lay before them. Even Exner winced at the scene.

Five men lay dead, one obviously the captain. Exner recognized two as the men who had been charged with his captivity. "Alan, I know two of these men. They were my guards."

"Same here," he said grimly.

"Dead men tell no tales," he continued, "and Wu Yang leaves no trails." He looked down at the men and noticed that three of them had been poisoned, as evidenced by their positioning. The men were on the floor in fetal positions, with white foam around their mouths. Cyanotic complexions indicated they were painfully asphyxiated.

They saw the fourth man at the same time. Bindhira nearly vomited at the sight. There was a large gaping hole where his left eye had once been.

Exner reached down and said, "Still warm. This must have been Yang's final solution for the failure of these men to find and execute us. He must have been in a hurry to leave. I'm sure the bastard has special plans for this vessel. He's not one for 'loose ends.'"

The NABS control went next to the dead ship's officer. "The captain took a bullet to the heart."

Bindhira went over to the bridge's console. "Alan, the ship is going in circles!"

Exner came over but was careful not to step into the widening pool of crimson liquid surrounding the captain's body.

"The ship's wheel is locked hard a-starboard," he observed.

"We must get off this vessel now!" Bindhira looked to him with hurried concern. "The ship's gyro has been electronically locked and tied into this." She pointed to a small black box attached to the console by a powerful magnet. "If you try to disengage the wheel, it will prematurely detonate. Neither could budge the unit from the console.

"There is only six minutes to detonation," she said as she pointed so Exner could see for himself.

Exner noticed that the unit was an ultra-modern state-of-the-art self-destruct mechanism. Wu Yang was too thorough in his ways. By killing the men on the bridge, Yang had purchased their silence and ensured the secrecy of his mission by taking care of the rest of the crew, and them, all in one fell swoop.

"We've got to get the radio operator and get off this tub!" Exner said. "Come on!"

"Alan, there is no time!"

"Never leave a man in the field; in this case, the lake. The operator is innocent. He doesn't deserve to die like this. Find something that'll float and meet me by the rail off the radio shack." Before she could argue, Exner left the bridge.

By the time he reached the radio room and extricated the man from his bindings, Bindhira had located three life buoys and firmly lashed them together with rope located under one of the life-buoy stations.

"Quick; over the side!" he shouted. Exner took the homemade raft Bindhira made and pushed Enrico in that direction.

Reaching the port side gunwale, Exner said, "Make damned sure you jump as far off and away from the ship as you can to avoid being sucked under or minced by the propellers. When I see where you end up, I'll heave the rings in your direction before I jump."

Bindhira nodded then directed Enrico to the railing. She helped him step up onto its top rung. The frightened man used her shoulder for balance. "Can you swim?"

"Yes, but—" Enrico was unable to finish his sentence as Bindhira pushed him over the side with all her might. She then turned to Exner and planted a kiss on his cheek. "See you below," then plunged far out into the churning water.

Enrico was struggling to keep his head above water. As Bindhira swam to him, the tied buoys slammed into the water not ten feet from her. She swam over and pushed the crude raft to the struggling radio operator. Swells were running now, and the two lost sight of each other at varying intervals. Groping frantically, the man managed to get an arm over one of the buoys.

Bindhira grabbed onto another section and said, "We must kick hard to get away from the ship before it goes down!" As they moved slowly away, Bindhira looked back, expecting Exner to be close behind.

She scanned the water's surface for several seconds. Her heart began to sink. Then as she looked up she saw his form as it ran along the top deck of the doomed ship.

"Where is your friend?" Enrico gasped, as he struggled to get his breathing under control.

Minutes later, the top of the old ship blew apart in a scathing blast of burning hot metal and thick black smoke. Almost immediately the hulk listed to port and began to angle down at the bow.

"Enrico: dive!" Bindhira let go of the makeshift raft and submerged as debris from the explosion began to rain down upon them.

Bindhira exhaled more to sink deeper below the water's surface to avoid being knocked unconscious by the heavy falling debris.

Only one thought filled her mind: *Had Alan Exner gotten off the ship in time?*

59

Trouble in Paradise

Six men huddled around a roaring fire pit at the rear of the motel. Nights in Tobermory were cold, and a roaring fire helped take away the bitter chill. Team one had returned unsuccessfully from their mission at Niagara-On-The-Lake. Team two had remained at the small abandoned hotel, awaiting their return. Together, the group sat behind the one-story structure hidden from view from either the side road or the main.

It wasn't unusual this time of year for campers to have fires in the area on cold, crisp nights such as this, thus the aroma of burning wood would raise little concern or suspicion as the sparse traffic passed by.

Choi Li and Chen Fa, leaders of teams one and two respectively, compared notes since Wu Yang sent them on their missions. It was with great relief that Choi Li and his men, Huang Fu and Carlos Rodriguez, returned to their secret base in Tobermory to find Wu Yang absent.

Chen Fa, Shing Shen, and Gino Vaselino were glad to see them again. The feeling was reciprocated by the returning team.

"We have learned that NABS has increased their efforts to discover the true nature of our mission. So far they have been operating on rumors, guesswork, and fear," Choi Li said as the men huddled closer to the warmth of the crackling fire before them.

"The NSA woman you failed to liquidate and the NABS control are currently missing," the Chinese agent said.

"So," Chen Fa said, "we have two missing leaders: our venerable master Wu Yang and Alan Exner, our sworn enemy. We have collectively failed in fulfilling our duties, comrades. It is my fervent hope that in light of the fact that we are all he has left to fulfill the Establishment's mission here, he will spare our lives and afford us another opportunity to orchestrate his success."

"Yes," Huang Fa said, "we would bring great honor to his name. We would then be well rewarded." This brought nervous smiles to most of them.

"Do not forget your Cuban brothers, my friend," Carlos Rodriguez said. "We are in this together. We have spent much time in this country seeking out the most effective places to plant the containers."

The night was still, the hour was late. The men were tired, but no one moved. Mosquitoes were feasting on the ankles and arms of the men. Despite their best efforts, it was impossible to keep them at bay. It was unsettling for them to experience the ease with which the virus they had worked so hard to unleash on others could be acquired.

The roaring fire and its warmth did little to comfort the small band of men. They sat there, each lost in thought; thoughts of uncertainty, thoughts of fear, thoughts of family, but always the thread of hope for the success of their mission and the triumphant return to their respective countries as heroes of their people.

In the distance came the sound of an approaching aircraft, a helicopter. The methodical whirring of its blades drew increasingly closer. Within minutes, the locust-like machine was directly over head. Loose branches and twigs swirled, gritty sand blew in their faces; even the hot embers of their campfire attacked them as the flying machine came in for a landing in the open field beside the motel.

The men shielded their faces with their arms until the sleek craft touched down. Its pilot powered down the engine. A lone figure emerged from the cockpit and headed in their direction through the darkness of the night, using his cane for support and carrying a thing folder. The men stood and waited expectantly, silently, questioningly. The figure slowly ambled into the glow of the fire, which had increased dramatically as the chopper blades brought the fire to a stronger intensity.

"It is time to regroup, gentlemen." It was Wu Yang!

Both Choi Li and Chen Fa came over to him. Yang put a hand on each of their shoulders.

"There have been arresting developments, both here and in Cuba," their leader said. "In light of them, your latest assignments were destined for failure, thus you are forgiven for your inability to complete your tasks. But know this: our cell is on an even tighter schedule. The noose, as they say, has been tightened."

Over the course of the next hour, the two team leaders discussed with Wu Yang the events that had shaped their past few days. The others remained by the fireside as their superiors conversed among themselves a short distance from the fire pit.

When the discussion ended, the men came back to rejoin the others.

"I have received an alarming report from the Establishment," Wu Yang announced. "The same strain of Ebola our scientists have developed has broken out in Jamaica. Initially two fishermen were found to have been affected. Soon thereafter, many more have suffered similar symptoms."

"Understandably," he continued, "this had caused great concern among the disease professionals there. It is our strain; of this there is no doubt."

"This could well compromise everything we have worked so hard for, even to the destruction of the Establishment, should our governments discover this for themselves, as they will."

"What do you mean, Yang?" Vaselino came out from behind Shing Shen so he could better see the Chinese man as he spoke.

"Regular Ebola takes several days to incubate," Wu Yang explained. This specific pathogen has taken hold in mere hours. Members of the Establishment assured me it was not by our hand."

The men stood silent and dumbfounded before their leader.

"What does this mean, Wu Yang?" Huang Fu asked.

Turning to face the entire group, Yang said, "This means, gentlemen that someone else has inadvertently managed to get their hands on our 'product'. This means that our plans are in definite jeopardy. This *means*," an unsettling fear was detected in the voice of the usually calm senior agent, "that we lose our element of surprise not only before our enemies, but our very governments as well. I fear the Establishment may well be in dire straits, and all of us along with it."

"What are we to do then, Yang?" Rodriguez had his back to the men and was briskly rubbing his hands in front of the fire as he spoke.

"The Establishment has adopted a contingency plan, Mr. Rodriguez," Yang replied. "There are others on their way to assist us from our base in Cuba."

"Even though the initial plan was devised for maximum shock and awe, we still have a slight advantage. At this point, disease control pathologists in Jamaica are struggling to determine where the Ebola originated from, and how it was able to present such advanced symptoms in so short a time."

Wu Yang drew near the fire. Balancing his cane against the side of his knee, he briskly rubbed his hands together. He looked over to the helicopter. The pilot sat in wait, the long thin propeller blades of his craft idle above him.

"We are dealing with an international network of professional antiterrorists. So far we have managed to confound them. But it appears that they are rapidly gaining ground and spiraling into an awareness of our actions. We must tread very carefully now my friends."

The men gave Wu Yang their full attention. No one dared interrupt him as he continued to speak. "Through a stroke of unexpected good fortune, I took a North American Bureau of Security chief and his female assistant captive aboard the *Étoile Profonde.* I need not bore you with the details," he smiled. "I should think they are quite dead now."

He paused for a moment. "I am happy to report the ship has served its purpose, and that most of its mission was successfully completed. However, it is with regret that I must tell you it has been destroyed."

Wu Yang smiled his evil smile, then his eyes narrowed. "Were it not for me, our mission would have ended in abject failure. However, there is still opportunity before us to ensure a successful completion." Yang fidgeted with the dragonhead of his cane.

"I think we deserve more than promised, Yang," Rodriguez said as he looked to his associates. "We have all been put through a lot over the past several weeks." The others said nothing, but Wu Yang saw that even his countrymen agreed and approved of this bold and greedy request.

This disturbed him greatly. Men who were not happy in their tasks were men who were lax in detail, and disgruntled men were a poison to the cause. Most unfortunate, he thought. But he was prepared for such an eventuality.

"Indeed. Your concern has been duly noted, Mr. Rodriguez," he lied. "You have all, for the most part, done well and I thank you for that." He looked over the group of men meditatively. Though he did not care for the overly confident Cubans, he had great respect for his countrymen. They were good soldiers who had served him well.

"I personally guarantee that you will get everything that's coming to you and more." Wu Yang's demeanor changed. He was lost in thought, but only for a few moments. "Your new orders as issued by the Establishment are contained within this pouch." He handed a thin folder to Choi Li.

"It is imperative that you peruse the folder's contents together inside the motel immediately after I depart. Within two hours an airship similar to this one will arrive to collect you. But for your safety, you are to wait inside until it arrives."

"Do you understand?" Wu Yang noticed that everyone nodded in understanding—all but Gino Vaselino. Looking at the Cuban he said, "Do *you* understand, Mr. Vaselino?"

Vaselino was visibly angered that he had been singled out in this manner. Looking around at the others, he turned to face the old Chinese man with a glare. "Yes, Wu Yang. I think I got it."

"That is good, Mr. Vaselino, very good indeed." Wu Yang's gaze turned to include the rest. "From here you will be routed to the final destination of your assignment. Once completed, you will have fulfilled your obligations to the Establishment and sent to wherever it is you would like to retire."

He paused to look at his illuminated watch. "I must take my leave now, gentlemen. Goodbye and good luck." He placed a gentle hand on the shoulder of Choi Li. Their eyes met not so much in duty, as in mutual respect, then Wu Yang limped his way back to the helicopter.

Swinging his cane, a smile crossed Wu Yang's face unnoticed by the others as darkness engulfed him. Two crew members disembarked to assist him into the helicopter.

Vaselino waited until Wu Yang had been swallowed by the night, then trotted off to relieve himself in the bushes. The others went into the motel office.

Within minutes, the pilot powered up the engine. The Apache helicopter lifted off from the motel ground with only its flashing beacon lights visible from the ground. Wu Yang requested the pilot to come around for a flyby but at a higher altitude. As they did so, Yang was pleased to see his operatives had obeyed his command and entered the building.

Once inside, Choi Lee pulled a small sheaf of papers from the pouch Wu Yang had given him.

Every page was blank.

60

Underwater Combat

Lee Hartley and Bill Travers glanced at each other at the sixty-foot mark. Buddies are to check each other frequently throughout a dive, and this was no exception. Pedro had brought an ops kit for the Canadians, which included several sticks of waterproofed dynamite designed for clearing harbors of dangerous wreckage. This was exactly what Lee needed to blow up the last deadly cargo of Ebola contained within the bowels of the *Cristóbal Colón*.

The original brass container still lay in place. Although its contents had been released, the container's cover had fallen closed. The box looked as though it was still intact. Lee carefully opened its lid. The divers must not have discovered it had been tampered with, for it was still empty. That was good.

By placing a charge around the second brass container that still housed viral-laced matchbooks, the sudden concussion from a detonation would render the unstable virus impotent while still under pressure at depth. Should any of the matchbooks survive the shock of the explosion, the fragile components of the pathogenic catalyst would quickly break down and harmlessly dissipate into the salt water. At least, that was the theory.

The water was clear and warm. Lee could easily see Travers descending about twenty feet below him as they drifted slowly down amidships. They had to be particularly cognizant of their air supply this time as they were using the last of their air tanks.

Lee thought of the men who had died on this wreck over a hundred years ago during the Spanish American War of 1896, men of the sea like him, like Travers. Caught up in a war they did not want and were ill-prepared to face, these sailors were brave men who wanted to make a difference for their country. Sadly, their contribution only created more widows and orphaned children.

War is never fair.

Lee knew he had to work fast. They had wasted precious time in their planning, and soldiers would be infesting the area very soon. Pedro and Juan hoped they would be able to hold off any interlopers with the plan they had devised. For all their sakes, Lee hoped they were right.

Dropping down into the hold, the divers switched on their powerful underwater lights. The boxes lay in the same positions as before.

Lee carefully laid a charge in series around the second container, so that the blast would blow the box, not out and away, but implode *into* itself. Upon detonation, this would atomize the contents before the water pressure had time to act on the catalyst.

Setting the fuses was always the most delicate part. Lee took a moment to clear his mask, stretch his neck, and loosen up his arms before he continued. It was a ritual he went through whenever he set such a delicate charge.

Suddenly Travers shook Lee's shoulder. Hartley looked over to his friend, who had drifted up to the opening of the hatch above. He pointed toward the surface. Lee carefully set the detonator down, switched off his light, and left it by the nearly rigged box. He then rose up to the hatch and Travers.

Lee now saw the reason for his buddy's concern. Two divers were heading their way, carrying long sticks in their hands. Spear guns.

The divers had come from the beach and not yet noticed their bubbles. Hurriedly Lee motioned to Travers who quickly understood. Travers would remain in the wreck under the still intact top deck. His bubbles would not rise to the surface there, but would simply travel along the ceiling of the hold, deeper into the wreck.

Lee exhaled deeply to avoid an air embolism due to the expanding air pressure in his lungs before he rose out of the hold. Holding his breath, he pulled himself low along and over the side of the wreck before inhaling slowly to avoid detection. His years of martial arts training paid off as his controlled breathing did not alert the approaching divers. Air pockets were not uncommon in shipwrecks, even old ones, thus slow, erratic exhalations should not bring unwanted attention.

Lee swam along the starboard side of the wreck and pulled himself along jagged beams and twisted metal until he arrived at the ship's bow. From this vantage point he could see the divers clearly. They hovered about forty feet abovc and sixty feet or so away above the main deck. Lee watched thankfully as they split up.

Lee knew what they were up to. One man would swim along each side of the ship's deck then converge upon their prey in a pincer movement. It was an old frogman trick, but effective against the unwary. Lee Hartley was not the unwary type.

Losing sight of one diver, Lee waited close to the hawsehole where the anchor chain came through the hull of the ship. The other diver, a little unsure of himself, slowly drifted down to the starboard bow of the ship. He checked his spear gun to ensure it was primed for firing and paid no attention to the uneven trickle of bubbles that rose where Lee waited for an opportune time to pounce.

He was partially protected by the massive metal ring of the hawsehole, and could see the man as he swam overhead. Lee hugged the side of the ship.

At the precise moment, and with all the strength he could muster, Lee explosively propelled himself upward, both fists held out tightly together. He caught the man directly in the solar plexus just above the wide waist belt of his buoyancy compensator.

The man dropped his spear gun and immediately doubled over in pain. Lee had timed it right. Hitting the diver at the exact moment he exhaled, the man was prevented from inhaling due to the involuntary spasms of his diaphragm.

He reached up and yanked the face mask off the stunned diver and dragged him back to the hawsehole. Releasing the Velcro buckle from a shoulder harness of the man's BC, Lee then quickly wrapped it around the anchor chain before refastening it, which effectively bound the man to the anchor chain.

The hapless diver slid slowly down the chain, still fighting to regain his breathing pattern as Lee knew he would.

Without his mask, the man was effectively blind underwater. One down.

Lee then dived fifty feet below to the sandy bottom. He was relieved to see that the man's spear gun had not gone off when it hit the ocean floor.

He retrieved it then swam carefully up to the afterdeck of the ship. He knew Travers would need assistance but didn't want to give his position away just yet.

The second diver's bubbles easily betrayed him. The man was directly over the hold where Travers was hiding, spear gun at the ready.

Throwing caution to the wind, Lee launched himself up and over the railing and into the hatchway just after the diver had dropped through the opening.

Bubbles issued profusely from the open hatchway. Lee dropped into the hold to assist his buddy, but the life-or-death struggle that ensued between Travers and the enemy diver greatly diminished visibility. Stirred up silt and rust flakes quickly clouded everything from view. Lee cursed himself at leaving his light at the bottom of the hold.

It was hard to tell who was who, and Lee didn't want to get caught up in the fracas. Unable to see, each would consider the other his foe.

Lee rose above and peered over the hatchway entrance into the clear water above. Good. No further reinforcements had been dispatched. He hung close to the hatchway opening. The combatants wrestled themselves deeper into the wreck.

Not liking the way this was going, Lee pulled himself back over the edge and down into the hold. He went directly to the deck floor and felt his way blindly in the murk for something, anything, he could use for a weapon.

His hand made blind contact with the handle of something smooth and heavy. It was a spanner wrench. Returning to the combatants, Lee held his ground until he was sure.

He caught a snapshot of a split-fin in the silty turbulence and attacked. Lee reached up to the figure wearing it, then spun the man violently around and drove the spike end of the wrench deep into the man's face mask. Its glass immediately shattered inward and into the man's wide startled eyes. The man thrashed about for a few moments, then drifted slowly to the deck.

Bill Travers hated split-fins.

Lee looked up just in time to see a lone figure fin his way slowly up toward the hatch. In seconds, Lee was out of the hold and beside his friend. The visibility was much better.

Travers was tough, but he was on the older side of life. Lee tapped him on the shoulder and looked deep into his friend's face plate. Travers nodded gratefully, then clung to Lee's shoulder.

Looking down at his gauges, Lee saw he had nine hundred pounds of air left, Bill probably less than that. He motioned Bill to hold his position.

Against his better judgment, Lee pulled himself back down and into the hold. Reaching the deck, he pushed the vanquished diver's body out of the way. Frantically, he groped around in an effort to find his light. Several moments later, he felt the familiar shape and switched it on.

With its powerful Xenon beam, Lee quickly located the box and the dynamite charge beside. Carefully, he finished interfacing the fuses, then set the timer for forty-five minutes. He prayed that would be sufficient. He wasn't crazy about having his vital organs liquefied before he could get out and away from the wreck.

Lee gently pulled the diver's body over to the top of the container, careful not to pull any wires from the dynamite. The diver lay perfectly over the charge. His body would help maximize the implosion of the contents in the box.

He was a staunch advocate of recycling.

He quickly returned to the afterdeck where Travers had remained as requested. His friend had rallied by this time and pointed to his air pressure gauge. Five hundred pounds remained in his tank. Lee acknowledged and pointed in the direction of the stern.

As the two reached the wreck's stern, they continued past on a course that would take them around the point at the far end of the beach. Lee hoped their point of egress would sufficiently shield them from whoever was farther up the shoreline.

He checked his air pressure gauge: seven hundred pounds. It was too little, but Lee hoped, not too late.

61

A Death And A Resurrection

Bindhira looked frantically over the swells of Lake Huron searching for any sight, listening for any sound of Alan Exner in the nearby waters around her. The only sights she saw however, were the roving whitecaps, the only sounds that of the unearthly death groans of a dying ship as it began a slow descent to the grave awaiting her at the bottom of the cold, deep lake.

Suddenly, another massive explosion as water entered the ship's boilers, tearing the already mortally wounded ship apart amidships. Again Bindhira dived deep to avoid being struck by the heavy, jagged metal shrapnel from hitting her. She hoped Enrico had the presence of mind to do the same.

Bindhira surfaced in just time to witness the *Étoile Profonde* as she unceremoniously slipped beneath the rolling swells of the mighty Great Lake.

Alan . . . Alan.

From her right in the distance she heard sputtering and coughing. In anticipation she turned, but was somewhat disappointed when she saw that it was Enrico, not Exner, floundering in a desperate attempt to keep his head above water.

Bindhira scanned the water's surface. Moderate swells were running which made it difficult for her to fix her gaze on any one area for long. Then, about fifty feet away, she thought she spotted something orange. She did! But it was the life-buoy raft she had constructed.

Although a strong swimmer, Bindhira was weakening rapidly. She could feel the early tendrils of hypothermia clawing at her body as she swam over and grabbed onto the raft in the 66 °F water.

She paddled back to where Enrico had been. Bindhira knew he'd be gone if she didn't act swiftly. Her body protested every inch of the way as the numbing coldness of the water sought to drive her aching muscles into submission.

The radio operator was still there, but much lower in the water. Just as he slipped from the surface for the last time, Bindhira reached down, grasped his collar, and with superhuman effort, pulled him back to the surface. She helped him place an arm around one of the three rings in the makeshift raft.

For several minutes the two just hung off the raft. Both were beyond exhaustion. Enrico tried to say something to his rescuer, but was unable. Bindhira simply nodded. Neither had the strength to speak and their teeth chattered too much to have made any sense anyway.

Dark clouds were gathering formidably in the west and heading their way. Swells were now running several feet high and increasing in both frequency and intensity. The makeshift raft heaved, dipped, and bobbed. It was all they could do to hang on.

Bindhira looked up just in time to see Enrico as he slipped once again. She reached over and grabbed under his armpit with all the strength she could muster. Hope had all but abandoned her. She had accepted the fact that this was her time to die, then . . .

Bindhira thought she was becoming delusional, for it sounded like a loud buzzing over her head. She dared not look up for fear she would lose her grip on the radio operator. The water around them suddenly became a violent frothing, roiling cyclone as heavy air pressed down upon them. She looked up. It was something else orange this time above the lake. It was the fuselage of a Canadian Coast Guard rescue chopper!

Even Enrico in his weakness looked up. Each lowered their head into the rings of the raft to protect themselves from the stinging froth of the lake water the whirring blades of the Eurocopter EC-175 drove down up them as it hung suspended above.

A man's voice, barely audible above the sound of the whirring blades and roiling water said, "Lady, give me your hand."

A crewman suspended on a winched cable reached down to try to assist her into a harness. She grabbed it but secured Enrico into it instead. The crewman signaled to the winch man above. The winch was thrown into reverse which pulled the radio operator up and into the safety of the large flying machine.

Within minutes Bindhira too was safely aboard the coast guard aircraft. As the crewman slid the side door of the chopper closed, a disembodied voice said, "Took you long enough."

Even above the finely tuned noise of the twin Pratt and Whitney turbo shaft engines, Bindhira knew that voice. With great effort, she stumbled around the bulkhead in the direction of the voice.

Exner reached over and caught her just as she collapsed into his arms. Even though he too was cold and wet, he noticed her body was colder still.

"Alan! Oh, Alan! How—"

"Shhh . . ." He enveloped her in the blanket he had been given and held her tight in his arms to help warm her shivering body. It felt strangely good. He hadn't held a woman since . . . Marlissa . . .

The brief comfort Exner felt holding her was broken when one of the crewmen directed them over to the bench behind the pilot's cabin where it was a little warmer. He handed each of them a thick wool blanket and a warm, not hot, cup of coffee.

Looking to the crewman Exner said, "Have the pilot radio in to your dispatch and inform them you have NABS agents on board. Our Niagara-On-The-Lake office must be notified at once. I have vital information they imminently need in the interests of national security."

"Will do, sir." Turning, the crewman rapped on the pilot's door, slid it slightly open, and relayed the information as directed.

Two other crewmen were tending to Enrico, who wasn't faring too well. They bundled him into several blankets and lashed him to a gurney.

"We're twenty minutes out from Parry Sound," said one of the crewmen as he came back to the two agents. "Your friend is hypothermic. Much longer and he would've gone into shock. There's an ambulance at the base standing by."

Exner peered out a window at the fury of the Lake Huron below. The coast guard airship valiantly navigated its way through the heavy winds and hammering sheets of rain toward the warmth and safety that awaited them on the mainland.

62

A Startling Revelation

"I am sure you are quite aware of what the DGI does to traitors," Major Dayana Torrado said as she paced slowly around Pedro Ramirez and Juan Zayas. Two soldiers had their weapons trained on the men, while a third man in a suit directed his binoculars out over the Caribbean Sea in the area where the *Cristóbal Colón* lay.

The counter-revolutionists said nothing. Juan and Pedro knew they had an ace up their collective sleeve if they could stall these people on the beach. They only hoped Hartley and Travers had time to set the charge before the FAR divers got to them. The two NABS collaborators were not alarmed by the "surprise visit."

They had intel that DGI was aware of two tourists who had gone missing from the state-run resort they had checked into, with diving tanks and weights missing from its dive shop inventory.

Due to airline luggage weight restrictions, all tourists coming to Cuba for scuba diving brought all their underwater equipment save for tanks and weights, the heaviest components of their kits, so this was not unusual. What was unusual, were two diving tourists who had not returned and who vacated the resort with their belongings without informing management of their departure.

Several hundred yards to the left of the Cubans on shore and unnoticed by them, Lee and Travers struggled in the surf. They were pummeled by the frothing incoming waves as they fought their way to the lee of the point. The Canadians knew their extraction would probably go unnoticed here by the "welcoming committee" that no doubt was waiting for them at their point of entry.

The Canadian divers kept a low profile in the surf so as not to be seen. With great exertion, they managed to remove their fins in the strong undertow that threatened to suck them back into deeper water. Each time the surf rolled in, they ran with it until finally they reached knee-deep water and broke free of the suction as the crashing waves withdrew from the beach and back out into the deep.

Once on the beach, they tossed their fins to the sand and dropped to their knees, then removed their tanks and weighted BCs.

Catching his wind somewhat, Lee got up and pulled Travers by the arm to a standing position. "Come on, Bill. Juan and Pedro are going to need our help."

The Canadians grabbed their gear and stashed it under nearby scrub brush. Travers covered their tracks as best he could. He used palm leaves to rake their footprints into the sand. Looking around, and satisfied that their tracks had been sufficiently covered on all fronts, they headed back to the area of their original entry, in the hope that their two friends would still be there, and alive.

There wasn't much cover on their return. After rounding the point, they had to belly crawl over open sand from one outcropping of vegetation to the next along the long undeveloped beach to avoid detection. Moving as stealthily as possible, the Canadians managed to get within a hundred feet of the small congregation standing at the mouth of the grotto.

They saw a man with binoculars at the edge of the shoreline looking out toward the area of the shipwreck. He was dressed in a dark blue suit and expensive looking shoes—not exactly beach wear, probably DGI.

He'll be waiting a long time for his divers to surface, Lee thought ruefully.

Two soldiers held Juan, Pedro, and Mercedes at gunpoint. A woman officer in the Cuban army stood before them. They could hear the conversation but it was in Spanish. All they could discern from it was that it was heated, and unless they acted fast, there could be some untoward gunplay.

Lee and Travers maintained their position as they weighed their options. Unexpectedly, one was provided for them however, when the binocular man spotted one of his divers on the surface. He called out to the female officer, who came over to him. The guards maintained their position at the grotto, covering Zayas and Ramirez.

"How much time, Lee?" Travers asked

Lee looked down at the black face of his Rolex Submariner. "Five minutes by my count, Bill."

They could see that the diver was losing his battle in the pounding surf. He managed to remove one fin, but couldn't seem to break the suction holding the other to his foot. He spun around several times in vain, then stood in place for as long as he could to recover his balance. The surge drew him a little farther out as each crashing wave returned from shore.

"Sucks to be him," Travers said.

Lee caught the double entendre. He felt for the man though. Lee had shaken him up pretty good before lashing him to the anchor chain by his BC strap.

The man in the suit began to wade out to help the frogman, but was restrained by the female officer. She shouted a curt warning to him, and he backed out again to the safety of the shore. She was aware of the dangers in these waters. The surge would surely have pulled him out. It was all the diver could do to hold his ground in the undertow.

No sooner had the diver finally reclaimed land when a loud explosion erupted from the wreck site. A huge narrow plume of heavy angry spray rose from the center of the *Cristóbal Colón* as the charge detonated right on time.

"Let's move!" Lee grabbed Travers' arm and they dashed out in the ensuing confusion. The three at the beach dropped to the ground and covered their heads. The surprised soldiers were locked in conflict with Zayas and Ramirez as they fought for their lives.

Mercedes ran into the grotto, hands covering her ears.

Reaching the epicenter of the struggle between the two armed soldiers and their friends, Lee and Travers each took a guard, who were quickly overpowered and summarily knocked to the ground.

"Cover them!" Lee ran to the shore knowing the female officer was armed, but not sure of the other man.

The woman saw Lee as he rushed toward her and reached for her holster. Lee pulled an old ninja trick. He shoulder rolled onto the beach and scooped up a fistful of sand in the process. Two steps later, he was upon her and hurled it into her face.

Blinded, yet with ancient revolver drawn, Major Torrado attempted to get a shot off from where she last saw him. Lee anticipated her movement however, and directed the forearm of her gun hand skyward. Spinning inside under her arm, he twisted her wrist into an agonizing wrist lock, which sent the weapon to the ground.

He wasn't prepared for the knee she planted hard onto his coccyx, however. Lee dropped to his knees in pain as the woman blindly threw a kick to his head, but it was weak and glanced off the side of his face. She rubbed her eyes wildly in an effort to regain her vision.

In the meantime, Travers tackled the binocular man to the ground. Throwing a back fist into his face, the Canadian reached into the man's suit coat and removed an old WWII-era Colt .45 auto loading pistol from his shoulder holster.

The Cuban diver meanwhile, still weak from his experiences that day, had just enough energy to slug Travers hard from behind with interlocking hands. This knocked the wind out of the aging diver. Travers spun into his opponent and threw a reverse elbow into the diver's solar plexus, which dropped the surprised man to the sand gasping for breath.

The woman let out a war whoop and proceeded to choke a surprised Lee when two shots rang sharply out. Everyone instinctively stopped what they were doing. Pedro Ramirez yelled a command in Spanish, rifle in hand. The woman released Hartley. Both the diver and the man in the suit struggled slowly to their feet. The man in the suit held his bleeding nose. The diver remained in place but remained doubled over, still trying to regain his breath.

Travers assisted Lee to his feet as Juan Zayas approached them, rifle at the ready. He instructed the others to remain where they were.

"Your timing is *impeachable*, *señors*," said a beaming Juan.

"Uh, that's impeccable, Juan-man," Travers said, correcting him on his English vocabulary.

"*Señors*; this man! He is Alberto!" Pedro remarked, nervously elated. "We have captured the head of Santiago's DGI! He is a dangerous man, *señors*. Do not take your eyes off of him!"

"Luis . . . Luis," the Cuban diver lamented over the loss of his dive buddy. The fight had left him exhausted physically, but it was apparent to the others that the death of his friend had also exhausted him emotionally.

Lee explained to his Cuban associates what had taken place underwater, and how the other diver had been killed in self-defense. But Lee was secretly glad to see that the other diver made it back. The frogman had merely carried out orders, however misguided they were. Still, Lee rationalized; the man would have killed them given the chance.

The group drifted back to the grotto, with the armed counter-revolutionaries bringing up the rear. Their captives offered no resistance.

Mercedes stared warily at the uninvited guests as they came her way.

Travers smiled to himself with glee.

"What's so funny, Bill?" Lee really didn't want to hear it, but he let the man have his say.

Travers was quick to comply. "You let a woman get the better of you. A Cuban woman with big—"

"It has been a long day, *if* you don't mind," Lee said, visibly irritated.

Successful at achieving the desired result, Travers continued. "Yeah, I know. But you, a black belt in karate—and a Cuban chick almost takes you out! Jeez, Lee!"

Travers knew his friend was more than capable of holding his own in a confrontation, but it was a rare treat to get him going once in a while.

Lee said nothing in reply. Travers almost felt sorry for his friend, almost, then shook his head and smiled again as the scene repeated itself in his mind's eye.

As the men talked, Mercedes could not help but overhear. "This man; he is *Alberto*?" She rushed over and would have scratched

Alberto's eyes out had it not been for Travers. He grabbed her around the waist and wrestled her back until he was able to restrain her arms, at great peril to himself.

In spite of the gravity of the situation, Lee had to repress a smile at the strength of the Cuban woman and the effort it took for Travers to restrain her. "Back at ya," he smiled. Travers was not amused.

"*Señors*," she said, "you must *kill* this man! He murdered my child!" Mercedes' violent struggle to break free of Travers' viselike grip devolved into deep despair and the woman went totally limp. Travers released his grip and let her fall gently to the ground. In shock, she began to cry hysterically.

Not long after, Travers helped the grief-stricken woman up and guided her away from the others. They went over to a small grove of palm trees with large fronds that provided a welcome relief from the searing heat of the midday sun. Together they sat down in the sand. No words were exchanged; no words were required. He sat and silently held her as she wept. Her feelings of revenge had morphed into a debilitating grief.

If the world didn't suck we'd all fall off, Travers thought, hanging his head in helplessness as he watched her shake in loss and trepidation.

Lee noticed that the faces of this female army major and her men were devoid of any emotion. These were stone-cold killers playing a completely different game, he thought. Who was backing them?

"*Señor* Lee," Juan said. "That one: the woman. She is Major Torrado of FAR. She is very close to the Castros."

Lee strode over to the woman officer. "I don't know what's going on here, but from what I saw, you people are not exactly patriotic. Those containers down there were meant for your own people. I don't think Fidel condoned this, do you major?"

"What are you planning Major, and with whom?" Ramirez snapped as he came over to them.

Major Torrado leaned in until she was almost face to face with Lee. Ignoring their line of questioning the major said, “We have been looking for you, and now you have been found. You will pay for what you have done here. The tables will soon turn, *señor*, and when they do I assure you, you shall all die a most torturous death!”

“We will get nothing from this one, *señor*,” Pedro said, looking at her with disdain. He pulled her back from Lee, then spat on the ground beside her. Looking deeply into her eyes he said, “Torture would be too good for these scum, *señors*, and a waste of our valuable time.”

“Maybe,” Lee said. “But I think they’re going to tell us *exactly* what the hell they’re up to and why.” Turning to Juan he said, “Bind the men up.”

“With what, *señor*?”

Lee said, “There are some large zip ties in my dive kit.”

Zayas left the group and disappeared into the grotto. Returning with the zip ties, he bound them hand and foot, then pushed the diver and the two soldiers into the grotto. Lee left Zayas to stand guard and returned to the others.

“You—Alberto!” Lee grabbed his dive knife. He walked over to Alberto, and with his right hand, stuck its blade behind the man’s ear. With his left, he grabbed the man by the hair and bounced his face off the rock wall of the grotto. Tiny bits of stone were imbedded in his bleeding cheek from the impact.

Lee’s face was a mere two inches from that of Alberto’s. “I’ve got to be honest with you. I’m not an overly violent man Alberto, but frankly, I have no qualms whatsoever about killing you right here, right now. You cold-bloodedly killed an innocent child, Alberto. A young child, an innocent girl: that woman’s daughter.” Lee grabbed him by the hair once again, and forced the man to look at Mercedes de Quesada who was still sitting with Travers.

"Either you tell me what the hell's going on down here, or I'll bring so much fire and brimstone down on you even God himself will be jealous. *Comprende, amigo*?"

Travers looked over, a smile below a squinty eye and said, "You don't want that, Alberto. He does fire pretty good. Brimstone's my specialty."

The DGI operative was strangely silent at this. He was still spitting sand from being tackled to the ground. The agent cowered slightly at Lee's icy stare. A killer knows the face of another killer; at least that was the impact Lee wanted to have on the Cuban, and it was working.

"Kill him, *Señor* Lee; *kill him*!" Mercedes cried out maniacally. She suddenly jumped up to attack Alberto and nearly made it had Travers not jumped up to restrain her once again.

Pedro kept his gun trained at both Alberto and the major. Directing a question to Alberto with a curt upward nod in his direction, Pedro said, "What have you to say for yourself, slimy one? You had your men out for us, now we have you!"

Alberto looked among his captors, then slowly said, "You think you have us, but your victory shall be short-lived. I will tell you nothing," he snarled.

Suddenly and without warning, Major Torrado lunged at Pedro. She knocked his gun to the ground. He scrambled for it. Alberto tried a similar move on Lee, but Lee was too fast for the older man. Jumping straight upward, Lee threw a vicious double knee strike into Alberto's solar plexus as the latter attempted to tackle him. The man fell to his knees and clutched his stomach, both fight and wind knocked out of him.

Meanwhile, Pedro and the major were at a stalemate as each attempted to wrestle the rifle from the other. The woman was wiry and stronger than she looked. She would have wrested the rifle from Pedro had Lee not walked over and socked the Cuban FAR officer squarely on the jaw, knocking her out. She fell lifeless to the ground.

Suddenly, the men heard a mysterious muffled crackling. Perplexed at hearing the strange noise, Lee was quick to realize the curious sounds were coming from Alberto's coat pocket. The man quickly stood up and tried pushing Lee's hand away as he reached for his pocket but Pedro, still holding the gun on the major, stomped down hard onto the DGI man's instep. The counter-revolutionary then stepped back to better cover his two prisoners.

Alberto cursed him in Spanish then reflexively reached down to rub the top of his foot, but not before Lee pulled a transceiver from his pocket.

Surprisingly small, it was a modern high-powered unit. The radio crackled again, the static giving way to a man's voice.

Surprisingly the voice spoke in English. "Alberto, damn it, come in. This is Raul, your commander-in-chief. *Respond at once!*"

63

A Little Something To Remember Me By

The motel exploded into a huge ball of white fire, scattering debris hundreds of feet into the air. Contentment crossed Wu Yang's face. He raised a forefinger and saluted off his brow through the window as the Apache punched a hole through the billowing smoke above its fiery remains.

Yang tossed the cell phone used as a detonator to the floor of the chopper as they swung out on a southwesterly course over Lake Huron. He then made a call on his sat-phone.

The Apache whined eerily as the pilot set a new course into the wind. The four main rotors and four blade tail rotors screamed in protest until the craft stabilized.

Wu Yang sat smugly in the cabin of the Boeing AH-64 Apache helicopter which sported the latest in stealth technology, including the Ventriloquist array. It carried a pylon station on the stub-wings at each side of the craft, which held AGM-114 Hellfire air-to-surface missiles, each employing a semi active laser-honing guidance system. The Chinese operative was not one to take chances.

The black chopper bore dull gray Canadian Air Force markings to allay suspicion while in Canada. A mere month prior, it had operated in Pennsylvania sporting U.S. Air Force insignia.

The Establishment had roots in North America. Cutting-edge technological equipment, men, and resources had been deployed to the continent's heartland over a span of several months. But the whole undertaking had taken the Chinese years.

It was imperative now to have a close offshore base of operations close to the continent to provide a safe haven for their scientists and operatives once Project Vector was hot. Cuba jumped at the chance. Several million American dollars formally thrown to the Cuban government to restore their infrastructure, a few million more to the Castros, and it was a done deal. If all went as planned, it would come back to the Peoples' Republic a hundredfold; the Establishment, a thousand.

The Establishment had managed to appropriate, without detection, several packets of the experimental virus through inside operatives who had managed to infiltrate the tight network of both Chinese and Cuban doctors and scientists commissioned by their governments to develop an Ebola derivative sufficiently virulent to paralyze not just a country, but a continent.

Where the finalized series of packets ended up however, was of great concern to Wu Yang. Without them, the Establishment was powerless to carry out phase three; that of bringing their own governments to their knees at the appropriate time.

With the weaker pathogenic material the Establishment had already managed to smuggle into Canada, the *Étoile Profonde* had fulfilled its mission. Ten containers had been successfully planted in shipwrecks at depths varying from eighty to 140 feet.

The stage had been set. The rest was up to Alberto and him.

The viral outpouring they were about to unleash would no doubt go down in history as the Black Plague of the twenty-first century.

The death toll would be staggering. Wu Yang liked death. It was so inevitable, so final. Death did not leave the loose ends life did. Death provided no pardons, no reprieves, and no second chances. Death was, in effect, a most cost-effective way for controlling a rebellious free society that demanded its rights. Death was not concerned with rights. It was only concerned with finality.

Content with the loose ends he had tied up the past few days, Wu Yang reached into the case beside him, withdrew a laptop, and set about encoding the next phase of the operation.

The Apache maintained a low altitude as it cut through the sky at its cruising speed of 165 miles per hour.

Wu Yang had but one final loose end to tie up. Secrets could be kept by a group of men as long as all but one was dead . . .

64

Unnerving Developments

"With all due respect, our men in Cuba are in danger imminent and need to be extracted ASAP, Mr. Prime Minister," Alan Exner said from a sat phone link at the NABS Ottawa headquarters. He listened patiently before responding. "That is correct, sir. Our men were sent to Santiago de Cuba. The last communiqué received stated they had been compromised, but were still at large."

Exner listened for several more minutes before speaking into the receiver. "I see. Yes, sir; they *have* been invaluable to this mission . . . yes, sir. I will definitely relay the information to them when they arrive . . . yes; you as well, sir. Good day, Mr. Prime Minister." Exner ended the conversation and shut down the communication system.

"Well," Bindhira asked. "What did your prime minister have to say?"

Exner got up from behind the desk of Ottawa NABS Control Jayden LaPlante. He motioned LaPlante to reclaim her desk. The statuesque middle-aged woman nodded eager for his response.

Walking around the desk, Exner addressed the two women. "The Royal Canadian Navy has just completed a major refit of one of their Victoria class diesel-electric submarines, the HMCS *Windsor*. Coincidentally the crew of the SSK 877 is conducting sea trials off the Florida Keys as we speak. The Windsor has been given the go-ahead to proceed to Cuba at flank speed then standby off shore at a predetermined extraction point, at which time they'll deploy Zodiacs for a dash-and-grab." He paused. "All we have to do now is get word to Hartley and Travers."

"I'll have my people alert them, Alan. Hopefully your men will be in a position to get back to us soon," Jayden LaPlante said. She picked up her phone and issued the appropriate orders.

"Your plan might be a tall order, Alan," Bindhira interjected. "The coastline has been regularly patrolled by Cuban gun boats since the Missile Crisis. The NSA still routinely monitors their frequencies. The Cubans maintain a highly efficient coast guard, even though it is primarily designed to keep their people hemmed *in*."

"Still in all," Jayden said, looking highly professional in her expensive teal-colored pantsuit and darkly tanned olive skin, "we must make every effort to get those men back." Looking to Exner, LaPlante said, "Alan, if anything were to happen to those men, you are aware that we could be facing a lawsuit from their families. They're not trained NABS agents."

Exner smiled and patted her on her shoulder. "These men have no families, Jayden. We've used their services on many occasions in marine situations where even NABS divers would fear to tread. Don't worry, no matter what happens, believe me, they're solid. In fact, there've been many occasions that Hartley took no remuneration from us in spite of the dangers involved. He likes the challenge. He's a true Canadian patriot."

"Lee's father served with Canada's Queen's Own Rifles during WWII," Exner continued, "and took part in Operation Overlord at Juno Beach during the invasion of Normandy on June 6, 1944. He survived, unlike many of his comrades. But the man rarely spoke of it. He even refused to take his army pension, which he was certainly entitled to."

Exner looked deep into her eyes. "Lee took his father's death from cancer quite hard. They were tight. As they say, the apple doesn't fall far from the tree."

Bindhira was not aware of this facet of Lee Hartley's life. Like his father, Lee was not one to talk about his past. But knowing this, and the fact that he had no other family, endeared him to her more than ever. These feelings however, quickly morphed into a deep-seated concern for his wellbeing. She hoped he was wearing the gift she had given him before he left for Cuba.

The coast guard helicopter that carried Exner and Bindhira had been rerouted directly to Ottawa at LaPlante's request. The two agents were set up in VIP suites within the NABS Ottawa complex. They were provided with fresh clothes, an excellent meal, and a thorough briefing before the prime minister was contacted by Ottawa's control, Jayden LaPlante.

LaPlante had served with the RCMP for twenty-one years. The French-Canadian woman originally from Rimouski, Quebec, relinquished her post with the counterterrorist squad to accept a directorate in the newly formed North American Bureau of Security a few years prior. She was a tall, lithe woman whose fresh, natural beauty belied her true age.

The experience gleaned from years of profiling and tracking terrorists and subversive organizations throughout Canada provided her with the perfect skill set for her present post. She had a sixth sense when it came to subversives, and many were brought to justice directly through her efforts.

Jayden and Alan Exner had met many times with other NABS controls throughout North America, and in joint meetings with both domestic and foreign antiterrorist organizations. Both LaPlante and Exner had a healthy respect for each other.

Enrico, the *Étoile Profonde's* radio operator, after treatment for hypothermia, was personally interrogated by LaPlante. They determined that the Cuban merely signed on as the ship's radio operator as he maintained, and had not been privy to the true nature of the ship's operations in the Great Lakes. Much of the correspondence according to him, was sent and received in code, and he was not responsible for deciphering it.

For the time being, LaPlante placed him in protective custody in the Hilton a few miles from the NABS federal building. The top floor of this particular Hilton was owned exclusively by NABS for billeting visiting foreign dignitaries and informers. The floor was highly secured, monitored, and regularly patrolled by NABS enforcement agents. The Cuban was never left alone. An armed agent was present with him at all times, and Enrico was never allowed to leave the floor he was on.

Jayden LaPlante filled Exner and Bindhira in on the events that had transpired since their abduction. She told them how CIA sub-director Scott Culp had set up temporary operations in Canada from Exner's office at Niagara-On-The-Lake. She also told them about the last contact NABS had received from Lee and Travers, and that no further transmissions had been received since.

Exner asked, "What's our next play, Jayden?" He walked over to a small bookcase by her desk and picked up a black obsidian dagger.

"I'd be careful with that if I were you Alan," Jayden said. "That was used in a triple homicide and might still have traces of curare on the blade tip."

She smiled to Bindhira as Exner hastily replaced the object. He bent down to closer inspect the knife, then instinctively looked at his hands. He grabbed a small tube of hand sanitizer off the woman's desk and proceeded to do a thorough job of cleaning his hands.

The women had a good laugh in spite of themselves and Exner, his face blushing in Technicolor, returned behind the desk, plopped himself down, and sat facing them, hands folded on the desktop.

"The material found on the bridge of the *Étoile Profonde* is disturbing, to say the least," Exner said, trying to reclaim some dignity. "We know basically what the Chinese-Cuban connection is, but we have no information on this *Establishment*. From what I managed to harvest from the ship just before I ah, escaped, it seems as though the Chinese have a different game plan."

"How so," LaPlante asked.

Bindhira eyed him suspiciously, and Exner did his best not to notice. But he knew she would eventually corner him for an explanation as to how he got off the ship and was picked up by the coast guard before Enrico and her.

Exner looked to Bindhira before he spoke. "This Wu Yang character comes across as a diehard Chinese nationalist, but from what little information we have on the man, that may not be the case." It's going to take a group of Bletchley Park cryptologists to get to the bottom of this one, I'm afraid."

"How do you mean, Alan," LaPlante asked.

Bindhira caught Exner's eye and smiled. "Bletchley Park at Buckinghamshire, England, was where wrens worked during WWII at decoding ciphers generated from the German Enigma and Lorenz machines. They intercepted many ciphers that greatly aided the Allies in tracking U Boats in the North Atlantic as well as German troop movement in North Africa. Without the high intelligence produced at Bletchley Park, codenamed *Ultra,* the war was certain to have lasted several years more. Its outcome would have been very different without their efforts."

They were interrupted by a brief knock on the door and the entrance of LaPlante's aide.

"Ma'am, we've managed to establish communications with Mr. Exner's team in Cuba. I'm afraid it doesn't sound good."

65

Disturbing News

The infamous Roof Club on West Street in Port Antonio, Jamaica, is perhaps the busiest, and raunchiest, nightclub on the island. Located in the middle of town, the Roof Club is situated on the second floor of a nondescript industrial building. No need to buy *ganja* here. Potent fumes of the marijuana derivative flowed freely throughout the club, sufficient enough to bring a smile to anyone venturesome enough to cross its threshold.

Soca and reggae thundered from the club's core nightly. One needs to constantly have their wits about them here though, as the unwary are never the same again. Port Antonio's most crowded nightclub, the Roof Club is a crowded noisy den of iniquity, and definitely not a place to bring one's mother while on holiday.

The early hours of the morning usually brought out the most unpredictable behavior in patrons, but this night was different. People were leaving in groups because they felt ill, not because they had exceeded their personal limits.

Blood dripped from the facial orifices of many who were compelled to leave earlier than expected. Few picked up on the increasing frequency of the anomaly. Within an hour of the first to leave, the Roof Club was increasingly tamer as the morning wore on, its patrons leaving in favor of the local hospital.

News of the strange phenomenon spread quickly around the world as Jamaican health authorities made an international plea for assistance, while the local constabulary did their best to isolate the affected area.

Word of a possible terrorist attack reached the ears of many of the world's greatest intelligence gathering agencies. England's MI6, Israel's Mossad, France's Douxieme Bureau, Russia's SVR Foreign Intelligence Service, Spain's Centro Superior de Informacion de la Defensa, even the Chinese ChIS and Cuban DGI. All received similar communiqués regarding the mysterious plague in Jamaica.

The World Health Organization scrambled a crack team of bio-terror experts to Jamaica to examine the victims firsthand. Within twenty-four hours, the world was both aware and dumbfounded as it received developments of the mysterious outbreak.

NABS control Jayden LaPlante ushered her aide out of the room, much to the chagrin of Alan Exner and Bindhira Shankar. During the time of her absence, they listened to, and were shocked at, the latest news broadcast live from Jamaica as they watched from a TV monitor in her office.

"A tsunami, though one not of the water variety, has crashed upon the northeastern shore of Jamaica in the Caribbean," the young female reporter said. "Millions of tourists flock to the island nation each year to get their fix of sun, sand, warmth, and fun. This year, however, their fix was met with unexpected repercussions."

"Airlines have been grounded. People are stuck in the island's airports, as federal officials ordered a lockdown of the island. Medical teams have arrived from all over the free world to pool their resources to determine just what caused such widespread sickness at the nation's most famous nightspot, the Roof Club."

"It all began a few days ago when two local fishermen came into the Port Antonio Hospital complaining of advanced flulike symptoms, bleeding from bodily orifices, and complaining of severe headaches. The older of the two succumbed, but the other, younger man, remains in hospital in serious condition."

"Then a day later," the TV reporter continued, "the outbreak at the Roof Club. Dozens of patrons experienced simultaneous symptoms. Fourteen have already succumbed to the illness."

"The World Health Organization is conducting tests of all food, water, and beverages served at the nightclub in an effort to find out just what caused dozens of revelers to suddenly fall ill."

"Many have been ferried to other hospitals, most notably, the Kingston Public Hospital and the University Hospital of the West Indies in Saint Andrew. All of these hospitals are in lockdown in a desperate bid to contain the strange disease."

"Fear and uncertainty have gripped the island, and rumors of terrorism have been rife. All flights into and out of Jamaica have been cancelled indefinitely until the source of the infection has been located and contained. Federal Aviation authorities are asking everyone with family members visiting Jamaica to exercise calm and to pray for a quick solution."

"We will continue to keep you abreast of all the local happenings here as they unfold. This is Sandy Bunson, GNN, live at UHWI Hospital, Saint Andrew, Jamaica. Back to you, Robert . . ."

Just then NABS Control Jayden LaPlante returned to the room.

Exner and Bindhira eagerly met her halfway. "What is the word?" Bindhira asked.

LaPlante replied, “Your agents in Cuba have fallen under attack, Alan. They did manage to blow up a cache of biological material concealed in a wreck off the southwestern coast, and captured a DGI agent along with a major in the Cuban Revolutionary Armed Forces, both with direct ties to the Castros.”

“But reinforcements arrived and overwhelmed them. Somehow your Hartley and Travers managed to escape, albeit barely. There’s a massive manhunt currently underway for them. I fear they don’t have much time.”

Exner looked at Bindhira, then to the floor. She put a hand on his shoulder. “What about the HMCS *Windsor*? Do they know about the *Windsor*?” Exner’s concern for his friends was clearly etched on his face.

“We received word that our hunter-killer submarine is on its way at flank speed, Alan,” LaPlante said. “It should be outside Cuban territorial waters very soon. The message then became garbled and intermixed with high-pitched squeals.”

“The Cubans were attempting to jam their transmission signals,” Bindhira interjected. “Sequoia is designed to enable verbal communication through the heaviest of artificially generated static. The system reflects the jamming waves back to the original sender, damaging their equipment in the process.”

“Sooo, did the com get any clearer as a result?” Exner asked.

“I did manage to get through regarding the submarine rendezvous,” LaPlante said. “We received coordinates from them for two locations suitable enough for a rendezvous at sea.”

“Two things,” she said. “First, they have two Cubans with them. They are men in the underground counter-revolutionary movement who know the area quite well.”

“Second, the Sequoia automatically tracks and records the movements of all its systems, and is programmed to issue better-than-military-grade GPS coordinates.” She paused to gather her thoughts.

"The bad news, Alan, is that their Seqpod is running low on power, and was no doubt damaged in an altercation they had on the beach. But at least we got our message through."

"Thank goodness for that," Bindhira said.

"At least they have some hope," Exner added.

"And extraction coordinates we can use for a pickup at sea," Bindhira said with hope.

"All they have to do is keep in front of the hounds for a few more hours, Alan," LaPlante said.

"This whole damned affair is going to the dogs, Jayden. They may not have two hours."

66

Beach Assault

Bullets were flying and sand was spitting up all around them. Lee and Travers with their Cuban compatriots were hunkered down; trapped between the high rock cliff on one side and the Caribbean Sea on the other. There were outcroppings of high rock formations as far as the eye could see along the beach, which kept them alive, at least for now.

Two jeeploads of soldiers from the Eastern Army's Third Armored Division of the Cuban Revolutionary Armed Forces, Major Torrado's unit, had just recently arrived on the scene and quickly relinquished the hold the Canadians and their Cuban friends had on Major Torrado and Alberto.

Lee and Travers had each managed to maintain possession of a rifle they had wrested during their surprise attack on the Cuban contingent who had lain in wait for them on the wrong part of the beach following their dive on the *Cristóbal Colón*. The Canadians had beaten the odds then, but they were currently stacked against them now.

Lee was with Zayas; Ramirez was with Travers. The Cubans stayed behind the Canadians as they were not able to secure weapons.

The two fired a few random bursts here and there to keep their attackers at bay. Their ammo was fast running out, as was their time, and they knew it.

"Looks grim for the Hardy Boys, *amigo*," Travers said as he looked over at Lee with a squinty eye. They were pinned down behind a massive, pitted rectangular boulder. Cuban soldiers managed to dig in on a plateau across the road that was not quite high enough to shoot over the rock protrusion the two men had taken cover behind.

"We've just got to hold on a little longer, Bill," Lee said. "At least we got the extraction intel before the radio was destroyed."

"At what price Lee?" Travers was visibly distraught. "The bastards got Mercedes, damn it! At this point, I really don't give a shit."

There was little time to dwell on the fact as a salvo of machine gunfire blasted stone chips at Travers' face with the ferocity of a jack hammer.

Travers got off three short bursts in the direction from which the withering fire had come from.

Twenty minutes prior, Mercedes de Quesada had sacrificed her life to save the Canadians in a last act of defiance. With the men facing the ocean, maintaining control over their captives on the beach, Mercedes had caught the glint of a rifle scope high in the rocks behind. She saw a soldier acquire a bead on Lee Hartley. With no thought for herself, she unexpectedly pushed Hartley aside. In the act, Mercedes received a barrage of machine gun fire which instantly killed her.

The valiant woman had time only to gurgle in shock before she dropped to the sand, dead. Bloody froth continued to issue from her drawn mouth. The corpse's eyes were still open in wide disbelief.

Even despite their current situation, the Canadians were devastated that the entire de Quesada family had been wiped out within a month.

Catching a glimpse of movement to their left flank, Lee's battered Soviet-made Kalashnikov AKM-S assault rifle coughed out. One Cuban soldier caught a 7.62 mm round in the left cheek. Another soldier close by was struck by a round to the throat. Both dropped heavily to the sand, the latter thrashing violently as he fought to regain his breath, but to no avail. Neither moved.

The Canadians then watched in horror as a covered troop truck screeched to a halt just past the curve in the road at the base of the mountainside.

"We are so screwed," Travers shouted to his friend.

It was only a matter of time now. Both Lee and Travers saw soldiers crouching low among the beach bramble, protected behind the rocks there. Lee had a clear shot on a soldier who thought he had sufficient cover. He squeezed off several more rounds before both the man and Lee's gun went silent.

"I'm out," Lee shouted. Travers squeezed off a few more rounds to keep his side clear of interlopers.

Looking back in Lee's direction, Travers cried out. "Lee!" He pointed nervously out to sea.

They looked out over the ocean in dismay. Two black rubber Zodiacs threw up twin plumes as they rushed at flank speed to the beach from the point to their left.

"We've had it, Lee. Shit! Shit! *Shit!*" Travers was now out of ammo as well. They held tight against the rock slab, waiting for the inevitable.

Suddenly Pedro Ramirez broke cover from behind Travers and ran toward the mountain to draw fire from the ground soldiers. He was immediately cut down in a hail of bullets mere feet from a huge boulder that would have afforded him protection from the relentless gunfire.

"Pedro!" Zayas cried and would have run out had Lee not grabbed his shoulder and pulled him back. "He's gone, Juan. No time for heroics brother," he shouted.

"Incoming," Travers cried.

Unexpectedly two RPGs, rocket propelled grenades, whistled over their heads, one from each Zodiac, hitting both the troop transport and a jeep! Both exploded in huge fireballs. Heavy black smoke temporarily obstructed their view.

Then a voice from the direction of the Zodiacs: "Hartley! Travers! Get your asses out here on the double!"

Not waiting for a second invitation, Lee cried out, "Don't need to be asked twice. Bill! Juan! Hang close!" The men threw down their now useless weapons and ran toward the beach as the Zodiacs swept in as close as they dared.

When they got to the water's edge, where the drifting smoke had cleared, the three saw that the men in the Zodiacs were wearing blue navy-issue camouflage coveralls with no identification swatches. They were engaged in sending withering fire to several areas on the beach wherever movement was detected, save for the three unarmed men rapidly racing toward them.

Then came another two whistling flashes, and another two explosions. This time, the sniper nest on the mountain face had been obliterated. Rock and debris combined with body parts rained down on the beach, as far as the shore itself.

One of the boats broke formation and veered into the shallows where the Canadians and Juan Zayas struggled against the surf. The desperate men felt the powerful suction as the receding waves attempted to drag the three under and out to sea.

A seaman reached out and latched onto Travers' wrist with one hand while throwing a line to Lee with the other. He quickly yanked the lighter Travers up and into the boat.

Zayas struggled to hang on to the rope that surrounded the Zodiac's upper hull. He was trying to pull himself into the boat when he was peppered in the back by a barrage of bullets. Several would have punctured the rubber side of the Zodiac had it not been overlaid with heavy Kevlar, the same material used in bullet-proof vests. The bullets ricocheted harmlessly off the sturdy rubberized fabric.

There was no time for goodbyes. A seaman in the Zodiac reluctantly pushed Zayas away from the bow. Within seconds the small craft sped out to sea.

"*Juan!*" Lee cried out, but he had all he could do to hang on for dear life himself as they raced around the corner of a rock outcropping. The second Zodiac followed close behind, laying down a massive wave of withering firepower before it too disappeared around the rock point, leaving their attackers in total dumbfounded disbelief.

The boats slowed to a crawl. Two brawny hands reached out and plucked a water-logged Lee Hartley out of the sea and into the relative safety of the Zodiac.

"Major General Jim Harris, JTF2, sir," he announced as he swung the shoulder strap of his Heckler and Koch MP5A3 submachine gun out of the way to shake the exhausted Canadian's hand.

"Hartley, Lee Hartley. Glad to make your acquaintance, sir. Boy, are we glad to see you."

"I second that!" Travers said as he reached up from where he was sitting to shake the man's bear paw.

"How'd you find us?" Lee asked, utterly amazed at how they had been able to pinpoint their exact location.

"Long story, sir; mostly classified I'm afraid. Suffice it to say that you are considered valuable assets of the Canadian government. Somebody back home moved heaven and earth to get your asses back alive. Submarine HMCS *Windsor* is standing by a few miles out in international waters, awaiting our arrival." He smiled and put a hand on Lee's shoulder.

Major General Harris then pointed at the coin on the gold chain around Lee's neck. "You must have someone in lofty places who cares enough about you to have given you that, sir." He smiled and pointed to the gold coin that hung around Lee's neck.

Surprised at this, Lee removed the necklace. Upon closer examination of the coin it supported, Lee noticed that along the coin's edge, a very tiny slit was etched all the way around. "A miniature GPS transmitter had been embedded in the coin! Well, I'll be damned!"

Bindhira had given it to Lee prior to his leaving for Cuba. Although it was indeed as she had said, a gold coin uncovered by Mel Fisher during his recovery of the Spanish Galleon *Nuestra Senora de Atocha* during the late 1980s, it ingenuously contained a wafer-thin high-powered homing device.

The unit emitted signals at frequent intervals that were picked up and monitored by the Sequoia computer system's emergency locator frequency database. All Lee knew however was that it was a tool of the NSA. He just hoped they wouldn't be mad at Bindhira for 'borrowing' it."

The major general looked up to the man at the helm of his Zodiac. Giving him an upturned twirling index finger, he said, "Get us the hell out of here, Dave."

The helmsman caught the signal from his superior officer and then waved over to the pilot aboard the other Zodiac. He relayed the same hand signal. "Aye that, sir," the man said. Both boats' twin 150 HP Evinrude V6 motors roared to life at maximum throttle.

The Zodiacs swung around and headed out to sea. But as they did so, a Cuban gunboat appeared over the horizon and bore down on them at flank speed.

67

Special Delivery

"The president and prime minister have been formally briefed on the developing situation in Jamaica, and have sent their leading virological scientists down to assist, as many more fall ill to the mysterious plague threatening the island nation."

Exner was walking down the hall and past the open door of the situation room at NABS headquarters in Ottawa where a large eighty-inch monitor continued to blare out TV coverage of the *Jamaican Plague*, as it had come to be known.

He carried flight bags and ticket in hand, when Bindhira came around the corner. She too carried a luggage bag along with a slim handbag by her side. They nearly collided. Exner took her arm and steered her to the elevator.

They had been reassigned to Tobermory, where a mysterious explosion had occurred at a derelict motel several miles south of the picturesque little village.

"There's more happening in Tobermory than we were lead to believe Bindhi," Exner said, taking up her luggage bag.

"Yes, and we must somehow locate the missing gym bag that contained those matchbooks, Alan," she said grimly.

A few minutes later, the two emerged onto the rooftop of the building. They headed toward the black, white, and gold helicopter awaiting them that bore the markings of the Ontario Provincial Police. As soon as the two clambered in, the chopper gracefully lifted off the helipad and headed west to Tobermory.

Inside they were greeted by none other than OPP Detective Sergeant Jane Hardcastle. Once the craft reached cruising speed, the detective sergeant briefed them on the latest developments at Tobermory.

"A most unusual incident, to say the least," Detective Hardcastle said. "It was a very sudden and intense explosion directed at the motel office."

"'*Directed,'* Detective?" Bindhira caught Hardcastle's deliberate use of the word.

"Well," Hardcastle explained, "this explosion has all the indicators of an air-to-surface missile attack! But who would possess such a weapon in Canada, and why would they want to blow up an abandoned motel," Detective Hardcastle asked.

"Nothing surprises me about this case, Detective," Exner said as he looked to Bindhira.

"Rule out nothing during your inquiry, Detective Hardcastle," Bindhira said. "This is definitely the work of an international terrorist group we are attempting to locate."

"One more thing," Detective Hardcastle said. "We've also uncovered the remains of five hopelessly charred and dismembered bodies inside the motel office. Not much left of them I'm afraid.

The explosion was quite intense. Death came instantly for the poor bastards."

"Male? Female? Ethnic origin," Exner prodded.

"It's too early to determine at this point, sir. Forensics is combing the crime scene as we speak."

"These people, good as they are, have left a pattern; most do," Bindhira noted, smiling wryly. "The explosion and fire at the Scuba U in Fort Erie was set off by a crude bomb placed in, of all places, a toilet tank. The components used were not run-of-the-mill, do-it-yourself bomb items."

"No, and the incident here was a precision military air strike," Exner mused. Looking to Detective Hardcastle he said, "From what we've seen here, Detective, this attack appears to be the work of someone much farther up the food chain."

"Perhaps," she said. "Do you think the two incidents are related to one another?"

"No question," Bindhira stated. "Things are heating up in more ways than one, no pun intended."

"Detective," Exner ventured, "this may sound completely out of context, but did anyone happen to turn in a gym bag sporting a Fitness Revolution logo that had been left abandoned on Little Tub dock the past day or so?"

"Funny you should ask, Mr. Exner," the detective replied. "Why, just yesterday afternoon one of our patrol officers spotted a shabbily dressed little girl walking along Highway 6 after dusk, not far from where the motel is, or rather *was*, and she was carrying a gym bag."

"And what did your officer do, Detective?" Bindhira was taken aback at the unexpected revelation. Both she and Exner exchanged excited glances.

"Why, he picked her up of course. That stretch of highway is dangerous enough in a car, let alone for a little girl to be walking at night. He brought her to the OPP satellite station in Tobermory.

When the officers asked who she was, and where she had come from, she started humming, as if she hadn't heard them. For a little girl all alone at night, she seemed quite content in herself."

"Did she say anything," Bindhira asked, a genuine note of concern in her voice.

"Well, we didn't get a chance."

"What's that supposed to mean?" This from Exner.

"I mean, the child said she needed to go to the bathroom 'real bad.' When she didn't return, an female officer went to see if she was okay." Hardcastle left them hanging as she relived the strange event.

"And what did the child say when she was brought back?" Bindhira felt like she was a lawyer interrogating a witness.

"She didn't say anything," the detective said. She was gone. Disappeared. Never saw her leave, and no one has seen her since."

Exner turned from the two women and gazed out the window of the Eurocopter. "Any way she could have gotten out of the washroom without being detected? No window, no air vents, no attic access in the ceiling above the washroom?"

"There *is* a window, but it's far too small even for that little mite to have squeezed through."

Taking a different tact, Bindhira said, "Do you still have possession of the gym bag?"

"Oh yes, but that's another thing. The bag contains only old matchbooks, and nothing more. Initially we thought perhaps it was she who'd set the fire at the motel. But the fire was much too intense to have been set with matches alone," the detective said.

"We'll need that bag," Exner said. "Please contact your Tobermory office and inform them we need the bag for evidence. It's a matter of national security."

"Of course, sir," Detective Hardcastle said.

"*Now* if you don't mind, Detective."

The OPP woman nodded, rose, and knocked on the cabin door.

"The child again," Exner said, when the detective had left their ear shot.

"Yes. Mr. Travers was emphatic that a child fitting her description had freed him from the cave prison," Bindhira recalled.

"Funny, and I never paid much credence to it," Exner said, "but my chief forensics man, Mataeo, mentioned on the by that there was a child fitting her very description on site at the Scuba U when we picked up the Viper."

"If that is the case, Alan, how could she have gotten from here to Niagara-On-The-Lake and *back again* without anyone to assist her? It is just not logistically possible."

Exner, himself perplexed, was forced to put it on the back burner as he gratefully accepted a cup of hot coffee from a crewmember who also handed one to each of the women.

Just then the speakers crackled, and the pleasant voice of the pilot came over the intercom. "Tobermory in five. Please secure your seatbelts at this time, and thank you for flying Air OPP."

68

A Voluntary Capitulation

Gino Vaselino was tired, hungry, and cold, and not necessarily in that order. He had nearly frozen in the cool, damp Tobermory night air and almost blown up in the horrific motel explosion the night before. *That Chinese bastard Wu Yang! After all the cell members had sacrificed for him and his Establishment, he thanks them by killing them all. Well, almost all,* he thought as he walked back from the beach along Dunks Bay Road.

Fortunately for Vaselino, and despite Chen Fa's order the night of the blast, he had gone off into the bushes to relieve himself when he heard Yang's helicopter doubling back.

Moments later, the motel had erupted into a huge fireball. Even though he was several hundred feet from the building, Vaselino had been knocked to the ground by a searing blast of hot air.

Both the bath he took in the cool water of Georgian Bay and the long walk back to the highway did much to invigorate him. He had been through a lot the past few days, and it felt good to have a reprieve from cell activities.

It was just past noon when he heard another helicopter heading his way. Thinking it was Wu Yang, he dove for the cover of the woodlands to his right. Although his didn't see the chopper, he could hear it slowing down for a landing near the motel.

Vaselino quickened his pace and ran the rest of the way through the heavy forest back to the motel. If it *was* Wu Yang he thought, he would tear the man apart with his bare hands. The opportunity fueled him with rage and drove him onward with hatred.

As he approached the motel from the main road, he drew back into the woods that paralleled the roadway. Drawing as close as he dared, Vaselino saw that the chopper had landed. He remained out of sight and waited to see who came out.

To his utter surprise, he saw that it wasn't Wu Yang's helicopter after all. It was an Ontario Provincial Police unit, no doubt sent to investigate the motel explosion.

Vaselino continued to watch from cover as several officers combed the scene. Four police cruisers were on site. He rubbed his crotch in praise for the urgency of having to take a piss when he did the night before. His full bladder saved his life.

Although he could hear voices, he was too far away to discern conversations. Vaselino lowered himself down behind a cluster of white spruce trees. The ground was soft with the blanket of fallen pine needles beneath his feet. His body craved sleep but that would have to wait.

The Cuban entertained various options in his mind. He was orphaned from his cell with no backup and no weapons. Not that any of that would be of benefit to him now.

He wanted to turn himself in, to blow the whistle on Wu Yang and his damned Establishment. Vaselino realized that it was over for him. He'd been betrayed by the very cause that he so strongly believed in. Now he was in a foreign country with nowhere to go.

The Cubans who came to Canada soon after him were all killed, and their cell obliterated. What he had been led to believe, that he was doing a service for his impoverished nation, evaporated in the reality of his current situation.

At that moment, Vaselino experienced an epiphany. No matter the cost, no matter the price the Establishment would put on his head, for once in his life Gino Vaselino was determined to do the right thing.

As Exner and Bindhira exited the charred remains of the motel office, the NSA agent caught Exner's arm. Standing not a hundred feet from them was a man whose torn and soot-tinged clothes suggested he had been witness to the carnage.

The man walked cautiously toward them. Exner trotted over to meet him. "Get an officer to assist me here, Bindhi, and call an ambulance," he said over his shoulder.

Within minutes Exner and one of the provincial officers had Vaselino out to the car park as they awaited an ambulance. "Are you hurt anywhere, sir?" the officer asked as they guided the Cuban over to sit on the rear gate of a police SUV.

"My name is Gino Vaselino, and I wish to claim asylum in your Canada," he said in his heavy Latino accent.

"How's that?" Exner looked deep into the man's eyes. He had seen it all too often. In front of him no doubt stood a once powerful foreign operative who had gotten into something way out of his element only to be abandoned by his handlers. This was a man out of options, out of hope.

"I am a citizen of Cuba," Vaselino said, "and wish to tell you about things, terrible things, which are soon to happen to this country and to the United States if you do not take me seriously."

"Oh, don't you worry; we will take you *very* seriously, Mr. Vaselino," Exner said, a wry smile crossing his lips.

69

Point Of No Return

Detective Sergeant Hardcastle had an officer return to the nearby OPP satellite station to retrieve the gym bag the girl had left behind. The officer returned shortly thereafter and turned it over to Exner. With the bag safely in hand, the two agents, the detective, and their Cuban charge lifted off from the motel crime scene.

After refueling at their helicopter base in Orillia, the OPP chopper transported Exner, Bindhira, and Gino Vaselino to NABS Niagara headquarters at Niagara-On-The-Lake.

Upon arrival at the Niagara District Airport, Exner and Bindhira thanked the detective for her assistance before the OPP helicopter lifted off on a reciprocal course back to Orillia. A limousine with heavily blacked out windows awaited them for the drive back to NABS headquarters and Exner's office.

Few questions were asked of Vaselino on his arrival. On the one hand, Exner saw that the Cuban was in no shape for interrogation but he was also painfully cognizant that time was running out. The NABS control was also aware that although this man held the key to the whole affair, they first had to win his confidence and meet his physical needs before he would be of any use to them.

The Cuban was ushered into a room, where he enjoyed a hot shower, then was later treated to a hot meal of surf and turf. The Prince Edward Island lobster was among the tastiest he had ever had, and the steak was cooked medium-well, exactly to his liking.

Following his meal, the Cuban was ushered back to his room, where he quickly fell asleep, exhausted, but clean and well fed. For the first time in a great while, Gino Vaselino felt relaxed and yes, safe—for the moment.

After a hearty breakfast of bacon, scrambled eggs, toast, coffee, sausage, home fries, and fruit the next morning, the Cuban was then led to the interrogation room. Exner began to extract details of a complex series of operations: the Chinese-Cuban plan to destabilize the North American governments, the 'parasitic' plot of the Establishment, and most important of all, the finer details of Project Vector that was the common thread between them.

Control was confident the relevant knowledge the man had of his cell's activities would rapidly bring everything into focus. Being a good judge of character, Exner quickly discerned the man was telling them the truth to the best of his knowledge. From Vaselino, Exner extracted much concerning the activities of both the Chinese-Cuban connection and the Establishment in exchange for both a pardon and the granting of asylum in Canada.

NABS scientists thoroughly examined the gym bag's contents. The matchbooks found were indeed laced with an Ebola hybrid, but apparently much more virile than that wreaking havoc in Jamaica.

It was further determined that the catalyst, which was impregnated into the matchbook covers themselves, had been improved to hasten its reaction time with the pathogen-laced match heads, thereby allowing for a quicker release of hydrostatic pressure and still maintain its virility.

Summoned to his NABS lab, Exner admonished Bindhira to accompany him. The head of the viral unit was a tall, thin attractive brunette by the name of Dr. Charity Nelson.

Dr. Nelson was a thirty-something infectious disease specialist who had been recruited by NABS from the John Hopkins University School of Medicine in Baltimore, Maryland several years prior. Dr. Nelson specialized in biomedical research and had been one of the most foremost scientists in her field before signing on with NABS.

Wearing her usual white smock and infectious smile, she welcomed them into her world. "Hello, Mr. Exner," Dr. Nelson addressed NABS control as they walked in. She acknowledged Bindhira with a nod and polite smile.

"Dr. Charity Nelson, this is Bindhira Shankar," Exner said by way of introduction. "Ms. Shankar is acting as liaison between the U.S. Central Security Service branch of the NSA and our organization in this matter."

Again the pleasant nod which Bindhira reciprocated.

"What have you got for us, Charity?" The look on Dr. Nelson's face told Exner that whatever it was, it wasn't good.

"This is one nasty beasty, sir," the doctor said. "The pathogen we're dealing with is an Ebola hybrid and not just of one type. It's a combination the five known Ebola strains. Inherent within its DNA are components of the Bundibugyo, Ivory Coast, Reston, Sudan, and Zaire strains all rolled into one. As you may or may not know, Mr. Exner, Ms. Shankar, the Ebola virus is conventionally transmitted through close contact with either the blood or bodily secretions of the infected."

"This particular strain," she continued, "not only reduces the white blood cell count in the body, it causes the remaining white blood cells to *bond* to cells of the pathogen. As if this weren't enough, it also causes a massive enzyme buildup in the liver which seriously compromises its ability to function, shutting it down in a matter of days."

"From your experience in this field doctor, who would have the capability of developing such an insidious virus?" Bindhira asked.

Dr. Nelson pushed her glasses higher on the bridge of her nose. "Cuba's current scientific knowledge and capabilities in this field could definitely support a bioterror weapon such as this, at least as far as research goes. The country's biological technology is one of the most advanced in the emerging countries. However, by herself, I don't believe she's actually capable of developing such a weapon."

"What about China, Doctor?" Bindhira asked, waiting for confirmation to an answer she already knew.

At this, Exner nearly knocked a beaker of blue liquid all over the table when he attempted to rest a derriere cheek on the corner of its surface in front of them.

Charity Nelson gave him a depreciating frown.

"Sorry, Doc," he said in mock apology.

"Not to worry, Dr. Nelson said. "Had it spilled, we'd have been dead as soon as the vapors reached our nostrils," she said, smiling with a disturbing nonchalance.

Exner backed away from the table and came over to stand beside and behind Bindhira.

"Shades of *déjà vu*, Alan," Bindhira said drolly.

"China; yes, China is definitely a contender for this type of bioweapon," the attractive doctor said in answer to Bindhira's question. "Although their true capabilities are carefully cloaked in secrecy, the Chinese have the requisite means for the development, production, *and* dissemination of such an agent."

She paused for dramatic effect. "Regardless of origin, it must be emphasized that this is a virus for which there is no known vaccine."

"So, in your professional opinion doctor, do you believe the pathogen can be effectively delivered in the manner you have determined," Exner asked.

"Well, again, the virus is a trendsetter," Dr. Nelson said. "The strain has been genetically modified to remain dormant until pressurized within a liquid. With the graduated release of a highly variable hydrostatic pressure, and following a prescribed cure time, the agent would be free to enter the atmosphere, held in check only by a pressure detonator of some type or other."

"The most dangerous aspect of the virus is that upon its release, the finalized agent will maintain its virulence and not weaken as it spreads. So, ah, yes, this can definitely be delivered in the manner described and very effectively so."

Exner furrowed his brow as he looked back over to the blue beaker. "So, once released, the virus becomes the gift that keeps on giving somehow, is that it?"

Dr. Nelson thought for a moment then responded. "Although the virus is initially released as a deadly infectious gas into the atmosphere, it's really, *really* bad feature is that it's been modified to infect the larvae of insects indigenous to the region: mosquitoes, black flies, and the like. This serves to drive the virus ever further inland, and brings it to a whole new level."

"There are no options here, Alan." The only time Exner ever heard Charity address him this way was in dire situations. "You cannot allow this virus to spread, mutate, or infect the insect population. We have, at present, no means to combat its effects. You'd have to bend to any demands the perpetrators wish, because . . ." Dr. Nelson paused.

When she failed to continue, Bindhira asked, "Because why, Doctor?"

Charity Nelson let out a huge sigh. "Because once unleashed, there is no possible way on God's green earth that it can be recalled. It's designed as a 'final solution.'"

Exner heard all he needed. He punched a button on the lab communications console, looked at the two women, and then spoke into the instrument.

"Yes: Exner here. I want a full work-up on everything we have on a Chinese nationalist by the name of Wu Yang, as well as everything on an organization called the Establishment. I also want constant updates on the continuing interrogation of the Cuban. It is imperative that we keep the CIA in the loop as well." Then a pause before he added, "and keep us posted on the Jamaican problem." He rang off.

To the doctor, Exner said, "Thank you, Charity. You've been most helpful."

"Not as much as I'd like, I'm afraid."

"How long would it take to develop a vaccine should things go south now that you have a sample of the strain?" Exner asked with great trepidation.

The good doctor walked over to Exner and said, "Alan, with all the years of viral study and experimentation under my belt, and despite my nomination for the 2007 Nobel Peace Prize in the fields of physiology and medicine, I say to you with all the earnestness I possess: in my expert opinion, it can't be done."

70

The *Singing Woods*

The executive club house of the prestigious Singing Woods Golf Course in Erie, Pennsylvania, was host to a small group of men who had anything *but* golf on their minds.

Wu Yang sat among a small group of his peers as he waited for another to join them. These men were part of an organization as yet unknown, but soon to be recognized and feared around the globe. This was the inner circle of the Establishment.

There was little conversation as the men sat at the conference table with their laptops before them. Each silently perused their reports to preclude any mistakes before being called upon to address the group. The Establishment had zero tolerance for mistakes. Those that made them were seldom heard from again.

As Wu Yang had done, each team leader had liquidated cell members in their charge following the completion of their tasks. In attendance were the men who had chosen to make a daring gamble to siphon off a portion of the viral agent developed by the joint Chinese-Cuban endeavor known as Project Vector.

They had stolen from the project and placed it on a whole new level for private gain. Each man knew they were one step away from a gruesome demise should elements of either government uncover their plans.

The Singing Woods was owned by the Establishment. Of course it operated as an elite golf course, and today was no exception. The only difference was that on this particular day, the 'club attendants' milling about the entrance to the executive club house were carrying Ruger MP9 submachine guns beneath their well-tailored navy blue golf blazers. Each weapon carried a magazine of thirty-two 9 mm Hydra-Shok expanding bullets, and was capable of spitting them out at a rate of 650 rounds per minute. Each man also carried two spare magazines. Carrying a seven-pound weapon system, although not bulky, took its toll by day's end.

Inside the club house, the air was thick and stale, and smelled of old beer and pine. The heavy brown drapes were drawn over the two medium-sized bay windows of the meeting room, one on the east side wall, and the other on the west.

It was not because of the early afternoon bright sun that the drapes had been drawn. It had to do with security. Every three months, Establishment members met in this off-the-beaten-path club house. However, due to the near completion of phase one, they met a month early.

The door to the kitchen opened. At the sight of the man entering the room, all rose from their seats and afforded him a formal bow from the waist. The distinguished looking middle-aged man nodded in kind. At this they uniformly resumed their seats.

After a few minutes of prerequisite rustling, the man in the loosely fitting suit assumed his position behind a lectern that faced the men, seated six to a side at the table before them.

"Gentlemen," the late arrival began. "It is good that you were able to attend on such short notice. It appears that there is another party in this business of ours; a party who has prematurely tipped our hand necessitating immediate implementation of phase one." The room was unsettlingly still as their leader continued. "I wish to assure each of you that the breakout in Jamaica was not of our doing." The man looked around the room at the other members.

No questions were raised, so he continued. "I have alerted our contacts in Cuba and they were equally perplexed, which is why we are still alive right now. I have read each of your dossiers. I am pleased you have all performed your due diligence in matters pertaining to Establishment procedures and protocol."

"All boxes have been carefully placed at the prescribed locations and at the depths required for our purposes, is this not so," the man asked.

Everyone in attendance nodded. One of the men put his hand up and was given a nod to proceed. He rose to put forth his question. "There have been disturbing reports coming out of Wu Yang's section in Tobermory. It has been rumored that they have not as yet taken possession of the 'finalized product'."

Wu Yang slowly raised his head to stare at the man speaking. Sheepishly, the man quietly resumed his seat.

"Is this true, Wu Yang," the man queried.

It was several moments before Wu Yang slowly stood up and said, "Yes, Alberto, it is true."

The room became a montage of hushed whispering. Wu Yang remained standing until he was satisfied Alberto had no further questions for him. Hearing none, he reclaimed his seat and leaned on his ever-present cane. The room went deathly quiet.

"This is most unfortunate," Alberto said, glaring at Wu Yang. "The final shipment was the kingpin to the success of our entire operation, because the components of that shipment were especially designed to provide us with an override to nullify our governments' detonation capabilities, thereby giving us complete control over the entire system."

"The matchbooks saturated with the catalyst are thicker, and the viral coating on the match heads is *blue*, as opposed to red. The blue strikers contain a series of forced-pair detonators that provide us with the means to override the system employed in the Chinese-Cuban design through the use of specially encoded triggering devices, of which two are needed to remotely activate the release mechanisms on the containers."

"We *would* have been able to control the virus in ways that would overtly expose the plot as being of Chinese origin. The United States would 'discover' clues implicating them and they would then act accordingly."

Alberto continued. "With the wrath of the United States and the world upon them, we would then be in a position to strike while everyone cries *'peace and safety'*. Our collective governments would be laid bare before us."

Alberto could feel the intense collective gaze focused on him as everyone hung on his every word. It would have been a good plan—no, a perfect plan. Alberto paused as he looked as those before him.

"I had managed to convince Raul to hold off on the original timetable, so that back in my country, our divers had time to retrieve containers from original placements off the Cuban coast ahead of their incubation period, and replace them with our own, which gives us total control in Cuba. Even the Cuban military assigned to the task had no knowledge of our true actions."

"Prior to my leaving for the United States, we came face-to-face with North American government agents operating in Cuba. Not only did they succeed in uncovering our operation, they also managed to blow up the box we had most recently placed within the *Cristóbal Colón*."

An uneasy stir descended upon the group of men. "I myself was present," Alberto continued, "as was Major Torrado, an officer in FARS who is loyal to the Castros'. Unexpectedly, North American Black Ops commandos in inflatable boats stormed the beach at the wreck site and extricated two of their agents with heavy firepower and great cost to the Eastern Army's Third Armored Division."

"This is most disturbing," Alberto said, disgust etched on his face. "In my position as DGI quadrant commander for the Santiago region, I received *no* intelligence whatsoever of such a commando unit working within our province."

"One of our patrol boats in the quadrant picked up the unusual activity on their radar. They managed to destroy one of the inflatable boats, before they were themselves destroyed by an unseen presence."

He paused for several moments to gather his thoughts. "You will proceed to your assigned stations around the lakes and await further instructions. Make the necessary preparations so we can release the packages manually if need be."

I will remain and coordinate from here. As you all know, I have Raul Castro's ear. I do not know how much longer we can proceed before we are discovered, but we must prepare ourselves for such an eventuality. If we fail to act promptly, we will lose our window."

"If we lose our window, all will be lost." Alberto paused to find the right words. "I assure you gentlemen, should that happen, it will not just be my head that rolls."

71

One Sub To Go, Please

"We've a bogey on our six, Commander," Major General Harris shouted to his helmsman. A Cuban patrol boat was bearing down on the two JTF2 Zodiacs as they sped away from the Cuban coastline to international waters and safety.

Grabbing the waterproof Sequoia high-powered handheld transceiver from a case on his belt, the major general shouted into it, "Commander Byrnes, protect the package at all costs. I repeat, protect the package!" He looked over to the other Zodiac.

Commander Byrnes, piloting the other Zodiac replied, "Protect the package, aye, sir!" The major general saw the commander salute him as his Zodiac immediately broke formation, throwing up a huge plume of foamy spray as it swung far right in a bid to come behind the patrol boat. The Zodiac containing the major general and his "package" broke left. Both Zodiacs zigzagged to make it harder for the patrol boat gunner to get a bead on them.

One of Commander Byrnes' men stood up and fired off an RPG at the rear flank of the patrol boat just as it swung around to present its

20 mm deck gun to them. The RPG just missed its portside bow and the patrol boat continued to close in on them.

Lee and Travers hugged a side of the Zodiac while their pilot took evasive maneuvers as the patrol boat's forward machine gun opened fire.

The major general's radio crackled, but the message was inaudible through the roar of the engines, the splashing of their zigzag maneuvers, and the machine gun fire.

The captain of the patrol boat proved himself to be a worthy seaman and accurately anticipated their every move. Despite the best attempts of the two JTF2 commanders, they were unsuccessful at maneuvering the Cuban vessel into a pincer movement.

"Commander, don't play with these men," the major general said. "Evidently they don't take kindly to visitors!" Just then he caught a huge wall of spray directly in the face as their sturdy little rubber craft cut suddenly to starboard.

More machine gun fire. Neither Lee nor Travers said a word. The only thought that had time to cross Lee's mind was that they were now out of the frying pan and thrown directly into the fire. He regretted having these hearty Canadian JTF2 warriors risking their lives for Travers and him, but the men of this taskforce were professionals to the core.

A man in Lee's boat took aim at the patrol boat with his RPG launcher. Their boat veered hard to starboard as another deadly volley was sent their way. After another sudden abrupt turn, the commando lost his rocket launcher to the depths.

The situation was not good. For every measure the JTF2 commanders took, the Cuban patrol boat seemed to have a countermeasure. Personnel in both Zodiacs had become totally drenched by the life-prolonging evasive maneuvers of each.

As the patrol boat closed in on the Zodiac that carried Lee and Travers, the small craft suddenly veered to port and then pulled ahead in a bid to get as far from the other Zodiac as possible, thereby making it more difficult for the Cuban gun crew.

Then, unexpectedly, and to the utter astonishment of the men in the second Zodiac, they saw a huge flash at the side of the attacking vessel. The thought processes of each man went into *tachy-sight syndrome*. The men originally thought the patrol boat had been hit. But then everything seemed to slow down considerably. The cacophony of noise around them and the screams of their shipmates all became a slow, muffled, and tangled blur of disassociated sights and sounds.

The Zodiac's back had been broken when it was violently upturned by an RPG launched from off the portside of the gun boat's bridge. The rocket propelled grenade found its mark. Limbs, torsos and chunks of the heavy black rubber that was once a JTF2 Zodiac were thrown high into the air. Black smoke rose from the flotsam and occluded the vision of the men in the Zodiac that carried Lee and Travers.

The gun boat veered sharply to starboard to avoid hitting a large piece of wreckage as it zipped through the area where the Zodiac had once been. The crew of the Cuban vessel savored a victory and intended to return to base as heroes. With the taste of blood on their tongues, their boat steadily bore down on the other foreign rubber boat.

The remaining Zodiac continued its seemingly fruitless attempts at ditching the patrol boat. Aside from their wet side arms, the commandos in the Zodiac were now defenseless after losing their RPG launcher. The gun boat had now positioned itself off their port stern quarter.

"We're nearly to the international boundary line!" The commander of the Zodiac shouted over his shoulder as machine gun fire erupted again. It seemed as if they might just make it. But would the patrol boat break off its attack once they reached international waters?

"Incoming!" Major General Harris shouted over his shoulder as he pointed to a white bubbly plume fishing its way just below the surface toward their starboard quarter.

Seeing the menace at the same time as the major general, his commander threw the boat full a starboard. The plume whistled just astern of the Zodiac as the patrol boat began to veer along a parallel vector, but it was too late for the slower maneuvering larger vessel.

By the time the captain of the gun boat detected the same plume, it was too late. The boat exploded into a thousand pieces as a Mk. 48 torpedo carrying the equivalent of 1,200 lbs. of TNT ripped through its bowels.

The commander of the Zodiac immediately dropped the rpms of his twin motors and brought the bow of his rubber craft to bear as a large wave from the explosion crashed in upon them. This quick action allowed the Zodiac to ride harmlessly over the huge wave rather than be swamped by it.

"What the bloody hell was THAT?" Bill Travers said as he pulled himself up from the floor of the boat.

Major General Harris paid no attention but put his ear closer to the speaker of the small transceiver in his hand. "Roger that sir, and thanks," he said into the little instrument before returning it to its holster.

"Dave, make a sweep." Turning to the other crewman, Harris said, "Humble, keep your eyes peeled for anyone in the water." The major general handed the commando a pair of waterproof binoculars from the Zodiac's contingency kit.

"What just happened, sir?" Lee asked, looking from the commander to the major general. Lee removed his saltwater-soaked shirt.

Harris just smiled. "A miracle, Mr. Hartley," he said as their pilot brought their craft over to the area they had last seen their compatriots.

They then made a slow pass in the area of the patrol boat flotsam. Seeing no bodies, alive or dead, floating in the water, they came about in time for a spectacular sight.

The bow of a massive black cigar-shaped object suddenly lifted high out of the water not a hundred yards from their position. The majestic Canadian Victoria-class submarine HMCS *Windsor* gracefully splashed back down into the water as its stern leveled off into the calm Caribbean Sea.

Two men appeared in the sail of the huge underwater ship. By now the Zodiac had come within twenty yards of the sub. Its commander powered down his motors.

All eyes in the little craft were trained on the sail of the former UK submarine as it lay patiently in waiting.

One of the men shouted down to the occupants of the Zodiac. "Want a ride, boys? Michael Dunne, commander of the HMCS *Windsor* and your chauffeur for the day. Major General Harris, I've orders to relieve you of your charge. They're to be picked up by chopper once we pull out of these waters."

"Aye, sir. You sure are a sight for sore eyes."

"Any sign of the rest?" The commander asked as he leaned close to the rail, scanning the periphery with his binoculars as he did so.

"Negative sir. The boys in two won't be coming home," the major general reported, a crackle in his voice. Then, he straightened up. "Request permission to come aboard, Commander Dunne."

The commander paused for a moment out of respect for the fallen commandos, then said, "Very well." He slowly removed his hat as he looked over each of the five men in the Zodiac and saluted them. The commander's executive officer, who had accompanied him to the sail, followed suit. "Welcome back, men," Commander Dunne said, "permission granted."

Turning to his exec, Commander Dunne said, “Get these men aboard quickly Bob, and see to it that they have fresh clothes and the best cuisine in the restaurant. Time to get the hell outta Dodge.”

“Aye, that sir,” the exec said, saluting him.

The commander of the Windsor returned the salute, and then disappeared back into his boat, his exec close behind.

Within minutes a hatch opened three feet above the waterline at the sub’s stern quarter. The men in the Zodiac were quickly lifted aboard, and two of the sub’s crew winched their small craft inside.

Within minutes the HMCS *Windsor* was underway, diving as it picked up speed on a return course to the safety of international waters.

72

A Second-Hand Presidential Address

A helicopter had rendezvoused with the Canadian submarine HMCS *Windsor* in the open Caribbean Sea the day previous, and whisked Lee Hartley and Bill Travers to Palm Beach International Airport in Florida. From there they boarded a waiting CSIS Learjet 85 for a nonstop flight to Niagara-On-The-Lake.

The Canadian divers arrived the next day for their debriefing at NABS headquarters. Alan Exner, Bindhira Shankar, Dr. Charity Nelson, CIA Sub-Director Scott Culp, Dr. Juanita Cortez from the bioterrorism branch of the Infectious Diseases Society of America out of Arlington, Virginia, as well as several others from agencies not common to the general populace, all went silent as the two divers entered the situation room.

Without prompt, everyone in attendance stood up and applauded. Exner and Bindhira rushed over to greet them. After hearty slaps on the back between the men, and an overtly warm "welcome home" hug awarded Lee by Bindhira, Exner went to the head of the long rich mahogany boardroom table as everyone resumed their seats.

Lee and Travers sat down on either side of Exner. Culp sat on Travers' right. Bindhira was positioned to Lee's left.

An expectant hush ensued as Culp stood and said, "As you well know, it never been, nor will it ever be, the policy of the United States to negotiate with terrorists. Presently however, we stand on tenuous ground."

Many in attendance had their cell phones on the table in front of them so as to record the briefing. Culp paused to look around the room at the agents in attendance. Many had been instrumental in keeping the president in the loop as they delved into the recent activities of the Chinese in Cuba at the behest of NABS.

Exner took a sip of his cold café mocha. Travers scratched an itchy armpit. Lee tried to maintain focus as Bindhira slipped off a shoe and softly rubbed a nylon encased foot up and under his pant leg.

"Ladies and gentlemen," Culp continued, "through a rather amazing turn of events, we have uncovered a confirmed act of bioterrorism on the shores of the Great Lakes region. The president of the United States will be making a televised address within the next few minutes to this effect." He looked over to a man standing in the far rear corner of the room. "Kevin, if you would please?"

At this, a man punched a button on the remote he was holding. The wall at the front of the situation room parted to reveal a huge screen. Kevin punched another button on his remote, and images from a prominent American news channel appeared on the eighty-four inch screen before them.

While waiting for the president's broadcast, Culp said, "Both the Chinese and Cuban governments have flatly denied any knowledge of a joint act of bioterrorism between them to be carried out in the heartland of North America. What they don't know is that we have irrefutable evidence that they're lying through their teeth."

At this, the seal of the president of the United States appeared on screen. Without fanfare, Culp quietly reclaimed his chair to watch the special bulletin with the others. Those seated at the head of the long table watched little screens installed in the table in front of them so they didn't have to crane their necks to see the monitor behind them.

A close-up image of the president behind his desk at the Oval Office in Washington occupied the huge screen. Looking up from his notes and with a look of grave concern, the most powerful man on earth began.

"Good morning, my fellow Americans. This government has maintained a close surveillance of the activities of the People's Republic of China on the island of Cuba. Within the past week, unmistakable evidence has established the fact that a bioterrorist plot has been developed and designed to invade North America from that impoverished island. The purpose of this attack can be none other than to provide a total destabilization of the Western Hemisphere."

"Upon receiving the first preliminary hard information of this nature Sunday morning last at 10:00 a.m., I directed that our surveillance be stepped up. Evidence of the introduction of a deadly biological agent deliberately released into the region of Port Antonio, Jamaica, resulting in the death of dozens of innocent civilians has prompted us to take a closer look at the recent activities of the two aforementioned countries. And having now confirmed and completed our evaluation of the evidence and our decision on a course of action, this government feels obliged to report this new crisis to you in fullest detail."

The president paused to slowly sip from a glass of water in silent contemplation before he resumed his address.

"The characteristics of this bioterror threat indicate two distinct types of attack. The first type of attack is a virulent strain of pathogen resistant to treatment being released into the atmosphere at predetermined points around the Great Lakes region. The second type of attack is of an entomological nature."

"Through a deliberate viral impregnation of millions of mosquito, black fly, and wasp larvae naturally scattered throughout the humid Great Lakes topography, it will be possible for the pathogen to travel much farther inland. Additional sites as yet uncovered appear to be in the workings with an even more potent strain of the virus."

"Chinese military scientists have manifested their presence on the island of Cuba under the guise of conducting *a* joint *scientific research and development venture of a peaceful biological nature* on their soil. The People's Republic of China has provided the island nation with a biological agent developed by them, which was then refined and packaged in Cuba for dissemination at a time of their choosing."

"The urgent transformation of Cuba into an important strategic base used by China to unleash a heinous biological weapon of mass destruction constitutes an explicit threat to the peace and security of all the Americas, in flagrant and deliberate defiance of the Rio Pact of 1947, the traditions of this nation and hemisphere, the joint resolution of the 114th Congress, the Charter of the United Nations, and my own public warnings to the Chinese a few days ago."

"This action also contradicts the repeated assurances of Chinese spokesmen, both publicly and privately delivered, that the joint biological research currently being conducted in Cuba is strictly for the good of all mankind, and that the People's Republic of China has no interest in unleashing byproducts of the same on the territory of this or any other nation."

"However, the size of this undertaking makes clear that it has been planned for some months. Yet only since last Sunday, after I made clear the distinction between any introduction of a viral agent of any kind, good or bad, without formal notification, the Chinese government publicly stated, and I quote, 'the equipment and biological materials sent to Cuba have been designed exclusively for the betterment of all mankind.'"

"The reality is that there is no reason whatsoever for the People's Republic of China to reassign any of their chemical or biological materials or equipment to any other country, especially Cuba, and

I quote their government, 'the People's Republic of China already possess sufficient advanced chemical and biological agents of their own with powerful enough missiles to deliver such a type of warhead that there is no need to search for sites to develop them beyond the borders of the motherland of China.'"

"These statements are false. Neither the United States of America nor the world community of nations can tolerate such deliberate deception to covertly deploy offensive threats on the part of any nation, large or small. We no longer live in a world where only the actual dissemination of biological weaponry represents a sufficient challenge to a nation's security to constitute maximum peril. The unleashing of any bioterror weapon is so final that any substantially increased possibility of their use or a sudden change in the deployment may well be regarded as a definite threat to peace."

"For many years, both the People's Republic of China and the United States, recognizing this fact, have handled chemical and biological weapons with great care, never upsetting the precarious status quo that insured that these weapons would not be used in the absence of some vital challenge. Our own biological agents have never been transferred to that territory or that of any other nation under a cloak of secrecy and deception; and our history since the end of World War II, demonstrates that we have no desire to dominate or conquer any other nation or impose our system upon its people."

"Nevertheless, American citizens have adjusted to living daily in the bull's-eye of Chinese weaponry located inside the People's Republic, and stored in the warheads of Chinese nuclear submarines. In that sense, chemical and biological weapons in Cuba add to an already clear and present danger, although it should be noted that the nations of Latin America have never previously been subjected to a chemical or biological attack."

"But this secret and subversive means of transporting Chinese biological agents cleverly concealed under ordinary objects into the heartland of North America, is a deliberately provocative act that cannot be accepted by this country if our courage and commitments are ever to be trusted again by friend or foe."

"The 1930s taught us a clear lesson: aggressive conduct, if allowed to go unchecked and unchallenged, ultimately leads to war. This nation is opposed to war. We are also true to our word. Our unswerving objective, therefore, must be to prevent the use of these horrific weapons against this or any other country, and to secure their safe elimination from the Western Hemisphere and their total, safe destruction."

Everyone in the situation room sat with rapt attention as the president presented an address that stunned both the nation and the world.

"By United Nations decree a ban has been imposed on chemical and biological weapons, but for the most part this has been ignored by many nations. Our policy has been one of patience and restraint, as befits a peaceful and powerful nation that leads a worldwide alliance. We have been determined not to be diverted from our central concerns by mere irritants and fanatics."

"But now further action is required and is already under way, and these actions may be only the beginning. Acting, therefore, in the defense of our own security and of the entire Western Hemisphere, and under the authority entrusted to me by the Constitution as endorsed by a Resolution of the Congress, I have directed that the following initial steps be taken immediately."

"First, to halt this offensive action on the part of the People's Republic of China, a strict quarantine of all shipments of products and raw materials coming into this country from China will be immediately initiated. We will board and inspect, as we deem fit, every Chinese ship entering our ports. This will be undertaken for an indeterminate period of time. This quarantine will be extended, if needed, to other types of cargo ships and carriers."

"Second, I have directed the continued and increased close surveillance of Cuba and the expansion of Chinese scientists and military into that island nation ninety miles from our coastline. The ministers of the OAS (Organization of American States), in their communiqué of a few days ago, rejected secrecy on such matters in this hemisphere. Should this offensive's so-called scientific operations continue, thus increasing the threat to our hemisphere, further action will be justified. I have directed the armed forces to prepare for any eventualities, and I trust that in the interest of both the Cuban people and Chinese scientists in that country, the hazards to all concerned of continuing this threat will be recognized."

"Third, it shall be the policy of this nation to regard any chemical or biological dissemination against any nation in the Western Hemisphere as an attack by the People's Republic of China on the United States, requiring a full retaliatory response upon the People's Republic of China."

"Fourth, as a necessary military precaution, I have reinforced our base at Guantanamo, and today evacuated the dependents of our personnel there, and ordered additional military units to be on a standby alert basis."

"Fifth, we have called today for an immediate meeting of the Organization of Consultation under the Organization of American States to consider this threat to hemispheric security and to invoke articles 6 and 8 of the Rio Treaty in support of all necessary action. The United Nations Charter allows for regional security arrangements, and the nations of this hemisphere decided long ago against the military presence of outside powers. Our other allies around the world have also been alerted."

"Sixth, under the Charter of the United Nations, we are asking today that an emergency meeting of the Security Council be convoked without delay to take action against this Chinese threat to world security. Our resolution will call for the prompt dismantling and withdrawal of all offensive chemical and biological materials in Cuba under the supervision of UN observers before the quarantine can be lifted."

"Seventh and last, I call upon Chinese President Zhu Guangmei to halt and eliminate this clandestine, reckless, and provocative threat to world peace and to continue stable relations between our two nations. I call upon him further to abandon this course of world domination, and rather to pursue more productive and peaceful ways of bringing his great nation to the fore."

"This present threat made either independently or in response to our actions in the near future, will be met with utmost determination. Any hostile move anywhere in the world against the safety and freedom of peoples to whom we are committed, including our neighbor to the north, Canada, will be met by whatever action is deemed necessary."

"Finally, I want to say a few words to the captive people of Cuba, to whom this speech is being directly carried by special radio facilities. I speak to you as a friend, as one who knows of your deep attachment to your fatherland, as one who shares your aspirations for liberty and justice for all. Now your leaders are no longer Cuban leaders inspired by Cuban ideals. They are, once again, puppets of a foreign country that does not have your best interests at heart. And once again they have fallen prey to an international conspiracy from which no good can come, especially for the people of Cuba."

"The path your leaders are currently taking is not in your interest. It contributes nothing to your peace and wellbeing. It can only undermine it. But this country has no wish to cause you to suffer or to impose any system upon you. We know that your lives and land are being used as pawns by those who deny you your freedom. Many times in the past the Cuban people have risen to throw out tyrants who destroyed their liberty. And I have no doubt that most Cubans today look forward to the time when they will be truly free, free from foreign domination, free to choose their own leaders, free to select their own system, free to own their own land, free to speak and write and worship without fear or degradation. And then shall Cuba be welcomed back to the society of free nations and to the associations of this hemisphere."

"My fellow citizens, let no one doubt that this is a difficult and dangerous effort on which we have set out. No one can foresee precisely what course it will take or what costs or casualties will be incurred. Over the next several days, weeks, maybe even months, both our patience and our will shall be tested. But the greatest danger of all would be to do nothing. The path we have chosen for the present is full of hazards, as all paths are, but it is the one most consistent with our character and courage as a nation and our commitments around the world. The cost of freedom is always high, but Americans have always paid it."

"One path we shall never choose is the path of surrender or submission. Our goal is not the victory of might but the vindication of right; not of peace at the expense of freedom, but both peace and freedom, here in this hemisphere, and we hope, around the world. God willing, that goal will be achieved."

The president's fiery eyes of resolve burned through the camera lens for several seconds before the White House feed was cut and normal programming was restored.

73

A Digital Operation

The Chinese entourage walked off the scorching tarmac at terminal three of the Jose Marti International Airport nine miles southwest of Havana. The international terminal was officially opened in 1998 by then Canadian Prime Minister Jean Chretien and Cuban dictator Fidel Castro. It was as hot this day as it was back then, perhaps a little more so.

A moderate northeasterly breeze did little to comfort the group of eight as the two lead men were immediately assisted into a huge black Soviet-made Chaika limousine. The lumbering old vehicle pulled away from the curb in surprising quietness, its ancient Mercedes 0M602 diesel engine offering minimal protest despite the blistering hot temperature of this typical Cuban day.

The rest of the entourage was ushered aboard a modern air conditioned blue and white Viazul bus, complete with video terminals and small lavatory. The comfort of the entourage in the chilly atmosphere of the bus would have been a source of chagrin to the president of the People's Republic of China and his special attaché as they rode along with all four windows down.

The Chaika's air conditioning had been out of service for over three weeks, and the open windows offered little in the way of relief from the scorching midday temperature of the tropical Caribbean island.

Little conversation had exchanged in the first few miles of their trek to Fidel Castro's secluded jungle retreat. The aging dictator was reputed to have over fifty different residences within his island nation. *El Comandante* had always been on the run in his own country. Over the years, it had become a way of life for him to be constantly vigilant against the repeated but as yet unsuccessful assassination attempts by the CIA and others.

Even though the CIA had "officially" abandoned their murderous attempts on Fidel several years ago, relegating his demise to nature and advanced age, the octogenarian never took chances. It was this obsessive-compulsive fear of being murdered that had kept him alive all these years. He would not allow the United States the satisfaction of murdering him in humiliation through their numerous, almost comedic schemes over the years.

It was not without precedent that Castro harbored this fear. His longest-serving bodyguard, Fabian Escalante, estimated that the number of assassination attempts or schemes by the CIA through the years amounted to over 638.

Among the most notable: a mafia-type shooting, an exploding cigar, a fungal-infected scuba wet suit, and a jar of cold cream that contained, among its many soothing qualities, a special additive of ground-up poison pills.

In a moment of dark humor, Castro was once quoted as saying, "If surviving assassination attempts were an Olympic event, I would have won the gold medal."

Chinese President Zhu Guanghei looked back from the window to the aging Cuban sitting directly in front of him. "I cannot understand how the Americans caught wind of our plan, Raul. It was foolproof.

How is this possible?" The Chinese president allowed his attaché to wipe his sweat-laden brow with a handkerchief.

"Perhaps the answer lies in your question, President Guanghei," Raul Castro said, himself now looking out at the trees whizzing by as they sat in the decidedly uncomfortable heat of the limousine.

"Perhaps we have allowed fools to carry out our wishes." The Cuban head of state turned back to focus deeply into the eyes of his guest.

"The opportunity to secure ourselves against defeat lies in our own hands, but the opportunity of defeating the enemy is provided by the enemy himself," Guanghei said, quoting Sun Tsu.

"Only your real friends will tell you if your face is dirty," Raul Castro said, countering with a national proverb of his own. "Tell me, comrade president; is Cuba's face dirty?"

President Guanghei uncharacteristically turned away from his verbal sparring partner to ponder the double-edged question. "Two pigs wallowing in the mud are hardly qualified to judge the degree of each other's cleanliness, wouldn't you agree?" The Chinese head of state expertly redirected the ball into the Cuban's court.

Their limousine reduced speed as it approached a heavily guarded wrought iron gate that now lay before them. Two guards armed with fully automatic weapons approached the limo on either side. The guard at the driver's side started to ask questions. Then when he saw Raul in the forward passenger seat, he shouted to the other guard to open the gates, and the limo proceeded on its way undeterred.

The vintage, albeit stately vehicle, followed a smoothly paved path through a series of tall, straight royal palm trees. Within minutes, the limo pulled up to the curb of a palatial mansion with Cuban flags flying high at each of its tall corners, and one each on flagpoles to either side of the front entrance to the building.

The driver got out and opened Raul's door, then ran around to expedite President Guanghei's exit from the limo. The *Viazul* bus that carried the Chinese entourage pulled up soon thereafter.

Two more heavily armed guards were positioned at each side of the front portal to the mansion. The limo driver climbed into his vehicle and pulled away. As he looked about the premises, President Zhu Guanghei noticed several snipers in various locations around the perimeter, including two on the roof of the building.

A once tall but now stooped figure came out between his bodyguards. He wore his trademark army fatigues and pushed a walker as he slowly approached the top of the staircase. Raul Castro and the president of the People's Republic of China came up the steps to meet him. The elderly man at the top held out his arms in a welcoming embrace and wore a huge smile on his face.

"Welcome comrade president, welcome," Fidel Castro said in English. He bowed to the Chinese president when the man reached the top step.

"You are most gracious, Fidel," Guanghei said, returning the facade of smiling diplomatic politeness to his host. "You have a most impressive security arrangement around your premises, Fidel."

"In our line of work one can never be too careful, can one?" Fidel replied cagily.

A limited perfunctory conversation exchanged between the two leaders regarding the comfort of the Chinese president's trip as Fidel ushered both his brother and their foreign ally into an elegant walnut-paneled stateroom. Several others were in attendance and seated much farther down the long solid mahogany table completely topped in crystal clear glass. Among them was Major Dayana Eveline Torrado.

The smell of lemon-scented wood oil pervaded the huge meeting room. Once the special dignitaries had seated themselves, Fidel stood up to address the group.

"The President of the United States and his military advisors have discovered our 'foolproof' plan to subjugate North America," Guanghei said. "I am sure you have heard his public address."

"Yes, comrade president," Fidel said. "We too have heard the president's ultimatums. We now stand in the calm before an impending storm." Fidel looked first to his faithful brother and comrade-in-arms, Raul. Then his gaze moved on to include President Guanghei, Major Torrado, and then the rest of those in attendance.

"Project Vector has taken over three years to formulate and perfect," the aging Cuban said. "How can this be when we have taken such great care?" Again, *el Comandante* swept the room with his omnipresent glaring gaze. He remained quiet as he again scanned the men and women before him. He had entrusted his life to many of them over the years, and their unwavering devotion to the perpetuation of *la Revolución* had pleased him greatly.

His gaze rested on Major Torrado and locked onto hers for several seconds. The middle-aged, strong, attractive, and very capable major stirred uneasily in her seat as she returned his gaze with an unconvincing nervous smile.

"Major Torrado and her team were onsite where the commando attack occurred." Fidel looked to the major as he addressed the group.

"Major, I have read your report of the assault near Pilon at the wreck site of the *Cristóbal Colón*. Can you confirm the identity of your attackers?" Fidel watched her face intensely.

Major Torrado, who was not easily intimidated, had no defense for the piercing eyes of *el Comandante*.

"No, *el Comandante*. I only know that they wore blue naval fatigues and spoke English. They assaulted the beach in two inflatable boats. There were no discernible markings on either the boats or their uniforms."

The major was careful not to include her unsuccessful dealings with Lee, Travers, and members of the counter-revolutionaries. She knew they would deal with her ever so harshly should they discover her failure at their hands.

Raul now stood. He looked to his elder brother for consent to speak. Fidel nodded slowly, then sat down.

The younger Castro spoke—slowly and with sadness. "Are you not leaving something out, Major? Did you not forget to inform us about the two foreign agents who were snatched out of your custody at the hands of the raiding commandos despite a blistering gun battle with your Third Armored Division?"

The major blushed, which was very rare for her. She was totally at a loss for words because this was exactly what she feared would happen. Someone had betrayed her. She sat silently in nervous fear, afraid to speak, afraid to even breathe.

"And Alberto: where is he?" Raul continued. He was not one to be made a fool of. "Alberto was to report directly to me. I have heard nothing, *nothing* of these things even from him!" Raul pounded his fist on the stateroom table.

"He disappeared during the attack, *Señor* Presidente," the major said. "He did not even report to me. He just disappeared."

"Did you carefully search for him among the bodies of the dead, Major?" Raul hated to question her on the obvious.

"All bodies have been identified, *señor*. His was not among them." The major straightened her back and remained erect and proud of having at least done this.

The room was eerily silent. Raul strode over to Fidel so he could quietly confer with his brother. They whispered back and forth for several minutes. Then Raul returned to his seat. Fidel slowly rose up to speak.

"Major Torrado; up to this point, you have been an unwavering active supporter of *la Revolución* for which we are grateful," the aged warhorse said.

Major Torrados thanked the elder Castro for his compliment, and for the first time since the meeting began, allowed herself to relax. The respite did not last long.

Fidel continued with sudden catlike tenacity. "Do you not think all this odd, major? Do you not think it very odd indeed, that the very biological agent we have so painstaking developed with our Chinese comrades in secret somehow managed to find its way to *Jamaica*? And that now the *entire world* has, after all these years, once again turned to us in anger for our actions?"

Fidel's eyes became fireballs and burned through hers, and his raised voice boomed in anger. "The reason you could not find Alberto, my dear major, is because *you* arranged to have him spirited out of the country. Is *this* not so?"

She sat in sheer horror at the accusations directed at her. "No; *no*, *el Comandante.* That is not true! I—"

"*Silencio!*" Fidel Castro ambled over to her behind his walker. He stood behind her, watched her. She dared not turn around to look at him. Everyone sat transfixed at the accusations. Many had known the major for years, had known she could not be responsible for these terrible things.

Fidel was relentless. He put a hand on the back of her chair. "We have received word from our operatives in the United States, *the United States* that Alberto is currently in Pennsylvania! How is *this* so, Major?" Fidel now rested his hands on the major's shoulders.

"I cannot answer for Alberto," Major Torrado managed to spit out. "He does not answer to me, el Comandante. He is, after all, a control for DGI. My unit has little to do with his." She was not sure where this was going, and it scared her. She had never before experienced this level of fear. Her heart all but burst from her chest.

Fidel returned to his position at the head of the room. "Our findings are not good, comrades," Fidel said, addressing the rest of the group. "There is a group from amongst us that has been currently at work playing both ends against the middle. A group comprised of individuals from both our countries who have taken it upon themselves to steal from us and beat us to the punch as it were. They have taken the initiative away from us and have left us holding the proverbial bag."

Fidel's voice became infused with passion and his face turned a deep red as he continued. The Fidel of old had reemerged, even now in his late eighties. "I have been in deep dialogue with our honorable comrade here, President Guanghei. He too is aware of traitors within the People's Republic." President Guanghei nodded as Fidel continued.

"These traitors, Chinese and Cuban, have formed an alliance consisting of both ChIS and DGI agents. Rogue agents with whom we have entrusted our technology, and who have now gone missing in North America."

"Once again I ask you; how is this so? These renegades are carrying out an agenda of their own and the world is blaming *us* for their misdeeds!"

Fidel continued. "These traitors have tipped our hand to the world. Worse; they have plotted to turn our own weapon against us even as we were planning to deploy it against the imperialists!"

Then, to the surprise of all in attendance, Castro pulled a cigar out of his top pocket. He did not light it, simply sucked and chewed on it as he continued. "Major, at this point in time, and based on your record of service to your country and your fidelity to us, neither my brother nor I are totally convinced of your complicity in any of this. However, you must understand how this must look for you."

Major Torrado was speechless. She wanted to stand up, to run. But to run was to admit guilt, and she had no doubt the elder Castro would pull out his pistol and shoot her dead before she even got to the door. No, running was not an option.

"El Comandante, I assure you—"

Castro raised a hand. Major Torrado held her tongue. Raul was quite fond of her and she knew it. She thought this must be killing him as much as it was her. Still . . .

"Major Torrado," the elder Castro said. "You have served long and well. For this reason, your *presidente* and I are willing to overlook our suspicions on one condition."

The major slowly rose to her feet. Looking from one Castro to the other, she could only say, "Yes, of course. Anything el Comandante. You have but to name it."

"You will go to the United States," he continued; to Pennsylvania. You will seek out Alberto and you will kill him. You will kill him with the utmost prejudice."

"You would also do well to remember that our operatives are everywhere, Major. Do not forget this. Do not ever forget this."

"Si, el Comandante, si," she said, immediately relieved.

Fidel had not finished. "When this is accomplished, you are to return to me with his thumbs and deliver them personally to me. We will be able to easily determine if they belong to Alberto. If they do, you will continue in your capacity as before. But if they do not . . ."

The major's spirits immediately sank. How does one go about murdering a man who is a master of shadows and who wrote the book on covert assassinations? She was trapped and she knew it. Major Torrado had no recourse.

"*Si.* I *comprende.*"

74

Everything Old Is New Again

Without verbal cue, Kevin punched a few buttons on his remote in the NABS Niagara situation room. The walls slowly came back together and concealed the massive screen. The shades came up to reveal a beautiful summer's day out on the waters of Lake Ontario, and the lights came on.

Alan Exner stood up. "The president was very succinct and well spoken on the matter,"

Amid the stirrings in the room, CIA man Scott Culp stood up. He respectfully waited for Exner's acknowledgement. The NABS control acquiesced to Culp, and nodded his assent to take the floor. Exner resumed his seat.

Lee noticed that the man was still wearing the same red face, navy blue suit, red tie, and probably the same white shirt as when he had first met him.

Culp began. "NABS has broken the spine of this Chinese-Cuban affair, and both the United States and Canada owe them a deep debt of gratitude. Currently we have two men in custody: Enrico Estevez, a radio operator who was aboard the *Étoile Profonde*, a 'research' vessel that was instrumental in planting several containers of the viral agent around the Great Lakes, as well as one Gino Vaselino, the only surviving member of a Chinese-Cuban terrorist sleeper cell working out of Tobermory, and who has sought asylum here in Canada."

"We have determined through our usual channels that Estevez was a 'benign,' and had no prior knowledge of the operation his vessel was involved in. As for the second," Culp looked over to Exner, Lee, Travers, and Bindhira, "he came to us of his own volition. While the man was not savvy to the entire plot, as all sleeper cell operatives aren't, he nevertheless was able to unravel a number of mysteries for us."

"One name repeatedly came to the fore, Wu Yang. A Chinese nationalist, Wu Yang is head of the joint operation in Canada, but he is *also* a high-ranking member of the Establishment."

Looking to his right, Culp said to a woman sitting several seats down the table from him, "Elaine; we need to dig deep on this one. None of our agencies including Homeland has any dirt on this guy. If ever we need dirt, it's now!"

"Digging as we speak Chief," Elaine Deegan replied. She was a senior CIA analyst for domestic terrorism. The tall, attractive, smartly dressed middle-aged woman rose from her seat, withdrew a 'firm'-issue Sequoia scramble cell from her purse, and put it to her ear, as she left the room.

"Perhaps the most disturbing news to come out of these interrogations," Culp continued, "is that a third party, this *Establishment*, has planned a double-cross on its own governments. Although we don't know what their game is yet, we bloody well will within the next twenty-four hours."

"As to all the unusual occurrences in Tobermory, again; I am confident that we will soon connect the dots. If all *that's* not enough," he continued, "there has been a little girl, a child of about ten or eleven years old apparently with the ability to disappear through walls, and who has provided us with the actual viral agent."

Many now leaned forward in their seats, totally drawn in by this bizarre admission by a sub-director of the CIA. Several restrained chords of nervous chuckling pervaded the situation room. Chatter flowed nosily throughout the crowd, and Culp had to put up his hands as a nonverbal request for order. The crowd quickly complied, and the din of hushed conversation gave way to complete silence before Culp continued.

"I know. I know. I'm not a superstitious man, but this phantom child *has* been seen by both NABS agents and OPP officers. It was she who surrendered a gym bag that contained the viral agent to an OPP constable on patrol after NABS agents inadvertently lost possession of it through, I might add, no fault of their own."

"We have since learned that the innocent looking matchbooks contained within the gym bag have been treated with a hybrid of the Ebola virus." Culp then looked in the direction of the two female doctors he had asked to speak at this time. "Doctors?" He sat down.

Drs. Charity Nelson and Juanita Delgado looked to each other. Charity gave Dr. Delgado from the Infectious Diseases Society of America the nod. Smoothing her above-the-knee skirt down, the olive-skinned woman in a striking sleeveless bright yellow blouse stood up for her report. After introducing herself, she began.

"There are five types of Ebola virus bio-technical scientists are currently aware of. The matchbooks contained within that bag have been treated with the more virulent properties of all five."

Again the agents in attendance were abuzz. And again Culp stood up and raised his hands, and once again the crowd complied as he regained his chair.

"The Infectious Diseases Society of America has never seen anything remotely like this," the attractive middle-aged doctor said.

"As you may or may not know; aside from the HIV virus, Ebola is the deadliest pathogen known to man."

A man sitting at the middle of the long table raised a hand. Dr. Juanita Delgado paused to finish off the last of her bottled water before acknowledging him.

"What are the symptoms of Ebola infection?"

"It initially presents as flulike symptoms which gradually progress to impaired kidney and liver function, internal and external bleeding from bodily orifices, then a steady decrease in white blood cells, which are the body's soldiers against disease and infection."

Dr. Delgado looked to Culp who rose from his seat. She took hers.

"Thank you, doctor. Alan?"

Now it was Exner's turn. Looking to Lee, Travers, and Bindhira, he then nodded to Culp as the latter took his seat.

"Right," Exner said as he took a deep breath. "Our interrogations with the Cuban DGI agent in custody, one Gino Vaselino, have provided the locations of numerous pods of similar matchbooks concealed in known shipwrecks scattered throughout the Great Lakes. The virus-laden matchbooks contained within these pods, for lack of better words, have a shelf life and are not as virile as those found in the gym bag."

"In their haste, the Establishment had stolen numerous packets out of several batches from secret government sanctioned facilities in Cuba before their scientists had managed to stabilize the pathogen. In short, while the pods scattered around the Great Lakes are less virile, they are deadly nonetheless."

"The Establishment cell member revealed that brass pods have been planted in two shipwrecks beneath each of the five Great Lakes. The radio operator confirms this as he recalls the *Étoile Profonde* had anchored over ten wreck sites during his tenure, although he wasn't privy to the reasons why."

"As to times of release," Exner continued, "we do not know. However, it is our belief that the Establishment may step up their program now that they are aware their scheme is unraveling."

"Both the U.S. and Canadian Coast Guards have been tasked with locating and destroying all Ebola containers planted within the Great Lakes. We have two professional diving consultants retained by NABS who know the Great Lakes extensively, know the wrecks, and how best to locate and destroy them. They have so advised the other dive teams on how best to accomplish this."

"In addition, several agencies have been working around the clock to find the rock the Establishment is hiding under. As you know, there are operatives working to locate this Wu Yang. He is currently at the top of the U.S. Homeland Security's most wanted list."

"It is our fervent hope that the recent presidential address will send a crystal-clear message to the governments of both China and Cuba. Neutralizing the Establishment and openly publicizing it will expose them as well. In the eyes of the world, the Chinese will have no other choice but to disband and withdraw from Cuba. We will then go in and ensure the remaining Ebola strains and the equipment to refine them are destroyed."

"As before, CIA sub-director Culp will coordinate all inter-agency activities and you will report directly to his office. They will then upload detailed feeds to your agency chiefs on a minimum bi-hourly basis. The next time we meet, it will be to congratulate you all on a good job well done."

As he sat down, Culp regained the floor. He looked with admiration over the dedicated agents in the room. "For those of you who don't remember how great a president John F. Kennedy was, and unbeknownst to the masses, the speech our current president just delivered was a carefully re-edited version of the famous 1962 presidential public address JFK made during the Cuban Missile Crisis in October of that year, with a few minor tweaks here and there to reflect our current situation."

Culp paused for dramatic effect. "And just as President Kennedy's speech was no idle threat then, our current president's speech is backed by an even mightier U.S. military than President Kennedy had at his disposal."

"JFK's speech turned the tide then, and we're banking on it to pull our bacon out of the fire now. Let's just hope the major players in this current crisis have as cool a disposition as those of the sixties. We need time, and we're hoping this'll be the winning ticket. Our lives and those of our families depend on it."

75

Trapped!

"Lee, we can't go around and blow up every damn shipwreck in the Great Lakes," Travers said. "And why do you ask? Because it's bad for business, that's why!" Turning from the ship's wheel, he dusted off the back of Lee's head with his hat before resuming the helm.

The two were aboard Travers' dive charter boat, the *Titan II.* Originally an old fishing trawler, Travers had spared no expense restoring and equipping his vessel with state-of-the-art digital radar, sonar, GPS, and radio equipment. The *Titan II* also carried a five-ton crane at the stern, and could comfortably accommodate ten divers in full kit. It was considered the most popular dive boat in Southern Ontario.

Also aboard were Bindhira Shankar and two JTF2 divers, Jay Burwell and Mick Donahue. Jay was a marine engineer and Mick, a demolitions expert. Whether the containers would be safe to bring up in their grid, or by necessity have to be destroyed in situ, all possibilities would be covered with the expertise aboard *Titan II.*

"Bill, believe me, if there was any other way . . . ," Lee said, wiping his face from the spray as the bow of the boat dipped into a deep trough between swells.

The day was slightly overcast, and swells were running at three to five feet. As the clouds blew in from the west, they were getting darker.

Exner and Culp had assigned nine other vessels as well, two to each of the five Great Lakes, to locate and destroy the brass containers which contained the deadly viral materials. Each vessel had a similar crew.

"There are probably Chinese, Cuban or Establishment operatives in close proximity to each of the wrecks involved," Bindhira cautioned the men aboard the *Titan II*, "and we must tread carefully as we do not know the extent of their capabilities."

"That's why we've got Hartley here, darlin'," Travers said, looking back from the helm.

"But what if Mr. Vaseline is not correct about the locations of the shipwrecks," Bindhira asked.

"It's Vaselin-*O*, darlin'," Travers said, smiling.

Lee ignored the banter and interjected. "Bindhi, Vaselino has no reason to lie to us. Don't forget that we also have him in protective custody. The only variable that *does* concern me is the accuracy of his intel. Sounds like he's a loose end on Wu Yang's part, and Yang's not the type to leave them lying around."

"If Vaselino's still breathing, it could be because Yang is using him to sow misinformation."

"Never thought of that," Travers said, holding onto his hat as the *Titan II* pulled out of a deep trough between the swells.

"Exner's got a whole fleet of ships out on the lakes looking for wrecks that may or may not have the brass containers aboard. But it's all we've got to go on," Lee said.

"If these boxes are not in the locations specified, I do not think the president would hesitate to invoke retaliatory measures against the Chinese, and that scares me, Lee," Bindhira said. A wisp of long black hair stuck to the corner of her mouth from the spray that saturated them as the *Titan II* continued to plod through the moderate swells. Gracefully she pulled it away and shook her head in a vain attempt to position it away from her face.

"ETA, ten minutes Lee," Travers announced. Because the *Titan II* was berthed at the Bridgeburg Yacht Club at Crystal Beach and in close proximity to Buffalo, New York, their search grid was located in eastern Lake Erie. The first wreck on their list was the tugboat *Acme*, which sank off Buffalo.

As the three divers suited up, Mick Donahue spoke up, "So what can you tell us about the *Acme?*"

Travers was busy negotiating the *Titan II* over an abnormally large swell, but he managed to guide his boat over it. Lee saw that his friend had his hands full at the helm, so he gave the divers a brief history of the wreck.

"In the spring of 1902, the twenty-nine-ton tugboat *Acme* was struck by the Lehigh Valley Line steamer *Wilkes Barre.* Owned by the Great Lakes Towing Company and built in Buffalo, New York, in 1893, the Acme went down off Buffalo, but not before all four hands managed to abandon ship. The ship is small but located in a fairly inaccessible spot not far from the Buffalo break wall. The break wall is at the mouth of the Niagara River, where the current runs fast and deep."

"Yeah," Travers added, "no one in their right mind would dive the thing, much less try to moor a boat over it. Nothin' to see anyway—small wreck, broken up by the current. No one wants to risk their neck divin' somethin' that boring."

"Which is exactly why the Establishment would choose it," Lee added.

Within ten minutes the first dive team comprised of Lee Hartley and Jay Burwell of JTF2 left the stern of the *Titan II* and drifted to the *Acme*, a quarter mile upstream of the wreck. With proper navigation skills, trained divers simply allow the current to take them to their destination. The downside is that there's only one chance to hit a wreck when a current runs at seven knots, which it was. If a diver overshoots his mark, there's no second chance of returning to it.

The crew aboard the *Titan II* was unaware that a pair of binoculars had been trained on their boat as it pulled out of the current after it had deployed the two divers. Travers headed south into the deeper, calmer waters of Lake Erie proper. Wu Yang could hardly believe his eyes. Who in their right mind would attempt to dive this wreck and allow their dive boat to abandon them?

Yang was not a diver, but even he knew that to leave divers untended in a current as swift as it was at the mouth of the Niagara River was the height of folly.

An unsettling thought then crossed his mind. What if these men knew what they were diving for? Wu Yang grabbed his sat phone and made a hurried call.

Lee Hartley and Jay Burwell were tethered together by a buddy line to prevent being separated in the fast-moving current. Fortunately, both men were strong swimmers and excellent divers. Despite flying over massive boulders and submerged debris in the murky water, the team managed to avoid all the potential hazards around them.

Although the depth of water was only twenty-five feet, many dangers lurked. One moment's inattention could result in being knocked unconscious on a rock or wooden beam at this speed in such reduced visibility.

Suddenly the wreck came into view. The tugboat *Acme* listed to starboard with a twenty-degree cant. The 110-year-old wreck had taken a beating over the years as the current had relentlessly chiseled away at its ever-weakening superstructure. The metal was dangerously jagged in several places, most notably around the wheelhouse, a portion of which had been torn away.

Although Lee was used to the fast-moving river and its unpredictable current, Burwell was not. Lee watched helplessly as the JTF2 diver bounced off the superstructure like a de-stringed marionette puppet, but he was tough and managed to get a hand hold on the wreck.

Once they pulled themselves over the side of the hull and into the bowels of the ship, they were out of the current and could relax. They saw and heard debris rolling and bouncing off the ship as they caught their breath below.

Burwell activated his powerful underwater LED light and shone it into an open hold. A rusted cot in a corner here, an old coal stove in a corner there. Below a table lay an overturned coffee pot and three plates, one of which had shattered. The entire hold was rife with zebra mussels, tiny mollusks that were first discovered in the Great Lakes in 1988. They were introduced into the mighty waterway via bilge water dumped from ocean-going vessels, and over time had massively infested much of the Great Lakes.

Silt and sand had filled a good portion of the hold. Both divers were careful to frog kick with their fins inside the wreck to avoid a silt-out, which would quickly reduce the visibility to zero.

Burwell veered right, Lee swam left, as each carefully combed the interior of the ship for any sign of a brass container. Finding none, the men carefully exited the way they had entered.

Regaining sight of each other, Burwell signaled Lee he was going to swim around the perimeter of the ship's deck and for Lee to go forward to the bow. As the current was practically nonexistent inside the protection of the ship's confines, Lee acknowledged and reeled in the safety line as Burwell let it go. The men swam close along the top of the main deck but below the ship's gunwales to avoid any flying debris above the railing where the current was strongest.

Lee had difficulty undogging a hatch cover located fore of the wheelhouse, which had been rusted in place for decades. He strained against the crowbar he had brought with him for a short time, but was finally rewarded when he found that once the dogs had been loosened, the hatch offered no further resistance and he easily pulled it up and away.

Pitch darkness. He reached for his powerful halogen underwater light. Once activated, Lee pulled himself headfirst over and down into the hatch. The cabin was smaller in size than the hold aft of the wheelhouse. He found it contained more debris and much more silt.

Lee cursed into his mouthpiece as his leg brushed against a beam. Instantly the visibility that was behind him dissipated into a heavy cloud of murk as the silt on the beam's surface dislodged behind him. Even an experienced diver can get claustrophobic in such situations, and Lee was no exception.

He bit a little harder onto his mouthpiece. The task at hand took precedence over fear. He trained his light in every nook and cranny of the little cabin. Just before he retraced his way back to the hatch entrance and into the murk, Lee thought he noticed a faint glint under the skeleton of a frame that once held a mattress.

Swimming back to it, Lee began to pick away at the framework. He managed to pull the rusted frame—and spring-work from above the glint. Then he fanned the area with one hand to float the silt away while the other trained the light before him.

There it was! A brass box, complete with characteristic Chinese writing etched into its top. Elated, Lee brushed it off. He knew he had to have help in raising it. He checked his wrist computer and noticed they had another ten minutes before the *Titan II* would rendezvous to pick them up. Upon surfacing, they'd then get a lift bag from the *Titan* II, and with Burwell and Donahue's assistance, Lee would send the box to the surface, where Travers would winch it into the safety of his dive boat. Dynamite was out of the question as it was too close to the Peace Bridge.

Turning gently so as not to trigger a silt storm, Lee carefully finned his way toward the opening. The silt had dissipated enough that Lee could see the lighter colored water beyond the open hatchway.

He ascended toward it and freedom when darkness suddenly enveloped him. The hatch cover closed above him with a loud thud!

Lee threw his shoulder into the hatch. It moved a little! Then he heard a metallic grinding above him. Someone was dogging the hatch! He tried again, but this time it was solid.

Where was Burwell? Lee realized that any further struggling would only serve to deplete his already dwindling air supply. He let himself drift down to the deck of the hold and switched off his light. Lying prone, head on forearms, he closed his eyes and set about slowing his breathing down. He knew all too well that panic kills.

Lee Hartley, commercial diver, was trapped.

76

The Big Bang Theory

"What's with all this, Ms. Shankar?" Mick Donahue stood to Bindhi's side and surveyed all the complex equipment the NSA liaison agent had spread out over the large engine hatch cover on the aft deck of the *Titan II.*

Bindhira looked up at the JTF2 diver, smiled, and then returned to her equipment as she spoke. "We have a descrambler array patched into the Sequoia system's sat-link onboard. When it failed to decipher an encoded message just sent from somewhere nearby, I switched to ULTRA, our elite message interpreter."

"ULTRA can decode or descramble the most complex of signals in a matter of minutes through Sequoia's data banks. I have been monitoring all local chatter since our divers left the *Titan II.* At first it seemed like a lot of white noise, background static, and the like. It was an unusual amount of interference for a location here on open water. That got my curiosity up. I nearly overlooked it, but my training at the Central Security Service Signals Cryptology Branch of the National Security Agency came in quite handy."

Travers meanwhile pulled his feet out of the water at the stern dive platform where he had been sitting and came over to hear what Bindhira was explaining to the elite navy diver.

"I redirected these random frequency and modulation signals through the Sequoia sat-link once again, and this is what I came up with." The beautiful Indo-Caribbean woman punched a few buttons on her mobile console. The unit remained silent for a few seconds, then voices.

"That's impossible, Yang! I covered every possibility!" Static overwhelmed the frequency for several seconds and then, "Finally, something even *you* didn't foresee!"

"Alberto, one cannot purport to foresee everything in the future. You yourself are far from omniscient, as we both know." A long pause, then the same voice continued.

Bindhira, Travers and Donahue looked to each other in disbelief.

"I have already taken steps to eradicate this unexpected wrinkle. I assure you, those divers will not surface with the 'package.'"

"Yang, I think they're on to us. I'll blow it from the Singing Woods here. Then we'll have to implement our second option."

"NO!" the Chinese voice said. "I *told* you, I am dealing with this as we speak! And do not forget, you must have *my* codes as well as yours to undertake any such action." Wu Yang paused for effect. "Now you can see why such prudence was engineered into the system."

"Well," the Cuban huffed, "you will answer to *me* if your 'wrinkle' isn't smoothed out! The Establishment is too close to reaching its objective to fail now. You have sixty minutes to report back to me in the affirmative!" Alberto said.

A sudden loud burst of static, then several intermittent loud buzzes emanated from the speaker of Bindhira's equipment. "Their message intermittently sends out an automatic jamming signal," Bindhira said.

"Their communication system is quite advanced, but fortunately for us, not as advanced as Sequoia."

"Whoever these guys are, they must have unlimited funds and the latest gadgetry," Travers said.

"They know we have divers in the water then, Ms. Shankar! I'm going down," Donahue said decisively.

"I'd accompany you, Mick," Travers said, "but Ms. Shankar here doesn't know a thing about boats in heavy current. I'll bring 'er around to the drop zone."

"Very well, sir," Donahue said, ever the professional. As a safety diver, he was already suited up.

Travers brought the *Titan II* as close to the sunken *Acme* as he dared and still give Donahue a time window to ride the current and hit the wreck.

No sooner had Travers cut the engine than Donahue splashed over the gunwale.

Meanwhile below, Jay Burwell had his hands full. He had no sooner come out of the main hold of the sunken tug when he saw two divers heading his way on DPVs, diver propulsion vehicles. Where they came from he didn't know, but the JTF2 diver certainly didn't expect company in such a fast-moving current.

Burwell watched as one of the interlopers noticed bubbles rising from the forward hatch and veered off to *dog* it, which trapped Lee and narrowed the odds. Without waiting, the other diver was on Burwell. The two engaged in hand-to-hand combat. The lanky diver surprised Burwell with his unexpectedly superior strength.

By this time, the second diver arrived and pulled what looked like a sawed-off shotgun from a holster attached to the thigh of his wet suit. Burwell could see that it was a Farallon shark dart pistol that carried three razor-sharp spear-headed barbs propelled by powerful .357 magnum loads. The man had Burwell dead in his sights.

But the JTF2 diver was an expert in underwater combat. As the diver advanced for a more reliable kill shot, Burwell waited for the right moment. As the armed diver acquired his sight, Burwell unexpectedly swiveled sharply, exposing his attacker's back to the other man.

The powerful spear tip exploded upon impact at the base of Burwell's assailant's spine. Immediately, the diver released his chokehold on Burwell and arched backward and to the side in a grotesque gyration. He collapsed immediately and floated to the deck below.

Burwell was immediately upon the stunned shooter. A ferocious struggle ensued as both men engaged in an underwater dance of death in an endeavor to rip each other's mask and regulator from their faces so as to inflict a fatal blow. Burwell was very careful not to allow the man's gun hand to break free.

He was caught off guard by the superior strength of the lanky DPV diver. His only thought was to dislodge the shark dart pistol from the man's grip and somewhat even the score.

Burwell didn't get that chance.

The attacker caught the JTF2 diver full on with an elbow to Burwell's face plate. The blow shattered its glass which drove shards into the tissues of his face.

The diver was in the process of reloading his pistol when Mick Donahue arrived. He came behind the man and shoved an unpinned Mark 2 cast iron pyrotechnic fragmentation grenade between the surprised man's buoyancy compensator and scuba tank. Yanking his victim over the side of the ship and down, Donahue grabbed Burwell and pulled him behind the tugboat's smoke stack just as the grenade detonated.

Combined with the grenade's fifty-five-gram TNT charge and fragmentation properties, the force of the compressed air in the ruptured scuba tank ensured the threat was neutralized.

What was once a human being was relegated to a broken mass of bloody bits and bites. The piece of lower torso and upper left thigh that remained was little more than aerated jello as it drifted off slowly into the current accompanied by a steady red stream behind.

Donahue lost no time with Burwell. He was careful to make sure Burwell's mouthpiece remained in his mouth as he brought his injured mate to the surface. On the way up, Donahue pulled out and activated an inflatable dive sausage, a long, thin highly visible bright yellow float that would mark their position on the surface in the middle of this busy waterway that doubled as a boundary line between the U.S. and Canada.

"There! I see their marker. There, William!" Bindhira pointed off the aft port beam as Travers brought the *Titan II* around close enough for Donahue to grab the boat's trailing line.

Travers cut the engines and threw an anchor over the side, then ran back to lower the stern dive platform.

Upon seeing only two divers, Bindhira said, "Where is Lee?"

"Still down there, Ms. Shankar," Donahue gasped after he spit out his mouthpiece. Together, Bindhira and Travers wasted no time in hauling the JTF2 divers aboard.

"Bindhi, channel sixteen on the marine radio, U.S. Coast Guard medical assistance required at our GPS coordinates!" Travers barked as he eased Burwell into the recovery position. He covered the injured man up with a heavy wool blanket.

"I'm going back for Hartley!" Donahue was already in the process of changing out his tank for a fresh cylinder. He also grabbed a small nylon bag from his kit.

Despite his profusely bleeding facial injuries, Burwell struggled to speak. “Hartley—Hartley’s—trapped—in—forward—cabin . . .”

“We’ll get him, buddy,” Donahue said. “Right now just hang tight; help’s on the way,” Donahue patted his shoulder on his way to the stern. “Get me back to that wreck,” he shouted forward to Travers.

“On it,” Travers said. He ran over to haul in the bow anchor. The boat’s engines then roared to life, and the Titan *II* spun a full 180 degrees as it headed back downstream to the *Acme.*

Donahue had little trouble locating the *Acme.* The visibility was good as he fought the relentless current. He pulled himself hand over hand along the port gunwale of the tugboat to the bow. He swam past the hatch for several feet before letting go and smashing into the raised lip of the hatch cover as the current brought him back in the manner he had anticipated.

The JTF2 diver lost little time locking a leg around a solid protruding deck pipe. He then tapped out a message in Morse code. He hoped Lee still remembered the now officially retired ancient signaling system of alphabet assigned coded taps consisting of dots and dashes.

Donohue next attempted to loosen the dog clips by hand. Unable to budge them, he reached into his bag and produced what looked like a cake of gray Play-Doh. The JTF2 diver quickly formed a small ball of semtex plastic explosive over each of the eight separate wing bolts securing the hatch. He inserted a small detonator stick into each of the charges, then looped the connecting wire around several protrusions as he headed along the forward deck and over the bow of the ship.

The current slammed him hard against the hull as he pushed the small handle down into the electronic box he held. Instantly, eight miniature explosions detonated simultaneously. As he finned over the bow, Donahue saw that the hatch had blown out and above the deck, rolling over and over. It bounced off a gunwale and drifted to the river bottom below.

A shaken Lee Hartley slowly emerged from his watery tomb. When Donahue saw his man, he let go his hold at the bow and drifted back to him.

Donahue gave the signal to surface, which Lee groggily acknowledged, then once again inflated his marker buoy. Then the two drifted upward through the current to the waiting safety of the *Titan II* above.

77

A Change Of Plans

"I have established contact with NABS control," Bindhira said, watching Donahue and Travers tending to Burwell's facial cuts and contusions. "I have a lock on one of the scrambled transmissions. The primary originated from Buffalo, not far from here. Sequoia is still sifting through jamming frequencies to determine the secondary."

"That's reassuring," Lee said, still shaken from the blast that set him free. He was glad to see that they had stabilized Burwell, who seemed to be in fairly good spirits. "How's the puss, Jay?"

"Uglier than ever," Burwell replied. "But you should have seen the other guy." He grinned from beneath a severely lacerated face patched up as best as Travers could with what was available onboard. The diver was fortunate not to have suffered eye damage from the shattered glass of his face mask.

The air-chopping sound of helicopter blades came over the horizon from the east. It was a U.S. Coast Guard 60-T Jayhawk. As the waters swirled violently around the *Titan II,* a voice came over a bullhorn from above.

"Prepare your casualties. We're sending down a litter and a crewman to assist and to ground your vessel preparatory to evac. Do *not* touch the litter until it has made contact with the deck. Please signal your acknowledgment."

Travers stood up and cross-waved his arms. He knew that if he made contact with the litter prior to grounding, it could kill him from the static electricity generated . . .

"I'll go with Burwell," Mick Donahue said. Good working with you people. Good hunting and godspeed."

Lee smiled, nodded, and said, "Pleasure, Mick. One down, thanks to you men. Be safe, eh?"

"Your commanding officer will keep you in the loop, Mr. Donahue," Bindhira said. Her genuinely warm smile affected the commando as it did most men.

Within minutes and with the JTF2 commandos and coast guard crewman aboard, the powerful twin GE T700 turbo shaft engines thrust the craft up and away into the eastern sky. Within seconds the Jayhawk had disappeared from view. Lee Hartley had been admonished to go as well but declined.

"A hit of Newman's is all I need," he said, smiling at his two friends.

"Told ya, dude, that stuff'll kill ya," Travers said, and gave Lee his trademark squinty-eyed stare.

Several minutes went by as Bindhira worked the controls of her communications array. "Got it," she said triumphantly. "I have a lock on the secondary as well and am forwarding both sets of coordinates to NABS," Bindhira said, looking up and into the two divers' faces. "The origin of the other transmission is Erie, Pennsylvania."

"You're the man, er, lady, Bindhira," Travers said.

"Time to get wet, Bill," Lee said, still focused on the task at hand. "Hook me up with a fresh tank. We've got ourselves a cask of death to bring up."

With Bindhira's help, the three had little trouble raising the heavy brass container of Ebola-laced matchbooks, thanks in no small part to the winch aboard the *Titan II.* Neither diver wanted to blow up another shipwreck, especially in the middle of the Niagara River.

Travers received instructions from CIA sub-director Culp to deliver the container to a cement containment bunker located at a secret remote area of Canadian shoreline. The bunker had been hastily designed by NABS scientists to contain the boxes should they prematurely detonate.

Their counterparts in the other Great Lakes were successfully in the process of conducting similar operations concurrently as container after container was discovered. The intel provided by the Cuban, Gino Vaselino, proved to be the real deal.

Some dive teams reported trip-wire booby traps planted on some of the boxes, which were designed to detonate if a wire was disturbed by an unwary diver. One dive team had already fallen prey to such a trap.

Other divers were successful in locating and raising their boxes, but a few were found to be dummy plants placed in well-dived wrecks. In Lake Michigan, two such boxes were uncovered at great loss of time and resources.

The dummies were found to be lighter in weight because they were constructed of aluminum but painted to look like brass. To save precious time, this was defeated by ensuring that each diver scratch the surface of every container found to quickly determine the genuine from the fake. Brass was no doubt used in the genuine units as it was antimagnetic, strong, and impervious to any environment.

En route, Lee and Travers gathered around Bindhira as she worked her high-tech wizardry to hone in on the exact location of the transmissions.

Lee recognized the first. "That's the *Porthole*, Bindhi. It's not more than a few miles from here! They're world famous for their chicken wings and sauce. The man behind our attack was there, but no doubt long gone by now."

They immediately contacted Exner, who also knew of the *Porthole*. He promised to send men there from their Buffalo office at once.

Following delivery of its container to the designated facility heavily guarded by well-armed RCMP about thirty minutes away, the *Titan II* returned to its base in Crystal Beach, not far from Fort Erie.

Once the dive boat had docked, Bindhira and Travers agreed to stop at Lee's residence. Once there they each took a shower, and the men changed clothes. Travers managed to squeeze into an old outfit of Lee's. Then they drove Bindhira to a local woman's shop, where she picked up some things for herself.

Sternly warning the men to keep their eyes on the road ahead, Bindhira changed her clothes in the back of Travers' Hummer as they made their way to Niagara-On-The-Lake and NABS headquarters. Travers enjoyed the show through his rearview mirror, ever careful to avert his gaze whenever she glanced up to check on them. Lee smiled to himself. He eagerly anticipated his friend getting busted, but the old diver actually managed to pull it off, for she was none the wiser.

Halfway to their destination, Bindhira received an incoming transmission on her sat-phone. It was Exner, ordering them to reroute and proceed to the *Porthole* stat. At this, Travers took the next off-ramp and swung the Hummer around and back toward the Peace Bridge and Buffalo beyond.

Apparently, three NABS agents had discovered the man who sent the encoded message to Establishment headquarters from the restaurant. A struggle ensued and two agents were down.

"Carlisle said the man was an elderly Chinese male with a cane and briefcase," Exner, still on link, explained. Bindhira switched to speaker. "Carlisle survived, but Matthews and Bailey didn't fare so well. Seems the Oriental poisoned them somehow, and it wasn't pretty to say the least." Exner paused.

"Carlisle's still there. I need you three over there pronto. This has all the makings of Wu Yang. The U.S. Border Patrol and CBSA have been put on high alert. Get back to me when you can. You've been cleared to cross the border without inspection. Exner out." Bindhira secured her phone.

"He's some upset," Travers said.

"It very well could have been Wu Yang," Bindhira said solemnly. "If so, he will be very wary because he knows the net is closing in on him."

"Which necessitates another quick stop to my place," Lee said grimly. "We've some hardware to pick up."

78

Wu Yang Has Left The Building

The *Porthole* played host to several operatives by the time Lee, Travers, and Bindhira showed up. Criminologists were searching for clues and dusting for prints where the elderly Chinese man had sat.

Travers stared at the mouthwatering menu and made a mental note to order some takeout once they finished up here.

A man came over to where they were conversing with an agent. "I'm Ken Carlisle, senior NABS field officer out of Buffalo. Glad you got here so soon."

Lee introduced himself and the others with him. "What can you tell us concerning this man?"

Agent Carlisle steered them over to the front window where it was not so crowded. "Apparently the unsub came in and ordered a bottle of water, then sat over in the corner there," Carlisle said, pointing to where several agents were busy dusting the table and its environs for fingerprints and searching for other evidence.

"We got here soon after the dispatch was received from your coded message, Ms. Shankar," Carlisle said. "It wasn't hard to pick the guy out. The owner said the guy was still sitting in the corner, which narrowed our investigation down considerably. Bailey came up to him. The Oriental was preoccupied with his briefcase. Bailey's approach startled him somewhat. They engaged in brief conversation. Then the man got up with the assistance of his cane."

"By this time, Matthews had come over," Carlisle said, obviously shaken. "The unsub was belligerent when the agents started questioning him, as if they had interrupted him in something important. When he saw that they weren't going to leave, a witness saw the man poke each agent in the stomach with the bottom of his cane."

Carlisle looked down and paused to get his emotions under control. "The cane must have been equipped with a poison dart or something. Within seconds of getting poked both were in excruciating pain and went into convulsions. The owner called 911 right away but it was too late. Our agents had died a horrible death."

"Did anyone see this unsub leave, or the direction he took," Bindhira asked. Carlisle steered them back to the table where Wu Yang had sat.

"No, but in his haste, he left this."

It was a small valise containing several loose papers. Bindhira peered inside the leather pouch.

"Hmmm," she said. Travers peered over her shoulder. "Just several pamphlets from a golf facility in—you won't believe this—Erie, Pennsylvania."

Travers grabbed one and turned it over in his hand. "The Singing Woods," Travers said, more to himself than to the others. Then he added, "Hey, there's some handwriting on the back here, but it's all Chinese to me."

Lee and Bindhira each grabbed a pamphlet from the thin brown leather case.

"Yeah, same here," Lee said, turning to Bindhira "It's all in Chinese. What's on them, Bindhi?"

"At face value," she said, "these are copies of brochures promoting a prestigious golf course in Erie called the Singing Woods." She read from the one in her hand. "But on the back of this particular brochure, a handwritten note in Mandarin says 'return home when you've made your donations.'"

Agent Carlisle was first to speak. "Of course! Erie, Pennsylvania: the Singing Woods. It could be the nerve center of the Establishment!"

"Copies of these brochures must have been issued to the various teams assigned to each of the Great Lakes. When their missions were accomplished, they were to rendezvous 'home,' meaning the Singing Woods," Bindhira surmised.

"Yeah, so Yang could tie up loose ends and kill them," Travers said disgustedly.

"We have already compromised their plans here," Bindhira said. "There is no telling what the Establishment will do from that end."

Agent Carlisle was already on his sat-phone to Exner.

For the first time in a long while, Lee paused to take in Bindhira's beauty. She caught his affectionate gaze and smiled her devastatingly beautiful smile full-on in return.

"Thanks for the coin pendant Bindhi," Lee said, changing the subject. "You saved my bacon."

"I could not allow your bacon to fry now, could I?" Once again, she directed her resplendently beautiful smile his way.

Abruptly, Ken Carlisle re-holstered his sat-phone. Then he circled an index finger over his head and said to his agents, "Okay everybody, time to wrap it up. Party's moving to Erie, Penn. You'll get your briefing en route."

Carlisle turned to Bindhira, Lee, and Travers, "Chopper's at the waterfront a few minutes away. You're all cordially invited to attend."

With that they abruptly left the *Porthole,* much to the chagrin of Bill Travers, who had his heart set on a two-pound plate of world-famous chicken wings.

79

Situation Compromised

Disembarking from their helicopter a short distance from the Singing Woods Golf Course in Erie, Pennsylvania, Lee Hartley, Bill Travers, and Bindhira Shankar followed NABS Agent Ken Carlisle to a waiting late-model black Chevy Suburban.

"We've agents surrounding the clubhouse sir," the driver said, as they set out on their way.

"Hostiles," Carlisle asked, concerned about armed resistance.

"Multiple, and heavily armed sir," the driver replied. "We have snipers in position. We believe a Cuban Secret Intelligence officer is inside calling the shots."

"Are we still cold?" Carlisle asked as the Suburban pulled up behind several other unmarked agency vehicles several hundred feet away from the laneway leading up to the golf course.

"No indication our presence has been detected, sir," he reported.

The five exited the vehicle. A perimeter had been established and the road blocked off by a "local road crew" to keep unsuspecting motorists from driving into a potential hotspot. The crew consisted of FBI agents with sidearms and spare magazines concealed beneath their bright orange safety vests.

The "safety vests" the men wore were actually bulletproof, which when reversed, were combat black and displayed the agency acronym. Their "utility trucks" were heavily armored, and sported 20 mm cannons concealed inside that could electronically elevate though the roof to deliver serious firepower if need be.

When they reached the mobile command post in the guise of a utility trailer, they were greeted by Alan Exner! He stood at its entrance with a cup of café mocha in hand.

"Took you long enough," he joked as they all went inside.

"Our people confirm their readiness," Exner said with professional intensity. "The Sequoia system spit this place out as the nerve center that has been in communication with various locales around the Great Lakes; no doubt Yang's divers," he said.

"Could be just golf membership inquiries," Travers said half-seriously.

"The communiqués were kept short," Exner said, ignoring the levity, "and the final transmission went to Buffalo; not one sentence of which pertained to a golf inquiry," Exner said dryly in Travers' direction.

Turning to Ken Carlisle, Exner said, "We have a team in place to hit each side of the clubhouse simultaneously. Two additional sweeper teams will follow into the north and south entrances respectively."

"Standard shock-and-awe approach," Carlisle explained to the others.

“That is correct,” Exner said. Turning to his friends he said sternly, “Hartley, neither you nor Travers are to get involved in any type of fracas. Clear?”

“Crystal,” Lee said. The suddenness of the response surprised even Travers.

“Bindhira,” Exner said, looking past the two men to her. “You are to continue monitoring your NSA cryptological decoding array and report any chatter, however small. Keep us ahead of the action, Bindhi.”

“Understood Alan,” she replied.

Suddenly gunfire spilled over the grounds. Within minutes, the trailer door yanked open without warning, and a woman’s head popped in.

“Sir, one of our agents is down,” the woman said. “He was spotted through the trees as he was sneaking up to the clubhouse,” the young, out-of-breath, brunette female agent said.

Exner grabbed his Seqpod and spoke authoritatively into the instrument. “We are red. I repeat; we are red!”

As he exited the trailer, Exner turned back toward Lee. “Just remember what I told you!” Then to Carlisle; “Hold down the fort, Ken.” Turning to the young woman he said, “Follow my lead.”

Carlisle checked his weapon as Exner and the woman left the trailer.

More gunfire erupted, then shouts as operatives drew into a huddle preparatory to storming the double-storied clubhouse up ahead.

“We can’t just sit on our hands here,” a frustrated Lee Hartley said.

"You can and you will, Lee," Bindhira said, looking from Lee to Travers.

"Hey, I'm easy," assured Travers. He walked over and sat on a couch beside the communications array to demonstrate his compliance. Bindhira followed him, placed a set of headphones over her head and began to work the frequencies.

"I'll take up a position in the tree to our west corner," Carlisle said. Cautiously he opened the door and trotted off behind the trailer.

Gunfire once again erupted all around them. Whether friendly or hostile, it was moot as chunks of wood blew off trees too close for comfort. Thirty minutes went by. Continued sporadic yelling and gunfire gave testimony that the operation was not the cakewalk Exner had envisioned.

"Sounds like they are bringing the fight to us," Bindhira said as she temporarily raised the headphones to speak.

Lee and Travers strained to see any action through the twenty-eight-foot trailer windows. Neither could see anything, but the gunfire was getting too close for comfort.

Then Bindhira spoke as she put a hand to her left earphone. "Alan and his team have breached the clubhouse rear entrance. There are several agents down. Control reports they must have a 'bloody arsenal'—his words, not mine. I have been instructed to send in a full strike team if I do not hear back from him within ten minutes."

"Don't know why he'd waste the strike team's time when he's got Hartley standing by eh, hotshot?" Travers attempt at humor did not fly. Both Bindhira and Lee were lost on different trains of thoughts.

Bindhira strained through her headphones to detect and decipher any outgoing messages from the clubhouse. Lee just stared out a window. Travers knew that usually meant he was formulating a plan.

'You've got that 'deep in thought' look Lee," Travers remarked.

"Yeah, give me some time to decompress on the way up," Lee said.

For a few moments, all was calm. No gunfire, no shouting. Suddenly an explosion rocked the trailer, the concussion of which flattened one of the dual tires on the trailer's left side.

The blast, with the intensity of a small bomb, stunned the trailer's inhabitants. Everything became muffled to the three occupants within.

"Is everyone okay?" Lee, like the others, had been thrown to the floor. He assisted Bindhira to her feet. Travers just lay there. The blast had knocked off his hat.

"You good, Bill?"

"No hurry on the uptake Lee," Travers said. "Probably just gonna get knocked down again anyway." He found his hat and returned it to his head before getting up.

Bindhira replaced her earphones and resumed her post. Lee looked out the windows. Although he could see no one, he was sure the gunfight would eventually come their way as this was the only route in and out of the facility.

Bindhira put a hand to an earphone and said, "Lee, it's Alan. He's been hit! Two of his men are down and they're trapped on the first floor near the lounge!"

"Screw this!" Lee remarked. He kicked open the door, shouting over his shoulder, "I'll need you at my six, Bill." He pulled his .40-caliber Baretta Centurion from the pancake holster on the belt beneath his shirt.

"Already there," Travers said. A .45-caliber Glock 21 suddenly appeared in his hand. Each racked the slide of their weapon and then bolted out of the trailer.

"Wait! You must stay here," but Bindhira's words went unheeded as the two had already vacated the trailer.

"You ready?" Lee asked.

"At the risk of sounding cliché I was born ready, you Newman junky," Travers said. He was so glad Lee had had the foresight to stop and pick up his sidearms on the way.

"Hey, where do you knuckleheads think you are go—" An earsplitting shot rang out and Carlisle fell from his perch in the tree behind the trailer, eight feet to the ground below.

Travers started to head back to Carlisle, when Lee grabbed his shoulder. "NO! Exner needs our help now."

"Shit! This whole thing sucks, man," Travers said worriedly in his usual old hippie style.

"Come on Bill. Stay close, and for heaven's sake, stay low!" Lee took off at a trot, careful to hold tight to the well-manicured hedge which lined the driveway. Travers followed in like manner.

Bindhira lost no time. She sent out a signal to the strike team. No response. She tried again. Switching frequencies, she made another attempt, but still could not raise them. The NSA agent flipped switches and adjusted dials on the communications array, but nothing she did was able to enhance her sat-phone signal.

Shouting an unladylike expletive in her native dialect, Bindhira stormed out of the trailer unarmed and without backup.

80

Uninvited Guests

Wu Yang pulled up to the roadblock at Singing Woods Lane. He pulled his late-model rental BMW X6 to the side of the road. Yang decided to traverse the remaining quarter mile on foot when he noticed the damaged trailer. The ChIS agent reached into the X6 and grabbed a briefcase and cane.

Cautiously, he advanced toward the trailer. He stood still for a moment and listened. No sounds emanated from the unit. He was about to continue when he heard gunfire. Not wanting to be caught out in the open, he walked up to the trailer and threw open the door.

Empty, but what he did see put Yang on high alert. He recognized the high-tech communications system for what it was. The CSS equipment before him was so advanced he quickly realized how his jamming efforts in Buffalo had been to no avail.

As he exited the trailer, the ChIS agent was immediately tackled to the ground. Yang lost his briefcase as he fell, but managed to hang on to his cane. He realized that although he wrestled with a much younger man, the man was not as strong as he should have been. Then he saw the blood.

Carlisle had been shot in the shoulder, probably by a stray bullet, but his fall from the tree had left him with a severely sprained ankle.

Yang attempted to choke Carlisle with his cane, but the NABS agent managed to break the grip on one hand. He knocked the arm still holding the cane to the side. This enabled the young agile agent to regain his breath. Despite Carlisle steadily weakening from a steady loss of blood, he still managed to keep the surprisingly strong elderly man at a disadvantage.

Unexpectedly the NABS agent felt a sharp pin prick pierce a thigh close to his groin. Thinking nothing of it, he had the Chinese man on the defense now. As he rolled away to stand up, he suddenly felt nauseous. Carlisle staggered back from his opponent, thinking himself woozy from loss of blood.

Looking back to Wu Yang, who was standing now, Carlisle noticed that the man was smiling at him. Carlisle's throat suddenly felt thick, and he struggled for air. Gasping now, hands around his throat, the agent began to cough, bringing up frothy blood.

As he dropped to his knees in great distress, Wu Yang kneeled down before him face to face and said, "Not long now, my friend. The poison has no antidote and is guaranteed to deliver maximum discomfort. You are dead, my friend, you just haven't realized it yet."

As he stood back up, Wu Yang delivered a needless and cruel crescent kick to the side of the man's face. Carlisle fell over on his side, gasping for breath. He was drowning in his own bodily fluids and he entered into the early throws of violent convulsion. His body arched into one last powerful upheaval before it settled slowly and finally to the ground.

NABS Agent Ken Carlisle was dead.

Yang stooped to pick up his briefcase. Gunfire was prevalent all over the grounds. He began to formulate an alternate plan knowing that the Establishment had just lost another base of operations.

He disappeared into the relative safety of the dense woodlands that surrounded the clubhouse.

Alan Exner, shot and low on ammunition, felt embarrassed. He cringed at what the headlines would read if he survived this ordeal: *Prestigious Order of Canada Award Presented to Senior NABS Agent for Being Shot in the Ass in the Line of Duty.*

Then Exner's thoughts were jarred to the present. He heard two men speaking in Mandarin as they approached his position. They were whispering behind a large vending machine at the other end of the room. A man lay dead not ten feet from where Exner sat propped up against a wall. He reined in a carelessly extended leg tighter to his body.

But it was too late. Before Exner could react, the two suddenly popped into view, guns drawn.

Alberto was bewildered. His life literally flashed before his eyes. The plans he had worked so long and so hard to develop; the contacts he had so painstakingly nurtured with malleable elements of the Chinese and Cuban Secret Services; the endless days of sacrifice and caution—all had so suddenly unraveled before him.

The Establishment had operated successfully for years. Its members had grown quite adept at throwing wrenches into government workings worldwide for the furtherance of their selfish ambitions. Bringing the Western world to its knees would have been his, Wu

Yang's, and the Establishment's greatest triumph. Now their work had become a nightmarish albatross around their collective necks.

Where the devil was Wu Yang? It was not like the old Oriental to be tardy, thought Alberto. The man had been invaluable to China's Secret Service for decades. Alberto had worked alongside him on several occasions, but never liked him. The ChIS agent's methods were too brutal even for the tough Cuban to stomach.

But the old warhorse was getting old, which meant that he would soon become a liability to his handlers. Wu Yang may be many things, but he was no one's fool. He was well aware of his age and how his government dealt with elderly high-ranking officials who knew too much and no longer cared. It was inevitable. No one of his age and status ever retired from the Chinese Intelligence Service.

No doubt Wu Yang had fled, Alberto reasoned. Perhaps it was even Yang who had tipped off the Americans as to the whereabouts of the Establishment's headquarters, in the hopes of bringing the Cuban down and thus throwing them off his trail.

Several of Alberto's trusted bodyguards lay dead before him. He realized nothing remained for him here but capture. He took to the secret exit behind the wine rack in the basement of the clubhouse complex. It led to the Lake Erie shoreline, three hundred feet to the northeast.

The underground passageway had been dug during the Prohibition Era of the mid 1920s. It had come in quite handy at the time, when the original building had housed a lucrative bootlegging operation out of its basement.

During the war years however, the clubhouse and its property fell into disrepair and remained vacant until the early 1950s, when the very wealthy Kovach family restored it into a thriving private golf club, known as the Singing Woods.

A consortium bought the family out in 2012 with an offer they couldn't refuse, even though they weren't in the market to sell. This consortium, a shell corporation of the Establishment, was made up of very discreet secret service operatives from Cuba who worked as spies for Castro in the United States, but sought a better life for themselves.

This small band believed in oligarchy. They saw how easily corrupt governments had bilked their countries out of millions of dollars. So they set about bilking the bilkers. But they didn't go so far as to embrace the philosophy of Robin Hood.

The Establishment sought to steal from these rich, corrupt governments and channel these funds into furthering their own causes.

Alberto was a high-ranking member of the Establishment. The crowning achievement for him came when he stumbled onto Project Vector quite by accident. As control for the DGI section stationed in Santiago, he was entrusted with security for Chinese doctors, scientists and officials in his province who worked on the project with scientists from his own country.

He soon made friends with several like-minded Chinese officials, who, he carefully discovered, were very interested in his ideals. Wu Yang was the first. Several others followed his lead. Still working for their respective governments, they set about planning to undermine them, and to steal from them, little by little.

Together they assembled an officially sanctioned Chinese-Cuban cell that was sent to Canada. Alberto's plan was for the Establishment to set up a single network, steal packets of the virus, and then covertly send them to their cell in Canada. This was accomplished by concealing them behind works of art from another shell front, a Cuban art gallery run by Carlos Rodriguez. and sent to Canada by an unwitting mule; the old Canadian diver, William Travers.

If the Establishment could wrest control of Vector and unleash it in North America first, they would upstage their own governments' plans, and frame them for the crime. Then, when the time was right, they would make their move against the rest of the world.

But then Alberto caught wind of the fact that the virus they had painstakingly acquired was but an unstable weaker strain that would hit hard initially but break down shortly thereafter. They had to get their hands on the perfected virus or they would lose the initiative over their governments. Without the perfected pathogen and the right timing, the results would prove disastrous for them.

That was when Alberto had daringly stuck his neck out and stole a well-documented sample of the most virile pathogen known to man from the primary research facility in Santiago. That was the shipment his men never received in Canada, and that was when his plan began to fall apart.

Sweat saturated Alberto's shirt, even in the dank environment of the underground passageway. He had hoped to have met up with Wu Yang up before the unexpected raid.

The ChIS agent carried a briefcase that contained, among other things, the secondary codes needed to override the pressure detonators placed within the brass boxes so they could trigger them at will.

Alberto chided himself most severely. If Yang had not met with his "wrinkle," they could have triggered a box or two then escaped into Canada during the ensuing melee. Any further "wrinkles" in Establishment plans would be certain to expose them, and there would be literal hell to pay for their treachery from all corners.

Alberto realized that he now hated the word *wrinkle* almost as much as he hated the man who had imbedded it deep within his consciousness in the first place.

81

Pickup And Delivery

The silence was deafening. The carefully planned op didn't go as planned. Carefully planned ops seldom do, thought Lee.

The shooting had abated, at least for the moment, but both Lee Hartley and Bill Travers knew that the area around them was no less dangerous.

They skirted along the tree line surrounding the perimeter of the Singing Woods clubhouse, guns at the ready. The once stately building was full of holes from blasts and bullets. The grounds surrounding it were littered with bodies in various states of brokenness, and blood, lots of blood.

The two winced at the carnage spread over such peaceful surroundings. When they came to the back of the large two-story structure, Lee grabbed Travers' arm.

"I'll go in first," Lee said. "If I make it, get here as fast as you can, Bill." Without waiting for a reply, Lee broke out and away from the safety of the tree line.

It was about fifty feet from the perimeter of the woodland to the rear of the clubhouse. Lee was about halfway there when a pair of gunshots rang out. He dropped to the ground. Surprised he had not been hit, Lee raised his head and looked back from where the shots came. There stood Travers, who gave him a two-finger salute off his right eyebrow.

To Lee's left, he noticed a large marble water fountain. It was formed in the shape of a huge golf bag full of clubs, their heads spouting water. The water was a beautiful Caribbean blue color. But it wasn't the architecture of the fountain that caught Lee's attention. It was the body of one of Alberto's bodyguards strewn haphazardly beside it with two bullet holes in his chest that interested him the most.

Lee jumped up and sprinted the rest of the distance. He sought cover behind one of the huge stone pillars, and then motioned for Travers to follow. Without further incident, Travers reached Lee's side in seconds, breathing heavily.

"Right. We've got to get Exner and get the hell out," Lee said.

"Where's the cavalry?" Travers asked, surprised by this time that none was evident.

"Don't know, gotta go. Follow my lead," Lee said as he approached the rear door.

The solid rear oak door of the clubhouse opened for them without contest. Once inside, the two Canadians split up, one to the left and one to the right along the walls of a cavernous lounge room.

The room was furnished with expensive leather chairs, luxurious antique leather chesterfields, and oak end tables throughout. Paintings of prestigious golfers of the past adorned the walls of the white alabaster room. It had been a beautiful place before all this, Lee thought.

As if on cue, the two looked at each other in fearful uncertainty. A groan had issued forth from around the corner closest to Travers. Lee rushed over to Travers' side. They threw a quick glance at each other then, guns at the ready, rushed in low through the open door of an adjoining room.

They found Alan Exner propped against the liquor bar, one arm hanging off the bottom hoop of a bar stool. He had been shot. Lee saw that he was favoring his left ass cheek. Fortunately he would live through that one. Normally it would have been funny, but the men saw that their friend had been badly beaten. Both his eyes were swollen, and his head lolled to one side.

Beside him a female agent had been shot several times in the back. She lay face down, a pool of crimson liquid already coagulating around her body.

Travers continued on through the barroom. He checked over and behind everything in his path, his gun ready to spew death at the first sign of aggression.

Lee rushed to Exner's side. He slapped the man's face lightly on both cheeks and said, "Alan, Alan, it's me, Lee. Bill's here too. We're getting you out of here. Hang tight."

Exner looked slowly up into his face. "About time you got here, Hartley." He attempted a smile but his face was too swollen.

"Looks like they gave you a bloody good beating, Ex," Lee said.

Their eyes met in mutual concern and respect. Exner tried to speak but fell silent as he passed out.

By this time Travers had cleared the room. He came over to help Lee with their friend.

Exner faded into and out of consciousness. The divers led him to a plush loveseat along the far wall. They carefully positioned him on it.

"Too quiet," Travers observed.

"Say what?"

"Too damn quiet; almost like we've just walked into a trap."

Lee sprinted to a wall phone at the far end of the bar. "Dead," he reported.

The men pulled Exner to his feet and half walked, half dragged him to the rear door. Just as they rounded a corner, they were met by an Asian who held a hostage before them.

Exner looked groggily up. "Wu . . . Yang . . ."

"Yes, Mr. Exner. It is time we meet again," he said, with dangerous politeness.

"The pleasure is all yours, Yang," Travers seethed.

"Bindhi," Lee shouted. The Chinese agent had positioned the NSA agent as a shield in front of him. He and Travers stared in disbelief. A myriad of questions began to fill their minds. How had Wu Yang captured Bindhira? Where was Carlisle? And where was Alberto?

The elderly Oriental was far more powerful than his captive. The vice-like half-nelson chokehold he had on her kept her in compliance.

"Attempt nothing foolish gentlemen," Wu Yang said as he lowered his cane such that its tip rested against Bindhira's calf. "I assure you that this young lady will die a most horrible death if you try to intervene."

"Just like you to hide behind a woman, Yang. Let her go; you're not getting out of this one and you know it," Lee said.

Ignoring him, Wu Yang said, "you will do well to drop your weapons. I shall not ask a second time." The elderly ChIS agent's eyes narrowed more than usual.

Lee and Travers did not wait for a second invitation. They dropped their weapons to the floor.

"Most excellent, gentlemen, thank you. Now please kick them over to me and move clear of your friend." Wu Yang was careful to keep Bindhira in front of him at all times.

Through the whole melee, Lee noticed that Bindhira had managed to maintain her composure. He also knew that once the chance presented itself, she would make her move.

"You can't get far Yang," Exner said, now cognizant. He slowly stood up. "We're on to you and your damned Establishment." He had to use the chesterfield's arm as a crutch. "You know what they do to traitors within the Chinese Secret Service don't you, Yang?"

"I am no man's fool, Mr. Exner. Least of all yours," Yang said coldly. He looked warily from him to the other two men. "A contingency plan has been developed for just such an occasion and you, gentlemen, will do nothing to interfere."

Exner noticed that both Lee and Travers were slowly and carefully edging closer to Wu Yang stealthily from different angles. Exner knew he would have to engage the Chinese agent, draw him into a disturbing conversation to distract him from their intentions.

"Yang, you're right. You're nobody's fool. That said, what do you *really* expect to get out of this now?" Exner knew that one false move from any of them could trigger the desperate man into injecting Bindhira with his lethal poison.

"That, Mr. Exner, is none of your concern, for I fear your life expectancy and that of your friends has come to an end."

From outside the clubhouse, gunfire rang out once again. This startled Wu Yang sufficiently enough for Bindhira to throw her left leg behind his, breaking his balance. She then delivered a reverse elbow into his stomach. He released his grip on her neck and staggered back, dropping his cane in the process. The NSA agent quickly kicked it towards Exner.

Lee and Travers regained possession of their weapons. Bindhira took up a position behind the main entrance to the room. Exner reached down and picked up Yang's cane.

"Be careful with that damned thing Ex," Lee said. He went over and yanked the dazed Chinese agent to his feet.

"Our guys should have arrived by now," Exner said. "Can't be too many more of theirs left."

Walking up to Wu Yang, Exner said, "Where's Alberto, Yang?"

"Unknown, but the fool would have triggered the devices if he had the chance," Yang said.

"What do you mean?" Exner tightly grabbed the man's arm and gave it a shake.

"It all makes sense now, Alan," Lee said as he peered once again around the corner. Seeing no one in sight, he continued. "Yang carries a briefcase with him at all times. That case is not with him right now, but I bet it's not far away. I'd also bet his life that their 'launch system' requires two separate codes as a backup safety system and Alberto has the other. Am I getting warm, Yang?"

"I offer no resistance," Wu Yang said as he yanked his arm from Exner's grip. "You must find the man. He is most dangerous and may be able to override such safeguards. However, it would take even him time to accomplish this."

"Why the sudden spilling of guts, Yang," Travers piped up. He rechecked his pistol's magazine.

"I offer this information because the virus can destroy me as well and, I assure you, it will do its job most effectively," he said.

The quietness was suddenly shattered as heavy machine gun fire broke out in the courtyard. But it had a different pitch than before, and came with a much greater rapidity of fire. The whirling blades of a fast approaching helicopter cut the air.

"This just keeps getting better," Exner said ruefully as he rushed to the window for a cautious peek.

The others followed suit. Wu Yang was positioned between Lee and Travers, with Travers at the rear. Through the window, they saw black-clad Delta Force commandos taking up positions behind trees and life-sized marble golf celebrities as the chopper came in low for another sweep.

One of the commandos, armed with an *RPG,* took careful aim. As the black attack chopper came in low for another volley, the commando fired. The small rocket hit the apache's propeller shaft at its linkage. Strangely the helicopter began to twirl opposite the slowly decreasing whirl of its props. It plummeted from the sky over and away from the onlookers' field of vision, only to crash scant seconds later in a huge exploding ball of fire.

"Contingency that, asshole," Travers said as he spun the man around.

With lightning speed, Yang kneed Travers twice in the groin. He would have continued were it not for Bindhira's powerful open-handed *shuto* delivered to the Chinese agent's neck. Yang dropped to his knees.

Heavily armed commandos in full combat gear silently poured into the room from both sides, taking up strategic positions within. Seeing Wu Yang, the officer-in-charge had two of his men cover him with their submachine guns.

Travers gruffly yanked the Chinese agent up by the lapel and pushed him over to them.

"Are you okay, sir?" The commanding officer asked Exner.

"As well as any man who's just had the shit kicked out of him and been shot in the ass, commander," Exner said with obvious relief.

Ignoring the underlying humor, Lee said, "commander, there's another man, as dangerous as Wu Yang, still at large either on the grounds or not far from them."

"I know where he has gone," Wu Yang offered of his own volition. "I regret to inform you, but if he took the secret escape route, Alberto was probably on that downed helicopter."

Turning from Wu Yang to the Delta Force commander, Exner said, "Before you take this man to your interrogation center, squeeze the location of his briefcase out of him. It's imperative that we have it in our possession."

"Oh, and you'd better get a forensics team on that downed chopper stat, commander. I want to know if there was a Cuban DGI agent on board that downed bird ASAP."

A pair of Delta Force commandos grabbed Wu Yang, handcuffed him, and led him out of the building.

"Anything else sir," the Commander asked.

"No commander, but you and your men are to be commended for your timing today," Exner said, with a sigh of relief.

"Yes sir, thank-you sir," the commander said.

Exner saluted the man as did Bindhira, Travers, and Lee.

"Thank you, sir. I'll pass it along to my men," the commander said with a slight smile. "By the way sir, a paramedic team is on their way to tend to your, uh, wound." The commander did his best not to smile.

"Thank you, Commander, that will be all," Exner said with mock sternness.

The commander then spun on his heel, and with the rest of his men behind him, exited the room as silently as they had entered.

82

So Close, Yet So Very Far Away

Very early the next morning, Exner and his team arrived back in Canada via Learjet from Erie, Pennsylvania. It had been decided that Travers would stay at Lee's place until he could get back on his feet again.

By one o'clock that afternoon, the two "consultants" and Bindhira Shankar stood silently before control in his office. Exner was on the phone, and he was not happy.

"What do you mean," Exner asked, repeatedly clicking a ballpoint pen as he listened. "He was transferred under Delta Force escort," Exner said as he spoke into his communications console.

"Prisoners under Delta Force escort don't escape. Even if a rare opportunity did present itself, the prisoner wouldn't get far." From Exner's half of the conversation, it didn't sound like he was receiving very good news. "Well thank heaven for that! Bring the suitcase in ASAP. Yes, and keep me informed."

Exner rang off, then looked up and confirmed what they had already figured out. "Wu Yang escaped, wily devil that he is. We don't have the full details yet, other than Yang said he was going to be carsick. When the armored van pulled over, the commandos were gassed. When they came to, Yang was gone, handcuffs and all."

"Shit!" Travers was obviously upset. "How does an old dude like Wu Yang elude a whole friggin' commando unit?"

"He may not be as slippery as you think, Bill," Exner said. "He left his briefcase in the prisoner transfer van. He might have been startled by police cruisers with sirens running in the vicinity at the time of his escape. Could be he felt he had to choose between getting out and away clean or being slowed down with a briefcase. At any rate, it should be here within the hour."

"Could be another trick," Lee said. "Yang doesn't strike me as the careless type."

"Alan, what about Alberto?" Bindhira asked. "Did forensics find out if he was aboard the helicopter when it crashed?"

"There were three men in the chopper," Exner said by way of explanation. "Both the pilot and the gunner of the downed helo have been identified as AWOL airmen from the U.S. Air Force base in Niagara Falls, New York. The third body has yet to be identified."

Lee noticed that Bindhira looked well rested and fresh despite the events of the past few days. The bright yellow capped sleeve ruffled blouse and navy blue microfiber leggings she wore perfectly accentuated her physical assets.

He admired the way Bindhira took such great care of herself. She was ever so feminine but tastefully so, never to the point of empty seductiveness. Once again he had to repress his bubbling hormones.

Unexpectedly, she looked in his direction as if she sensed his gaze. Quite out of character for her, she blushed and smiled, then strolled over to look out at the lake through Exner's office window.

Exner rose from behind his desk and sat on its front corner, café mocha in hand, then said, “coast guard divers have uncovered seven of the brass containers, so far.”

“There were supposedly ten of the damn things,” Lee said. “We uncovered one, which means there are still two more to find.”

“*Supposedly* being the key word,” Travers said as he went over to the window beside Bindhira.

“Homeland Security is working the other side of the ‘creek’; CSIS this side of the lakes,” Exner said. “We exchange regular updates as fresh intel becomes available. As I’ve said, they’ve managed to uncover several of the containers, yet no arrests have been made,” Exner said with concern.

“Just one container left undiscovered would be disastrous,” Bindhira said, as she turned from the window. “Once the pressure of the water cures the viral catalyst at its predetermined time setting, the contents would not require a remote detonation to release it,” Bindhira said.

“Even so,” Exner said, “the members of the Establishment can override the system and blow it manually.”

“But,” Lee said, “if the detonation devices in the briefcases Wu Yang and Alberto carried have GPS coordinates of the containers programmed into them . . .”

“. . . we may be able to locate the remaining containers by pulling the coordinates out of the unit we seized from Wu Yang,” Bindhira said.

“You guys might be onto somethin’,” Travers said. “Kinda like that ‘football’ the president carries with him wherever he goes that contains nuclear warhead activation codes.”

“In a Scuba U sort of way,” Lee responded facetiously. Travers grunted and gave him his patented one-eyed squint-stare in return.

Fatigue and a growing despair shadowed each of their faces in varying degrees.

Exner was proud of his inner circle team. Bindhira, an NSA/CSS agent not trained for this type of assignment. Lee Hartley, a man of action but getting older, albeit gracefully so, and never one to say he had had enough. Then there was Bill Travers, pondered Exner; a friend of his friend, Lee Hartley.

Travers was prone to spontaneity, which had, on several occasions, been to his undoing. Here was a man who just lost his home, his livelihood, and nearly his life on this case. Yet the man never once complained. As crusty as he came across, Travers was a class act when the chips were down.

"Time's a-wasting," Lee said to no one in particular. "If Yang's briefcase turns out to be a red herring, I don't think any of us are going to have a very good day."

Just then the phone rang. Exner returned behind his desk and picked up the receiver. He listened silently for a few minutes then hung up.

"That was forensics. Yang's briefcase is the real deal," Exner settled down into his plush leather desk chair.

"Why then do you look so unhappy," Bindhira asked.

Exner looked up at her, then over to the men. "Because to deactivate the manual detonation system, we need an additional code set in addition to the one we pulled from Yang's device; a code set only Alberto has, and I'm willing to bet my life that he already has the codes Yang carried."

83

And A Child Shall Lead Them

The end exit to the underground passageway was locked tight. So tight in fact, that despite Alberto's best efforts at throwing his shoulder into the heavy wooden door, it wouldn't budge.

Other than Wu Yang, only Alberto knew about the secret passageway and exit point. Each time he returned to the Singing Woods, Alberto made a point of taking the fairly long stroll to the lake to ensure the exit's continued concealment and the door's functionality. What could possibly have caused its impediment?

If that wasn't enough, his powerful lithium-ion battery powered light gave out without warning. To retrace the several hundred feet back though the passage in pitch-blackness would be very hazardous at best.

Hewn of solid rock, the tunnel had many twists and turns, and portions of the ceiling were in danger of letting loose. Piles of jagged rock had already collapsed into the tunnel over the years, and its successful navigation was perilous even with a light. Without one . . .

Alberto hoped the helicopter had made it through the gunfire and picked up his body double. It was a good plan. He prided himself in ensuring his safe, certain, and undetected escape. This latest turn of events, however was not in the script; another unexpected wrinkle. Damn, he hated that word!

Alberto threw his briefcase to the ground in disgust. Trapped like a rat in the pitch-black tunnel, he knew it would only be a matter of time before the commandos discovered the secret entrance and him.

He cursed himself for his carelessness. He had a small light on his keychain, but its small button battery had expired a few days previous. He had made a mental note to replace it, but didn't. The tendrils of fear and panic began to close around him.

Alberto began to wonder if he and Wu Yang would ever pull off their double-cross. In the isolation of the cool musty dampness of the dark tunnel with no way out, he was not so sure.

Suddenly a moving light, dim at first, permeated the passageway. It gradually grew brighter as its owner drew closer. Thinking the worst, Alberto hunted around for a stick, a piece of rebar, even a rock with which to protect himself. With renewed urgency, he felt around and at least had managed to reclaim his briefcase.

Although the case was perfect for carrying important documents, one of its more practical attributes was that it was bulletproof. At least that's what his DGI superiors had told him.

The light grew nearer, and Alberto crouched behind a large piece of fallen ceiling stone not fifty feet from the blocked exit and the lakeshore beyond. If he was fast enough, he would have the element of surprise and catch his pursuers off guard.

Alberto gasped when a little girl about ten years old silently and suddenly appeared around the small bend a few feet from where he stood. Startled, the briefcase fell from his hands.

In spite of his desperate situation, Alberto could not help but feel sorry for the small child. Standing now before him, he could better see her in the light she carried. The clothes she wore were tattered and threadbare. She carried a flattened out teddy bear that hung off one hand, and an old dim two-cell tubular flashlight in the other.

"How did you get here, child?" Alberto found himself slightly unnerved at her calm demeanor.

The young girl simply smiled as she hummed a little tune. Alberto was stunned by the fearless innocence of this child, who boldly faced a stranger in such surroundings. His first inclination was to seize her and snap her fragile neck at the first sight of the commandos who surely put her up to this.

But she was alone. Perhaps the child had somehow stumbled into the tunnel by accident. Even so, how could she remain so calm after passing through all the broken bodies, mayhem, shooting, and death on the outside?

"Did anyone follow you down here child," Alberto snarled.

The girl remained silent, and he could see that she was neither intimidated by him nor concerned for her safety.

This unnerved him even more. The Cuban wrenched the flashlight from the little girl's grasp, then without word, trotted off the way the child had come, leaving her alone in the darkness.

He ran nearly a third of the way down the tunnel. A little farther on, he stopped and listened. There was no sound of rushing footsteps or anyone else ahead. All was calm, but not all was right. He had abandoned a child in the hellish dark of a narrow tunnel with no way out, and she was not crying, not even a sob.

The briefcase!

The flashlight was glowing dimmer now. Alberto cursed himself for not remembering to pick up his briefcase when he left the girl.

Very strange things were happening with increasing frequency, and it spooked him.

As he retraced his steps along the narrow passage, he determined that if the child tried to cling to him he'd slap the little bitch unconscious, maybe even do her a favor and kill her. He, like Wu Yang, was not one to leave loose ends. Loose ends were *wrinkles.*

He reached the end of the tunnel where he left the girl. But the child was nowhere to be found! Could there be other passages he wasn't aware of? No. The old blueprints showed only this one.

Where the hell was she? More importantly, *where was the briefcase?*

In frantic despair he crawled around on hands and knees. Yes, this was definitely the spot where he had dropped it.

What he saw next paralyzed him in fear. Training the dying flashlight on the ground around him, he saw only adult footprints on the silty ground: his footprints and those of no other.

Alberto felt he was going insane. What the devil was going on?

He finally gave up his frantic search. The briefcase was gone, and with it the manual detonation device. He called out to the child, pleaded with her.

That was when his flashlight died. In panic, he blindly ran back in the direction of the clubhouse. He hadn't gone far when he tripped and fell, striking his forehead on the rock face of the tunnel.

Pain, fear, and unconsciousness ensued immediately thereafter.

84

"A Very Weird Case"

"It's the weirdest thing I've ever come across in my thirty-two years as a police officer," staff sergeant Michel Nadeau said to Bindhira Shankar.

Alan Exner had been summoned the next morning to the Niagara Parks Police Station, a mere quarter mile north of the Canadian brink of the Horseshoe Falls. But he was unable to attend however, as he was locked into a hastily scheduled teleconference with other top North American security agencies. Bindhira and Lee offered to go in his stead.

Travers meanwhile, had a meeting with his insurance company to discuss options over his written-off home and business, and so declined their invitation to tag along.

NPP officers were commissioned with policing the thirty-mile stretch of Niagara Parks Commission property that ran parallel along the Niagara River from Niagara-On-The-Lake in the north to Fort Erie in the south.

Staff sergeant Nadeau had been strangely cryptic in his request to NABS.

Nadeau shook each of their hands in turn, and after inspecting Bindhira's NSA/CSS credentials, gestured them to take a seat in front of his brightly lit desk. He took his place behind a well used and very old desk.

The staff sergeant was a husky French-Canadian with well-groomed pure white hair and a serious demeanor. Powerfully built, the man was in his late fifties, but possessed the body of a much younger man. Dark brown eyes exuded a wisdom acquired through years of policing experience. His intense eye contact and equally intense handshake left no doubt that this was a police officer you would not want to mess with.

After pleasantries were exchanged, the staff sergeant got down to business. "One of our officers picked up a little girl all alone on a lonely stretch of the Niagara Parkway a little after 3:00 a.m. last night. She was heading north to the falls, and carried a rather heavy briefcase."

Lee and Bindhira looked to each other eagerly. Lee was first to speak. "Staff Sergeant Nadeau, this may sound a little silly, but did the little girl also carry a well-worn yellow and brown teddy bear with her as well?"

The staff sergeant was visibly surprised by this. "Why, now that you mention it, yes." Then he added, "Do you know her, Mr. Hartley?"

"In a manner of speaking," Lee said.

"What are the contents of the briefcase?" Bindhira cross-examined.

Nadeau replied. "Several documents typed in a curious mixture of Spanish and Chinese." He paused to recollect. "Yes, and it seemed the briefcase perhaps belonged to a mathematics professor or like kind."

"Why do you say that," Lee quizzed.

"Because there were several sheets of both typed and handwritten numerical equations."

"Do you still have them," Bindhira asked with a note of urgency.

"But of course, Ms. Shankar."

Nadeau hit a button on a console in front of him and spoke into its microphone. Within minutes an attractive young constable knocked and then entered her staff sergeant's office carrying a well-worn black briefcase. It clunked heavily on the desk as she placed it in front of Nadeau. Smiling at the two guests, she then resumed her post outside his office.

He beckoned the two visitors to come behind his desk and view the contents of the case as he opened it in front of them.

"If you do not mind sir," Bindhira said as she slid the case closer to the end of the desk so that it sat in front of her. She went through the case's various pockets and folder sections. She even sniffed at the paper within.

"Part bloodhound, sir," Lee said to the staff sergeant, which brought a chuckle to them both.

Looking up to the men, Bindhira said, "I do not wish to sound melodramatic, staff sergeant, but this briefcase is a matter of international security, and I am afraid we must take it back to NABS headquarters for a more thorough analysis."

"But of course, Ms. Shankar. My due diligence regarding this matter is now complete," Nadeau said, rising from his chair.

Lee stood up as Bindhira closed the case and hefted it up to a standing position on Nadeau's desk. "By the way," Lee said, "about the girl. Where is she now?"

"Well, that's the strangest part of this whole thing, Mr. Hartley. The child never spoke. She was not even afraid being out alone on a lonely, dark highway in the middle of the night."

"One of our female officers tried to befriend her, but the girl remained silent, distant. Cindy attempted to converse with her in the several languages she knows, but the child remained silent throughout." The staff sergeant shook his head. "Then, when Cindy asked in English if the child needed to go to the restroom, she nodded, so we knew she wasn't deaf. She was shown the restroom and that was it, she was gone."

"What do you mean 'gone,' sir," Lee asked, but already knew what his answer would be.

"Never saw the child again. She never came back out," Nadeau said.

"Probably got out through the restroom window," Bindhira offered, to gauge his reaction.

"That's where the weird part comes in, Ms. Shankar. There isn't one."

85

A One Room Suite In A Crowbar Hotel

Heavy fire from the Blackhawk helicopter had all but destroyed the armored van's front end. The vehicle had jumped a small ditch and came to an abrupt stop when it crashed into the sturdy barbed wire fence that ran parallel to the road.

The helicopter circled, then came around again. Hovering twenty feet off the ground, the Blackhawk held its position in front of the vehicle. After a minute to ensure the scene was "dormant", it slowly touched down horizontally across the road not thirty feet from the rear of the van.

As it idled on the pavement, a disoriented Wu Yang stumbled out of the rear of the van, his cane dangling from his arm, albeit precariously. He walked a few paces, staggered, and then fell.

A man in a flight suit rushed over to the van, lobbed a gas grenade into it, and slammed its armored door shut. There was a muffled pop. He then ran up and checked the front cab. Both men lay unconscious and bleeding.

Coming back to the man on the ground and seeing it was Wu Yang, the man helped him to his feet. Slowly they made their way to the helicopter.

When they got within ten feet of the airship, a pair of sirens became increasingly more audible as two police cars rapidly approached from their rear. The Blackhawk lifted off just as two OPP cruisers came to an abrupt stop at the scene of the wreck.

An officer jumped out from each of the vehicles, guns drawn. But the chopper was already far and above the range of their tiny handguns.

Wu Yang knew Alberto would be nothing short of furious at this, another *wrinkle.* The Chinese ChIS agent looked over and noticed his cane hung on the side of his seat. He pulled it into his lap and inspected its mechanism and the number of charges left within.

There was still one injection of the deadly poison, tetrodotoxin, left in the weapon. He hoped it was one he would not have to use.

The pilot laid in a course for a small airstrip just outside Toronto's Pearson International Airport. There was a small plane at the ready to spirit him away to Mexico City. Yang had contacts there who would keep him safely underground until things blew over. Such was Wu Yang's contingency plan.

Twenty minutes later, the Blackhawk touched down beside the tower of a small airstrip. A plane was on the runway awaiting its passenger.

The co-pilot of the helicopter climbed out and slid open the side door for Yang. He then assisted his passenger down, then tapped his head to ensure he kept low and clear of the rotor blades. Finally, the man handed the agent a small envelope. Yang gave the man a curt nod. The co-pilot secured the hatch, trotted back, then resumed his position in the cockpit.

Within seconds the Blackhawk was a mere speck in the southern sky.

Scant seconds later, a late model gray Rolls Royce limousine pulled up on the tarmac and came to a stop at the front of the plane.

Immediately, two men in black uniforms and bulletproof vests jumped out, submachine guns in hand. One stood beside the plane, his weapon trained on its pilot. The other man directed Wu Yang into the darkened interior of the immaculate vehicle, then returned to the plane.

The powerful Rolls then quickly pulled away. The corners of Yang's mouth suddenly turned down in direct proportion to the interior lights, which had been turned up.

Across from him sat a very fit Delta Force lieutenant holding a pair of handcuffs in one hand, a Glock 21 in the other.

"Welcome aboard, Mr. Yang," the man beside him said without facial expression. "We've been long overdue for this get-together. I'm CIA sub-director Culp and this is Delta Force lieutenant Mandziuk."

Yang attempted at this point to subtly direct the tip of his cane to his own leg, but the power of the man in front of him was too great.

Nudging the commando's shoulder, Culp said to him. "Lieutenant, relieve this man of his cane, and if he as much as twitches, you are authorized to react with extreme prejudice."

"Roger that, sir," the commando said. He handed the cane to Culp, then handcuffed their prisoner.

"Where are you taking me, gentlemen?" Wu Yang, astonished at this most unexpected turn of events, tried to remain calm and dignified in spite of the inner turmoil raging within. His maniacal anger quickly eroded when the answer came.

"Cuba. We know you've spent a lot of time there, so we'd like to send you back, all-expenses paid of course, courtesy of the United States government."

Warily Wu Yang said, "Back to Cuba?" Then his eyes narrowed. "Where in Cuba?"

"Ever hear of Guantanamo Bay?"

86

Opaque Transparency

“The Cuban *presidente*, Raul Castro, has accused the United States government of kidnapping the head of their Santiago DGI control, one Alberto Cabrera,” Alan Exner said from his office over his Sequoia sat-link console to Bindhira, who was with Lee in the TaZeR.

She put the conversation on speaker so Lee could hear as well. She slowed the vehicle as they approached a red light. “Not soon after that,” Exner continued, “the Chinese had the audacity to make a request of their own. It appears they want their ‘diplomat’ Wu Yang returned to them at once.”

“And my government’s response,” Bindhira questioned.

“The U.S. government stated that their warning was explicit, and that these men are guilty of espionage and terrorism,” Exner said, “and that neither the United States nor the rest of the free world will tolerate any further acts of hostility or aggression, either covertly or overtly by the People’s Republic of China.”

"What the Cubans don't know is that we haven't been able to get our hands on Carbrera yet. While we know he *was* in Erie, Pennsylvania at the Singing Woods golf course, he's since dropped off the radar."

"Come on, Ex," Lee leaned closer to the speaker, "you can't tell me neither NABS *nor* the CIA can get the drop on this guy."

The traffic light changed, and the TaZeR quickly and quietly accelerated as Bindhira resumed the cruise control.

"On a lighter note," Exner said, "Culp and Delta Force managed to reclaim Yang just as he was about to leave the country by private plane."

"Seems the pilot was a little lax and failed to encode his transmissions. We found out Yang had a plane waiting in Toronto to take him to Mexico City. Culp and Delta Force were waiting."

"Where will they take him Ex," Lee asked.

"Culp has his ass on a flight back to Cuba—Guantanamo Bay to be exact."

"If that is the case, it will not be too long before the proverbial canary sings," Bindhira said. "Their ways are most persuasive."

"And just how would you know 'their ways', Bindhi," Lee asked, half in jest.

"To extract the truth *out* of a terrorist, one has to use the methods *of* a terrorist. I have studied such methods well and used them on occasion," she said casually and without emotion.

"Oh . . . ," Lee said, a little unsettled.

"Here's another one for you," Exner said. "The briefcase found in the Delta Force transport van really *was* Wu Yang's 'football.' Hidden in a false bottom of the case were several documents, all in Mandarin, and all directly related to the Establishment."

"Sooo," Lee said, "what you're saying Ex, is that we now have a complete set of 'bookends.'"

"With both briefcases in our possession," Bindhira said, "we now have the coded information needed to neutralize the remaining containers."

"On a different note, was Alberto a confirmed casualty in the Blackhawk helicopter crash, Ex," Lee asked.

"The bodies were burned beyond recognition," Exner replied. "If we checked into dental records, we could determine a positive ID."

"Good luck getting Cuban dental records," Lee said with a snort.

"True that," Exner said. Then, changing the subject, he said, "What's your ETA?"

"About an hour and thirteen minutes Alan," Bindhira said with a straight face. Lee knew from experience that she was probably not exaggerating.

"As long as you're not an hour and fourteen, we're good," Exner replied in kind.

87

'As It Was In The Days Of Rome'

It was another beautiful summer afternoon the next day, and Lee was pining to have this affair over with so he could do some wreck diving with Travers. But he knew his old buddy had too much on his mind to even consider a dive trip just yet.

Travers was locked in conversation with control when Lee and Bindhira arrived at Exner's office. Within seconds of their arrival, Exner's desk phone rang. With Exner on the phone, Lee leaned over to Bindhira, who stood silently off to one side of the desk, rubbing her arm. "So, Bindhi, how are you holding up through all this?"

"Just as every day: very well, thank you." She smiled warmly. "You owe me a night out when this is all over," she added, batting her eyes deliciously at him.

"You're on, me pretty," Lee said with relish. He pulled out his flask and took a swig.

"Won't happen," Travers said abruptly.

"Excuse me," Bindhira asked, slightly put out by the comment.

"To my knowledge," Travers continued as he squinted an eye, "no restaurants are licensed in this province to sell Newman's parmesan and roasted garlic salad dressing on tap, and it seems that's all he's been sucking back of late. So, you're SOL on that promise, little lady." Travers remained stoic for a few seconds, then even he laughed with the others. Lee pointed and wagged a finger at his friend.

They turned their attention back to Exner who was still engaged in conversation on the phone. He said little as the voice at the other end continued. After several minutes, Exner replaced the instrument to its cradle.

"That was Culp. Wheels are up on Yang's plane. He's on his way to Guantanamo."

"Good riddance," Travers said.

"*IF* he in fact gets there," Bindhira said dubiously. "He is a very wily operative. I will not be convinced until I hear he has been so incarcerated."

"Yeah, I second that motion," Travers said.

"Not our concern at this point, kids," Exner said. "New problem."

"We're all ears," Lee said.

"CIA moles operating within high levels of both the Chinese and Cuban governments have uncovered disturbing news," Exner began. "From their end, it appears that this whole Establishment thing has been a scapegoat concocted by the Chinese government to exonerate them and the Cubans of their complicity in the plot."

The others in the room listened with rapt attention as Exner continued. "Establishment operatives meanwhile have been setting up the Chinese by ensuring all the containers have Mandarin labeling on them to lead investigators into believing that the People's Republic of China are the perpetrators."

"If Project Vector is compromised, which it now is, both the Chinese and Cuban governments are prepared to recall their operatives, try them as 'traitors,' then turn them over to firing squads before their stories can be told."

"That's a fine kettle of fish," Travers blurted out. "Each is pointing the finger at the other."

Lee took out the metal flask hooked to the belt under his shirt and downed a swig of salad dressing.

"So where do we stand in the midst of all this, Alan?" Bindhira's mind raced to formulate a revised 'big picture' of the situation.

"First things first," Exner replied. "Coast guard dive teams have located all but two of the viral containers in shipwrecks in the Great Lakes, as we were led to believe. If the intel we have remains solid, that two boxes were placed on two wrecks in each of the five Great Lakes, then we still have a live one in Lake Ontario here and another somewhere in a Lake Michigan wreck."

"Smart," Lee said. "Satellites can't see what's below the waves, and the containers are concealed inside wrecks in the inland waters of the Great Lakes where submarines don't operate. Plus the special brass alloy the containers are made of does not allow conventional metal detecting devices to pick it up.

"The official stance of the United States government is one of aggressive nonaggression," Exner said. but there is undeniable intel that the Soviets are also tooling up once again for another kick at the global can," Add the Chinese, the North Koreans, and the Iranians into the mix, all with nuclear capabilities and all with similar aspirations, and you can readily see that these are once again desperate times."

"The president has televised his position and drawn the line in the sand. It's a position he means to enforce."

"One of his close aides remarked to Culp recently that this global terrorism shit will no longer be tolerated in the free world," Exner said. "The stance of the United States government will soon be that the 'rights of the people' and freedom as we know it will be subjugated for the sake of 'heightened national security in the face of worldwide terrorism'."

"And that will become the stance of all the governments of the free world," Bindhira said. "The mega corporations, the ones *really* pulling the strings of the major democracies of the world, are very close to drawing them into a singular world government, and they cannot have freelance rogues running around trying to conquer the world in their own way."

"Not good," Travers remarked.

Bindhira continued. "If—I should say *when*—these mega corporations successfully deceive the world populace to the point of embracing a world government, then those in corporate power stand to make not millions, but *trillions* of dollars, all legal, tax and tariff-free."

Exner further expounded on Bindhira's train of thought. "Initially, citizens will be thrown a few bones so they will accept such a global pact. But soon thereafter the real agenda will be revealed, and definitely not one in the public interest."

"The major news networks, run by very powerful people with very different agendas than you or me, will do their best to convince the general populace that a global government will be the answer to eradicating poverty, reducing greenhouse gas or—fill in the blank; *anything* to dupe the masses into peacefully accepting a blanket world government scheme."

Lee grabbed his flask. He guzzled its remaining contents. Although not a drinking man, Lee wished this time that it contained rum instead of Newman's salad dressing.

"Here's another 'coincidence,'" Exner went on. "Countries have been accepting new immigrants since their inception; no biggie there.

And that's all good; people deserve a new start, especially if they've been repressed or live in fear of their lives.

Exner continued. "However, within the past decade, immigration into western countries has increased exponentially, to the point that Australia has closed its borders, and now for the first time in the history of the country, England has more foreigners than domestics. In a few short years, foreign interests will totally, legally, and peacefully infiltrate our governments at great cost to us and all the things we hold dear."

"The terms *political correctness* and *discrimination* were invented to shame us into accepting foreign interests into our countries, which will soon relieve us of our very way of life. Our health, education, and welfare rolls are already burgeoning to the point that public healthcare plans and government pensions will not be able to keep up."

"It doesn't take a rocket scientist to see the result of their experiment with the European Union. Many countries that jumped in with both feet and gave up their own independent currencies became bankrupt and had to be 'bailed out.'

Exner was on a roll. Aside from Bindhira, neither Lee nor Travers had any idea that these things were part of an elaborate plan on the part of the big corporations to foist a unilateral world government on the peoples of the world.

"And what about the ever-increasing 'sudden' global stock market collapses and massive 'downsizings' that have affected nearly every working man? Again: cleverly orchestrated. Some of the less intelligent orchestrators have been exposed and thrown to the dogs as scapegoats."

"Some of the earlier 'financial crises' were experiments by the global movers and shakers to monitor the reactions of world markets and populations to see just how far they can push. Once they've their scheme is perfected however . . ."

"Here's another point to ponder," Exner continued, "why is it that all our jobs have gone to China? Answer, it's cheaper. Corporations no longer have to shell out for emissions control, union payoffs, employee safety, high wages, benefits, pensions, or having to constantly conform to government regulations. And that's just for starters."

"So the mega corporations have given China most of our industrial jobs," Exner continued. "Nearly everything we buy now comes from China. China is a world nuclear power. And now China is subversively taking steps to bring North America to a complete standstill. If that happens, stocks will fall the world over, the global economy will crash, and the stage will be set for a world government, run by the Chinese."

"Rank-and-file citizens have gradually witnessed an erosion of their way of life for years. After 9/11 though, how many times have you heard it said, 'Sure, I'd give up some of my freedoms for increased safety, who wouldn't?'" Exner paused at the thought of such naiveté. "Well, be careful what you wish for."

This triggered a nerve in Travers. "Ex, do you think the planes that crashed into the twin towers in 2001 were masterminded by Islamic terrorists?"

"Never believe *anything* you see and only *half* of what you hear buddy," Lee said. "If we're told enough times that something is true, even if it isn't, we eventually come to believe it, especially if the information comes from 'reliable official sources.'"

"Should a world government form," Bindhira said picking up on Exner's train of thought, "no one anywhere, except those in power and their cronies of course, will have any rights or freedoms at all."

"The Romans were the last to enjoy total world control, and you see how well that went," Exner said.

"Hitler's plan for a 1000 year reign of the Third Reich barely got off the ground. His idea will eventually fly, but through 'diplomacy', not through guns and tanks," Bindhira said.

The room fell silent for a time, then Lee spoke up. "The Bible predicted hundreds of years ago that Rome would be the last of the world empires until a *final* world government would rise up in the distant future. This world government will herald in the most horrific era in the history of human existence—not a good thing."

No one dared speak. Politics and religion do not a combination make. A respectful silence pervaded the office.

"But the Chinese government does not want that," the NSA analyst said. "The Chinese government wants to be king of the castle. Once Project Vector enters phase two, the Chinese will 'discover' an antidote that only they control, and which will ensure total world dominance. This will be the time they say 'good-bye' to their Cuban comrades."

"We have a chance," Exner said zealously, "right here, right now, to stave off mass hysteria and death *if* we can round up the rest of those damned containers *before* they're released; not that I'm putting pressure on anyone," Exner concluded wryly.

"Is this the point where I should be worried?" Travers looked into everyone's faces questioningly.

88

A Chink In The Armor

A pin falling to the floor would have been deafening in Alan Exner's office.

"There still remains the Ebola 'epidemic' currently going down in Jamaica," Exner said, "which was directly initiated by a certain pair of NABS consultants we sent to Cuba."

"We had no idea, Alan," Lee said soberly.

"Not your fault, and not on record," Control said. "Had this not occurred, we would never have had the chance to observe and develop a strategy against it," Exner said. "The concern here is that the Chinese have duped the Cubans into finalizing the 'perfect plague' for them. In unsurprisingly back-stabbing fashion, the Chinese plan to unleash its full fury into Cuba as well once they've brought North America to her knees."

"That would make sense," Bindhira said. "Cuban scientists are the only others who are savvy to the Ebola derivative; how it is manufactured, how it is disseminated, and how the trail leads directly to the Chinese."

"This is really starting to get scary," Travers said with growing concern.

Just then there was a knock on the doorframe as Dr. Charity Nelson peered around the corner. At Exner's beckoning, she entered the room. Charity closed the door behind her. Travers, Lee, and Bindhira came around behind control, who was standing at the front corner of his desk.

"I have just received the tox results from the Jamaican outbreak," Dr. Nelson said. "This Ebola variant appears unstable, and has very limited properties inherent within its biological composition at the cellular level."

"In English please, Dr. Nelson," Exner said, a faint smile crossing his lips.

Dr. Nelson returned the smile. "In essence, the Ebola virus, although dangerous to humans, has no effect on either insect or animal life. Not a real showstopper there, as mutations between species is uncommon."

"However, what *is* newsworthy is that although the virus that found its way to Jamaica appears to have the inherent properties to replicate exponentially, its DNA is flawed." In a word, Chinese virologists screwed up. It seems they were in too big a hurry to get this off and running. Although the virus has definite potential to massively replicate itself, it falls short of the goal."

She paused as if she didn't want to continue. "I sincerely hope that the Ebola packets contained within that gym bag haven't been unleashed. If humankind is exposed to the finalized variant, it'll be the deadliest plague mankind has ever seen."

"What are you saying, Dr. Nelson?" Travers asked.

Looking at everyone's blank faces, she explained. "Okay." Charity took a deep breath then continued. "This pathogen has the ability to mutate between species. Insects infected with this Ebola variant land on and inject or bite humans. Humans get infected. Humans die. That's bad."

"With a capital B," Travers interjected.

"What's really bad," Charity said, "is that not only do infected insects not die prematurely from the virus they carry, their offspring will *also* continue to propagate the full potency of the parent viral pathogen. The virus deeply imbeds itself within the cellular structure of its host's DNA and *becomes* a component of the host insect's reproductive system."

Silence pervaded the office for several moments as everyone within was left to reflect on the ramifications of the insidious man-made virus.

Lee was the first to break in. "So what you're saying is North America and wherever else this stuff is released will become devoid of all human life: the ultimate perpetual weapon of destruction at its diabolical best."

"That will make a very bad day for everyone," Travers said with a squinty eye.

"I can't believe even the Chinese would unleash something *that* devastating," said Exner. "What could they possibly hope to get out of killing nearly every man, woman, and child on our continent?"

Charity spoke. "It is the collective assumption of my fellow virologists that even the Chinese haven't realized the true ramifications of what they've achieved here."

"Surely there must be *something* you can do," Bindhira said, looking optimistically to the doctor.

"There may be," Dr. Nelson said. "The viral agent under compression is very weak, very fragile, until its pressure is relieved, and that's its Achilles heel. It came somewhat as a surprise to us that the Ebola outbreak in Jamaica eventually weakened. Initially we did not think this possible."

"That's a good thing, right?" Travers seemed lost in the explanation.

"Well, for it to become totally virulent, it must mature under pressure, water being the ideal facilitator due to its abundance. But Jamaica had a massive rain the past few days. Once the rain abated, new cases of Ebola markedly decreased."

"Water giveth, and water taketh away," Lee remarked.

"Exactly," Dr. Nelson said. "As powerful an agent as this is, the strain's 'kryptonite' is water. But not just water: Jamaican rainwater. The air over Jamaica is not only laden with salt from the seawater, but also microscopic coral dust from the coral that naturally surrounds the island."

"The unique pH of the moisture in the Jamaican air along with the coral dust it carries is acted upon by the ultraviolet rays of the sun. This acts as a natural catalyst with the fresh rainwater to break the virus down at a cellular level."

"Great. All we need to do is import thousands of tons of Jamaican rainwater to the Great Lakes region and we're good to go," Travers remarked.

"As strong as this particular pathogen is," Dr. Nelson said, "we *also*, and quite by accident, discovered that if it is either *rapidly* depressurized, or subjected to a sudden explosion, the agent will readily break down to a point of impotence."

"Well done, doctor. I think you've earned your pay this week," Exner exclaimed, excited at the prospect. "Charity, I knew you could do it! This is the backdoor we've been looking for."

"So," Lee said, picking up the thread, "basically what the good doctor is saying is that if we shoot this stuff to the surface at a greatly accelerated rate we can kill it by giving it an embolism."

"At the cellular level, that would be correct," Dr. Nelson said, rather impressed. "In layman's terms, that actually sums it up perfectly."

"Right then." Exner decided to put everything into perspective. "From the information we currently have, the following seems to be our current status."

"*One*. We are now well aware of Project Vector and its convoluted history, projected dissemination, and ramifications of release."

"*Two*. We have discovered that the Establishment is now being used as a scapegoat behind which the Chinese and Cuban governments are attempting to paralyze North America. But the reality is that the Establishment has already beaten them to the punch. They have seized the initiative and have already disseminated the virus. Once they go live with it, they'll let the world put the blame on the Chinese. At present we have largely foiled their plans, but the question remains as to whether there are other containers still out there that we don't know about."

"*Three*. We've successfully cracked the Establishment's primary cell, and have uncovered the identity of its two ringleaders. One has been removed from the playing board, with the other still missing and presumed dead."

"*Four*. So far divers have managed to recover eight of the ten boxes, with two more at large; one somewhere in Lake Ontario and one somewhere in Lake Michigan."

"*Five*. Through an unwitting and unfortunate release of the virus that drifted from Cuba over to Jamaica, our virologists have managed to uncover a means of rendering impotent, a viral agent heretofore believed to be perpetually virulent and indestructible."

"*Six*. At present we have no definitive confirmation that Alberto Cabrera, a Cuban DGI control and Establishment mastermind, was killed in a helicopter crash. If he somehow managed to survive, he may still have a 'final solution' in the workings we are not currently aware of."

"*Seven*. Although we have both 'footballs,' we've been unsuccessful so far at decrypting the codes needed to remotely disable the remaining Ebola containers."

"Eight. We now have a shot at neutralizing this damn Ebola variant to the point of eliminating it completely. This is where we must concentrate our efforts: seek-procure-destroy." Exner paused, "Any comments, questions, or clarifications?"

"*Nine*." Lee added. "Who is our mystery child, and how and why did she drop crucial pieces of the puzzle into our lap only to disappear?"

"And *ten*." Travers piped up, "I'd like to know the answer to that one myself. If it wasn't for that kid I wouldn't be here now."

89

A Not-So-Bad Day

Alberto Cabrera stumbled in the dark toward his goal. Wiping a warm sticky substance from above his left eye, he felt along the rough stone walls with bloodied fingertips to find his way safely back to the secret entrance of the Singing Woods clubhouse.

He cursed audibly in the inky darkness at both his bad luck and this strange turn of events. *How could a child; a miscreant little nose-miner, get the better of me?* Then a second thought entered his head: Another *wrinkle.* The implications of that word seemed to be a curse on him, thanks to Wu Yang!

In what seemed like an inordinate amount of time, the Cuban spymaster finally reached the last bend in the passageway that now led straight to the secret entrance to the clubhouse. He hastened his step along the wall, ever careful not to trip over anything else in his path.

Reaching the rear of the wine rack that lead to the basement, he listened cautiously for sounds of activity on the other side. Nothing.

Cautiously he slid the wine rack to the side. Its tiny wheels groaned in protest, but he managed to get through. He could hear voices upstairs, but none in the immediate vicinity. Ever so quietly, Alberto crept up the well-worn wooden steps leading to the first level. He rubbed an itch over his left eye. A small crusty patch of blood fell from his face, which caused his wound to bleed again, although not profusely.

Alberto noticed a pair of old coveralls and well-worn ball hat that sported the logo of the Singing Woods golf course hanging on the wall by the rear door of the kitchen. He stripped to his underwear and donned them. They were a size too big for the fit Cuban. He next bent down and wiped the floor with his sweat-soaked shirt.

Wiping his face with it, dirt caked over his features as he hoped it would. Then he rubbed his hands on it. *There,* he thought. *Instant gardener.* Taking his clothes back to the wine rack, he slid it open, tossed them into the darkness, and then slid it back into position.

Cautiously he retraced his steps and opened the door to the kitchen. With no one in sight or earshot, he wasted no time exiting the rear entrance of the building. Alberto was careful to walk slowly and methodically. Although there were several trees and statues on the grounds he could use for cover, he was too professional to make an obvious run for it. Sure enough, two men in suits and armed with Uzi submachine guns ran up to him from his left quarter. As he turned to face them, he slowly pulled the hat lower over his brow.

"Where the hell do you think you're going?" one of the agents challenged him. A second agent frisked him roughly.

Alberto quietly and patiently allowed this, and then responded. "*Yo no hablo Ingles, amigos; jardinaro*—gar-den-er," he lied.

The two men eyed him suspiciously. Dirty, disheveled, and wearing oversized clothes, it appeared to them that this man was who he claimed to be.

"That cut over your eye; how'd you get it?" The first agent tapped above Alberto's left eye with the muzzle of his Uzi.

Playing the dumb immigrant routine, Alberto stupidly reached up and felt his brow. Slowly, deliberately, Alberto said, "*Rosal, señors,* rose *boosh.*" He was careful to act scared around their weapons. But he knew he couldn't play this dumb act much longer. Anger welled up within him. He wanted to take them out as quickly and as painfully as he could, but he restrained his temper. Anger caused mistakes, and he couldn't afford to draw any further attention to himself.

The agents stared into Alberto's face in an effort to read him. Alberto stupidly pointed to a small gardening shed at the rear corner of the over-manicured property. The agents looked to each other and then smiled condescendingly at him. One of them waved him on with his Uzi. As Alberto started on his way, the other man kicked him in the rear, which knocked him to the ground.

Alberto lay face down as though dead, palms on the ground in a push-up position, and remained there. The two men holstered their weapons to help him up. With lightning ferocity, Alberto spun around low with his right foot, knocking both feet out from under the surprised agent to his left. Continuing the motion, he then came up facing the second agent to his right and head-butted him deep in the stomach before he could draw his weapon. This knocked the wind out of him. Alberto, still in motion, then stomped hard onto the face of the man behind him as he attempted to get up to acquire a firing position.

Grabbing the downed man's Uzi, which had fallen to the ground beside him, Alberto tossed it into the air, grabbed it by the muzzle, and then hit a home run on the face of the bent-over man with the butt end of the weapon.

Both agents lay groaning on the ground before him. Looking to the clubhouse, Alberto was amazed that no one had rushed to their assistance. He lay the weapon down beside him and went over to each man in turn. As he did so, he smiled into their horrified faces then broke each of their necks in turn with a violent neck snap.

He then ran for the cover of the woodland, hoping against hope that only a two-man detail had been assigned to the rear of the clubhouse. *This turned into a not-so-bad day after all*, he thought as he disappeared into the woods.

90

But Wait; There's More . . .

"All ten boxes have now been located and rendered harmless," Exner reported, with a huge sigh of relief to a very tired group of agents, including Lee, Travers, Bindhira, and Dr. Nelson. An emergency meeting had been held at the NABS situation room to update all operatives on the case and to determine their next course of action.

"Both the prime minister and the president are breathing much easier as we speak," Exner continued. "As expected, both the Chinese and Cuban governments have expressed righteous indignation at our accusations, and are demanding proof of their complicity in this fiasco. Aside from the Chinese stamp on the containers, we have none.

"So it would appear that both Wu Yang and Alberto Carbrera *were* acting on their own behalf," Bindhira deduced, "and that the Establishment has no affiliation to those governments."

"Another wrench has just been thrown into the mix," Exner said. "Two Homeland Security agents were recently found dead behind the clubhouse of the Singing Woods. No witnesses came forth, and no one untoward was discovered on the premises."

"How were they killed Alan," Bindhira asked, obvious concern in her voice.

"Necks broken, both in the same fashion," Exner replied.

"Sounds like the work of one individual Ex," Lee said.

"True that. There's a search party deployed there searching the surrounding woodlands, but I doubt they'll find much," Exner said.

"Is that form of execution not a trademark of DGI operatives, Alan?" Bindhira asked.

"Yes, but it's not like a 'go around and break necks to keep in shape' thing," Exner answered. "And in answer to the question Bill's going to ask, yes, Vaselino is still in custody. I just had it confirmed."

"How'd you know what I was going to say?" Travers asked, a perplexed look on his face.

"Wasn't that what you were going to ask?" Exner quizzed.

"Yeah, but . . ."

"Shut up then." Exner had him on the run and he loved it.

"There's another possibility," Lee said, bringing seriousness back to the table. Everyone in the room grabbed a chair or a desk corner to rest on.

"Go on," Exner said.

"Alberto," Lee said.

"Yeah, I bet that cagey bastard's still on the loose," Travers said with a squinty eye.

"A very real possibility and one that's being investigated," Exner said.

"Both Yang and Cabrera are highly trained intelligence agents for their respective governments. Why risk going rogue and incurring their collective wrath," Exner asked without expecting an answer.

Just then, a series of short double buzzes sounded on Exner's desk.

"It's for you," Travers said, and he reached across the desk from the corner he was sitting on, picked up the handset, and handed it over to Exner.

The top NABS operative quietly listened for several minutes. All eyes were on him, and everyone watched as the concerned look on his face grew.

"Right. Thanks Scott. Yes; will do." Exner walked over from the opposite corner on the desk and hung up the instrument. "Turns out Alberto wasn't in that 'copter crash. He somehow managed to get through CIA scramble channels and reached Culp himself. Culp said he sounded almost maniacal. He said he used a body double on board the helicopter to throw us off his scent, but that it didn't matter anymore." Bindhira could sense that control had more on his mind.

"What else, Alan?" Bindhira vocalized the question that had formed in the minds of the others in the room.

"It seems that the Establishment does have a contingency plan, Bindhi," Exner said. "Alberto told Culp that there's *another* wreck; one that even Vaselino apparently didn't know about. One that makes the others pale by comparison."

"Where, Ex: any idea where?" Lee looked to Travers, then back to Exner.

"None," Exner said, "other than it's concealed in an as yet undiscovered wreck located somewhere in Lake Huron."

"That cuts down a lot of mileage," Lee said, "But Huron's a big lake, and quite deep in spots."

"He may just be bluffing, but he doesn't come across as the bluffing kind," Exner said. "Alberto's boys have screwed up big time, and he's all too aware of it. From all appearances, I bet he wants to go out in a blaze of glory. He's determined to make his plan succeed and take us with him."

Dr. Nelson put one hand to her mouth while the other grabbed the side of her chair.

"Here we go again," Travers said. "How do we know for sure that this *is* the last one?"

"We don't," Exner replied, "but Culp said Alberto sounded desperate; on his last legs, out of options, tired of running."

"Next question," Lee said. "Where can we even *begin* an educated search?"

"All Alberto said, because he knew Culp would have a trace on him," Exner continued, "was that the final 'surprise' was 'tamperproof,' and located inside a most unique shipwreck, and that by week's end it would be all over for everyone."

"Geez," Travers groaned.

"There was nothing in either Yang's or Alberto's briefcases to indicate this," Lee recalled. "It may just be a red herring, Ex."

"Or not Lee," Exner said. "We've invested a lot of man hours and resources working around the clock to get as far as we have. Finding that last container should have been game, set, and match."

"Bill!" Lee blurted out. "That wreck you discovered a few weeks back. The one you believed was LaSalle's *Griffon*. It doesn't get more 'unique' than that!"

"Yeah, but no. *I'm* the only one who knows where it is," Travers said, a questioning pall of disappointment etched in his voice that someone else may have discovered it as well.

"Ex," Lee said, "from what Bill's told me about this wreck, it definitely sounds like it is indeed La Salle's long-lost *Griffon,* and it's practically in our backyard, though it's off Manitoulin Island in *Georgian Bay.*"

"If we operate on this premise," Lee continued, "it would only be because Alberto isn't up on his geography of the Great Lakes and that Georgian Bay is its own body of water, closely bordering Lake Huron."

"If you're right about this, Ex, Bill knows where the *Griffon* is, and I can't think of anything more 'unique' under those waters," Lee said encouragingly.

"That would make perfect sense Lee," Bindhira agreed. "It is a shipwreck that has eluded discovery for centuries. But be forever mindful that Alberto's deep obsession to bring this warped plan of his to fruition may well succeed if you are not correct on this."

"Ex; Bill and I are on our way," Lee said. "Our gear's still packed, just need to charge the tanks—"

"No time for that, Lee. I'll have one of my operatives escort you and Bill to the airstrip. The Learjet's still there. I'll have dive gear and a boat awaiting your arrival at South Baymouth, Manitoulin."

Looking in Travers's direction, Lee said, "Any objections?" Before his friend could answer, he continued. "Didn't think so."

"This may not be the cakewalk you think it is, Lee," Exner said. "Our keywords for today are: *tamperproof.* It may be booby trapped."

"We can do tamperproof," Lee said grimly. "You locate Alberto; we'll do tamper-proof."

"Godspeed, gentlemen," Exner said. Swiveling on his office chair, the NABS control then punched a button on his desk phone and began issuing orders.

As Lee and Travers headed to the door of Exner's office, Lee turned and pointed a finger at Exner. "Just make sure there's a case of Newman's parmesan and roasted garlic salad dressing awaiting my return. I get miserable without my fix."

91

The *Griffon*

The Learjet took Lee and Travers as far as the OPP helipad in Hamilton, where they were then whisked by waiting helicopter to the south of Manitoulin Island at South Baymouth.

The two managed a quick snack en route, once again compliments of 'Air OPP'. As usual, Exner had left no stone unturned. The helicopter contained all the underwater equipment the men would require for their mission and then some. Lee and Travers spent the rest of the flight going over their gear.

"Exner said this box may be booby-trapped in more ways than one Lee," Travers said nervously.

"The good news is, if Dr. Nelson is correct," Lee said, "and we handle the material as she instructed before we left, we should be able to do major damage to the virus while inflicting minor damage to a national underwater treasure."

They were met at the South Baymouth helipad by a Captain Alexander Reay of the Canadian Coast Guard. The captain had his men transfer the dive gear from the OPP helicopter to his ship, the CG2350, better known as the *Limnos.*

The *Limnos* was a 489-ton inland waters oceanographic research vessel that would provide excellent surface support to the dive team, complete with recently fitted Sequoia sat-com capabilities to ensure Culp and Exner would keep in the loop as developments unfolded, good or bad.

Fortunately the *Limnos* had already been in the area conducting core sample studies of the lake bed under Lake Huron to determine percentages of various types of pollution advancement within the immediate eco-environment.

Within two hours of the equipment transfer, the *Limnos* had arrived over the GPS coordinates Travers had provided the captain for the wreck believed to be the *Griffon.*

As Lee, Travers, and a coast guard diver suited up on the back deck of the research vessel, Captain Reay came up to them. “Big hit on the LORAN Lee,” the captain said. “Might be the hull of a wreck or it might simply be one of many underwater plateaus in the area. Whatever it is, it’s in eighty-two feet of water.”

“That’s our ship Lee!” Travers said euphorically. “I found the *Griffon* at eighty feet,” he said before stuffing the mouthpiece of his regulator into his mouth.

“We’ll follow your lead, Bill,” Lee said as he checked to ensure the Coast Guard diver’s air valve was fully turned on. “Remember; once we reach the ship I’ll take over. That ship could be booby-trapped, and we definitely can’t take any chances at this stage of the game.”

The water was numbingly cold. Travers led the way as they descended down the anchor line of the *Limnos.*

The men were using a hybrid mixture of breathing gases called nitrox. By reducing the partial pressure of nitrogen in the mix and increasing that of oxygen, the divers would have a slightly extended bottom time with a reduced risk of incurring the bends. The theory being that the body would absorb less nitrogen into the bloodstream with a higher partial pressure of oxygen in the mix. And unlike nitrogen, oxygen did not build up in the system, but was simply metabolized by the body.

At the forty-foot mark, Travers motioned the other divers to follow him and left the line.

At fifty-one feet, Lee thought they had hit bottom. Puzzled at Travers, who left them and was swimming around seemingly aimlessly, it wasn't long before Lee realized what he was doing. Swimming back to the other divers, Travers motioned for them to follow. Not far from their descent line, Lee was dumbfounded at the realization that what he had thought to be the lakebed was merely a massive limestone overhang. Travers descended through a cavernous hole in the false bottom of the limestone. Lee and the coast guard diver followed suit.

Descending another fifteen feet, there she lay! The cold, dark freshwaters of Georgian Bay had been good to the wreck of the fabled French ghost ship, the *Griffon.* The famous ship was considerably smaller and rougher hewn than Lee had envisioned, but then he recalled Bill's excited explanation when told he had discovered the ship.

The *Griffon* had been hastily constructed out of raw timber without the luxury of proper ship-building facilities or craftsmen from France. It was built in the wilds of Black Rock just outside of what is now Buffalo, New York, near the Niagara River.

The three switched on their underwater lights, then split up. Travers swam to the intact bow. The coast guard diver finned to the area of the sand-covered stern as planned. Lee swam into the center hold.

Sand had filled much of the inner part of the wreck. Lee could only imagine what a proper archeological expedition would uncover. For the time being, he was only concerned with a single brass box.

Even though the nitrox dive tables for a 28 percent oxygen enriched breathing mix allowed them a fifty-minute no-decompression window at eighty feet, it was agreed upon that due to the bone chilling cold of the water they would allow a safety margin and return to the surface after forty minutes to avoid a potential dose of the bends.

The *bends* was a term used to describe a debilitating and painful condition brought on by exceeding the safe time at depth as determined by the US Navy No Decompression Tables. Exceeding these limits usually resulted in too much dissolved nitrogen in the tissues of an unwary diver.

Should a diver remain at depth past his no-decompression limits, and allow nitrogen to further accumulate in his tissues then surface without proper decompression stops to off-load tissue saturation of the gas, the situation could lead to permanent paralysis and death without *immediate* treatment in a hyperbaric chamber.

Without treatment, a diver's blood would become frothy foam, much like shaking up a carbonated Pepsi bottle then suddenly popping the top and releasing its built-up pressure. Nitrogen that had accrued in a diver's system during a dive needed time to come out of his capillaries and into his lungs gradually for a safe ascent to the surface.

Lee wasn't about to let this happen. He knew the rules of physics as applied to diving, yet he had been bent before. Few commercial divers worth their salt had been untouched by the bends. *Once bent, twice shy*, the old divers' adage went. Many divers never got that second chance.

Finding nothing in the main hold, Lee realized they would need a sand dredge to properly clear the hold and uncover anything of value. But he also knew that the container they were looking for had to be somewhere more easily accessible. It was planted only days ago, not years.

Lee pulled himself clear of the hold. He shook his head at the coast guard diver as he swam up to him. The diver likewise shook his head that he too had found nothing around the ship's stern.

Lee swam along the length of the sturdy little ship until he reached the bow. He saw Travers' bubbles emanating through the cracks in the upper deck from inside the forward hold. Lee looked down at the remaining time on his computer. They'd already been down for twenty-five minutes—still time enough to continue their search.

Swimming directly off the bow, Lee turned to look at the ship head on from a distance of about ten feet. He hovered before the majestic figurehead. It was indeed a mythological griffon, part eagle and part lion.

Griffons were traditionally known for guarding treasure and priceless possessions. Many of its fine features had eroded with time, but Lee could still make out fine flecks of gold paint around its eagle's beak and between the cracks of its lion's toes.

Just then Travers came up beside him. Lee chided himself for being startled at his friend's sudden appearance. He saw the coast guard diver swimming along the hull toward them. Lee was engrossed in studying the figurehead. Travers tapped him on the shoulder, signaling that it was time to surface.

Lee nodded, then signaled Travers to alert the coast guard diver and for them to return to the anchor line and ascend. The coast guard diver nodded in understanding and left. But instead of surfacing himself, Travers finned his way back to Lee.

On seeing Travers return, Lee knew his friend wouldn't leave his side. Lee couldn't blame him; he'd have done the same. They hovered just above the figurehead for several moments in awe of the discovery.

Then two men then swam back over the point of the bow and turned to face the rear of the figurehead.

Lee noticed what appeared to be a small cover along the back of the figurehead. While wiggling the wood at this point, the lower portion of the griffon's back end suddenly popped off. Were it not for Lee's lightning reflexes, he would have dropped the heavy metal cylindrical object that fell into his hands. The silver canister was about two feet long and one foot in diameter.

Lee's fingers were numb from the frigid water temperature by this time, and he was increasingly aware that their no-decompression bottom time margin was swiftly eroding. Travers shone his light over the object. Lee slowly turned it over in his hands, and was startled to see a series of blinking digits displayed through a clear crystalline acrylic display.

The bright red digits displayed 00:31:54 in its countdown to zero.

92

When In Doubt . . .

The NABS divers were in a lose-lose situation. On the one hand, if they didn't surface immediately, they could face an excruciatingly painful bout of the bends. The nearest hyperbaric chamber was in Tobermory over two hours away; too far to be of any use should they require its services. On the other hand, this was not the brass box they had anticipated finding. Lee knew it was a bomb; a bomb with a pressure sensor. The device had been rigged to explode upon a decrease in water pressure.

Unable to adequately communicate with Travers, Lee wanted him to surface, save himself, and get the *Limnos* as far away as possible in less than the thirty minutes that remained on the device's timer. But Lee knew Bill Travers too well. He was never one to run from danger, and he was certainly not one for leaving his best friend to die alone underwater.

Lee had to think fast. No wonder they couldn't locate a brass container. There wasn't one. The device no doubt contained the deadly pathogen. It had probably been under pressure long enough for the catalyst to have been adequately cured.

Not only did he have the crew of the *Limnos* to think of, he could not stand to lose the *Griffon* after the fabled ship had just been located.

Lee saw Travers out of the corner of his eye. Travers knew better than to break Lee's concentration in times such as these, and Lee knew that Travers' life also lay in his hands. Whatever decision he made had to be the right one.

Fourteen minutes remained on the timer. Turning the unit over and over in his hands, Lee was unable to find an opening into the sealed acrylic cylinder of death. Even if he could find a way to open the unit, his fingers were fast becoming too thick and dead from the numbing exposure in the freezing water to do anything about it.

Twelve minutes. Travers requested to hold it. Delicately, Lee placed the cylinder into Bill's quarter-inch neoprene gloves whereupon Travers immediately proceeded to swim away.

What-the-hell?

Lee finned after him. Travers had pulled himself up and over the bow of the ship. As Lee came up and over himself, he watched Travers drop down along the bow of the ship to the hawsehole. Lee watched as his friend yanked free a small bar he must have seen previously that was hooked into a link of the anchor chain.

Lee continued to watch as Travers turned the cylinder over in his hands. Lee focused his powerful LED light on the object. Then to Lee's sudden horror and dismay, Travers bashed the object—several times!

Suddenly the casing gave way in a plume of bubbles. Amazingly, the LED readout on the cylinder's digital timer still displayed the time remaining. Nine minutes.

The numbers on the display were now flashing. This was no doubt a warning that the final ten minutes were counting down before the thing exploded.

Travers pointed excitedly at the cylinder, then handed it back to Lee. He carefully placed it into Lee's numbed hands.

Lee now saw the cause of Travers' excitement. Beneath the face plate of the digital readout panel was an assemblage of wires partially illuminated by the reflective glow of the LED numbers. Six minutes remained.

Lee knew that the black wire went to ground. But he had to be sure he pulled the right ones if he was to successfully render the device harmless!

He hated to think about it, but here was the proverbial good news and bad news situation. Good news: two wires had to be pulled to render the unit inoperable. Bad news: they had to be pulled *in proper sequence* without touching each other and without breaking the ground contact.

Despite the numbing cold, Lee was perspiring. *What to do?* Three minutes. Lee realized the cold had not only dulled his dexterity, it had also dulled his mind.

Travers drew closer and fidgeted with his hands. The display now read *three minutes*. The two exchanged fearful glances.

In an unexpected gesture, Travers yanked the cylinder out of Lee's hands. Despite the numbing temperature of the water, Travers had removed his bulky neoprene gloves. Lee watched in horror as he saw Travers pondering over the wires. *He has no training in explosive devices,* Lee gasped.

Before Lee had time to wrestle it back, Travers had pulled two wires in rapid succession. Lee held on to the rail, expecting the worst. It didn't come. Nothing did.

Lee pulled himself over to his buddy. The readout on the digital display held at forty-five seconds! *Ignorance truly was bliss,* Lee thought as he sternly shook his head and then patted his friend on the back.

Now it was Lee's turn to spring into action. As Travers looked on, Lee pulled the quick releases to the weight pouches on each side of his buoyancy compensator jacket. Twenty-eight pounds of formed lead rocketed to the deck of the *Griffon.* Next, he removed his jacket-tank assembly.

Wrapping up the acrylic cylinder as tightly as he could into the webbing of the personal inflation device, Lee then took one last drag of air from his regulator, and then inflated the unit until it tore from his grasp in an unstoppable madcap spiral to the surface.

Lee hoped against hope that the acrylic cylinder did indeed house the Ebola pathogen Alberto had bragged about, and that Dr. Nelson had been correct in her hypothesis that a sudden decrease in water pressure to the unit would render the virus impotent when released before the maturity date of the pressurized cylinder of doom.

Lee dropped to the bottom and collected his weight pouches to help hold him down as his rubber wet suit would expand upon surfacing which would drastically increase his buoyancy. Travers met Lee and quickly offered him the back-up regulator to his emergency pony bottle supply.

The two swam back to the anchor line of the *Limnos*, then began their slow ascent, unaware of what awaited them on the surface.

93

Bad Things Come In Threes

According to their computer readouts, the two Canadian divers had a five-minute mandatory stop at fifteen feet. Without Lee's air supply, Travers' pony bottle would only last a few minutes more, and they would then have to buddy breathe off Travers' primary unit.

Ascending slowly from eighty feet to assist in the decompression process, they finally reached the fifteen-foot mark. The weights Lee had carried with him to this point now proved too much for him to hang onto with his now frozen hands. They dropped to the bottom of the lake. This proved cause for serious concern.

At this depth, his one-quarter-inch neoprene wet suit was extremely buoyant. They struggled until Lee managed to wrap both arms and legs tight around the anchor line. He was thankful the line was taut. With the pony bottle now empty, there was only one regulator between them. Lee was glad to have Bill in his corner on this one.

Already past numb, the two looked to each other in the anticipatory fear that only one of them would survive this dive unscathed, and Lee knew it would eventually result in a fight to see who *stayed* behind.

The men shared Travers' main air supply by passing the single mouthpiece back and forth between them, taking only two slow breaths at a time, even though they both knew their wasn't enough air in Travers' tank for the both of them to complete their decompression obligations.

They were startled to see a dark shadow enter their right periphery. It was an unconscious diver floating back-first down past them! Lee immediately left his buddy, completely exhaling the only breath he now had in a bid to remain less buoyant to cover the thirty feet or so to where the diver continued his graceful descent toward the bottom.

Lee saw that it was the coast guard diver who had initially accompanied them. The man had been hit by a tight grouping of machine gun fire, obviously at close range. Stunned but in survival mode, Lee had no time to process any further thought on the matter.

His lungs cried out for air and he was rising back to the surface. Quickly, he grabbed the man's air hose swaying limply by his side, and stuffed its life-giving mouthpiece between his lips. Air, sweet life-giving air reached Lee's lungs. Within seconds Travers was by his side. He held the deceased diver as Lee quickly donned the man's buoyancy compensator, tank, and regulator. The weights in the vest enabled Lee to finally achieve trim at depth.

Astonishingly, there didn't seem to be any collateral damage to the buoyancy compensator from the shotgun blast. Travers looked to Lee and was about to let the man go, but Lee had the presence of mind to know the body would rocket to the surface and inflate to grotesque proportions on its way to the surface.

They pulled the body to the anchor line of the *Limnos.* With his friend's help, Lee managed to release the man's right arm from his wet suit. He then used the arm of the rubber suit to tie the man fast to the anchor line at the twenty-foot mark.

Travers understood Lee's actions. If they allowed the body to hit the surface without its weighted buoyancy compensator and tank, it would alert whoever killed the man that there were other divers in the water; if they didn't know *already*.

As they sank deeper and their time at depth had now increased, they would have to hold off at the fifteen-foot mark for an additional period of time. Each man could clearly see the bow of the *Limnos* from this depth. The ship was bobbing up and down in the water, and this concerned both divers. The ship was large, and significant swells could present a serious problem for safe extraction.

Of greater concern was the knowledge that the ship was under some type of attack, as evidenced by the dead diver. Without a hydraulic lift or inflatable Zodiac to scoop them out of the water, it would be next to impossible to gain access to the ship.

Further, they were unarmed. They had no intel on their enemy as to number, weaponry, or motive. Lee hoped that Captain Reay had the presence of mind not to reveal that he had additional divers in the water. This would give them an element of surprise, *if* they succeeded in gaining access to the ship.

Lee's thoughts turned to the immediate as Travers had now run out of air. Lee took turns sharing his mouthpiece. He was amazed that his buddy's air supply had lasted as long as it did under these bizarre circumstances. He was grateful that Bill was an expert diver, and like himself, was not only in good shape, but also knew the secrets of air conservation.

After what seemed like an eternity to the men who had to undergo a *seven*-minute decompression fulfillment due to their compromised mandatory deco stop, they watched as the digits on their individual dive computers clicked to zero, signifying their decompression obligations were fulfilled.

Swimming under the keel so as not to be spotted, the men hoped the ship's underwater cameras were not activated. Surfacing at the bow in the midst of growing swells, the two communicated as quietly as possible. But it seemed that every time one of them opened their mouth to speak, it was quickly filled with water. They decided to swim back to the stern to the hydraulic lift in the hope it was still lowered to surface level.

It wasn't, however, but they were able to rest momentarily by hanging onto a line suspended from the lift, which unfortunately was in its sailing position ten feet above.

Lee could neither see nor smell any evidence of an explosion having taken place. That was good. The Ebola canister must have contained only a small charge sufficient enough to blow the canister open and away from the figurehead. If Dr. Nelson was wrong and the device they sent hurling to the surface had released its deadly payload without effect, it would become very apparent when they boarded the *Limnos.* They headed back to the bow.

In spite of the task that lay before them, Lee focused for a moment on the coast guard diver. He was a good man, brave and competent. He had unwittingly saved Lee's life, and Lee made a mental note to honor his memory.

Reaching the bow of the ship, the two divers quickly devised a plan of action. Lee found a compact collapsible snorkel in the pocket of the dead man's buoyancy compensator. He snapped it onto his mask. Travers meanwhile had completely purged the air out of his buoyancy compensating unit, and sent the empty tank assembly sinking to the bottom. Meanwhile, Lee swam down and tied off his tank assembly about ten feet below the surface to the anchor line in the event they needed to get off the ship in a hurry.

Lee surface swam close to the starboard side of the vessel. Travers, in like manner, stayed close to the port side to see if a launch had been moored somewhere along the ship.

Staying as close to the side of the ship as he could without getting hammered into the cold orange-painted iron of the ship's hull by the pounding swells, Travers spotted a Zodiac halfway along. From his vantage point, he couldn't see inside its small cabin. The launch was large, black, and had twin 350 HP Evinrude engines. It bore no government markings, so he knew it wasn't coast guard issue. He slowly and cautiously made his way up to it.

Rounding the bow, Lee immediately spotted the Zodiac. He noticed a man on board beside the cabin. He watched as the man flicked a cigarette butt over the side. Hugging close to the waterline of the *Limnos*, Lee allowed the white caps to engulf him as they slammed against the ship's hull.

Bad things truly do come in threes, Lee thought as he grimly made his way slowly to the small craft.

94

"And This Just In . . ."

"The world news agencies have just gone public regarding the recent activities of the Chinese and Cuban governments in North America," Exner said to Bindhira as he punched a button on the dashboard of the TaZeR, ending his communiqué via Sequoia sat-com to CIA sub-director Scott Culp who had returned to his office in Langley, Virginia. "Very few of any credence accept the Establishment as the sole perpetrator of this scheme to devastate the governments and people of North America."

"How did they come to that conclusion, Alan?" Bindhira asked as she pulled a wisp of long black hair away from the side of her face.

"A week ago," Exner said, briefly looking over at Bindhira as he piloted the TaZeR toward the Peace Bridge in Fort Erie, "a woman purchased a supposedly 'clean' painting that Travers imported and had for sale at the Little Tub Gallery in Tobermory. As it happened, the woman, a recently landed immigrant from Spain, inadvertently dropped the picture, smashing the frame. What she picked up among the pieces of wood and canvas was an unencoded document with an official-looking letterhead from the Cuban Ministry of the Interior.

It was a damning directive that should not have left Cuba, much less been planted in a painting and exported out of the country. The document directly implicated the two countries in a 'biological experiment' that was to be secretly conducted in North America. Upon reading its contents, the purchaser promptly surrendered it to a Toronto police precinct, which in turn contacted CSIS."

"What was the subject matter of the material?" Bindhira asked.

Exner slowed the TaZeR to safely negotiate a sharp corner in the road, then punched a button on the console to lower the air conditioner setting in the vehicle. "The document listed a number of safe houses operatives would have at their disposal should their mission be compromised. False passports and details for extraction to Havana were also provided. But this was a directive that had not yet been approved, nor encoded to be sent to their operatives abroad."

"Did the directive also list addresses for these safe houses?" Bindhira pressed.

"I was getting to that." Exner smiled as he turned onto the Niagara Parkway. Bindhira was good at what she did and was always ahead of the game. He wished he had her on his team. "There are three such safe houses, Bindhi. One located in Erie, Pennsylvania, what we now know to be the Singing Woods, which as you know has been compromised. Another is located in Toronto. The RCMP have already uncovered this one, which is near a private airstrip."

"That's two down," Bindhira counted.

"The last refuge, and the one closest to us, is located somewhere in the Fort Erie area, no doubt due to its proximity to the international border crossing at the Peace Bridge."

"Which is why we are currently headed there," Bindhira deduced.

"Spot on, Ms. Shankar; spot-on."

95

Drama On The High Seas

Lee Hartley waited until Travers swam up to him. Through a series of hand signals, Lee quickly explained his intentions. Travers nodded his acknowledgement. It was dangerous, but as good as any under the circumstances.

Travers dived down under the Zodiac. He pulled out a heavy steel dive knife from its sheath, and using the stainless steel butt end of the tool, hammered three times at the stern-most end of the hull. Then he swam under to the bow and repeated his actions.

This startled the Oriental in the Zodiac. Emitting a quizzical expletive in Mandarin, he peered over the sides of the Zodiac, looked out over the water, then directed his gaze up at the *Limnos*' gunwale far above. He readied his submachine gun and headed to the stern to inspect the motors. They were shut down, yet perhaps something has worked its way loose, he reasoned, as the launch was constantly being battered by the swells into the larger vessel's hull.

Now hearing a similar thumping beneath the launch's bow, he nervously paced the short distance forward. Each time the man was lured from one end to the other, Travers managed to get a few deep breaths before ducking back under the water. The old diver had him going and he knew it. He swam back to the Zodiac's stern, which is the lowest point to the water level due to the weight of the motors. Once again he hammered, this time for all he was worth. He could hear the man clumping his way back to the Zodiac's stern.

Travers then swam under amidships and held fast. The rest was up to Lee.

Noticing the Zodiac's rear starboard corner dipping lower than normal, Lee swam to the opposite side. He knew the man was peering down into the water at that point.

Lee took a series of deep breaths, then pushed upward with all his might. He knew he couldn't affect the heavy boat too much, but it was just enough. The man lost his balance and fell into the water. Quickly Travers swam over and punched the surprised man in the solar plexus. The Chinese operative still held tenaciously to his weapon. Lee swam the short distance around the motor array to the other side of the stern. The man struggled with both the weight of his weapon and with keeping his head above water.

In a surprise move Lee snatched the weapon out of the man's hands. Wrapping its shoulder webbing around the man's neck, Lee twisted the submachine gun from behind and allowed gravity to take them down. What little air the man had remaining in his lungs was quickly squeezed out. Lee had him in a tight neck lock, using the webbing as a noose. The man's wild gyrations in a vain attempt to free himself became less frequent, less intense.

He soon succumbed, and Lee left him to sink, the weight of the submachine gun quickly dragging the man to a bottom. Freed of his heavy scuba gear, Lee pulled himself up and into the Zodiac tired, frozen, and out of breath.

Travers remained in the cold water, numb as he was. The old diver kept a lookout above at the deck of the *Limnos* in case the boarders reappeared to make good their escape.

Meanwhile, Lee located the Zodiac's marine radio. Thankfully the boarding party had kept one on board, no doubt to monitor the coast guard frequency. Quickly he punched in the Ontario Provincial Police marine frequency. He dared not utilize the coast guard frequency in the likely event one of the terrorists had manned the *Limnos'* radio shack.

The OPP acknowledged Lee's transmission within seconds. He thought it odd how quickly they responded. They advised Lee that their ETA or estimated time of arrival at the GPS coordinates of the *Limnos* was fifteen minutes. The divers were ordered to stand down until their launch arrived.

Lee pulled Travers up and into the Zodiac and relayed the good news. He left out the part about standing down, however.

"Fire this thing up, Bill," Lee said as he ran to cast off the lines to the *Limnos.* "Keep her tight to the ship, and for heaven's sake, keep your head down!"

Before Travers could respond, Lee dived into the water in the direction of the ship's anchor line at the bow. When he reached it, he looked to Travers, who gave him the diver's OK signal, making a large O with his arms, meaning no action was observed on deck.

Though not as quick as he would've liked because he was so numb from the cold, Lee scaled up the anchor line. Pulling himself up as far as the hawsehole at the top of the chain, he wrapped his legs tight around it. A small knotted rope hung from the gunwale not far from the hawsehole through which the anchor line went.

After a few unsuccessful attempts at grabbing it, Lee finally managed to catch hold of the rope. Losing no time, he pulled himself up to just below the gunwale. Looking aft, he noticed a small group of men congregated amidships. No one noticed as Lee stealthily pulled himself up and over the railing, concealed by a huge capstan.

Quickly he ran back to the gunwale and peered down to the Zodiac below, shook his fist three times, then the OK sign. He knew Travers would now know that there were three militants visible and that everything was, as yet, OK. As Travers continued to look up at the bow, Lee displayed three fingers, then rotated his right index fingers several times. Then he disappeared.

Lee returned to his cover behind the capstan. He watched silently as three men armed with submachine guns conversed with Captain Reay. One of the men, apparently unhappy with Reay's response to a question, pushed the captain at the shoulders with both hands, whereupon he stumbled back and over a heavy coil of rope on the deck, which cushioned his fall in the process.

Lee quickly weighed his options. The captain was in immediate danger, and if the OPP were to suddenly arrive with a SWAT team, the men would crawl into the bowels of the ship and the police would have a devil of a time extracting them.

There'd be no doubt of a hostage scenario if he didn't do something. Lives would be lost. Lee also knew that these militants were desperate men. Should they fail in their mission, he knew they could never return home. They would be hunted down and liquidated mercilessly and without conscience.

Lee surveyed his immediate surroundings but could find nothing to use as a weapon. He unconsciously placed a hand on the white barrel-shaped automatic inflatable life raft shell to his left. Of course! Lee was crouched beside a military MK7 life raft. Unlike its commercial counterparts, Lee knew that this particular unit contained two cylinders, each holding 5,000 psi of compressed air.

The MK 7 life raft was normally actuated by a change in pressure sensed by a hydrostatic release device should the ship begin to sink. If triggered manually, the polyurethane shell would burst open, and the raft would fully inflate within thirty seconds in Arctic conditions, faster in warmer climes—the perfect diversion.

Looking aft, Lee saw that the captain had regained his feet. A militant stood to each side of him with one standing behind. Lee was afraid they were getting ready to enter the ship. He had to act fast. Locating the emergency actuator lanyard of the life raft, he gave it a stiff yank. Nothing.

Come on, Lee thought. He looked around past the capstan. In another few seconds Travers would fire up the Zodiac's motor and rev it up for all it was worth.

The men turned to head into the superstructure of the vessel. Lee grabbed the lanyard and pulled with everything he had. Almost simultaneously the Zodiac's twin motors revved up high then slowed down, revved up harder, and then slowed down again.

Instantly the thin polyurethane case housing the auto-inflatable raft exploded apart, sending Lee tumbling to the inside of the point at the bow. The raft hissed viciously as the air in its compressed gas cylinders bled out with incredible force, throwing it high into the air and over the side.

Lee recovered from his prone position at being knocked back in time to see the men peering over the gunwale. The sight and sound of the raft's shell exploding off the bow above and the motors of the Zodiac revving up below created the desired one-two punch Lee had hoped for.

One of the men turned in time to see Lee charging at them. But before any of them could bring their weapons to bear, Lee covered the remaining distance with a flying jump kick into the group. Two were knocked down. The third was met with a vicious elbow strike that all but shattered his jaw.

As the soldier started to fall backward, Lee grabbed the man's submachine gun by the barrel. With a circular yank of the weapon's shoulder strap, Lee pulled it free of his grasp. The momentum spun the man into the other two as they struggled to get into a position to fire their weapons.

The first man down recovered and nearly got a bead on Lee, but he managed to get a five-shot burst off first. The man was thrown back and to the deck, a deep crimson fluid oozing from several large holes in his chest and pooling around his body.

By this time Captain Reay had managed to throw a haymaker into the other man's face as he struggled to get up and around the first man who had fallen over him.

"The bastards shot my diver," Captain Reay said, holding a machine pistol on the two soldiers. "Jim had surfaced near their Zodiac. They had a man on their boat. He noticed Jim's bubbles right away and ordered him to get in. When the guy bent down to pull him in with one hand, Jim made a move to knock the gun out of his other hand. He didn't have a chance. Half in and half out of the inflatable in full gear, the man just shot him."

"I know Captain, I know," Lee said, putting a hand on the man's shoulder. "We found the body and tied an arm of his wet suit to your anchor line to hold him for now." Lee reached down and grabbed the other machine pistol.

"Thank you for that Lee," Captain Reay said.

A faint sound was heard in the sky, growing in intensity as it drew increasingly nearer. Captain Reay and Lee watched as a helicopter approached. The deck was awash with the heavy downdraft of the craft's rotors as it gently touched down on the stern helipad deck.

Travers shut the motors to the Zodiac down and hit the deck as he saw the approaching chopper. For reasons unknown, he rolled under a soiled, heavy canvas tarp. He hoped this would also help warm him up.

Back on board the *Limnos*, Captain Reay and Lee watched, fully expecting at least four heavily armed OPP SWAT officers to charge out of the helicopter, guns at the ready. But they weren't and they didn't.

To their collective surprise, an unarmed man in a loosely fitting suit emerged. He smiled at them, then turned back to the helicopter. The man assisted a middle-aged woman as she dropped down to the deck. The woman had long black hair and wore a knee-length army green skirt with a wide black leather belt and a plain beige blouse. Her shoes were flat black pumps.

The coast guard captain and Lee Hartley looked to each other questioningly. The differing thought processes of each man computed basically the same result: *as if this day hasn't been bad enough.*

The scene turned dramatically grim as two men jumped out of the chopper behind her, clad in green camouflage and fully decked out in assault gear, complete with submachine guns pointed in their direction.

Lee lowered his weapon then looked back at the subdued soldiers behind him. One tried to pull Lee down at the ankle. Lee stomped the man square in the face, knocking him out. This went unnoticed by the approaching party as they couldn't see the men who lay off to the side and out of their immediate sight.

The two soldiers swiftly positioned themselves: one in front and one behind the captain and Lee. Everyone stood silently in place until the man and woman came within speaking distance.

"*Señors*, please to toss your weapons down in front of you," the man in the suit said. Lee and Captain Reay had no recourse but to comply. Lee was careful to keep between the men at his feet and the guns they had tossed to the deck.

"*Gracias*," the man said pleasantly, and then continued in his suave nonchalant manner. "*Señors*; allow me to introduce Major Torrado of the Third Armored Division of the Cuban Revolutionary Armed Forces," the man in the suit said.

"Yes, the major and I have met before," Lee stated in a monotone, no fear in his voice.

The major stared evilly at the Canadian, but remained strangely silent.

"What the devil's going on here?" Captain Reay interjected. Lee saw that the captain was both perplexed and livid at this brazen act of piracy aboard his ship.

The man in the suit continued. "Permit me to introduce myself *señors*. I am Eladio Fuentes, a superior with the Cuban Ministry of the Interior."

"Translation, Captain; he's a Cuban Intelligence agent," Lee whispered.

"You're trespassing on a sovereign Canadian government vessel," Captain Reay said, looking uneasily at the armed men. "You are to leave this ship at once."

At seeing the men lying at Lee's feet, Fuentes barked to him, "Step away from those men and be quick about it!"

The two men struggled to their feet. One of them picked up the machine gun Lee had used and meekly followed the other man, who came to stand behind Fuentes.

"*Capitán*," Major Torrado said turning to Reay without acknowledging the two militants that had failed in their duties. "Your radio operator has been led to believe that he received a CSIS communiqué ordering your men to remain within the vessel and not to interfere with a 'secret transfer' about to occur on deck."

"The orders came from our operatives, of course, but unlike us, your radio operator has no knowledge of CSIS security protocol. She looked from Lee to Captain Reay, then sighed. "We are here for only one man gentlemen, the man Alberto Cabrera. Where would we find him?"

"How you managed to approach this vessel undetected is more to thc point, Major," Captain Reay said.

"Nothing is as it seems, *Capitán*. The message you sent to your Ontario Provincial Police was jammed and intercepted. It never reached its intended destination. You and your crew are quite alone," Major Torrado said as she walked slowly around the two men. "Ah, *Señor* Hartley. You've caused us irreparable harm, you and that old fool," the major said. "He is dead, no?"

Yeah, where is the old fool, anyway? Lee thought. "Naw, he's just sitting this one out, lady," he lied.

She stared at him for several moments before she continued. “Be that as it may, we are here for Cabrera. He is to be returned to Cuba on charges of insubordination, dereliction of duty, and treason. But you will also accompany us, *si, Señor* Hartley?”

Lee ignored her question. “More to the point, major, is that Alberto screwed up the crazy-ass plans your people and the Chinese cooked up.” Lee paused for dramatic effect. “You Cubans always seem to pick the wrong friends don’t you?”

At this, the major reached out and slapped Lee smartly on the side of his face. Blind rage filled the diver, and it took every ounce of willpower to restrain himself. The machine guns aimed at his chest convinced him that he had made the right choice.

“You will not talk to the major in this manner!” Fuentes said. “If you were in Cuba you would have been shot for this outburst!”

“Nothing changes for your countrymen, does it Fuentes,” Lee said rubbing his face. “How the devil can you still be enamored with a man who has repressed your people’s freedom and raped your resources for personal gain for over half a century?”

“Enough!” Major Torrado said emphatically.

“We must have Cabrera,” Fuentes said. “I assure you no harm will come to you.”

“Whatever,” Lee said. “Alberto eluded us at his compound in Pennsylvania. ”

“I don’t know of any man called Alberto,” the captain said truthfully.

“I can vouch for the captain, Major,” Lee said. “NABS is looking for the man as well. They want him just as bad as you do.”

“*No one* wants this man more than I!” the major hissed. “He and his Establishment have put me in a very vulnerable spot with my government.”

"Well I can't help you, Major," Captain Reay said emphatically. "He's not on my ship!"

Travers meanwhile, had managed to pull himself up to the bow of the *Limnos,* as Lee had done. He rolled up and over the gunwale and hid under a tarp where the raft had been stored. He had no plans to intervene, but steeled himself to help Lee when the time came.

At the right time he planned to yell to Lee, then lower himself back down to the Zodiac and fire up the motors to effect a hasty escape, *if* the interlopers didn't ventilate it beforehand with machine gun fire first.

To both Lee and Travers' horror, the major said to one of her soldiers in English, "There is a rubber dingy on the side of this ship that needs a few holes in it." She nodded in its direction.

The obedient soldier walked to the bow of the ship and peered over. Out of the corner of his eye, he was surprised by the quick flapping of the heavy tarp at his side as Travers rolled out from underneath and bowled the man down.

The soldier cried out in surprise. The man standing at Fuentes' side raised his weapon and would have run over to assist his comrade had Major Torrado not restrained him by the shoulder. "NO!" she said. "These things have a way of sorting themselves out." She smiled evilly.

Travers was no match for the highly trained Cuban commando. The man easily managed to break out of the pin that Travers had struggled to apply. He jumped up and struck Travers with the butt of his machine gun. The old Canadian went down with a moan.

The soldier looked down at him for a moment. Seeing that the fight had gone out of him, the man calmly walked over to the gunwale and fired several short bursts into the Zodiac below. Within minutes the rubber boat was dragged to the bottom of the lake as the weight of the twin stern motors won the battle over the now empty air cells of the deflated craft.

The commando then returned to Travers. Slinging his machine gun over a shoulder, he pulled Travers up by one hand and slapped him on the face with the other to bring him to. Pushing the Canadian ahead of him, the soldier walked back to the waiting parties.

"Thank you Sergeant," Fuentes said. Turning to Lee and Captain Reay, he said, "Sergeant Gomez is an expert in, how you say, the mixed martial arts?" He looked to the sergeant and smiled. The sergeant smiled back like a Cheshire cat. "Had the old man got the better of him, I would have shot the sergeant with his own weapon before killing your friend."

The smiled immediately drained from the sergeant's face.

"So your friend was just 'sitting this one out' was he, *Señor* Hartley," Major Torrado asked. "I have a mind to kill you both right where you stand! However, you two will serve me better as insurance to safely leave your country with Carbrera in our custody!"

"I say again major," Lee reiterated, "Carbrera's not aboard this ship, and none of us know where the man is."

"I will quickly get his whereabouts from one of you or the other *señor*," Fuentes said fiercely. His face turned red and his eyes bulged.

This guy's a psychopath, Lee thought, then said calmly, "To save you some work Fuentes, you can hammer us until the cows come home. But no matter what you do to us, Alberto still isn't aboard, and we still can't tell you anything," Lee then increased his volume and tone, "*because we don't know*!"

Lee could see that Fuentes wanted to break them. But he was given a stern look by Major Torrado. It was clear who was in charge here.

"If the authorities here have not found him, Eladio," Major Torrado said, "my guess is Alberto will make his way to one of our safe houses here."

She thought for a moment, then said, "My guess is the neutral safe house. Even Carbrera wouldn't be stupid enough to go to the one in Toronto. Canadian agents may be aware of its existence."

The major turned and barked orders to her men in Spanish. Soldiers grabbed Lee and Travers tersely by the arms as the major said, "*Capitán* Reay, I thank you for your most gracious hospitality."

Nodding to Fuentes, the man became a blur. In a nanosecond, the man produced a large switchblade and shoved it deep under the captain's ribs. The sadistic Cuban then pulled the captain up to face level by the knife still embedded in his side until their faces almost touched. Fuentes smiled amicably at him, then shoved him down to the deck by the hilt of the knife.

Fuentes then bent down and wiped the blade off with the captain's own coat sleeve before retracting and replacing the weapon. The captain dropped to the ground in extreme pain, blood immediately issuing from beneath his coat. Looking over to Major Torrado, he smiled. Interestingly, Lee noticed that she didn't smile back.

The armed men forced the divers toward the helicopter. Spotting a fire alarm pull station just before the open area leading to the stern heliport deck, Lee suddenly broke rank and pulled it. The deck of the *Limnos* immediately became awash in a piercing series of successive air horn blasts.

Lee was knocked to the ground, kicked, and then grabbed by two men who tossed him roughly into the helicopter bay. They hopped in, followed by Travers, then the others.

By the time confused crewmembers poured out onto the deck from a side hatch, the helicopter had already lifted off and pulled away.

Some crewmembers watched quizzically as it disappeared into the evening sky, while others tended to their seriously wounded captain, who lay bleeding and unconscious amidships.

96

Illegal Immigrants

Alberto was a fortunate man. He had managed to elude the government agents at the Singing Woods. He then escaped through the woods of the golf course in Erie, Pennsylvania, to a major highway. Finally, having concealed himself from unmarked vehicles potentially containing government agents as they passed him by, Alberto had the good fortune to flag down a Canadian trucker bound for Canada who agreed to take him as far as the border. A good-natured man, the rotund middle-aged happy-go-lucky trucker was grateful for the company.

Alberto found that he actually liked the man. The Cuban liked Canadians in general because they didn't have the senseless prejudices that had been bred into Americans. Canadian tourists had done much to bolster the Cuban economy, unlike the Americans who still enforced their draconian law making it illegal for its citizens to 'spend money', that is, to visit Cuba, since the early 1960s.

Those in the upper echelons of the Cuban government were actually glad of this. They didn't want corporate America infiltrating the country and setting up fast food franchises or big box chain stores on practically every major street corner like they had in North America.

The two had a pleasant conversation along the route to the Canadian border. Alberto was grateful for the trucker's affinity for country music that blared from the speakers of the tractor cab's satellite radio system. The odds of the driver tuning in to a news station were remote, thus the man would have no knowledge of current events, such as that his passenger was wanted by the authorities for acts of terrorism.

With each passing mile however, Alberto was increasingly concerned about how he would get back across the border from Buffalo, New York, into Canada at Fort Erie.

But he knew he had to get there. A Cuban safe house had still been maintained in the sleepy little Canadian border town. It hadn't been used for several months, but Alberto knew it was the only place left for him to go. The safe house had a sat-com concealed inside a bathroom wall which he could use to send a coded message to Establishment operatives to initiate their emergency evacuation protocol.

Alberto hoped their secondary helicopter was still functional or all would be lost. The Establishment maintained a network of landing pads along the eastern seaboard. The ventriloquist array installed in the chopper would ensure its unimpeded flight to North Miami, Florida, by throwing phantom coordinates of their location miles away from their actual position.

It was in North Miami that the Establishment retained a $500,000 fifty-foot 2009 Cigarette Marauder V-hull, one of the largest Go Fast boats ever built. The powerful center engine and rear twin 1,075 sci Mercury motors were capable of delivering speeds in excess of 130 MPH, more than adequate to evade any coast guard or naval vessel.

Early in the evening on the outskirts of Buffalo, the trucker pulled into a Jimmy Dean's restaurant where the men had a satiating dinner.

In an appreciative gesture for his company, the trucker covered the cost of their meal.

After the bill had been paid, the two headed toward the Peace Bridge that linked the U.S. with Canada. When they arrived at the plaza on the American side of the bridge, the trucker dropped Alberto off, wished him well, then proceeded across the border into Canada and home.

Within minutes, Alberto was in the backseat of a cab headed to a marina on the Niagara River not far from where the truck driver had dropped him off. He paid his fare, then casually walked along the fence surrounding the land portion of the marina.

There was a simple numerical lock on the gate and a gangway on the other side which led to the numerous docks and slips of the vast marina.

Seeing no other access in, Alberto walked back and stood near the gate, feigning interest in the various types of boats berthed there. Within minutes a car pulled into the nearby parking lot. A young couple in their early twenties got out and came up to the gate. They exchanged pleasantries with the Cuban. Alberto told them he was from out-of-state and that he was looking to buy a small sailboat.

The young man explained to Alberto that although he could not let him into the marina, a salesman would be on duty in the morning and would be glad to discuss his interests at that time. Alberto thanked the young man and wished them well. He had positioned himself near the lock and watched as the careless girlfriend dialed in their four digit code. The girlfriend waved as she closed and locked the gate behind them.

There was a fast food restaurant down the street from the marina. It was a busy place, and it was easy for Alberto to be lost in the busyness of the place. He spent some time sitting in various areas of the restaurant, coffee in hand. He even walked around the block a few times. Then darkness fell.

Alberto headed briskly to the marina gate. Seeing no one in the vicinity, Alberto entered the code, 6053. A click of the gate, and Alberto was in. He wasted no time. Ever careful of watchful eyes, the Cuban discreetly conducted a methodical search from slip to slip, looking for a boat, any boat that had a key left carelessly in its ignition.

He avoided those slips that contained boats with bright lights and people on their decks. Alberto was annoyed at the slapping of the water against the boats that at times lent his imagination to thinking someone was sneaking up on him.

At last, at long last, Alberto found a boat, an incredible boat, unmanned, with keys still in the ignition switch. It was a sleek thirty-seven-foot Intrepid Cuddy Thirty-Seven, powered with not one, but three supercharged Mercury 275 HP Verados motors. It looked to have a beam of no less than ten feet.

Alberto hopped back off the boat and took a casual look around. The darkness was full, and even though there were lights at the ends of each dock, it would be impossible to notice an interloper among all the owners and their guests in and around the vessels of the marina. Anyway, it was a secure area. They had a coded access gate!

With no one in the immediate vicinity, Alberto stealthily cast off the bow and stern lines, pushed the boat out and away from its slip, and fired up the engines. Within seconds he was away from the marina, and across the Niagara River to the Canadian side, where he proceeded south under the Peace Bridge and into the waters of Lake Erie.

He passed by old Fort Erie, a fort that had been instrumental in the War of 1812-1814 between American and British soldiers. Built in 1764 by the British during Pontiac's rebellion, the garrison at Fort Erie participated in the American Revolution from 1776-1783.

Seeing the fort reminded Alberto of Cuba's battle with the United States during the Spanish-American war of 1898. *The more things change, the more they stay the same,* he thought. He reduced speed and made his way past the fort at a crawl to avoid undue attention.

As he rounded a small outcropping, he saw the bright lights of what looked to be a lakeside pub off to starboard. How he longed for a bottle of spiced rum. He was very tempted to pull up and indulge himself, but knew it was a dangerous thought.

The Cuban could not have known that this was Lee Hartley's watering hole, the Sea Shack, and that had he stopped he would have walked right into a trap of his own making. Alan Exner and Bindhira Shankar at this very moment had just finished a light meal here on their way to a reputed Cuban safe house somewhere along the Thunder Bay Road that ran parallel to Lake Erie.

Alberto putted by undetected as loud music emanated from the lively business. Even if, by chance, someone were to look out onto the water, they wouldn't have been able to see past the bright lights that were trained onto the outside patio from the end of the dock.

No one followed him; no one knew he was there.

A large tree was still on the beach in front of the safe house. Good. The tree was old and had split in two during a vicious lightning storm several years back. Without this landmark, the Cuban would not have located the safe house in the dark from the water.

Looking at the black face of his Boliva watch, the old radium analog dial read nine forty-five. He brought the Cuddy in to about waist-deep water, then put it in neutral. He lashed the wheel for a southerly bearing and hoped the boat with its powerful engines would run out of gas somewhere in the middle of the lake. He threw the throttles full ahead, slammed it in drive, then quickly dived over the side.

Instantly the engines came to life and within seconds, the thirty-seven-foot boat was gone, its sound reduced to a faint buzzing somewhere out over the lake.

Alberto decided he would lay low here for a few days until things died down a bit. Soon his men would contact him by sat-phone. If they hadn't done so within the designated time frame of the emergency extraction protocol, he would have to try to get to their Toronto safe-house.

For the first time, Alberto was scared. Surely word had reached Raul that things were not going well up here. He knew he had to return to his beloved Cuba, but what would he face on his return?

It was no use lying to his superiors. They were masters of lies themselves and would see through him in an instant. He had to work on a scenario they would buy; a scenario they would not be able to contest.

Reaching the rear of the lakeside estate, Alberto was pleased to find the hidden key exactly where it was supposed to be.

He went inside.

97

Frenemies

The sleek TaZeR rounded a tight curve as it purred along Thunder Bay Drive on the northeastern Lake Erie shore. The various lakeside estates that lined the road were separated from each other by thickly wooded areas, which afforded excellent privacy. The road that ran several hundred feet from the Lake Erie shoreline had been recently paved, and the engine of the high-powered vehicle was whisper quiet as it neared its destination under Exner's guidance.

"Not much farther Alan," Bindhira said. "Our sat-co indicates the safe house is five hundred yards ahead on the left."

"Right," Exner said as he pulled the TaZeR into a small car park that provided access to the public beach. The safe house was but a few hundred feet away from their position. Before powering down the TaZeR, Exner depressed a button below its stick shift. A screen popped horizontally out and up from what should have been a DVD player slot. The screen automatically activated and displayed an infrared map of the surrounding area. Exner looked over to his passenger and smiled.

Bindhira looked on with curious interest. Although she knew many features of this most unusual car, she had come to realize that there was much more to it than she was led to believe. "I did not notice that feature in the manual," she said lightly.

"This, my dear, will not only map out for us the most direct route through the forested area, but will also reveal any humanoids that may be lying in wait along the way."

"How novel," Bindhira said, "a satellite coordinate system incorporating an infrared thermo-graphical imaging device. Would I be correct in assuming this device can also discern between man and beast?"

"Your assumption would indeed be correct." He looked over and smiled. "No beasts to be concerned about in these parts, though," Exner said, as he punched another button and removed the portable screen portion of the device. "Let us see what we shall see." They exited and locked the vehicle.

Through the woodland they reached the outer perimeter of the estate without incident. Like others in the area, the large building was well back from the road. The rear deck of the house had a commanding view of Lake Erie, complete with a large fenced-in private beach.

Tapping the ITID's screen to enhance its image, Exner said, "Looks like we have a 'mouse in the trap' already, Bindhi. Be prepared."

"I am always prepared Alan," she said matter-of-factly.

The two watched as the imaging screen of the portable sat-co device revealed a man in a rear room of the house with a cell phone to his ear. He was bent over as if rooting through a drawer. He pulled something out and stuck it inside the rear waistband of his pants.

"Gun," Bindhira observed.

They continued to observe the man on the screen from under concealment of both the darkness of the night and the heavy foliage to the side of the estate. The man came outside onto a deck just off a second floor bedroom.

Exner powered the sat-co off and hid it behind a large ornamental boulder just inside the well-manicured property. They then skirted the building along the trees and foliage that bordered the property, still in sight of the upper floor.

The man was standing against the balcony railing, cigarette in hand, looking out over the lake. He looked behind him and carelessly tossed the cell phone onto a lounge chair. It bounced onto the deck.

The night was warm, and a cool, mild breeze blew off the lake. A near full moon now revealed itself in naked, unashamed glory above, occasionally concealed by broken formations of wispy dark clouds.

The man stood there for several minutes just staring into the black nothingness that was the lake as stars twinkled high overhead. The only noise that disturbed the quiet idyllic setting was the steady lapping of water as it rhythmically nipped at the toes of the shoreline.

The silence was soon violated by the whirring blades of a helicopter coming in low from the north. As it drew closer, Exner grabbed Bindhira's arm and guided her deeper into the woods, close enough to see from their vantage point, but far enough in not to be seen.

The helicopter swooped low over the lakeside estate, showing no running lights as it then boomeranged back to the beach in a head-on attitude with the balcony at the rear of the building upon which the man stood, unperturbed by the approaching craft.

"He must have been in contact with the helicopter, Alan." Bindhira said. Exner produced a small pair of infrared binoculars and trained them on the air ship.

The chopper slowly descended and delicately set down on the smooth, sandy beach to the rear of the estate. The man on the balcony calmly remained where he was. As the pilot powered his machine down, the loud chopping sound of the decelerating rotor blades became more of a quiet, chirping whirr.

Through his binoculars, Exner was taken aback when he saw that the first two figures to jump out of the helicopter were none other than Lee Hartley and Bill Travers!

"*What the . . . ?*" Exner exclaimed. He passed the binoculars over to Bindhira, who gasped in like manner. They silently watched as the divers were closely followed by two soldiers with submachine guns leveled at their spines. No longer needing the binoculars, Bindhira handed them back to Exner.

A lean, middle-aged woman was next to emerge from the helicopter bay. She wore a knee-length olive green skirt and beige blouse with a stunning gun belt and .45 caliber handgun in a holster at her side to complete her wardrobe.

The woman was followed out by still another person, an older middle-aged man in a poorly fitting suit. Ducking low as had the others to avoid being struck by the slowly spinning blades above, the man stepped up his pace to catch up with the rest of the small contingent.

"Ahhh, *Señor* Hartley; *Señor* Travers, so good of you to come," the man from the balcony called down to them. The soldiers at their sides prodded the Canadians toward the house with the barrels of their weapons. As the small group entered into the warm glow of the balcony lightning, Lee saw that the man addressing them was none other than Alberto!

A similar surprise under the same lighting at the same time beset Alberto at the sight of Major Torrado and Eladio Fuentes.

"M-M-Major Torrado . . . *Señor* Fuentes, this is a . . . a humble surprise to see you, here, of all places," Alberto tittered nervously. Fear was clearly etched in his voice. All he received from his Cuban guests was a cold stare, which served to unnerve him even more.

Playing on the man's obvious fear Lee said, "It's over Alberto, you're done, man—*finito*."

"It is never over until it is over, *señor*. Is this not what you Westerners like to say?" Alberto basked in the empowerment of the phrase. It made him feel a little more in control. Perhaps the FAR major and the senior intelligence man hadn't discovered his double-cross after all; perhaps they had merely captured the divers and had come to the safe house to gut them before returning home to Cuba.

At least this was his hope. Somehow this line of reasoning brought him little comfort. Alberto looked down, all eyes trained on him. "Yes, it is never over until it is over," he softly repeated. From deep within, he then seemed to muster some courage. Alberto raised his head and addressed the two Canadians again ever mindful of the Cuban ears his words would cross.

"Well, it *is* over for you two, *señors*. You have destroyed years of development, years of planning, years of hopeful anticipation." Then in a much more menacing tone, "You have yet to pay, and you *will* pay, of this I promise you."

"Fabio!" Fuentes barked and pointed from one of the soldiers to Carbrera. He trotted toward the rear of the beach house.

"How you say in North America?" Travers asked in his best Latino accent loud enough for Carbrera to hear. "You are in deeep sheet; is thees not so, *señor*?"

Alberto menacingly jabbed a forefinger at the two divers, then left the balcony. The remaining guard then nudged each of the divers further on with the barrel of his machine pistol until they reached the rear lower deck of the large dwelling.

Alberto came out the first floor patio doors just as Fuentes' man was about to enter. Carbrera was thoroughly frisked. He offered no resistance. A WWII era Colt 1911A1 .45-caliber pistol was removed from the rear waistband of his pants.

Major Torrado and Fuentes came over to him. “You have much to explain, *Señor* Carbrera,” Fuentes said. Then in a more menacing tone, “You have *much* to explain. I fear this may not bode well for you.”

Alberto looked from the major to Fuentes. Carbrera cringed when he saw the hungry look of anticipatory torture on the face of the intelligence man.

Turning in desperation to the major, Alberto pleaded, “I am not a traitor, Major.” He then looked to Fuentes, then to each of the soldiers, and finally to Lee and Travers. “It was . . . it was Wu Yang! Yes; it was he who let these two meddlers discover our secrets. It was his carelessness, not mine. You should be looking for him, major!”

“Enough!” Major Torrado said angrily. “You would do well to hold your tongue, *Señor* Carbrera, until such time as we decide whether or not to cut it out.”

“*Si,* Major,” Alberto sighed resignedly, and in near-shock. “I only ask that you hear me out.”

“How best to proceed, Alan?” Normally self-composed, Bindhira’s concern for Lee and Travers was beginning to manifest itself in her uneasiness as the situation grew increasingly tenser.

Exner thought for a moment then said, “I’ll get as close as I can. You get back to the TaZeR, Bindhi. In the trunk, you’ll find some toys. Pick your favorites. Then I want you to bring the TaZeR into the driveway. Make sure you engage its ‘whisper mode.’ Take the sat-co with you. We’re going to need it to track the chopper if things go south.”

“What about you, Alan?” she asked.

Exner pulled out his .45-caliber Glock 21. “I’m good.” He smiled at her.

In a moment of unexpected emotion, Bindhira gave Exner a hug. “Try not to start the party without me.” With that, she disappeared into the darkness of the woods.

98

Two Thumbs Up

Exner managed to skirt along the property, moving carefully so as not to snap a twig or stumble on his way through the trees and foliage that defined the side perimeter of the estate. He was also careful to freeze whenever the brightness of the moon broke through the passing cloud cover to reveal the well manicured back yard that bordered the beach.

Exner was now no more than fifteen feet from the group that congregated around the lower rear deck of the house.

From his vantage point, he could just see a small portion of the semicircular driveway at the front of the building.

Alberto was pushed down the short stairway of the back deck by the soldier. Fuentes motioned for Alberto to be brought beside Lee and Travers. Exner continued to observe the action from the safety of the bushes close by. Major Torrado and Eladio Fuentes stood several feet away from their captives. The armed commandos took up positions, one on each flank but a step behind, with their weapons at the ready.

Fuentes broke the silence. "So your Establishment failed, and now here you are, before us, your countrymen." He paused for effect. "You stupid, poor excuse for a man."

"Wu Yang . . . ," Alberto began.

". . . is *already* in Cuba, but at Guantanamo Bay!" To calm his nerves, Fuentes pulled out a large *Cohiba*, flicked his lighter, then proceeded to slowly roll its tip in the fire. He replaced the lighter, then took a long, slow drag.

"The Oriental was the lucky one. The rest of the primary cell has been killed off. Others, their work successfully completed, have crawled back into the proverbial woodwork. The remainder, these two soldiers and the pilot, are here fulfilling the last of their duties in this country." Fuentes looked to the soldiers with admiration. He blew a perfect smoke ring in their direction.

"What happened to Pepe and Ricardo?" Alberto asked meekly.

"The soldiers grew bored on the way and tossed them out of the helicopter," Travers blurted out. "Can't you people do anything without killing?"

"They knew the penalty for failure when they signed on for this mission," Major Torrado said without remorse. "Your Lee Hartley got the better of them. Second place is for first place losers," she said with audible malice. My commandos do not make mistakes."

Looking to her, Fuentes kept up appearances. "Their families will be duly notified that their loved ones died for the cause of *la Revolución*," Fuentes lied.

"The families of those men can't eat platitudes," Lee said with disgust. "I'm sure your men here will also die in the 'line of duty' right, Fuentes?" Lee hoped to plant doubt and fear into the minds of the soldiers.

"Doesn't appear any of you guys got anything right on this one except for wasting your own guys," Travers said to the Cubans collectively.

Suddenly, a loud explosion permeated the heretofore quiet ambiance of the night. Springing into action, Lee and Travers crossed the short distance between them and the soldiers, tackling each. All four went to ground.

Fuentes drew his pistol and covered Alberto as the major restrained him by the arm.

Lee and Travers fought for their lives. During the struggle, Lee's man got the shoulder strap of his machine gun hopelessly wrapped around an arm in a desperate bid to unleash a hail of death upon him. Lee struggled to a half-standing position. He managed to throw several jaw-breaking elbows to the man's face. The man fell precariously back onto the barrel of his gun.

Jumping up, Lee quickly executed a stomp kick to the entangled man's arm. With the gun acting as a fulcrum to lock the soldier's arm out, Lee's kick snapped the man's elbow at the joint. His cry of intense pain shattered the quiet of the night.

Meanwhile, Travers and his opponent both struggled to a standing position. Just before the soldier drew a bead, Travers grabbed the barrel of the weapon and yanked it violently downward. This unorthodox maneuver was followed by a head butt that dropped the man to the ground.

Then; a gunshot! A warning round from Fuentes' pistol narrowly missed the moon that had just peeked out from behind a misty bank of clouds. He lowered his pistol at them. "Major Torrado," he said without turning to look at her, "do what you came to do, and be quick about it!" No one moved. Lee and Travers each had a look of uneasy desperation on their faces.

Then, another ear-splitting explosion rocked the quiet neighborhood, this time from the beach area. Everyone covered their ears after the fact.

"What the?" Fuentes was visibly shaken.

"You!" Major Torrado barked to Travers' man who sat on the ground rubbing his neck, "Check it out!" Reluctantly the man reclaimed his weapon, pulled himself up and trotted off into the darkness in the direction of the blast.

Lee's man meanwhile was still screaming in pain. Fuentes walked over, and said, "Let me help, comrade." He drew his old .45, and simply shot the man between the eyes! The man immediately went limp, still propped up by his weapon. "I can't concentrate with that incessant noise."

"You bastard," Lee cried out. He rushed Fuentes, but was abruptly stopped in his tracks, when the Cuban leveled his gun at Lee's chest. "I wouldn't, *señor*," Fuentes said quickly.

"You," he snarled to Travers, "get over by your friend. And neither of you try anything. My patience has run out!"

"What kind of animal are you, Fuentes," Travers said, but Fuentes' murderous stare held him in check.

Ignoring the mysterious blasts and commotion, Major Torrado spun the surprised Alberto around and placed a tight choke hold on him. Fuentes, his gun still trained on the Canadians, casually strolled over and kicked Alberto viciously in the groin. Still in the major's choke hold, the crumpled figure was then dragged over to the deck still gasping for air. She relaxed her grip on Alberto's neck. He fell face-first to the stairs in agony.

The man didn't look up. If he had, he'd have been horrified. The major produced a stiletto knife concealed beneath her jacket. Without hesitation, she cleanly hacked off Alberto's right thumb.

Alberto's moans devolved to hideous screams. "*Why* . . . Why do you do these things," he cried between gasps.

Saying nothing, the major then viciously smashed his head down onto the hard wood of the stairs. Calmly, deliberately, she then walked over to Alberto's left side. "You are a disgrace to *la Revolución*, and to your people. And what *el Comandante* wants, *el Comandante* shall have!" As he looked groggily up at her, she proceeded to hack Alberto's left thumb off in similar fashion.

Alberto's pitiful screams were mercifully silenced by a bullet to the back of the man's head by Fuentes. The disgraced Cuban's body collapsed onto the stairwell. His blood spilled liberally over the stairs and pooled on the ground below.

"*That's* for Mercedes!" Travers almost cheered, but realized that the monster standing in front of him was probably worse than the one that had just expired before him.

Producing a baggie from her pocket, Major Torrado reached down and collected the bloody stumps. She dropped the digits into the bag, zipped it shut, then nonchalantly replaced it.

"We have what we came for, Eladio," Torrado said, "It is time to depart."

"Lady, I gotta tell ya: you guys are pretty harsh!" Travers could barely keep his stomach in check.

Looking with utter contempt at the two Canadians, the major turned to Fuentes and said, "Finish up here. I will await you in the helo. Be quick about it" She then turned and jogged off for the safety of the helicopter.

"End of the line, *señors*." Fuentes said. He walked closer to Lee, his gun still aimed at Lee's chest, so as not to miss.

Suddenly, Fuentes felt a small, cold barrel of steel pushed into the base of his skull. "Unless you want a shit-head busting .45-caliber hollow point bullet relieving you of your life, put the damn gun down!" The increased pressure of Exner's barrel convinced Fuentes to drop his weapon.

"Your timing's a little off Ex," Lee said with obvious relief."

"Better late than never though, eh?" Exner replied.

"Ex; the major, she's getting away," Travers shouted.

"Oh I don't think so, Bill." Exner said, smiling.

A cacophony of Spanish expletives came out of the darkness and into the light. The divers looked up in surprise as Bindhira appeared into light of the patio deck. She pushed Major Torrado ahead of her. The woman's hands had been handcuffed behind her back.

"It was you with the flash bangs," Travers exclaimed, relieved.

"Sorry, but a diversion is a diversion," she said, focusing her gaze on Lee. He smiled his gratitude.

"What about the pilot," Lee asked.

"Oh, he's tied up at the moment, along with a soldier I found milling about the grounds. They're currently taking a nap," she said smiling.

"You're amazing, girl," Lee said as he picked up Fuentes' handgun and covered the man while Exner placed him in handcuffs.

The moon lay bare above them as the passing cloud cover had completely disappeared to reveal a blanketing plethora of stars above.

A heavy truck noisily entered the front driveway of the estate. A blinding arc of light was seen as the truck's headlights came to a halt. Several doors could be heard opening, then the sound of footsteps as several men rushed toward them.

"Ahhh, the cavalry has arrived . . . ," Exner said, as an RCMP SWAT team poured around the sides and to the rear of the lake house. Other of the team continued down the beach to the helicopter.

"In their usual late tradition," Travers added with mock disdain.

"I don't know about that Bill; the RCMP always gets their man," Lee said, smiling.

"And their woman," Exner said with a smile.

The captain of the SWAT team and several of his men came over to where Exner was standing.

"You, Exner?" the captain asked.

"One and the same Captain," Exner said, shaking the burly middle-aged man's hand.

"Orders from the top, sir," the captain said without emotion. "You are to allow the Cuban major and her aide unrestricted passage back to their country."

"On whose authority Captain?" Exner and his team were flabbergasted.

"The PM himself sir. Word came up from Washington. They are to be permitted unimpeded passage back to Cuba."

"Surely Captain, you realize I can't simply allow them to walk just like that," Exner protested.

"Duly noted sir," the captain said. "That's why I've been issued this court order mandating their release."

The captain handed him a document. Pulling out a small flashlight, Exner grabbed it from him and examined it closely.

"Probably fake," Travers said impulsively.

"No . . . no it's quite genuine," Exner said after a few minutes of intense scrutiny.

"Remove their cuffs, Bindhi," Exner ordered at length. Looking to Lee and Travers, she reluctantly obeyed.

Major Torrado spoke up. "Yes, we are to return to Cuba to present *El Comandante* with these," she said. She pulled the bloody baggie containing the two thumbs out of her pocket.

"*Señor* Castro requires these as proof of the traitor's execution. That was my sole mission here. As ordered, you are to release us at once." She replaced the baggie.

"If they are not allowed to return to Cuba sir, there will be an international incident that will most certainly involve the Chinese." the Captain said to Exner by way of explanation.

"Dammit," Lee said. "Ex, it was the major and Alberto who were responsible for the deaths of the entire de Quesada family. If she's allowed to return, you'll compromise our men down there."

"No, Lee. We must let them go," Bindhira cut in, afraid Lee would reveal anything further in their presence. "While I was in the TaZeR," she said, "an urgent message came through to contact your headquarters, Alan. When I did so, they patched me directly through to sub-director Culp who had just received this mandate from the president himself. There were no options given or allowed."

"But Major Torrado, Fuentes, and her men are illegally on sovereign Canadian soil. Cuban military have boots in our country! Not to mention they're an integral part of a terrorist conspiracy to attack our citizens and disrupt our governments," Exner said incredulously.

Bindhira came over and gently squeezed Exner's arm. "Alan, it is out of our hands," she whispered to him. "Our work here is done. We have fought the good fight. If you do not permit these people to leave as ordered, you will be charged with insubordination at best, incarceration at worst."

By this time, the SWAT team had rounded up the others and radioed for ambulance and coroner assistance. Major Torrado and Fuentes were flanked by Exner, Bindhira, Lee, and Travers on one side, the captain and two heavily armed members of the SWAT team on the other.

"I cannot say it was a pleasurable experience gentlemen, but we are glad you see reason," Fuentes said.

The major boldly walked up to Lee and Travers. "Just a word of advice. If I were you *señors*, I would not make any visits to Cuba in the future."

"No," Travers said calmly, "I agree with you there, darlin'. I'm happy to say that Cuba's off my bucket list."

"Mine too," Lee chimed in.

Looking to the men with sober finality, she caught Fuentes' eye, nodded in the direction she was heading, then the four of them walked back to the beach and the helicopter.

Within minutes, the chopper powered up. In a swirling vortex of gritty sand, the air machine pulled straight up off the beach, running lights on. It hovered above them for several seconds, then disappeared into the blackness of the southwestern sky.

"Unbelievable," Exner said.

Bindhira held on to Lee's arm with both of hers. "I am just glad this is over."

"That makes two of us Bindhi," Lee said dourly.

"Ex; what'll happen to your contacts down in Cuba?" Travers asked.

"I've made arrangements with sub-director Culp to have them put up at Guantanamo Bay," Exner said. "From there, they'll be flown to Canada, courtesy of the US Air Force, where we'll accept them as refugees. Their families won't be far behind. I knew we'd have to do something when everything started going south at their end."

"Well, if it's any consolation," Lee said, "I wouldn't bet on Fuentes and Major Torrado living to see retirement."

"My thoughts exactly, Lee," Exner replied ruefully.

"Those two will be scapegoats for the failure of the joint mission," Bindhira said. "Fidel will deal with them far more harshly than we would. Their blind devotion to him will be their undoing."

Sirens grew increasingly louder. "Let's call it a night, team," Exner said as he combed his hair straight back with the fingers of both hands. Suddenly he felt very tired—no, exhausted.

"I'll power up the TaZeR," Travers said.

Bindhira pulled away from Lee. "NO! If you do not engage it in proper sequence, it will release a nerve gas and kill you instantly!"

"Holy crap," Travers said. "Really?"

"That's what I like about you, Bill," Exner said, managing a smile. "You always were a gullible old soul."

99

Terms and Conditions

Several days later, a formal debriefing in Langley on the Project Vector affair was concluded. NABS Control Alan Exner, Lee Hartley, and Bill Travers, along with NSA/CSS liaison Bindhira Shankar, were all given special recognition from a grateful U.S. government for their work at exposing and neutralizing the heinous plots of both the Establishment and the Chinese-Cuban alliance.

The President of the United States, along with Canada's Prime Minister, met with Chinese President Guangmei and a "high-ranking" member of Raul Castro's government at an undisclosed location.

While not openly admitting to being in collusion with Cuba in a terrorist act upon North America, President Guangmei did make known that both the Chinese and Cuban governments had "uncovered the workings of a rogue element" in their midst who had "stolen and distilled the findings of their viral research to suit their own ends." He assured the American president that the "traitorous element" had been identified and would be "dealt with most severely."

While the leaders of the U.S. and Canada were terse during the meeting, they were careful not to tip their hand as to how much they had really learned about Chinese affairs in Cuba. Of course, the alphabet soup mix of North American intelligence agencies would step up their surveillance of all things Chinese and Cuban for some time to come.

As a result of the meeting, and to allow the two countries to save face in the eyes of the world, the "ground-breaking" joint effort on viral research and virology on the subtropical island nation by the Chinese was to be immediately suspended. Its dismantling would be monitored by a U.N. team of inspectors. The U.S. president was emphatic about this. There was no opposition to the contrary.

President Guangmei assured North American leaders that the Chinese would fulfill their promise to immediately curtail and dismantle their research and development laboratories in Cuba and return their scientists promptly to the Peoples' Republic. Guangmei, however, was not privy to the fact that American CIA operatives were already in place in both his country and in Cuba to assure the promise was carried out, and that the inspection team would be protected against anything untoward.

By giving the Chinese a backdoor to withdraw gracefully and peacefully, and thus save face in the eyes of the world, the Americans had once again managed to avert a global incident of apocalyptic proportions, much as they had back in the early 1960s, albeit with a higher degree of discretion.

Cuba was officially ostracized by both the American and Canadian governments. Then, at the request of the U.S. government, Canada was admonished to severely restrict trade with the island nation. However, the prime minister would not consent to a complete trade severance as the American president had hoped.

Further, it was mutually agreed upon by the U.S and a reluctant Cuban government that upon the death of Raul Castro, an international board of representatives would be sent to Cuba to ensure a fair and democratic election by and for the people of the impoverished island nation for the first time in over fifty years of repression.

Of this, the U.S. government was adamant and the Cuban high ambassador was given no opportunity to appeal, much to his great chagrin.

The ambassador reluctantly assured them that the Castro government would give their assent to such a condition, but would do so grudgingly and under "official protest." At the searing glare of the American president, the Cuban representative offered no further comments.

100

An Informal Debriefing

The following day, Friday, Exner invited Lee, Bindhira, and Bill Travers to his home in Niagara-On-The-Lake later in the evening for drinks. His was a beautifully restored heritage home one street back of Queen Street, the quaint main street of the historic little village situated on Lake Ontario.

Travers came an hour early and made sure he had a head start on the finger foods Exner had provided for them. Lee had picked up Bindhira and arrived on time.

Throughout the evening, the highlights of the recent affair were replayed and bounced off one another. In addition they discussed, among other things, the senseless deaths of the de Quesada family, the recovery of old Mrs. Braithwaite's body from the cold, deep waters of Georgian Bay by an RCMP dive team, and the good and faithful Cuban anti-revolutionists who had given their lives selflessly for the cause they so strongly believed in.

It was a sober evening. Many lives had been lost, and some were good honest people. But were it not for the sacrifices made, thousands more would have been in dire jeopardy. Those who had fallen were people that Alan Exner and his team would never forget.

It was their collective hope that through all of this, coupled with the American president's stern demands, the good people of Cuba would see their dream of a truly free homeland come true, and soon.

"Say Ex," Travers asked, "What's happening down in Jamaica with the virus that, uh, found its way there?" Exner looked at the two divers for a few moments before speaking. "There were several deaths, and a lot of suffering. Fortunately for all concerned, although the Ebola strain was quite virulent, the best Chinese and Cuban scientists failed to factor in variants, such as the effects that the unique Jamaican salt air would have on it. Within an hour of its arrival over the island, the pathogen had rapidly started to break down."

Exner went on to say that he had also received a report that very day, concerning the health status of Captain Reay of the Canadian Coast Guard, who had been stabbed aboard the *Limnos.*

The ship's doctor got the bleeding stopped. A medi-vac helicopter was called in and Captain Reay was immediately transferred to hospital in short order.

The knife had messed up his intestines, but hadn't punctured any vital organs. He remained in guarded but stable condition in hospital, but was expected to pull through.

Captain Reay's actions aboard the *Limnos* were those of a truly brave man, as were those of his diver, whose body had been carefully brought up before they weighed anchor for port.

"What'll happen to that Cuban fellow who gave himself up, Ex," Travers asked as he munched down another handful of cheesy puffs.

"Gino Vaselino asked for and has been granted asylum in Canada in return for exposing the main players and schemes of both the Chinese, and the Establishment," Exner said. He removed the cheesy puff bowl from in front of Travers and handed it to Bindhira, who in turn placed in down on the bar in front of Lee.

"Culp alerted his CIA operatives in Cuba as to the whereabouts of Vaselino's family. U.S. covert forces stationed at Guantanamo Bay have been placed on high alert and ordered to mobilize should the Cuban FAR so much as blink in their direction.

In light of the 'accidentally unencrypted communiqué sent by the president to Gitmo, I'm sure Castro's goons won't go anywhere near them."

"Vaselino also told us that it was Travers' Cuban art gallery friend, Carlos Rodriguez, who drove the Viper the night you were attacked, Lee," Exner continued. "And of course, he was also the one who was responsible for the kidnapping of Bill."

"From what Vaselino told us, Rodriguez and Wu Yang were constantly at odds with one another. Seems Wu Yang won game, set, and match on that one when he blew up Rodriguez along with his own countrymen at the old hotel they were using as their headquarters up in Tobermory."

"Oh," Exner continued, "and the car that just about ran you over, Bindhi? It was driven by one of Wu Yang's men. Yang wanted to take out at least one of us to slow our investigation. We were getting too close too fast to their operations in Tobermory. Anyway, the driver was in the hotel the night Yang fired a missile into it."

"Karma at its finest, Alan," Bindhira said simply.

A silence pervaded Exner's rec room for several minutes as each nursed a glass of wine and helped themselves to the finger foods before them.

"Alan," Bindhira asked, "did you check to see how the Applegate couple was doing?"

"Funny you should ask, Bindhi." Exner paused to down a sauced-up piece of shrimp. "Poor old Mr. and Mrs. Applegate sure had their share of action."

"After we left, Wu Yang's men stopped by, only they weren't so discreet. Seems they weren't far behind us. The old couple was in their stateroom when their yacht was boarded. The Applegates weren't harmed, not really, just a little roughed up before being trussed and locked in their stateroom. Yang's goons had also cranked up their TV so no one could hear them inside."

Exner paused. "They were lucky Yang's thugs didn't take their frustrations out on them at not finding the matchbooks we'd already taken from behind the stateroom painting. Had they have gotten there ahead of us . . ."

"Fortunately for the Applegates, the Little Tub harbormaster stopped by their yacht to address several complaints of loud music emanating from the *Forever Young*. Somehow, over the blaring television, he managed to hear their muffled cries for help. He kicked the door in and found them bound and gagged. Freeing the elderly couple, the harbormaster then called police, who were quick to notify us."

"Oh, I am so glad no real harm came to them. A classic case of being in the wrong place at the wrong time," Bindhira said.

"Indeed," Exner agreed as he dipped another shrimp into the sauce bowl.

Bindhira turned to Lee, who seemed lost in thought. "What seems to be troubling you, Lee Hartley?" she asked, partly in jest.

Lee's gaze was focused on the bar in front of him. "I can't help thinking that we haven't seen the last of Wu Yang." He diverted his gaze to Exner who stood further down the bar.

As if on cue, Exner said, "Culp confirmed Yang's incarceration at Gitmo Lee, and he won't be out at least until his 110th birthday."

"Alan," Lee said seriously, "is that what you *really* believe?"

Exner took a sip of wine and stared into his glass for a few moments, then returned the gaze. "Lee, in all honesty, I don't think even Guantanamo Bay will hold the man, but it's not for me to say."

"The man is most resourceful, and I too do not believe we have seen the last of Wu Yang," Bindhira said with conviction.

"Yeah, the guy's probably stirring up lackeys down in Gitmo for another Establishment go-round as we speak," Travers chimed in.

At this, the other three laughed. Lee almost lost his mouthful of wine. Travers' face turned red.

In an effort to change the subject to one he was more comfortable with Travers said, "So what about the *Griffon,* Ex?"

"I was wondering when one of you guys was going to bring that up," Exner said. His gaze took in the two men. "Parks Canada has been informed of this historic national treasure, and an underwater archaeological team will be assembled."

He noticed the look of grave disappointment as it eclipsed Travers' face. "The team will be carefully chosen of course," Exner continued as he played it up. "It will take them several months to survey the ship and carefully document every item uncovered within."

Exner chuckled inwardly at seeing Travers' face turn white. The old diver was not an archaeologist, but he *had* found the *Griffon* and it was the find of a lifetime. To simply be overlooked during its exploration would be too bitter a pill for Travers to swallow.

"*However,*" Exner continued, "they *do* have need of two professional divers to act as underwater coordinators and technically advise the dive teams for which they will be well remunerated. Any candidates come to mind?"

Lee picked up on Exner's cue and fanned the flames directed at Travers. "No one immediately comes to mind, Ex—"

"What d'ya mean, ya dumb Muppet," Travers piped up indignantly. "I'm one of those divers, and yer gonna be the other!"

"I guess you have your two divers, Alan," Bindhira said, laughing. She witnessed ecstatic jubilation on Travers' face. Lee winked in her direction. Exner laughed. Travers knew he had been played, and once again his face flushed.

Bindhira poured herself a glass of white wine, then turned to face Exner. "Alan, you never did tell me how you managed to get off the *Étoile Profonde* in one piece."

Exner looked at his friends but remained silent for several moments. He then sat his glass down on the bar, a look of mock incredulity on his face. "My dear, I'm supposed to be resourceful. After all, I *am* control for the North American Bureau of Security in these parts."

Bindhira turned to the others and explained how she and the ship's radio operator had narrowly escaped when the explosion rocked the ship before taking on water at an alarming rate, and how she lost contact with Exner in the melee, then was surprised to see him alive in the helicopter after their rescue.

"So what's the 411, Ex?" Travers asked, happy to turn the tables on his friend.

"Right," Exner began. It was disturbingly apparent to Lee that his friend was hesitant and unsettled as he spoke. He reasoned it must have been more traumatic than he let on.

"When Wu Yang's explosive charge blew the bottom out of the *Étoile Profonde*," Exner continued, "Bindhira threw the radio operator over the side with a homemade raft hastily constructed of life buoys and rope before she did likewise. I ran back to the bridge to see if I could find a portable emergency locator beacon, which I did. I activated it and ran back out."

"By this time, the bow was starting to nose up out of the water. Through the smoke and fire, I noticed a fire hose cabinet positioned just outside the bridge. I opened it and ran with the hose. Lucky for me it was a hundred feet long. I threw it over the side and clambered down. Even with that length, I still had to drop a good twenty feet to the water. I swam away as fast as I could to avoid being sucked down."

Again that hesitation: that sense of uncertainty, almost fear. "Being on the other side of the ship, I could only hope that Bindhira and the radio operator had the presence of mind to do likewise."

"When the ship went under, a huge wave from the aftermath of the suction as the vessel went under must have spread us several hundred feet apart."

"Within about fifteen minutes though, a coast guard chopper appeared," he continued. "They had not only picked up the signal, but also saw my beacon flashing through the pounding waves, and pulled me out of the freezing water."

Exner turned to Bindhira. "If it wasn't for that brightly colored homemade raft, we'd probably have never found you in that storm." He took a sip of wine. "There, see? Mystery solved."

"If you say so," Bindhira said dubiously.

101

Lucrezia

Lee couldn't help but notice on the wall behind the bar that Exner still prominently displayed photos of his deceased wife Marlissa.

"I have to say, this is the weirdest case I've ever been involved in to date," Exner said.

"In what way, Alan," Bindhira asked as she poured herself another glass of white wine.

"The child." Exner said. "There's no way a child of that age could have possibly known or understood anything about our activities. It was simply impossible for her to have just shown up when she did, where she did, provide us with timely assistance and crucial evidence, only to vanish into thin air without a trace afterward."

"Well she *did*, and I'm living proof," Travers added.

"Yeah, it'd take a little girl to get you out of your jams," Lee kidded. As expected, Travers gave him the evil eye, this time with a grin. The others chuckled in response.

"Is it possible that any of you have come across the child somewhere before," Bindhira quizzed. "Mayhap one of you has a tie to her from somewhere in your past." Even she had been affected by the tiny specter's benevolent actions in their favor.

"Just thinking about this whole 'ghostly girl' thing gives me the creeps," Travers said. "But without her help, we'd probably all be *Ebolized* by now."

"*Ebolized?* That's not even a word, knucklehead," Lee said.

"William is right," Bindhira said, ignoring the obvious. "Had the child not assisted us when she did, there would have been many deaths and mass panic throughout North America by now, including ours."

The group fell silent.

"Hey, look at this," Travers said, pouring over the photos on the wall behind the bar. It was a four-by-six-inch faded color photo housed in a simple birch frame. The snapshot had obviously been taken several years ago. It was of four people in a lake in waist-deep water and had been taken by someone standing on shore. Exner had his wife on his shoulders and she was "wrestling" a child who was atop the shoulders of Marlissa's father. Others were frolicking in the water around them.

"Chicken fighting, eh?" Travers observed. "Looks like you guys are about to go down, Ex."

"When was this photo taken, Alan," Bindhira asked.

They parted as Exner came in for a look. He leaned across the bar for closer scrutiny. He stared at the picture for a long while; lost in thought at how happy he and Marlissa had been during those years.

"It was taken in the early eighties," he said slowly. "We—Marlissa and I—had only been married a few months. We were up at her Uncle Chet's cottage in the Muskokas. All her family; aunts, uncles, and cousins, made the sojourn up there every summer. Her Uncle Chet made sure everyone always had a great time."

"Ex; who's the girl?" Lee pointed to the lower-right corner of the photo's foreground. A young girl sat on the beach at the water's edge and held a brown and yellow teddy bear up into the face of an older girl. The children were both laughing, apparently because the bear was dripping wet. He was well stuffed, had both eyes, and looked new unlike the bear Travers picked up then discarded back at the grotto.

"What the . . . ?" Exner stared in stunned disbelief.

"That must be the same girl!" Bindhira said, a chill running up her spine.

"No way," Travers said slowly in fearful denial. "No-friggin'-way."

"Whoever it is, it's her, Ex. But she'd be ohhh, about forty-something—*today*," Lee remarked coolly.

Alan Exner walked away from the bar and from his friends, visibly disturbed. He pulled up Marlissa's family's history on the memory banks of his mind. The troubled man paced slowly and aimlessly around the rec room, head bowed, chin in hand.

"The girl with the bear," Exner said slowly, deep in thought. He jabbed a finger repeatedly at the ground then picked up his pace as his recollections became clearer. "The girl with the teddy bear was the younger sister of the older girl in the photo."

"*Was?*" Travers said uneasily. "Already I'm not so sure I want to hear this."

Exner returned to look at the photo in question. "I can't remember their names," he said. "The older girl was a good friend of Joy, Marlissa's younger cousin." He paused to reflect.

"Not long after this picture was taken, Marlissa, her father, Joy, Joy's friend, and her friend's little sister, the girls in this photo, were out in her dad's boat. Marlissa's father piloted his nineteen-foot fishing boat far out into the bay at a fair clip when they struck a huge log floating low in the water. All five were thrown from the boat."

Exner paused to gain control of the mists of his emotions. "Everyone could swim except Joy's friend and her little sister," he continued. The boat flipped over but was still afloat. Thankfully the motor conked out when water flooded it. Young Joy managed to pull Marlissa's dazed father over to the boat."

"While she helped her uncle hold on, Marlissa saw the other two sisters struggling for their lives. The little one went under. Marlissa dove down and managed to get the girl's head above water but the sister, in blind panic, grabbed on to Marlissa and pulled her under. She became so embroiled in her own struggle for survival that she lost her grip on the little one's arm. She managed to save the older sister, but the little girl disappeared beneath the waves in the melee."

"They never found the poor little thing's body; lake was too dark, water too deep." Exner crossed his arms and leaned over the bar. "My wife was a hero but she never forgave herself for failing to save the younger girl. She never forgot the desperate wide-eyed panic in the poor little thing's eyes. There were many sleepless nights. It haunted Marlissa right up until her death."

Exner looked lovingly back up to the photo. He walked around the bar, kissed a finger, and then placed it reverently over Marlissa's face.

"I know this sounds weird man," Travers said, "but the spook kid's protecting you and your interests Ex, and I for one am glad to be one of those interests."

"If that's true," Exner asked, "then why didn't she save Marlissa when those murderers broke into the house? Why wasn't she there then? It was my wife who tried to save her, not me."

Lee changed the subject. "Ex; the night your wife was murdered. You said the intruders were looking for something but you didn't know for what."

"I still don't, Lee," Exner said. "But if the ghost of the child Marlissa tried to save really wanted to show her gratitude, she'd help me make sense of it all."

"Stranger things have happened buddy," Lee said.

"It could be the kid wanted you to know she doesn't blame Marlissa for not saving her Ex, Travers waxed philosophically, "and now that your wife is gone, maybe it's her way of sayin' thanks."

"Whatever the reason Alan, some things are best left to the unknown," Bindhira offered sagely.

Soon thereafter everyone said their goodbyes to Exner and then left. Lee had "adopted" Travers for the time being until he could get back on his feet and so went home with him, but not before they returned Bindhira to her room at an inn on Queen Street.

Once alone, Exner let out a huge sigh of relief. It'd been a very busy several days. He returned to the photo on the wall, which had been the center of discussion. All he cared to remember about the incident so long ago was the fact that Marlissa had returned to him alive. He had forgotten about the loss of the little girl, and he chided himself for it.

Indeed this had been the most bizarre and dangerous case he had ever worked on. He no longer thought Travers crazy. He believed the man when he said the child rescued him, just as he *knew* the girl had saved *him* when he jumped from the *Étoile Profonde*. Chills ran up and down his spine at the thought. He hadn't told his friends the *real* story of his rescue.

At the moment he'd let go of the fire hose, the vessel was hit with a huge crashing wave. He struck his head on the side of the ship and fell to the water's surface twenty feet below. Stunned, he slipped beneath the waves.

The shock of the cold water quickly revived him however, and he surfaced. Twice more he went under. Exner tried to swim away from the sinking ship but the cold water, combined with nearly being knocked senseless, had left him impotent to do so. The portable locator beacon slipped away from his grasp.

The battle to keep his head above the waves had weakened him greatly and as he went under again, he knew his time had come. He was going to die.

It was then that Exner felt a strong pair of hands pulling him to the surface. He was quickly and superhumanly pulled far from the sinking ship as she slipped beneath the waves in a roiling, frothing swirl.

When the coast guard chopper arrived and the crew members pulled him into the safety of its cabin, Exner asked how they managed to find him in the rising swells. He was dumbfounded when they told him they had simply followed a phosphorescent series of bright blue underwater lights, similar to those outlining an airstrip.

As for locating Bindhira and the radio operator, it was as if they had a high-powered underwater beacon shining up from the deep beneath them, which spotlighted their position.

Neither Bindhira nor the radio operator had mentioned anything about this. Thinking fast, Exner strongly admonished the crew of the rescuc chopper not to relay any of these strange phenomena to anyone, sternly instructing them that it was in the interests of "national defense."

But he knew. He knew that somehow Marlissa had been watching over them.

The NABS control retired to his bedroom. Just before he switched on its light, a radiant blue hue emanated from the ensuite bathroom that was straight ahead through the bedroom. Standing at the threshold of the bathroom stood the child in Exner's photo, silhouetted in its glow! Startled, Exner was immediately immersed in a surreal blanket of peaceful calm.

"She couldn't save me, Mr. Exner. But I was able to save you and your friend," the child said slowly, calmly, deliberately. The ever present teddy bear hung off her right hand.

Exner said nothing. He felt paralyzed; unable to move, unable to speak.

"She loves you, you know. She loves you very much, Mr. Exner. I wanted to please her by helping you," the girl said matter-of-factly. Exner stood transfixed, as if a spell had been cast on him.

"Oh," as if she had just remembered something. "I'm Lucrezia. Mrs. Exner wanted you to know. My name is Lucrezia."

The calming surreal glow began to withdraw and fade through the rear wall of the bathroom, taking the child with it. Then Lucrezia's disembodied voice, "She will always love you. She shares your pain Mr. Exner, but you must leave her in your memories and move on."

"Wait, Lucrezia," Exner cried out in desperation.

But the child had disappeared, as she had on so many occasions before.

Alan Exner staggered back and collapsed on his bed, the bed he had shared with Marlissa for too short a time.

That night, Alan Exner fell into the deepest, most tranquil sleep he had ever experienced.

102

Loyalty Has Its Rewards

The following night found Bindhira in Lee's bed. Both knew their time together had come to an end. The NSA required her return to their headquarters in Fort Meade, Maryland, that day. They froze time that night as each savored the other with a passion borne of unwilling finality. At Lee's request, Travers had stayed the night at another friend's.

The next morning, and within an hour of them sharing a hearty breakfast of bacon, eggs, home fries, and fruit, Bindhira had dressed and packed. Lee had summoned a taxi to take her to the airport at Niagara-On-The-Lake, where the Learjet awaited her arrival.

As they sat on the double glider swing on Lee's front porch awaiting her ride Lee said, "I don't want this to end, Bindhi. I've never felt as alive as I do when I'm with you."

Bindhira smiled her beautiful East Indian smile. "It is a sad time for me also, Lee. Perhaps we will work on another case soon." They looked deep into each other's eyes.

"If you are ever in Maryland . . ." The moment was lost as her taxi pulled into Lee's driveway.

"Oh," Bindhira said as she got up, "I almost forgot." She pulled two envelopes from her clutch and handed them to Lee. "These are complements of a most grateful government." She pecked him on the cheek.

Lee tossed the envelopes onto the swing, grabbed her up into his strong arms, and converted the peck into a passionate embrace.

No words were exchanged as Lee walked the American agent to her taxi, bag in hand. He wanted to, but the words couldn't come for fear of losing his composure.

The driver exited his vehicle and opened the taxi's trunk. Lee gingerly placed her bag inside. The driver slammed the trunk shut then returned to his seat behind the wheel.

Bindhira climbed into the back and powered her window down. "You are a wonderful, talented man, Lee," she said with a smile he would never forget.

Lee bent down to the window, caressed the side of her face, and said ever so softly, "I'll make myself available for you anytime, anywhere, Ms. Bindhira Shankar."

"I will count on it my love," she said, looking deep into his eyes. "And I will never lose track of you as long as you wear my gift, Lee."

Just as the taxi slowly backed down the driveway Bindhira called out, "Promise me you will always wear the coin, Lee."

Lee had almost forgotten! He pulled the chain up from beneath his shirt and looked at the gold coin that hung around his neck, the coin she had given him which contained an embedded GPS microchip.

"I promise, Bindhi. I promise," he called after her.

She blew him a kiss as the taxi pulled out and drove away. Lee walked out and stood in the middle of the street and watched her leave. She looked back at him sadly, wantonly.

A car came up behind him. The miffed driver sounded his horn then veered around. Lee paid no attention, nor did he leave the street until her taxi turned a corner and disappeared from view.

Sadly, he walked back to his front porch. Then he noticed the envelopes Bindhira had left on the seat of the swing. He absentmindedly picked them up and went inside the house.

Lee then pulled a shot glass out of his kitchen cupboard, opened his fridge, and poured a half-shot of Newman's parmesan and garlic salad dressing. He savored its taste, and downed it slowly before retiring to his den, envelopes in hand. He tossed them on the desk. For several minutes he sat lost in thought, of what could have been, then suddenly realized just how tired he really was.

He started to nod off, and would have, but the envelopes suddenly came to mind. Lee pulled them off the desk. One was addressed to "William E. Travers." He noticed with mild jealousy that Travers' envelope was much thicker than the envelope addressed to him.

Lee opened his. Enclosed with a letter of extreme gratitude from the office of the Canadian prime minister, was a cheque sporting six figures.

Overcome with curiosity, he opened and read the contents of his friend's thick envelope. A broad smile crossed his face. Several minutes passed in quiet contemplation. Then he picked up his desk phone and dialed Travers' cell.

"Hello, Bill? Lee. Listen; I'm coming to pick you up in about an hour." Lee looked at his cheque and smiled. "Yeah, I'm buying." He listened for Travers' reply. "Yeah, yeah, I know, the Caddy's dead. I said I'll be there in an hour, so I'll be there in an hour—and I've got something for you."

Lee smiled into the receiver. He listened to his friend for a few moments, then responded into the instrument. “Don’t worry how I’m going to pick you up. Word on the street has it there’s a late-model Cadillac CTS Coupe in my imminent future.” He listened silently to Travers’ reply. “I don’t *know* what color. How many new CTS Coupes are there in town anyway?” Another pause as Travers spoke. “No I haven’t lost it, but you’re gonna.” Without waiting for a response, Lee hung up.

Moments later, a car horn sounded outside. He went to the front window and saw a brand-new jet-black Cadillac CTS Coupe sitting in the driveway. Lee returned to the den and carefully stuffed the contents of Bill’s envelope back inside. He tucked it under his arm then exited the front door.

Travers’ envelope contained a deed to a vacant commercial building on the waterfront, complete with a fully furnished upstairs apartment, just off a busy section of town that was ideal for a thriving dive shop.

To contact the author

Email–

deepobsession21@gmail.com

CPSIA information can be obtained at www.ICGtesting.com
Printed in the USA
LVOW13s1344060714

393054LV00011B/917/P